Critical acclaim for James Lee Burke

'James Lee Burke is an exceptional writer' *Observer*

'He writes explosively about crime and elegiacally about America. And he does so with style and passion enough to turn admirers into addicts. Burke is the only author guaranteed to make me bolt meals and lose sleep. No one else in the business is creating fiction like this' *Literary Review*

'James Lee Burke is one of the best – hell, he is the best American crime writer' *Irish Times*

'367 pages of dynamite' *Time Out*

'Burke writes prose that has a pronounced streak of poetry in it' *New York Times*

'American crime fiction has no finer stylist . . . a born storyteller' *Los Angeles Times*

'Burke's most self-evident strengths are two: the luminosity of his writerly voice, and the rich, vivid, fascinating terrain of southern Louisiana, which that voice renders with both love and despair . . . James Lee Burke is something special' *Washington Post*

'The best of American writing, never mind just American crime writing' *The Times*

'James Lee Burke is a writer to be remembered' *USA Today*

'James Lee Burke has a sophisticated and brilliantly expressed vision of humanity and one can see, smell and taste the America of which he writes' *Times Literary Supplement*

'Among the best American writers working today' *Daily Telegraph*

Also by James Lee Burke

Dave Robicheaux novels:

The Neon Rain
Heaven's Prisoners
Black Cherry Blues
A Morning for Flamingoes
A Stained White Radiance
In the Electric Mist With Confederate Dead
Burning Angel
Cadillac Jukebox
Sunset Limited

Other fiction:

Half of Paradise
To the Bright and Shining Sun
Lay Down My Sword and Shield
Two for Texas
The Lost Get-Back Boogie
The Convict and Other Stories
Cimarron Rose

James Lee Burke is the author of sixteen novels, including ten featuring Detective Dave Robicheaux, and a volume of short stories. *The Lost Get-Back Boogie* was nominated for a Pulitzer Prize, and he won the Edgar Award in 1989 for *Black Cherry Blues*. He divides his time between Missoula, Montana and Louisiana.

Dixie City Jam

JAMES LEE BURKE

ORION

An Orion paperback
First published in Great Britain by Orion in 1994
This paperback edition published in 1998 by
Orion Books Ltd,
Orion House, 5 Upper St Martin's Lane,
London WC2H 9EA

A CIP catalogue record for this book is available
from the British Library.

ISBN: 0 75281 651 9

Typeset by Deltatype Ltd, Birkenhead, Merseyside
Printed and bound in Great Britain by
Clays Ltd, St Ives plc

for Porteus and Alice Burke

chapter one

Not many people believe this, but in the early months of 1942 Nazi submarines used to lie in wait at the mouth of the Mississippi for the tankers that sailed without naval escort from the oil refineries at Baton Rouge into the Gulf of Mexico.

It was a shooting gallery. Because of wartime censorship the newspapers and radio carried no accounts of the American ships sunk off the Louisiana coast, but just after sunset people could see the oil fires burning on the southern horizon, like a quickening orange smudge low in the winter sky.

As a little boy in New Iberia, I heard shrimpers talk about the burned, oil-coated bodies of four merchant sailors who had been found floating like lumps of coal in an island of kelp, their sightless eyes and poached faces strung with jellyfish.

I had nightmares for many years about Nazis, who I imagined as pinch-faced, slit-eyed creatures who lived beneath the waves, not far from my home, and who would eventually impose a diabolical design upon the earth.

While scuba diving in college, on a calm, windless day, I accidentally found one of those submarines in sixty feet of water, resting at an angle on its keel, the deck rails and forward gun gray and fuzzy with seaweed, a chain of tiny bubbles rising from the stern.

My heart was tripping against my rib cage, the blood vessels tightening in my head, but I refused to be undone by my childhood fears, and I swam down to the twisted remains of the periscope until I could see the swastika and ship's numbers painted on the side of the conning tower.

I took my bowie knife from the scabbard on my side, and, like the primitive warrior who must touch the body of a slain enemy, I tapped with the butt of the knife on the conning tower's rim.

Then one of the strangest occurrences of my life took place.

I felt a bone-numbing coldness in the water, where there had been none before; then a sound, a vibration, like a wire cable snapping, rang through the entire length of the submarine. The conning tower began to right itself in the current, the metal plates on the hull grating on the sand, and clouds of silt and trapped oil rose from under the keel. I watched in horror as the submarine seemed to poise itself just above the gulf's floor, streamers of moss fanning back from the tower like tattered battle flags, then dip its bow downward into the darkness and slide over the edge of the continental shelf, my bowie knife toppling onto the rising stern, while sand sharks spun like minnows in the wake of its screws.

I discovered later that there was no mystery about the U-boat. It had been caught recharging its batteries on the surface, shelled by a U.S. Navy destroyer, then blown out of the water by depth charges, its spine broken; since that time it had scudded and bounced with the currents up and down the floor of the gulf along the Louisiana coast.

But sometimes in a dark moment I wondered about the crew that had gone down in a scream of sirens and whistles and torrents of water bursting through the ruptured plates or cascading down the tower that no one could close in time. Did they claw one another off the ladders? Were they willing to blind or maim or kill one another just to breathe air for a few more seconds? Did they regret embracing the scheme that would make the lights go out all over the world?

Or were they still sailing beneath the waves, their skins pickled in salt, their uniforms nests for moray eels, their plan to turn the earth into a place of concertina wire and guard towers still on track, as certain in prospect as the phosphorescent and boiling wake of a torpedo streaking toward a distant ship silhouetted against an autumnal moon?

It had been a strange day out on the salt. The wind was hot and sere out of the south, and in the swells you could see the shiny backs of stingrays and the bluish pink air sacs of jellyfish, which meant a storm was probably kicking them in toward shore; then the barometer dropped, the wind died, and the sun looked like a white flame trapped inside the dead water.

It rained for only about five minutes, large, flat drops that struck the water like lead shot, then the sky was clear and hot again and the sweat and humidity ran off your skin like snakes. Far to the south I could see the storm become stationary. Gray clouds were anchored low on the horizon, and right where they met the water there was a white line of surf and an occasional fork of lightning, like silver threads trembling inside the clouds.

While Batist, the black man who worked for me, put out the lines for gafftop catfish, I slipped on my air tanks, flippers, and mask and went over the side, following the anchor rope down through the cone of translucent green light, down to a level of water that was suddenly cold and moving and gray with silt, spinning with yellow blades of seaweed, perhaps alive with sand sharks that could whisk past you with such energy and force that you felt you had been struck by an invisible hand.

The anchor rope was taut and hard when I touched it. Above me I could see the silhouette of my boat's hull wobbling against the light, the bow dipping into the chop against the pull of the anchor. I blew my mask clear and

3

went down ten more feet along the rope, into a barrel of darkness, of swirling silt that had been blackened with oil, into sounds that shouldn't have been there – metal knocking against itself, like a ball peen hammer bouncing idly off an anvil, steel plates grinding across hard-packed sand, perhaps wire cables lifting in the current and lighting on twisted spars.

I gave it up and headed for the surface, rising once more into water bladed with sunlight, into the predictable world of wind and salt spray blowing against the mask, of gulls and pelicans gliding overhead, of Batist straining with both hands against a stingray he had foul-hooked through the stomach.

I pulled off my tanks and rubbed my head and face dry with a towel. Batist was stripped to the waist, his back knotted with muscle, his cannonball head popping with sweat as he got the gaff into the stingray and lifted it over the gunwale. The gaff had gone all the way through one of the ray's leathery wings. Batist flopped it on its back, shook the gaff loose, then knelt on one knee and sawed the treble hook out of its stomach. He wiped the blood off his knife, looked at the bent prongs on his hook, then flung the ray overboard with both hands.

'How far down was you, Dave?' he said.

'Thirty or forty feet maybe.'

'Ain't smart. They's a lot of trash down there. They's even trees, yeah, you know that? They float all the way down the Miss'sippi. Some big as your house.'

'I suspect you're right.'

'Well?' He put a cigar in the corner of his mouth.

'What?'

'You found that sub down there?'

'I heard some metal banging around, but I don't know what it is. It's too murky to see anything.'

'Maybe it's a wrecked oil rig down there. You t'ink of that? Maybe you gonna get tangled up in it, lose your life, Dave, all 'cause that Hippo fellow wavin' ten

4

t'ousand dollars around. He want that sub, let him get his fat butt out here and look for it.'

'Okay, Batist.'

'It don't do no good to be rich in the graveyard, no.'

'I'm getting your drift. I really appreciate it.'

'You ax me my opinion.'

'How about we catch some fish?'

'That's what I been tryin' to do. Except somebody been swimmin' around under my line.'

Hippo Bimstine was a mover in the state Democratic party and probably owned half of the drugstores in New Orleans. His girth was elephantine, his bejeweled, pudgy fingers and yellow-and-black checkered sports coats legendary. On any given afternoon you could see him in the Pearl on St. Charles, eating anywhere from five to eight dozen oysters on the half shell, washing them down with pitchers of beer, his thick neck powdered with talcum, a purple rose in his lapel, his jowls freshly shaved and glowing with health, his eyes squinting almost completely shut when he smiled. Years ago I had told him the story about the wreck of the German U-boat I had discovered on a calm summer day when I was in college. Last week a friend of Hippo's, a charter skipper out of Cocodrie, said his sonar had pinged a huge metal object just south of Grand Isle. Hippo remembered the story about the sunken sub, called me in New Iberia, and said he would pay a ten-thousand-dollar finder's fee if I could locate the sub and he could salvage it.

'What are you going to do with a World War II U-boat, Hippo?' I said.

'Are you kidding? You ever see this Geraldo guy on TV? He had millions of people watching him dig into a basement wall under a Chicago hotel where Al Capone used to live. He had everybody believing there was a car, dead bodies, gold bars, machine guns, all kinds of bullshit, buried in this underground vault. The show went on for three hours. It was so boring you had to keep slapping yourself awake. You know what he found? A

5

big pile of wet sand and some old bottles. He also almost punched a hole in the retaining wall that keeps Lake Michigan out of the city of Chicago.

'You know what I could do with a sub full of drowned Nazis? Use your imagination, Dave.'

But I had struck out. And it was just as well. Hippo's projects were usually as grandiose and thespian as his epicurean consumption of seafood in the Pearl, and if you became involved with him for very long, you began to realize that perhaps you had not successfully avoided the role of court jester in this life after all.

Batist and I caught and gutted over a dozen gafftop, ripped out the stingers and peeled the skin with pliers, fileted the meat in long, pink strips, and laid them out in rows on the crushed ice in the cooler. Then we ate the po'-boy sandwiches we'd made with fried oysters, mayonnaise, *sauce piquant*, sliced tomatoes, and onions and wrapped in waxed paper that morning; then we headed back toward the coast as the afternoon cooled and the wind began to blow out of the west, smelling of distant rain and speckled trout spawning and beached shellfish and lines of seaweed drying where the tide had receded from the sand.

As the late red sun seemed to collapse and melt into a single burning ember on the horizon, you could see the neon glow of New Orleans gradually replace the daylight and spread across the darkening sky. The clouds were black-green and low over the city, dancing with veins of lightning, roiling from Barataria all the way out to Lake Pontchartrain, and you knew that in a short while torrents of rain would blow through the streets, thrash the palm trees on the esplanades, overrun the gutters in the Quarter, fill the tunnel of oak trees on St. Charles with a gray mist through which the old iron, green-painted streetcars would make their way along the tracks like emissaries from the year 1910.

New Orleans was a wonderful place to be on a late evening in August.

That's what I thought, anyway, until I called Hippo Bimstine to tell him that he'd have to hire somebody else to dive the wrecks of Nazi submarines.

'Where are you?' he said.

'We're having supper at Mandina's, out on Canal.'

'You still tight with Clete Purcel?'

'Sure.'

'You know where Calucci's Bar is by St. Charles and Carrollton?'

'Yeah, it's across from your house, isn't it?'

'That's right. So right now I'm looking out my window at a shitstorm in the making. I'm talking about they got a SWAT team out there. Can you believe that? A fucking SWAT team in the middle of my neighborhood. I think they could use a diplomat out there, before the meat loaf ends up on the wallpaper, you get my meaning?'

'No.'

'The salt water still in your ears, Dave?'

'Look, Hippo—'

'It's Clete Purcel. He went apeshit in Calucci's and ran one guy all the way through the glass window. The guy's still lying in the flower bed. They say Purcel's got two or three others in there on their knees. If he don't come out, there's a supervising plainclothes in front says they're gonna smoke him. I got fucking Beirut, Lebanon, in my front yard.'

'Who's the supervising officer?'

'A guy named Baxter. Yeah, Nate Baxter. He used to be in Vice in the First District. You remember a plainclothes by that name? ... Hey, Dave, you there?'

chapter two

Calucci's Bar had been fashioned out of an old white frame house, with tin awnings on the windows, in an old residential neighborhood at the end of St. Charles by the Mississippi levee. The rain looked like purple and green and pink sleet in the neon glow from the bar, and on the far side of the levee you could see mist rising off the river and hear horns blowing on a tug-boat.

The street in front of the bar was filled with a half dozen emergency vehicles, their revolving lights reflecting off the shrubs and wet cement and the palm trees on the esplanade. When Batist and I parked my pickup truck by the curb I saw Nate Baxter in the midst of it all, rainwater sluicing off his hat, his two-tone shoes and gray golf slacks splattered from passing cars. His neatly trimmed reddish beard was glazed with wet light, his badge and chrome-plated revolver clipped on his belt, his body hard and muscular with middle age and his daily workouts at the New Orleans Athletic Club.

A flat-chested black woman plainclothes, with skinny arms and a mouthful of gold teeth, was arguing with him. She wore a rumpled brown blouse that hung out of her dark blue slacks, makeup that had streaked in the rain, and loafers without socks. Nate Baxter tried to turn away from her, but she moved with him, her hands on her thin hips, her mouth opening and closing in the rain.

'I'm talking to you, Lieutenant,' she said. 'It's my

opinion we have a situation that's gotten out of hand here. The response is not proportionate to the situation. Not in my opinion, sir. If you persist, I plan to file my own report. Are you hearing me, sir?'

'Do whatever you feel like, Sergeant. But please go do it somewhere else,' Baxter said.

'I'm responding to the call. I resent your talking to me like that, too,' she said.

'All right, I'll put it a little more clearly. You're a nuisance and a pain in the ass. You want to make a civil rights case out of that, be my guest. In the meantime, get out of here. That's an order.'

A uniformed white cop laughed in the background.

Baxter's eyes narrowed under the brim of his hat when he saw me.

'What are you doing, Nate?' I said.

He ignored me and began talking to a cop in a bullet-proof vest and a bill cap turned backwards on his head.

'What are you trying to do to Clete Purcel?' I said.

'Stay behind the tape, Robicheaux,' he said.

'I can talk him out of there.'

'You're out of your jurisdiction.'

Even in the rain his breath was heated and stale.

'Nobody needs to get hurt here, Nate,' I said.

'Purcel dealt the play, not me. You know what? I think he's been looking for this moment all his life.'

'Have you called him on the phone?'

'That's a good idea, isn't it? I'd really like to do that. Except he tore it out of the wall and wrapped it around a guy's throat. Then he rammed the guy through the front window.'

'The Calucci brothers are mobbed up. It's some kind of personal beef between them and Clete, you know it is. You don't call out a SWAT team on barroom bullshit.'

'We've got a vigilante loose in New Orleans, too. I think Purcel's a perfect suspect.'

I could feel my palms open and close at my sides.

Baxter was talking again to the cop in the vest, pointing at a high area on the levee.

'You're not going to get away with this,' I said.

'End of conversation, Robicheaux.'

'Clete stuck your head in a toilet bowl in a bar on Decatur,' I said. 'You didn't report it because he knew you were taking freebies from street hookers in the Quarter. That's what all this is about, Nate.'

Four white cops, as well as the black woman, were staring at us now. The skin around Nate Baxter's right eye was pinched like a marksman's when he sights along a rifle barrel. He started to speak, but I didn't give him the chance.

I held my Iberia Parish Sheriff's Department badge high above my head and walked toward the front door of the bar.

Clete had dropped the venetian blinds over all the windows and was leaning on the bar counter, one foot on the rail, drinking Mexican rum from a shot glass and sucking on a salted lime. He wore his powder blue porkpie hat slanted on the front of his head, his pants hanging two inches below his navel. His round, pink face was smiling and happy, his green eyes lighted with an alcoholic shine. Through one eyebrow and across the bridge of his nose was a scar, as thick as a bicycle patch, perforated with stitch holes, where he had been bashed with a pipe when he was a kid in the Irish Channel. As always, his tropical print shirt looked like it was about to split on his massive shoulders.

The bar was empty. Rain was blowing through the broken front window and dripping off the venetian blinds.

'What's happenin', Streak?' he said.

'Are you losing your mind?'

'Harsh words, noble mon. Lighten up.'

'That's Nate Baxter out there. He'd like to paint the woodwork with both of us.'

'That's why I didn't go out there. Some of those other guys don't like PI's, either.' He looked at his watch and tapped on the crystal with his fingernail. 'You want a Dr Pepper?'

'I want us both to walk out of here. We're going to throw your piece in front of us, too.'

'What's the hurry? Have a Dr Pepper. I'll put some cherries and ice in it.'

'Clete—'

'I told you, everything's copacetic. Now, disengage, noble mon. Nobody rattles the old Bobbsey Twins from Homicide.' He took a hit from the shot glass, sucked on his sliced lime, and smiled at me.

'It's time to boogie, partner,' I said.

He looked again at his watch.

'Give it five more minutes,' he said, and smiled again.

He started to refill his glass from a large, square, brown bottle that he held in his hand. I placed my palm lightly on his arm.

'Look, let me give you the big picture, noble mon,' he said. 'I'm involved with a lady friend these days. She's a nice person, she never hurt anybody, she's intelligent, she goes part-time to the Ju-Co, she also strips in a T and A joint on Bourbon owned by the Calucci brothers. We're talking about Max and Bobo here, Dave, you remember them, the two guys we ran in once for pulling a fingernail off a girl's hand with a pair of pliers? Before I met Martina, my lady friend, she borrowed two grand off the Caluccis to pay for her grandmother's hospitalization. So when she didn't make the vig yesterday, Max, the bucket of shit I put through the window glass, called her in this morning and said it was time for her to start working out of the back of a taxicab.'

He took off his porkpie hat, combed his sandy hair straight back on his head, clipped the comb in his shirt pocket, and put his hat back on.

'The Caluccis aren't going to make a beef, Dave, at least not a legal one. They get along in police stations like shit does in an ice cream parlor,' he said. He filled his shot glass, knocked it back, and winked at me.

'Where's the other one – Bobo?'

He glanced at his watch again, then looked across the counter, past a small kitchen, toward the massive wood door of a walk-in meat locker.

'He's probably wrapping himself in freezer foil right now,' he said. 'At least that's what I'd do.'

'Are you kidding?'

'I didn't put him in there. He locked himself in. What am I supposed to do about it? He's got an iron bar or something set behind the door. I say live and let live.'

I went to the locker and tried to open it. The handle was chrome and cold in my hand. The door moved an inch, then clanked against something metal and wouldn't move farther.

'Bobo?' I said.

'What?' a voice said through the crack.

'This is Dave Robicheaux. I'm a sheriff's detective. It's over. Come on out. Nobody's going to hurt you.'

'I never heard of you.'

'I used to be in Homicide in the First District.'

'Oh yeah, you were dick-brain's partner out there. What are you doing here? He call you up for some laughs?'

'Here's the agenda, Bobo. Let me run it by you and get your reactions. I'm holding a forty-five automatic in my hand. If you refuse to open the door, I'll probably have to shoot a few holes through the lock and the hinges. Do you feel comfortable with that?'

It was silent a moment.

'Where is he?' the voice said.

'He's not a player anymore. Take my word for it.'

'You keep that animal away from me. He's a fucking menace. They ought to put his brain in a jar out at the medical school.'

'You got my word, Bobo.'

I heard an iron bar rattle to the floor, then Bobo

pushed the door open with one foot from where he sat huddled in the corner, a rug wrapped around his shoulders, his hair and nostrils white with frost, clouds of freezer steam rising from his body into the sides of beef that were suspended from hooks over his head. His small, close-set black eyes went up and down my body.

'You ain't got a gun. You sonofabitch. You lied,' He said.

'Let's take a walk,' I said, lifting him up by one arm. 'Don't worry about Clete. He's just going to finish his drink and follow us outside. Believe it or not, there're cops out there who were willing to drop one of their own kind, just to protect you. Makes you proud to be a taxpayer, I bet.'

'Get your hand off my arm,' he said when we reached the door.

Batist and I stayed overnight in a guesthouse on Prytania, one block from St. Charles. The sky was red at sunrise, the air thick with the angry cries of blue jays in the hot shade outside the French doors. Nate Baxter had held Clete for disturbing the peace, but the Caluccis never showed up in the morning to file assault charges, and Clete was kicked loose without even going to arraignment.

Batist and I had beignets and café au lait in the Café du Monde across from Jackson Square. The wind was warm off the river behind us, the sun bright on the banana and myrtle trees inside the square, and water sprinklers ticked along the black piked fences that bordered the grass and separated it from the sidewalk artists and the rows of shops under the old iron colonnades. I left Batist in the café and walked through the square, past St. Louis Cathedral, where street musicians were already setting up in the shade, and up St. Ann toward Clete's private investigator's office.

Morning was always the best time to walk in the Quarter. The streets were still deep in shadow, and the water from the previous night's rain leaked from the wood shutters down the pastel sides of the buildings, and you could smell coffee and fresh-baked bread in the small grocery stores and the dank, cool odor of wild spearmint and old brick in the passageways. Every scrolled-iron balcony along the street seemed overgrown with a tangle of potted roses, bougainvillea, azaleas, and flaming hibiscus, and the moment could be so perfect that you felt you had stepped inside an Utrillo painting.

But it wasn't all a poem. There was another reality there, too: the smell of urine in doorways, left nightly by the homeless and the psychotic, and the broken fragments of tiny ten-dollar cocaine vials that glinted in the gutters like rats' teeth.

The biscuit-colored stucco walls inside Clete's office were decorated with bullfight posters, leather wine bags, *banderillas* that he had brought back from his vacation in Mexico City. Through the back window I could see the small flagstone patio where he kept his dumbbells and the exercise bench that he used unsuccessfully every day to keep his weight and blood pressure down. Next to it was a dry stone well impacted with dirt and untrimmed banana trees.

He sat behind his desk in his Budweiser shorts, a yellow tank top, and porkpie hat. His blue-black .38 police special hung in a nylon holster from a coatrack in the corner. He pried the cap off a bottle of Dixie beer with his pocketknife, let the foam boil over the neck onto the rug, kicked off his flip-flops, and put his bare feet on top of the desk.

'You trying to leave the dock early today?' I said.

'Hey, I was in the tank all night. You ought to check that scene out, mon. Two-thirds of the people in there are honest-to-God crazoids. I'm talking about guys eating their grits with their hands. It's fucking pitiful.'

He pushed at a scrap of memo paper by his telephone.

'I was a little bothered by something Nate Baxter said last night,' I said.

'Oh yeah?'

'This vigilante stuff. He thinks you might be the man.'

He drank out of his beer and smiled at me, his eyes filled with a merry light.

'You think I might actually have that kind of potential?' he said.

'People have said worse things about both of us.'

'*The Lone Ranger* was a radio show, mon. I don't believe there's any vigilante. I think we're talking about massive wishful thinking. These hits are just business as usual in the city. We've got a murder rate as high as Washington, D.C.'s now.'

'Five or six of them have been blacks in the projects.'

'They were all dealers.'

'That's the point,' I said.

'Dave, I've run down bond jumpers in both the Iberville and Desire projects. Life in there is about as important as water breaking out the bottom of a paper bag. The city's going to hell, mon. That's the way it is. If somebody's out there taking names in a serious way, I say more power to them. But I don't think that's the case, and anyway it's not me.'

He took a long drink from the beer. The inside of the bottle was filled with amber light. Moisture slid down the neck over the green-and-gold label.

'I'm sorry. You want me to send out for a Dr Pepper or some coffee?' he asked.

'No, I've got to be going. I had to bring my boat up from New Iberia for some work. It'll be ready about noon.'

He picked up the slip of memo paper by his phone and rubbed it between thumb and forefinger.

'I ought to save you a headache and throw this away,' he said. But he flipped it across the desk blotter at me.

'What is it?'

'That black broad, the sergeant who was in front of Calucci's, called this morning. She didn't know how else to get ahold of you. My advice is that you pitch that telephone number in the trash and go back to New Iberia. Forget New Orleans. The whole place is just waiting for a hydrogen bomb.'

'What's the deal?'

'She's a hard-nosed black broad named Lucinda Bergeron from the projects who doesn't take dog shit from white male cops. That's the deal.'

'So?'

'Last night she evidently got in Nate Baxter's face. So today he's trying to kick a two-by-four up her ass. He wrote her up for insubordination. He says she cussed him out. She says she's innocent and you can back her up.'

'She didn't cuss him out while I was there. In fact, she really kept her Kool-Aid.'

'Don't get sucked in, mon. Messing with Baxter is like putting your hand in a spittoon.'

I picked up the slip of paper and put it in my pocket.

'What do I know?' he said.

I called the dock from the guesthouse and was told that the mechanic had gone home sick and my boat would not be ready until the next day. Then I called the number on the slip of paper, which turned out to be Garden District police headquarters, and was told that Lucinda Bergeron was not in. I left my name and the telephone number of the guesthouse.

Batist was sitting on the side of his bed, his big, callused, scar-flecked hands in his lap, staring out the French doors, his face full of thought.

'What's troubling you, partner?' I asked.

'That nigger out yonder in the lot.'

'That what?'

'You heard me.'

'What'd he do?'

'While you was still sleepin', I got up early and went down to the dining room for coffee. He was eatin' in there, talkin' loud with his mout' full of food, puttin' his hand on that young white girl's back each time she po'ed

16

his coffee. Pretendin' like it's innocent, like he just a nice man don't have no bad t'oughts on his mind, no.'

'Maybe it's their business, Batist.'

'That kind of trashy nigger make it hard on the rest of us, Dave.'

He walked to the French doors, continued to stare out at the parking lot, peeled the cellophane off a cigar, and wadded the cellophane up slowly in his palm.

'He leanin' up against your truck,' he said.

'Let it go.'

'He need somebody to go upside his head.'

I knew better than to argue with Batist, and I didn't say anything more. He took off his short-sleeve blue denim shirt, hung it on the bedpost, and lathered his face with soap in front of the bathroom mirror. The muscles in his shoulders and back looked like rocks inside a leather bag. He began shaving with a pearl-handled straight-edge razor, drawing the blade cleanly down each of his jaws and under his chin.

I had known him since I was a child, when he used to fur-trap with my father on Marsh Island. He couldn't read or write, not even his own name, and had difficulty recognizing numbers and dialing a telephone. He had never been outside the state of Louisiana, had voted for the first time in 1968, and knew nothing of national or world events. But he was one of the most honest and decent men I've known, and absolutely fearless and unflinching in an adversarial situation (my adopted daughter, Alafair, never quite got over the time she saw him reach into a flooded pirogue, pinch a three-foot moccasin behind the head, and fling it indifferently across the bayou).

He walked back to the French doors, blotting a cut on his chin with a towel, the razor still in his hand. Then he folded the razor, dropped it in the back pocket of his denims, and began buttoning on his shirt.

'What are you doing, Batist?'

'Take a look out yonder.'

A tall, thin mulatto with skin the color of a new penny was talking to a half dozen black kids by my truck. He wore striped brown pants, with a braided black belt, and a lavender short-sleeve shirt with a white tie. He grinned and jiggled, and his hands moved in the air while he talked, as though a song were working inside him.

'A man like that just like a movie star to them raggedy kids, Dave.'

'At some point they'll learn he isn't.'

'It won't be no he'p then. He's a dope dealer or a pimp, don't be tellin' me he ain't. He'll use up them young boys' lives just so he can have money for a nice car, take womens out to the racetrack, put dope up his nose ... Hey, you t'ink I'm wrong? Come see.'

The mulatto man rubbed one kid on his head, the way a baseball coach might, then hooked two fingers inside the kid's belt, drew the kid close to him, and stuffed something small inside his pants. Then he cupped his hand around the nape of another kid's neck, his face beaming with goodwill and play, and shoved something down inside his pants, too.

'I be right back,' Batist said.

'Leave this guy alone, Batist. I'll call the locals and they'll send somebody out.'

'Yeah, in t'ree hours they will.'

'This isn't our pond, partner.'

'Yeah? How come you run across town last night to get mixed up with Purcel and them dagos?'

He picked up his dry cigar from the ashtray, put it deep in his jaw, and went out the door.

Oh boy, I thought.

Batist walked from the guesthouse through the shade of the mulberry tree to the edge of the parking lot. The mulatto man was leaning against the headlight of my truck, entertaining his audience by one-handedly rolling a half-dollar across the backs of his fingers. He propped one shined shoe behind him on the truck bumper and gingerly squeezed his scrotum. I don't know what he said to Batist. It may have been a patronizing remark or perhaps even a pleasant greeting; he was smiling when he said it. But I don't think he expected the response he got.

The flat of Batist's right hand, which could curve around a brick and shale the corners off it, seemed to explode against the side of the man's head. His face went out of round with the blow, and the blood drained from his cheeks; his jaw hung open, and his eyes were suddenly small and round, shrunken in his head like a pig's. Then Batist hit him with his open hand again, harder, this time on the side of the mouth, so that the bottom lip broke against the teeth.

Batist waved his hands in the midst of the black kids like someone shooing chickens out of a brooder house. They ran in all directions while the mulatto man held the back of his wrist against his mouth, one palm turned outward in a placating gesture.

Batist pointed his finger into the man's face and walked toward him silently, as though he were leveling a lance at him. The man broke and ran through the parking lot toward a cottage on the opposite side of the street. Batist ground a tiny glass vial into the cement with the heel of his boot, then walked past a group of stunned tourists who had just emerged from the guesthouse dining room; his perspiring face was turned away in embarrassment.

I called my wife, Bootsie, in New Iberia and told her that I would be at least another day in New Orleans, then I tried calling Lucinda Bergeron again at Garden District headquarters. She was still out, so I decided to drive over there, file a statement, and be done with the matter. I didn't know that I would end up talking to Sergeant Benjamin Motley, who used to be in Vice when I was a homicide lieutenant in the First District.

He was a rotund, powerful black man, whose clothes always smelled of cigar smoke, with a thick black mustache and glistening fire-hydrant neck, who had little sympathy for the plight of his own people. One time a black wino in a holding cell had ridiculed Motley, calling him the white man's hired 'knee-grow,' and Motley had sprayed the man from head to foot with a can of Mace. Earlier in his law-enforcement career he had been the subject of a wrongful death investigation, when, as a bailiff, he had escorted seven prisoners from the drunk tank on a wrist chain to morning arraignment and a fire in the courthouse basement had blown the circuits and stalled the elevator between floors. Motley had gotten out through the trap-door in the top of the elevator; the seven men on the chain had died of asphyxiation.

His office was glassed in and spacious, and several merit and civic citations were framed on the walls. Outside was a squad room filled with uniformed cops doing their paperwork at their desks. Motley leaned back in his swivel chair, one shoe propped on his waste-basket, and ate a half-peeled candy bar while I finished writing out in longhand what little I could report about the exchange between Nate Baxter and Lucinda Bergeron.

I signed my name at the bottom of the form and handed it to him. His eyes went up and down the page while he brushed at his chin with one knuckle.

'What are you doing in New Orleans, anyway, Robicheaux? I thought you were a plainclothes in Iberia Parish,' he said.

'I'm on leave for a while.'

'You couldn't stay out of New Orleans?'

'You need anything else, Motley?'

'Not a thing. Use your time any way you want to.'

'What's that mean?'

'You think this is going to bail that broad out?' He shook the page between his fingers.

'I don't know. But she didn't cuss out Nate Baxter while I was there. In fact, in my opinion, it was Baxter who was out of line.'

'Baxter got you suspended without pay when he was in Internal Affairs. You even punched him out in a squad room at First District. You should have written this on toilet paper and put it in the john.'

'You haven't lost your touch, Motley.'

He chewed on the corner of his lip and rolled his eyes sideways.

'Look through the glass,' he said. 'Count the white officers in the squad room, then count the black officers. When you get done doing that, count the female officers in the room. Then count the black female officers. Is the picture coming clear for you?'

'Do they give her a lot of heat?'

'You didn't hear it from me.'

I looked at his face and didn't speak. He wiped the chocolate off his fingers with the candy wrapper and threw the wrapper into the wastebasket.

'Dog shit in her desk drawer, a dildo Scotch-taped to a jar of Vaseline in her mailbox, phony phone messages from David Duke's campaign headquarters, that kind of stuff,' he said. 'She seems like a stand-up broad, but they'll probably run her off eventually.'

'It sounds like she could use some friends,' I said, and got up to go.

'You mean the brothers? Like me?'

I shrugged.

'Last hired, first fired,' he said. 'That's the way it is, my man. It doesn't change because you wear tampons. And let's be clear, the only reason you're involved in this is because of your buddy Purcel. So go pull on your own pud, Robicheaux.'

That evening Batist and I walked over to St. Charles and took the streetcar up to Canal, then walked into the Quarter and ate at the Acme on Iberville. It was crowded and warm inside and smelled of flat beer and the piles of empty oyster shells in the drain bins. We heard thunder out over the river, then it started to rain and we walked in the lee of the buildings back to Canal and caught the streetcar out on the neutral ground.

As we clattered down the tracks around Lee Circle, past the equestrian statue of Robert Lee, St. Charles Avenue opened up into a long green-black corridor of moss-hung oak trees, swirling with mist, touched with the red afterglow of the sun. The inside of the streetcar was cool and dry and brightly lit, the windows flecked with rain, and the world felt like a grand and beautiful place to be.

Back at the guesthouse we watched a movie on television while the rain and wind shook the mulberry tree outside the French doors. I paid no attention to the sirens that I heard on the avenue, nor to the emergency lights that beat angrily against the darkness on the far side of the parking lot. We were picking up my boat in the morning, and with luck we would be somewhere south of Terrebonne Bay by noon, on our way back to New Iberia, our baited jigs bouncing in the trough behind us.

Sheets of lightning were trembling against the sky, and I lay down on the pillow with my arm across my eyes. Batist began undressing for bed, then walked to the French doors to close the curtain.

'Hey, Dave, they's a ambulance and a bunch of policemens over at that cottage where that nigger run to,' he said.

'I'm hitting the sack, partner. Clete's right. Leave New Orleans to its own problems.'

'They carryin' somebody out of there.'

'Tell me about it in the morning. Good night.'

He didn't answer, and I felt myself drifting on the edges of sleep and the sound of the rain blowing against the windows; then I heard him click off the lamp switch.

It must have been an hour later that we were awakened by the knock on the door. No, that's wrong; it wasn't a knock; it was an incessant beating, with the base of the fist, the kind of ugly, penetrating sound sent by someone whose violation of your sleep and privacy is only a minimal indicator of his larger purpose.

I walked to the door in my skivvies, turned the dead bolt, and opened the door two inches.

'Take off the night chain, Robicheaux.'

'What do you want, Nate?'

'What's this look like?' He held a warrant up in front of me. His chrome-plated .357 Magnum hung from his right hand. The skin of his face was tight with fatigue and muted anger, beaded with rainwater. Three uniformed white cops stood behind him.

'For what? That beef at Calucci's Bar?' I said.

'You never disappoint me. Tell me stink and shit don't go hand in hand.'

'Why don't you try making sense, Nate?'

'We just hauled away a carved-up boon from across the street. Guess who knocked him around in front of a half dozen witnesses today? It's great having you back in town, Robicheaux. It's just like old times.'

He pulled his handcuffs from his belt and let them swing loosely from his index finger like a watch fob. Behind me, Batist sat on the edge of his bed, his big hands splayed on his naked thighs, his eyes focused on a sad and ancient racial knowledge that only he seemed able to see.

chapter three

There are those who, for political reasons, enjoy talking about country club jails. But any jail anywhere is a bad place to be. Anyone who thinks otherwise has never been in one.

Imagine an environment where the lights never go off and you defecate in full view of others on a toilet seat streaked with other people's urine, where you never quite fall asleep, where you are surrounded by the sounds of clanging iron, irrational voices resonating down stone corridors, a count-man or irritated turnkey whanging his baton off steel bars, or the muffled and tormented cries of an eighteen-year-old fish being gang-raped behind a shower wall.

Perhaps even a worse characteristic of jail is the denial of any identity you might have had before you stepped inside a piece of geography where time can sometimes be measured in five-minute increments that seem borne right out of Dante's ninth ring. Here you quickly learn that the personal violation of your *self* is considered as insignificant and ongoing an occurrence as routine body cavity searches, as the spraying of your genitals for crab lice, or as a wolf telling the server in the chow line to spit in your food, until you no longer think of yourself as an exception to the rules of jailhouse romance.

Batist spent the night in the tank and wasn't booked until the next morning. I sat on a wood chair in a waiting area next to a squad room and a row of glassed-in offices, one of which was Nate Baxter's. Through a doorway at the back of the squad room I could see the holding tank where Batist was still being held, though he had already been fingerprinted and photographed.

I had been waiting an hour and a half to see Nate Baxter. Then Sergeant Lucinda Bergeron walked past me, in navy blue slacks, a starched white short-sleeve shirt, and a lacquered black gunbelt with a leather pouch for handcuffs. She carried a clipboard in her hand, and if she noticed me, her face didn't show it.

'Excuse me, Sergeant,' I said.

She stopped and looked at me but said nothing. Her eyes were turquoise and elongated, like an Oriental's, and her cheekbones were rouged high up on her face.

'Could I talk with you a minute?' I asked.

'What is it?'

'I'm Dave Robicheaux. You left a message for me with Cletus Purcel.'

'Yes?'

'I came in and filed a report with Sergeant Motley yesterday.'

She looked at me, her face as still and expressionless as a picture painted upon the air.

'I was at Calucci's Bar,' I said. 'You asked me to come in and file a statement.'

'I understood you. What can I help you with?' she said.

'I have a friend back there in the tank. The black man, Batist Perry. He's already been booked.'

'What do you want from me?'

'How about getting him moved into a holding cell?'

'You'll have to talk to the officer in charge.'

'That's what I've been trying to do. For an hour and a half.'

'I can't help you. I'm sorry.'

She walked away to her desk, which was located in the squad room, among the uniformed officers, rather than in an enclosed office. Ten minutes later Baxter stepped out of his office door, studying some papers in his hand, then glanced in my direction and beckoned to me with one finger.

While I sat down across from him, he tipped his cigarette ashes in an ashtray and continued to concentrate on the papers on his desk blotter. He looked rested and fresh, in a sky blue sports coat and a crinkling shirt that was the color of tin.

'You're really charging Batist with murder?' I said.

'That decision comes down from the prosecutor's office, Robicheaux. You know that.'

'The man's never been in trouble. Not in his whole life. Not even for a misdemeanor. What's the matter with you?'

'Well, he's in trouble now. In a big way.' He leaned forward and tipped his ashes into his ashtray, cocking his eyebrows at me.

'I don't think you have a case, Nate. I think this is all smoke.'

'His prints are on the door at the crime scene.'

'That's impossible.'

'Tell that to our fingerprint man. Does this look like smoke to you?' He removed a half dozen eight-by-ten glossy black-and-white photographs from his desk drawer and dropped them in front of me. 'You ever see that much blood at a crime scene? Check out the chest wound. Has your friend ever been into voodoo?'

'You're using a homicide investigation to settle an old score, Nate. Don't tell me you're not.'

'Is the light in here bad? That must be the problem. The killer sawed the guy's heart out. That wasn't enough for him, either. He stuffed purple roses into the heart cavity.'

'What's your point?'

'Your friend wears a dime on a string around his ankle,' Baxter said. 'He carries a shriveled alligator's foot in his pocket. He had bones in his suitcase. The murder has all the characteristics of a ritual killing. If you were in my place, who would be your first suspect? Is there any chance it might be a superstitious backwater black guy who had already assaulted and threatened the victim the same day of the homicide and then left his prints at the crime scene? No, don't tell me. Just go think about it somewhere and drop me a card sometime.'

'I want to see him.'

'Be my guest. Please. By the way, I saw the black broad blow you off. In case you want to get more involved with her, I hear she's starting up a charm school. Take it easy, Robicheaux. You never surprise me,' he said.

But while I had been talking with Nate Baxter, Batist had already been locked to a wrist chain and taken to morning arraignment. By the time I got to the courtroom the public defender, who did not look to be over twenty-five, was trying to prevail upon the judge to set a reasonable bail. He was methodical, even eloquent, in his argument and obviously sincere. He pointed out that Batist had no arrest record and had been employed for years at a boat-rental dock run by a law officer in Iberia Parish, that he had lived his entire life in one small community and was not apt to leave it.

But Judge James T. Flowers was a choleric white-knuckle alcoholic who stayed dry without a program by channeling his inner misery into the lives of others. His procedures and sentences kept a half dozen ACLU attorneys occupied year round.

He looked at the clock and waited for the public defender to finish, then said, 'Hell's hot, my young friend. Perhaps it's time some of your clients learned that. Bail is set at fifty thousand dollars. Next case.'

An hour later Sergeant Motley arranged for me to see Batist in an interrogation room. The walls were a smudged white and windowless, and the air smelled like refrigerated cigarette smoke and cigar butts. Batist sat across from me at the wood table and kept rubbing his hands on top of each other. The scars on them looked like tiny pink worms. His face was unshaved and puffy with fatigue, his eyes arterial red in the corners with broken blood veins.

'What's gonna happen, Dave?'

'I'm going to call a bondsman first, then we'll see about a lawyer. We just have to do it a step at a time.'

'Dave, that judge said fifty t'ousand dollars.'

'I'm going to get you out, partner. You just have to trust me.'

'What for they doin' this? What they get out of it? I never had no truck with the law. I ain't even seen these people befo'.'

'A bad cop out there is carrying a grudge over some things that happened a long time ago. Eventually somebody in the prosecutor's office will probably figure that out. But in the meantime we have a problem, Batist. They say your fingerprints were on the door of that cottage across the street.'

I looked into his face. He dropped his eyes to the table and opened and closed his hands. His knuckles looked as round and hard against the skin as ball bearings.

'Tell me,' I said.

'After you was gone, after I bust that man's lip, I seen them kids t'rew the window, hangin' round his cottage do' again. When I call the po-lice, they ax me what he done. I say he sellin' dope to children, that's what he done. They ax me I seen it, I seen him take money from somebody, I seen somebody lighting up a crack pipe or somet'ing. I say no I ain't seen it, you got to see a coon climb in a tree to know coons climb in trees?

'So I kept watchin' out the window at that nigger's do'. After a while he come out with two womens, I'm talkin' about the kind been workin' somebody's crib, and they got in the car with them kids and drove round the block. When they come back them kids was fallin' down in the grass. I call the po-lice again, and they ax what crime I seen. I say I ain't seen no crime, long as it's all right in

28

New Orleans for a pimp and his whores to get children high on dope.

'This was a white po-liceman I was talkin' to. So he put a black man on the phone, like nobody but another black man could make sense out of what I was sayin'. This black po-liceman tole me to come down and make a repote, he gonna check it out. I tole him check out that nigger after I put my boot up his skinny ass.'

'You went over there?'

'For just a minute, that's all. He wasn't home. I never gone inside. Maybe he went out the back do'. Why you look like that, Dave?'

I rested my chin on my fist and tried not to let him read my face.

'Dave?'

'I'm going to call a bondsman now. In the meantime, don't talk about this stuff with anyone. Not with the cops, not with any of those guys in the lockup. There're guys in here who'll trade off their own time and lie about you on the witness stand.'

'What you mean?'

'They'll try to learn something about you, enough to give evidence against you. They cut deals with the prosecutor.'

'They can do that?' he said 'Get out of jail by sendin' somebody else to Angola?'

'I'm afraid it's a way of life, podna.'

The turnkey opened the door and touched Batist on the shoulder. Batist stared silently at me a moment, then rose from his chair and walked out of the room toward a yellow elevator, with a wiremesh and barred door, which would take him upstairs into a lockdown area. The palms of his hands left tiny horsetails of perspiration on the tabletop.

It was going to cost a lot, far beyond anything I could afford right now. I had thirty-two hundred dollars in a money market account, most of which was set aside for the quarterly tax payments on my boat-rental and bait business, four hundred thirty-eight dollars in an account that I used for operating expenses at the dock, and one hundred thirteen dollars in my personal checking account.

I went back to the guesthouse and called every bondsman I knew in New Orleans. The best deal I could get was a one-week deferment on the payment of the fifty-thousand-dollar bail fee. I told the bondsman I would meet him at the jail in a half hour.

I couldn't even begin to think about the cost of hiring a decent defense attorney for a murder trial.

Welcome to the other side of the equation in the American criminal justice system.

Our room was still in disarray after being tossed by Nate Baxter and his people. Batist's cardboard suitcase had been dumped on the bed, and half of his clothes were on the floor. I picked them up, refolded them, and began replacing them in the suitcase. Underneath one of his crumpled shirts was the skull of what had once been an enormous catfish. The texture of the bone was old, a shiny gray, mottled with spots the color of tea, polished smooth with rags.

I remembered when Batist had caught this same mud cat three years ago, on a scalding summer's day out on the Atchafalaya, with a throw line and a treble hook thick with nutria guts. The catfish must have weighed thirty-five pounds, and when Batist wrapped the throw line around his forearm, the cord cut into his veins like a tourniquet, and he had to use a club across the fish's spine to get it over the gunwale. After he had driven an ice pick into its brain and pinned it flat on the deck, skinned it and cut it into steaks, he sawed the head loose from the skeleton and buried it in an anthill under a log. The ants boiled on the impacted meat and ate the bone and eye sockets clean, and now when you held up the skull vertically, it looked like a crucified man from the front. When you reversed it, it resembled an ecclesiastical, robed figure giving his benediction to the devout. If you shook it in your hand, you could hear pieces of bone clattering inside. Batist said those were the thirty pieces of silver that Judas had taken to betray Christ.

It had nothing to do with voodoo. It had everything to do with Acadian Catholicism.

Before I left the guesthouse for the jail, I called up Hippo Bimstine at one of his drugstores.

'How bad you want that Nazi sub, Hippo?' I asked.

'It's not the highest priority on my list.'

'How about twenty-five grand finder's fee?'

'Jesus Christ, Dave, you were yawning in my face the other day.'

'What do you say, partner.'

'There's something wrong here.'

'Oh?'

'You found it, didn't you?'

I didn't answer.

'You found it but it's not in the same place now?' he said.

'You're a wealthy man, Hippo. You want the sub or not?'

'Hey, you think that's right?' he asked. 'I tell you where it's at, you find it and up the fee on me? That's like you?'

'Maybe you can get somebody cheaper. You know some guys who want to go down in the dark on a lot of iron and twisted cables?'

'Put my schlong in a vise, why don't you?'

'I've got to run. What do you say?'

'Fifteen.'

'Nope.'

'Hey, New Orleans is recessed. I'm bleeding here. You know what it cost me to get rid of—when he was about to be our next governor? Now my friends are running a Roto-Rooter up my hole.'

(Hippo had spent a fortune destroying the political

31

career of an ex-Klansman who had run for both the governor's office and the U.S. Senate. My favorite quote of Hippo's had appeared in *Time* magazine, during the gubernatorial campaign; he said of the ex-Klansman, '—doesn't like us Jews now. Check out how he feels after I get finished with him.')

'I won't charge expenses,' I said.

'I'm dying here. Hemorrhaging on the floor. I'm serious. Nobody believes me. Dave, you take food stamps?'

Hippo, you're a jewel, I thought.

Batist and I picked up my boat and left the dock at three the next morning. The breeze was up, peppered with light rain, and you could smell the salt spray breaking over the bow. The water was as dark as burgundy, the chop on the edge of the swells electric with moonlight, the wetlands to the north green and gray and metamorphic with mist. To the southeast I could see gas flares burning on some offshore rigs; then the wind dropped and the sky turned the color of bone and I could see a red glow spreading out of the water into the clouds.

It was completely light when I cut the engine and drifted above the spot where I had dove down into darkness and the sounds of grinding metal three days earlier. Batist stood on the bow, feeding the anchor rope out through his palms, until it hit bottom and went slack; then he tied it off on a cleat.

The water was smoky green, the swells full of skittering bait fish, the air hazy with humidity. I had fashioned a viewer box from reinforced window glass inset in a waterproofed wood crate, and I lowered it over the side by the handles and pressed it beneath the surface. Pockets of air swam across the glass, then flattened and disappeared, and suddenly in the yellow-green light I could see schools of small speckled trout, like darting silver ribbons, drumfish, as round and flat as skillets, a half dozen stingrays, their wings undulating as smoothly as if they were gliding on currents of warm air, and down below, where the light seemed to be gathered into a vortex of silt, the torpedo shapes of sand sharks, who bolted and twisted in erratic circles for no apparent reason.

Batist peered downward through the viewer box over my shoulder. Then I felt his eyes studying me while I strapped on my tanks and weight belt.

'This don't make me feel good, Dave,' he said.

'Don't worry about it, partner.'

'I don't want to see you lunch for them sharks, no.'

'Those are sand sharks, Batist. They're harmless.'

'Tell me that out yonder's harmless.' He pointed past the cabin to the southwest.

It was a water spout that had dropped out of a thunderhead and was moving like an enormous spinning cone of light and water toward the coast. If it made landfall, which it probably would not, it would fill suddenly with mud, rotted vegetation, and uprooted trees, and become as black as a midwestern tornado coursing through a freshly plowed field.

'Keep your eye on it and kick the engine over if it turns,' I said.

'Just look up from down there, you see gasoline and life jackets and a bunch of bo'rds floatin' round, see me swimmin' toward Grand Isle, that means it ain't bothered to tell me it was fixin' to turn.'

I went over the side, swam to the anchor rope, and began pulling myself downward hand over hand. I felt myself sliding through three different layers of temperature, each one cooler than the last; then just as a school of sea perch swept past me, almost clattering against my mask, I could feel a uniform level of coldness penetrate my body from the crown of my head down to the soles of my feet. Clouds of gray silt seemed to be blowing along the gulf's floor as they would in a windstorm. The pressure against my eardrums began to grow in intensity; it made a faint tremolo sound, like wire stretching before it breaks. Then I heard iron ring against iron, and a groan like a great weight shifting against impacted sand.

I held the anchor rope with one hand and floated motionlessly in the current. Then I saw it. For just a moment.

It was pointed at an upward angle on a slope, buried in a sand-bar almost to its decks, molded softly with silt. But there was no mistaking the long, rounded, sharklike shape. It was a submarine, and I could make out the battered steel flanges that protruded above the captain's bridge on the conning tower, and I knew that if I scraped the moss and layers of mud and shellfish from the tower's plates I would see the vestiges of the swastika that I had seen on the same conning tower over three decades ago.

Then I saw it tilt slightly to one side, saw dirty strings of oil or silt or engine fuel rise near the forward torpedo tubes, and I realized that years ago air must have been trapped somewhere in a compartment, perhaps where a group of terrified sailors spun a wheel on a hatch and pretended to themselves that their friends outside, whose skulls were being snapped like eggshell, would have chosen the same alternative.

I felt a heavy surge in the current from out in the dark, beyond the continental shelf. The water clouded and the submarine disappeared. I thought I heard thunder booming, then the anchor rope vibrated in my palm, and when I looked up I could see the exhaust pipes on my boat boiling the waterline at the stern.

When I came to the surface the chop smacked hard against my mask, and the swells were dented with rain circles. Batist came outside the cabin and pointed toward the southeast. I pushed my mask up on my head and looked behind me; three more water spouts had dropped out of the sky and were churning across the surface of the water, and farther to the south you could see thunder-clouds as thick as oil smoke on the horizon.

I climbed up the ladder, pulled off my gear, tied the end of a spool of clothesline through a chunk of pig iron that had once been a window sash, and fed the line over the gunwale until the weight bit into the bottom. Then I sawed off the line at the spool and strung it through the handles of three sealed Clorox bottles that I used as float markers. The rain was cold and dancing in a green haze on the swells now, the air heavy with the smell of ozone and nests of dead bait fish in the waves. Just as I started to fling the Clorox bottles overboard, I heard the blades of a helicopter thropping low over the water behind me.

It passed us, flattening and wrinkling the water below the downdraft, and I saw the solitary passenger, a blond man in pilot's sunglasses, turn in his seat and stare back at me. Then the helicopter circled and hovered no more than forty yards to the south of us.

'What they doin'?' Batist said.

'I don't know.'

'Let's get goin', Dave. We don't need to be stayin' out here no longer with them spouts.'

'You got it, partner,' I said.

Then the helicopter gained altitude, perhaps to five hundred feet directly above us, high enough for them to see the coastline and to take a good fix on our position.

I left the Clorox marker bottles on the deck and pulled the sash weight back up from the bottom. We could return to this same area and probably find the sub again with my sonar, or 'fish finder,' which was an electronic marvel that could outline any protrusion on the gulf's floor. But the sky in the south was completely black now, with veins of lightning trembling on the horizon, and I had a feeling that the Nazi silent service down below was about to set sail again.

chapter four

We lived south of New Iberia, on an oak-lined dirt road next to the bayou, in a house that my father had built of notched and pegged cypress during the Depression. The side and front yards were matted with a thick layer of black leaves and stayed in deep shade from the pecan and oak trees that covered the eaves of the house. From the gallery, which had a rusted tin roof, you could look down the slope and across the dirt road to my boat-rental dock and bait shop. On the far side of the bayou was a heavy border of willow trees, and beyond the willows a marsh filled with moss-strung dead cypress, whose tops would become as pink as newly opened roses when the sun broke through the mist in the early morning.

I slept late the morning after we brought the boat back from New Orleans. Then I fixed coffee and hot milk and a bowl of Grape-Nuts and blackberries, and took it all out on a tray to the redwood picnic table under the mimosa tree in the backyard. Later, Bootsie came outside through the screen door with a glass of iced tea, her face fresh and cool in the breeze across the lawn. She wore a sleeveless white blouse and pink shorts, and her thick, honey-colored hair, which she had brushed in swirls and pinned up on her head, was burned gold on the tips from the sun.

'Did you see the phone messages from a police sergeant on the blackboard?' she asked.

'Yeah, thanks.'

'What does she want?'

'I don't know. I haven't called her back.'

'She seemed pretty anxious to talk to you.'

'Her name's Lucinda Bergeron. I think she probably has problems with her conscience.'

'What?'

'I tried to help her on an insubordination beef. When I asked her to do a favor for Batist, she more or less indicated I could drop dead.'

'Maybe it's just a misunderstanding.'

'I don't think so. Where's Alafair?'

'She's down at the dock with Batist.' She drank from her iced tea and gazed at the duck pond at the foot of our property. She shook the ice in the bottom of the glass and looked at it. Then she said, 'Dave, are we going to pay for his lawyer?'

'It's either that or let him take his chances with a court-appointed attorney. If he's lucky, he'll get a good one. If not, he can end up in Angola.'

She touched at her hairline with her fingers and tried to keep her face empty of expression.

'How much is it going to cost?' she said.

'Ten to twenty grand. Maybe a lot more.'

She widened her eyes and took a breath, and I could see a small white discoloration, the size of a dime, in each of her cheeks.

'Dave, we'll go into debt for years,' she said.

'I don't know what to do about it. Nate Baxter targeted Batist because he couldn't get at me or Clete. It's not Batist's fault.'

The breeze blew through the mimosa, and the shade looked like lace rippling across her face. I saw her try to hide the anger that was gathering in her eyes.

'There's nothing for it, Boots. The man didn't do anything to deserve this. We have to help him.'

'All this started with Clete Purcel. He enjoys it. It's a

way of life with him. When are you going to learn that, Dave?'

Then she walked into the house and let the screen slam behind her.

I hosed down some boats at the dock, cleaned off the telephone-spool tables after the lunch crowd had left, then finally gave in and used the phone in the bait shop to return Lucinda Bergeron's call. I was told she had gone home sick for the day, and I didn't bother to leave my name. Then I called three criminal attorneys in Lafayette and two in New Orleans. Their fees ran from eighty to one hundred and fifty dollars an hour, with no guarantees of anything.

'You all right, Dave?' Alafair said. She sat on a tall stool behind the cash register, her Houston Astros cap on sideways, her red tennis shoes swinging above the floor. Her skin was dark brown, her Indian black hair filled with lights like a raven's wing.

'Everything's copacetic, little guy,' I said. Through the screened windows the sun looked like a wobbling yellow flame on the bayou. I wiped the perspiration off my face with a damp counter towel and threw the towel in a corner.

'You worried about money or something?'

'It's just a temporary thing. Let's have a fried pie, Alf.'

'Batist is in some kind of trouble, Dave?'

'A little bit. But we'll get him out of it.'

I winked at her, but the cloud didn't go out of her face. It had been seven years since I had pulled her from the submerged wreck of an airplane carrying illegal refugees from El Salvador. She had forgotten her own language (although she could understand most words in Cajun French without having been taught them), and she no longer had nightmares about the day the soldiers came to her village and created an object lesson with machetes and a pregnant woman in front of the medical clinic; but when she sensed difficulty or discord of any kind in our home, her brown eyes would immediately become troubled and focus on some dark concern inside herself, as though she were about to witness the re-creation of a terrible image that had been waiting patiently to come aborning again.

'You have to trust me when I tell you not to worry about things, Squanto,' I said.

Then she surprised me.

'Dave, do you think you should be calling me all those baby names? I'm twelve years old.'

'I'm sorry, Alf.'

'It's all right. Some people just might not understand. They might think it's dumb or that you're treating me like a little kid or something.'

'Well, I won't do it anymore. How's that?'

'Don't worry about it. I just thought I ought to tell you.'

'Okay, Alf. Thanks for letting me know.'

She punched around on the keys of the cash register while blowing her breath up into her bangs. Then I saw her eyes go past me and focus somewhere out on the dock.

'Dave, there's a black woman out there with a gas can. Dave, she's got a pistol in her back pocket.'

I turned and looked out into the shade of the canvas awning that covered the dock. It was Lucinda Bergeron, in a pair of faded Levi's that barely clung to her thin hips, Adidas tennis shoes, and a white, sweat-streaked T-shirt with the purple-and-gold head of Mike the Tiger on it. She wore her badge clipped on her beltless waistband; a chrome snub-nosed revolver in an abbreviated leather holster protruded from her back pocket.

Her face was filmed and gray, and she wiped at her eyes with one sleeve before she came through the screen door.

'Are you okay?' I said.

'May I use your rest room?' she said.

'Sure, it's right behind the coolers,' I said, and pointed toward the rear of the shop.

A moment later I heard the toilet flush and water running, then she came back out, breathing through her mouth, a crumpled wet paper towel in one hand.

'Do you sell mouthwash or mints?' she said.

I put a roll of Life Savers on top of the counter. Then I opened up a can of Coca-Cola and set it in front of her.

'It settles the stomach,' I said.

'I've got to get something straight with you.'

'How's that?'

She drank out of the Coke can. Her face looked dusty and wan, her eyes barely able to concentrate.

'You think I'm chickenshit,' she said.

'You were in a tough spot.'

'But you still think I'm chickenshit, don't you?'

'I know you're not feeling well, but I'd appreciate it if you didn't use profanity in front of my daughter.'

'Excuse me. Did you have a reason for not returning my phone calls?'

'When I called back, you were already gone. Look, Sergeant, I appreciate your coming down here, particularly when you're sick. But you don't owe me anything.'

'You've decided that?'

I let out my breath. 'What can I say? It's not my intention to have an argument with you.'

'You sell gas? I ran out down the road. My gauge is broken.' She clanked the gasoline can on the counter.

'Yeah, I've got a pump for the boats at the end of the dock.'

'Your friend, the black man, Batist Perry, they're sticking it to him. Nate Baxter held some information back from you.'

'Alafair, how about telling Bootsie we'll go to Mulate's for supper tonight?'

She made an exasperated face, climbed down from the stool, unhitched Tripod, her three-legged pet raccoon, from his chain by the door, and went up the dock toward the house with Tripod looking back at me over her shoulder.

'The murdered man had his heart cut out,' Lucinda Bergeron said. 'But so did three other homicide victims in the last four months. Even one who was pitched off a roof. He didn't tell you that, did he?'

'No, he didn't.'

'The press doesn't know about it, either. The city's trying to sit on it so they don't scare all the tourists out of town. Baxter thinks it's Satanists. Your friend just happened to stumble into the middle of the investigation.'

'Satanists?'

'You don't buy it?'

'It seems they always turn out to be meltdowns who end up on right-wing religious shows. Maybe it's just coincidence.'

'If I were you, I'd start proving my friend was nowhere near New Orleans when those other homicides were committed. I've got to sit down. I think I'm going to be sick again.'

I came around from behind the counter and walked her to a chair and table. Her back felt like iron under my hands. She took her revolver out of her back pocket, clunked it on the table, and leaned forward with her forearms propped on her thighs. Her hair was thick and white on the ends, her neck oily with sweat. Two white fishermen whom I didn't know started through the door, then turned and went back outside.

'I'll be right with y'all,' I called through the screen.

'Like hell you will,' I heard one of them say as they walked back toward their cars.

'I'll drive you back to New Orleans. I think maybe you've got a bad case of stomach flu,' I said to Lucinda.

'Just fill my gas can for me. I'll be all right in a little bit.' She took a crumpled five-dollar bill from her Levi's and put it on the tabletop.

'I have to go back for my truck, anyway. It's at a dock down by Barataria Bay. Let's don't argue about it.'

But she wasn't capable of arguing about anything. Her breath was rife with bile, her elongated turquoise eyes rheumy and listless, the back of her white T-shirt glued against her black skin. When I patted her on the shoulder, I could feel the bone like coat hanger wire against the cloth. I could only guess at what it had been like for her at the NOPD training academy when a peckerwood drill instructor decided to turn up the butane.

I carried the gas can down to her Toyota, got it started, filled the tank up at the dock, and drove her to New Orleans. She lived right off Magazine in a one-story white frame house with a green roof, a small yard, and a gallery that was hung with potted plants and overgrown with purple trumpet vine. Around the corner, on Magazine, was a two-story bar with a colonnade and neon Dixie beer signs in the windows; you could hear the jukebox roaring through the open front door.

'I should drive you out to the boatyard,' she said.

'I can take a cab.'

She saw my eyes look up and down her street and linger on the intersection.

'You know this neighborhood?'

'Sure. I worked it when I was a patrolman. Years ago that bar on the corner was a hot-pillow joint.'

'I know. My auntie used to hook there. It's a shooting gallery now,' she said, and walked inside to call me a cab.

Way to go, Robicheaux, I thought.

It was late evening after I picked up my truck down in Barataria and drove back into the city. I called Clete at his apartment in the Quarter.

'Hey, noble mon,' he said. 'I called you at your house this afternoon.'

'What's up?'

'Oh, it probably doesn't amount to much. What are you doing back in the Big Sleazy, mon?'

'I need some help on these vigilante killings. I'm not going to get it from NOPD.'

'Lose this vigilante stuff, Dave. It's a shuck, believe me.'

'Have you heard about some guys having their hearts cut out?'

He laughed. 'That's a new one. Where'd you get that?' he said.

'Lucinda Bergeron.'

'You've been out of Homicide too long, Streak. When they cancel them out, it's for money, sex, or power. This vampire or ghoul bullshit is out of comic books. Hey, I got another revelation for you. I think that Bergeron broad has got a few frayed wires in her head. Did she tell you she went up to Angola to watch a guy fry?'

'No.'

'It probably just slipped her mind. Most of your normals like to watch a guy ride the bolt once in a while.'

'Why'd you call the house?'

'I'm hearing this weird story about you and a Nazi submarine.'

'From where?'

'Look, Martina's over here. I promised to take her to this blues joint up on Napoleon. Join us, then we'll get some étouffée at Monroe's. You've got to do it, mon, it's not up for discussion. Then I'll fill you in on how you've become a subject of conversation with Tommy Blue Eyes.'

'Tommy Lonighan?'

'You got it, Tommy Bobalouba himself, the only mick I ever met who says his own kind are niggers turned inside out.'

'The Tommy Lonighan I remember drowned a guy with a fire hose, Clete.'

'So who's perfect? Let me give you directions up on Napoleon. By the way, Bootsie seemed a little remote when I called. Did I spit in the soup or something?'

* * *

The nightclub up on Napoleon was crowded, the noise deafening, and I couldn't see Clete at any of the tables. Then I realized that an exceptional event had just taken place up on the bandstand. The Fat Man, the most famous rhythm and blues musician ever produced by New Orleans, had pulled up in front in his pink Cadillac limo, and like a messiah returning to his followers, his sequined white coat and coal black skin almost glowing with an electric purple sheen, had walked straight through the parting crowd to the piano, grinning and nodding, his walrus face beaming with goodwill and an innocent self-satisfaction, and had started hammering out 'When the Saints Go Marching In.'

The place went wild.

Then I realized that another event was taking place simultaneously on the dance floor, one that probably not even New Orleans was prepared for – Clete Purcel and his girlfriend doing the dirty boogie.

While the Fat Man's ringed, sausage fingers danced up and down on the piano keys and the saxophones and trumpets blared behind him, Clete was bopping in the middle of the hardwood floor, his porkpie hat slanted forward on his head, his face pointed between his girlfriend's breasts, his buttocks swinging like an elephant's; then a moment later his shoulders were erect while he bumped and ground his loins, his belly jiggling, his balled fists churning the air, his face turned sideways as though he were in the midst of orgasm.

His girlfriend was over six feet tall and wore a flowered sundress that fit her tanned body like sealskin. She waved bandannas in each hand as though she were on a runway, kicking her waxed calves at an angle behind her, lifting her chin into the air while her eyelids drifted shut and she rotated her tongue slowly around her lips. Then she let her mouth hang open in a feigned pout, pushed her reddish brown hair over the top of her head with both hands, flipped it back into place with an erotic challenge in her eyes, and rubbed a stretched bandanna back and forth across her rump while she oscillated her hips.

At first the other dancers pulled back in awe or shock or perhaps even in respect; then they began to leave the dance floor two at a time and finally in large numbers after Clete backed with his full weight into another dancer and sent him careening into a drink waiter.

The Fat Man finished, wiped his sweating face at the microphone with an immaculate white handkerchief, and thanked the crowd for their ongoing roar of applause. I followed Clete and his girl to their table, which was covered with newspaper, beer bottles, and dirty paper plates that had contained potatoes French-fried in chicken fat. Clete's face was bright and happy with alcohol, and the seams of his Hawaiian shirt were split at both shoulders.

'Martina, this is the guy I've been telling you about,' he said. 'My ole bust-'em or smoke-'em podjo.'

'How about giving that stuff a break, Clete?' I said.

'I'm very pleased to meet you,' she said.

Her face was pretty in a rough way, her skin coarse and grained under the makeup as though she had worked outdoors in sun and wind rather than on a burlesque stage.

'Clete's told me about how highly educated you are and so well read and all,' she said.

'He exaggerates sometimes.'

'No, he doesn't,' she said. 'He's very genuine and sincere and he feels very deeply for you.'

'I see,' I said.

'He has a gentle side to his nature that few people know about. The people in my herbalist and nude therapy group think he's wonderful.'

Out of the corner of my eye I saw Clete study the dancers out on the floor as though he had never seen them before.

'He says you're trying to find the vigilante. I think it's disgusting that somebody's out there murdering colored people in the projects and nobody does anything about it.'

'Clete doesn't seem to give it much credence.'

'Look, mon, let me tell you where this vigilante stuff came from. There's a citizens committee here, a bunch of right-wing douche bags who haven't figured out what their genitalia is for, so they spend all their time jacking up local politicians and judges about crime in the streets, dope in the projects, on and on and on, except nobody wants to pay more taxes to hire more cops or build more jails. So what they're really saying is let's either give the blacks a lot more rubbers or do a little less to stop the spread of sickle-cell.'

Martina had taken a pocket dictionary from her purse. She read aloud from it: '"Credence – belief, mental acceptance or credit." That's an interesting word. It's related to "credibility," isn't it?'

Clete widened his eyes and looked at her as though he were awakening from sleep. Then somebody on the opposite side of the dance floor caught his attention.

'Dave, a guy's coming over to our table,' he said. 'He just wants to talk a minute. Okay? I told him you wouldn't mind. He's not a bad guy. Maybe you might even be interested in what he's got to say. It doesn't hurt to listen to a guy, right?'

Through the layers of drifting cigarette smoke my eyes focused on a man with two women at a table. His solid physique reminded me of an upended hogshead; even at a distance his other features – his florid, potato face, his eyes that were as blue as ice, his meringue hair – were unmistakable.

'You shouldn't have done this, partner,' I said to Clete.

'I provide security at two of his clubs. What am I supposed to say to him, "Drop dead, Tommy. My buddy Dave thinks you're spit on the sidewalk, get off the planet, sonofabitch"?'

'He's not just an eccentric local character. He was up on a murder beef. What's the matter with you?'

'The guy he did with the fire hose was beating up old people in the Irish Channel with an iron pipe. Yeah, big loss. Everybody was real upset when they heard he'd finally caught the bus.'

'Fire hose?' Martina said, and made a puzzled face.

There was nothing for it, though. The man with the red face and the eyes that were like flawless blue marbles was walking toward our table.

Clete mashed out his cigarette in a paper plate.

'Play it like you want, Dave,' he said. 'You think Tommy Bobalouba's any more a geek than Hippo Bimstine, tell him to ship out.'

'What about Hippo?' I said.

'Nothing. What do I know? I thought I might bring you a little extra gelt. You're too much, Streak.'

Tommy Lonighan hooked two fingers under an empty chair at an adjacent table without asking permission of the people sitting there, swung it in front of him, and sat down. He wore a long-sleeve pink shirt with French cuffs and red stone cuff links, but the lapels were ironed back to expose the mat of white hair on his chest, and the hair on his stubby, muscular forearms grew out on his wrists like wire. He had the small mouth of the Irish, with downturned corners, and a hard, round chin with a cleft in it.

'What d'you say, Lieutenant?' he said, and extended his hand. When I took it, it was as square and rough-edged as a piece of lumber.

'Not much, Mr. Lonighan. How are you this evening?' I said.

'"Mr. Lonighan," he says. I look like a "mister" to you these days?' he said. The accent was Irish Channel blue-collar, which is often mistaken for a Brooklyn accent, primarily because large sections of New Orleans were settled by Irish and Italian immigrants in the 1890s. He smiled, but the clear light in his eyes never changed, never revealed what he might or might not be thinking.

'What's up?' I said.

'Boy, you fucking cut straight to it, don't you?'

'How about it on the language, Tommy?' Clete said.

'Sorry, I spend all day with prizefighters down at my gym,' he said, glancing sideways at Martina. 'So how much is Blimp-stine offering you to find this sub?'

'Who?' I said.

'Hippo Bimstine, the beached whale of south Louisiana. Who you think I'm talking about?'

'How do you know Hippo's offering me anything?'

'It's a small town. Times are hard. Somebody's always willing to pass on a little information,' he said, and put a long French fry between his lips, sucking it deep into his mouth with a smile in his eyes.

'You're right, there's a Nazi sub out there someplace. But I don't know where. Not now, anyway. For all I know, it's drifted all the way to the Yucatán. The alluvial fan of the Mississippi probably works it in a wide circle.'

He set his palm on my forearm and looked me steadily in the eyes. There were thin gray scars in his eyebrows, a nest of pulsating veins in one temple that had not been there a moment ago.

'Why is it I don't believe you?' he said.

'What's your implication, Tommy?' I said.

'It's "Tommy" now. I like it, Dave. I don't "imply" anything. That's not my way.' But his hand did not leave my forearm.

Martina read from her pocket dictionary: '"Alluvial fan – the deposit of a stream where it issues from a gorge upon an open plain." The Mississippi isn't a stream, is it?'

Lonighan stared at her.

'I'm not sure why either you or Hippo are interested in some World War II junk, but my interest is fading fast, Tommy,' I said.

'That's too bad. Because both Hippo and me are going into the casino business. I'm talking about riverboats here, legalized gambling that can make this city rich, and

I'm not about to let that glutinous sheeny set up a tourist exhibit on the river that takes maybe half my business.'

'Then tell it to Hippo,' I said, and pulled my arm out from under his hand.

'*What?*' he said. 'You got your nose up in the air about something? I come to your table, you act like somebody's flushing a crapper in your face? You don't like me touching your skin?'

'Take it easy, Tommy. Dave didn't mean anything,' Clete said.

'The fuck he didn't.' Then he said it again: 'The *fuck* he didn't.'

'I'd appreciate your leaving our table,' I said.

He started to speak, but Martina beat him to it.

'I happen to be part Jewish, Mr. Lonighan,' she said, her face serene and cool, her gaze focused benignly on him as though she were addressing an abstraction rather than an enraged man at her elbow. 'You're a dumb mick who's embarrassing everybody at the table. It's not your fault, though. You probably come from a dysfunctional home full of ignorant people like yourself. But you should join a therapy group so you can understand the origin of your rude manners.'

The crow's-feet around Lonighan's eyes were white with anger and disbelief. I looked at Martina in amazement and admiration.

chapter five

I slept on Clete's couch that night, and in the morning I called Nate Baxter at his office and asked about the other homicides that involved mutilation.

Nate had never been a good liar.

'Mutilation? How do you think most homicides are committed? By beating the person to death with dandelions?'

'You know what I'm talking about.'

'Yeah, I do. You got to somebody under my supervision.'

'Your office is a sieve, Nate.'

'No, there's only one broad I smell in this. Nothing racial meant. Stay out of the investigation, Robicheaux. You blew your career in New Orleans because you were a lush. You won't change that by sticking your nose up that broad's cheeks.'

He hung up.

I got back home just before lunch. The air was already hot and breathless and dense with humidity, and I put on my tennis shoes and running shorts, jogged three miles along the dirt road by the bayou, then did three sets of arm curls, dead lifts, and military presses with my barbells in the backyard. My chest was singing with blood when I turned on the cold water in the shower.

I didn't hear Bootsie open the bathroom door.

'Do you have a second?'

'Sure,' I said, and twisted the shower handle off.

'I acted badly. I'm sorry,' she said.

'About what?'

'About Batist. About the money. I worry about it sometimes. Too much, I guess.'

'What if I had a wife who didn't?'

I eased the water back on, then through the frosted glass I saw her undressing in muted silhouette. She opened the door, stepped inside with me, and slipped her arms around my neck, her face uplifted, her eyes closed against the spray of the shower over my shoulders.

I held her against me and kissed her hair. Her body was covered with tan, the tops of her breasts powdered with freckles. Her skin was smooth and warm and seemed to radiate health and well-being through my palms, the way a rose petal does to the tips of your fingers, but the reality was otherwise. Lupus, the red wolf, lived in her blood and waited only for a slip in her medication to resume feeding on her organs and connective tissue. And if the wolf was not loosed by an imbalance in the combinations of medicine that she took, another even more insidious enemy was – temporary psychosis that was like an excursion onto an airless piece of moonscape where only she lived.

She was supposed to avoid the sun, too. But I had long since given up trying to take her out of the garden or force her back into the shade of the cabin when we were out on the salt. I had come to feel, as many people do when they live with a stricken wife or husband, that the tyranny of love can be as destructive as that of disease.

We made love in the bedroom, our bodies still damp and cool from the shower, while the window fan drew the breeze across the sheets. She moved her stomach in a circular motion on top of me, her arms propped against the mattress; then I saw her eyes close and her face become soft and remote. Her thighs tensed, and she bent forward suddenly, her mouth opening, and I felt her heat spread across my loins just as something crested and burst inside me like water edging over a dam and cascading in a white arc through a dark streambed.

She was one of those rare people for whom making love did not end with a particular act. She lay beside me and touched the white patch in my hair, my mustache, the rubbery scar high up on my chest from a .38 round, the spray of lead gray welts along my right thigh where a bouncing Betty had painted me with light on a night trail outside a pitiful Third World village stinking of duck shit and unburied water buffalo.

Then I felt her hand rest in the center of my chest.

'Dave, there was a man outside this morning,' she said.

'Which man?'

'He was out by the road, looking through the trees at the gallery. When I opened the screen, he walked back down the road.'

'What did he look like?'

'I couldn't see his face. He had on a blue shirt and a hat.'

'Maybe he was just lost.'

'Our number and name are on the mailbox by the road. Why would he be looking up at the gallery?'

'I'll ask Batist if he saw anyone unusual hanging around the front.'

She got up from the bed and began dressing by the back window. The curtains, which had the texture of gauze and were printed with tiny pink flowers, ruffled across the arch of her back as she stepped into her panties.

'Why are you looking at me like that?' she said.

'Because without exaggeration I can say that you're one of the most beautiful women on earth.'

When she smiled her eyes closed and opened in a way that made my heart drop.

Later, I went down to the dock to help Batist clean up the tables after the lunch crowd had left. Parked by the boat ramp, pinging with heat, was a flatbed truck with huge cone-shaped loudspeakers welded all over the cab's roof. On the doors, hand-painted in a flowing calligraphy, were the words *Rev. Oswald Flat Ministries*.

I remembered the name from years ago when he had broadcast his faith-healing show from Station XERF, one of the most powerful radio transmitters in the Western Hemisphere, located across the Rio Grande from Del Rio, in old Mexico so that the renters of its airtime were not governed by FCC restrictions. Sandwiched between ads for tulip bulbs, bat guano, baby chicks, aphrodisiacs, and memberships in every society from the Invisible Empire to the Black Muslims, were sermons by Brother Oswald, as he was called, that were ranting, breathless pieces of Appalachian eloquence. Sometimes he would become virtually hysterical, gasping as though he had emphysema, then he would snort air through his nostrils and begin another fifteen-minute roller-coaster monologue that would build with such roaring, unstoppable intensity that the technicians would end his sermon for him by superimposing a prerecorded ad.

He and his wife, a woman in a print cotton dress with rings of fat under her chin, were eating barbecue at the only table in the bait shop when I opened the screen door. It must have been ninety degrees in the shop, even with the window fans on, but Oswald Flat wore a long-sleeve denim work shirt buttoned at the wrists and a cork sun helmet that leaked sweat out of the band down the sides of his head. His eyes were pale behind his rimless glasses, the color of water flowing over gravel, liquid-looking in the heat, the back of his neck and hands burned the deep hue of chewing tobacco.

'That's Dave yonder,' Batist said to him from behind the counter, seemingly relieved. He picked up a can of soda pop and went outside to drink it at one of the telephone-spool tables under the awning that shaded the dock.

Flat's eyes went up and down my body. His wife began

eating a Moon Pie, chewing with her mouth open while she stared idly out the window at the bayou.

'Looks like you're a hard man to grab holt of,' he said.

'Not really. I was up at the house.'

'Don't like to bother a man in his home.'

'What could I do for you, sir?'

'I belong to the Citizens Committee for a Better New Orleans.

I make no apology for hit. The town's a commode. But I don't like what got done to your colored boy.'

'*Boy*?'

His southern mountain accent grated like piano wire drawn through a hole punched in a tin can. He took a toothpick from his shirt pocket, worked it into a back tooth, and measured me again with his bemused, pale eyes.

'You one of them kind gets his nose up in the air about words he don't like?' he said.

'Batist is older than I am, Reverend. People hereabouts don't call him a boy.'

'He probably ain't gonna get much older if you don't take the beeswax out of your ears. There's something bad going on out yonder. I don't like hit.' He waved his hand vaguely at the eastern horizon.

'You mean the vigilante?'

'Maybe. Maybe something a whole lot bigger than that.'

'I don't follow you.'

'Things falling apart at the center. I think it's got to do with the Antichrist.'

'The Antichrist?'

'You got woodpecker holes in your head or something?'

'I'm sorry, but I have no idea what you're talking about.'

'There's signs and such, the way birds fly around in a dead sky right before a storm. You had a president with the numbers in his name.' He puffed out both his cheeks.

'I can tell you're thinking, son. I can smell the wood burning.'

'What numbers?'

'Ronald Wilson Reagan. Six-six-six. The Book of Revelation says hit, you'll know him by the numbers in his name. I think that time's on us.'

'Could I get y'all anything else?'

'Does somebody have to hit you upside the head with a two-by-four to get your attention?' he said.

'Stop talking to the man like that, Os,' his wife said, opening another Moon Pie, her gaze fixed indolently on the willows bending in the breeze.

'That colored fellow out yonder's innocent,' he said to me. 'These murders, I don't care if hit's dope dealers being killed or not, they ain't done by somebody on the side of justice. People can pretend that's the case, but hit ain't so. And that bothers me profoundly. God's honest truth, son. That's all I come here to tell you.'

'Do you know something about the murders, Reverend?'

'You'll be the first to hear about hit when I do.' His face was dilated and discolored in the heat, as though it had been slowly poached in warm water.

After he and his wife drove away in their flatbed truck, the exact nature of their mission still a mystery to me, I called up to the house.

'Hey, Boots, I'm going to Lafayette to talk to a lawyer, then I have to pick up some ice for the coolers,' I said. 'By the way, that man in the blue shirt you saw ... I think he was just in the shop. He's a fundamentalist radio preacher. I guess he's trying to do a good deed of some kind.'

'Why was he staring up at the house?'

'You've got me. He's probably just one of those guys who left his grits on the stove too long. Anyway, he seems harmless enough.'

If I had only mentioned his name or the fact that he

was with his wife, or that he was elderly, or that he was a southern mountain transplant. Any one of those things would have made all the difference.

chapter six

She had just changed into a pair of shorts and sandals to work in the garden when he knocked on the front screen door. He wore a blue cotton short-sleeve shirt and a Panama hat with a flowered band around the crown. His physique was massive, without a teaspoon of fat on it, his neck like a tree stump with thick roots at the base that wedged into his wide shoulders. His neatly creased slacks hung loosely on his tapered waist and flat stomach.

But his green eyes were shy, and they crinkled when he smiled. He carried a paper sack under his right arm.

'I wasn't able to give this to your husband, but perhaps I can give it to you,' he said.

'He'll be home a little later, if you want to come back.'

'I'm sorry, I forgot to introduce myself. My name's Will Buchalter. Actually this is for you and the little girl.'

'I'm not quite sure I understand.'

'It's a gift. Some candy.' He slipped the box, which was wrapped in ribbon and satin paper, partially out of the sack.

'That's very nice of you, I'm sure, but it might be better if you drop back by when Dave's here.'

'I didn't mean to cause an inconvenience. I'm a little bit inept sometimes.'

'No, I didn't mean that you were—'

'Could I have a glass of water, please?' He took off his hat. His fine blond hair was damp in the heat.

Her eyes went past his shoulder to the dock, where she could see Batist washing fish fillets in a bloody pan.

'Or I can just walk down to the bait shop,' he said.

'No, no, come in. I'll get you one,' she said, and opened the screen for him. 'Dave said he was talking to you earlier about something?'

He nodded, his eyes crinkling again, filling with light, focusing on nothing. When she returned from the kitchen, he was sitting on the couch, examining two seventy-eight rpm records that he had removed from the metal racks where I kept my historical jazz collection.

'Oh,' she said. 'Those are quite rare. They have to be handled very carefully.'

'Yes, I know,' he said. 'This is Benny Goodman's nineteen thirty-three band. But there's dust along the rim. You see, the open end of the jacket should always be turned toward the back of the shelf.' He slipped his large hand inside one of the paper jackets and slid out the record.

'Please, you shouldn't do that.'

'Don't worry. I have a big collection of my own,' he said. 'Watch my hands. See, I don't touch the grooves. Fingerprints can mar a record in the same way they cause rust on gun blueing.'

He rubbed the record's rim softly with a piece of Kleenex, then carefully inserted it back in the paper jacket. He looked up into Bootsie's face.

'I'm sorry. I shouldn't have handled them,' he said, twisting sideways and replacing both records on the rack. 'But a shudder goes through me when I see dust on a beautiful old record. You have some wonderful ones in your collection. I'd give anything to have those Bix Beiderbeckes and Bunk Johnsons in mine.'

'Dave's collected them since he was in high school. That's why I'm a little nervous if somebody picks them up.' She handed him the glass of water and remained standing.

'Well, I won't take any more of your time. I just

wanted to leave this little gift and introduce myself.' He took a small sip from the water glass and placed the box of candy on the arm of the couch. 'Before I go, could I show you something? It'd mean a lot to me.'

The hair on his forearms looked golden and soft, like down, in the shaft of sunlight that fell through the side window. He removed a silver leather-bound scrapbook from the paper bag and rested it in his lap.

'It'll only take a minute,' he said.

'I'm a little behind in my work today.'

'Please. Then I won't bother y'all any more.'

'Well, for just a minute,' she said.

She sat down next to him, her legs crossed, her hands folded on her knee.

'I know that Mr. Bimstine has talked to Dave, but unfortunately he's sometimes not a truthful man,' he said.

'Bimstine?'

'Yes, Hippo Bimstine. Sometimes he has a way of concealing what he's really up to. I'm afraid it might just be another racial characteristic with him and some of his friends.'

'I'm not making the connection. I'm not sure of what you're doing here, either.'

He patted his palms lightly on the silver leather of the scrapbook.

'I don't want to say something that's offensive to anyone,' he said. 'But Mr. Bimstine lies about the causes he serves. I doubt that he's told your husband he raises money for Israel.'

'You had better come back later and talk to Dave about this.'

'You're misunderstanding me. I didn't come here to criticize Mr. Bimstine. I just wanted to show you how a hoax can be created.' His thumb peeled back several stiff pages of the scrapbook to one that contained two clipped-out newspaper photographs of men in striped prison uniforms and caps, staring out at the camera from behind barbed wire. Their faces were gaunt and unshaved, their eyes luminous with hunger and fear. 'These are supposed to be Jews in a German extermination camp in nineteen forty-four. But look, Mrs. Robicheaux.' He flipped to the next page. 'Here are the same photographs as they appeared in a Polish newspaper in nineteen thirty-one. These were Polish convicts, not German political prisoners. This is all part of a hoax that was perpetrated by British Intelligence. ... I'm sorry. Have I upset you about something?'

'I mistook you for someone else,' she said rising to her feet. 'I have to go somewhere now.'

'Where?'

'That's not your ... Please go now.'

He rose to his feet. His face looked down into hers, only inches away. For the first time she noticed that there were blackheads, like a spray of pepper, at the corners of his eyes.

'I only wanted to help,' he said. 'To bring you and your husband some information that you didn't have before. You invited me in.'

'I thought you were someone else,' she repeated. 'It's not your fault. But I want you to leave.'

'I'd like to help you, if you'd let me.'

'I'm going out the door now. If you don't leave, I'll call—'

'Who? That black man washing fish? I think you're very tense. You don't need to stay that way, Mrs. Robicheaux. Believe me.'

'Please get out of my way.'

He rested both of his hands on her shoulders and searched in her eyes as a lover might. 'How does this feel?' he asked, then tightened his fingers on her muscles and inched them down her back and sides, widening his knees slightly, flexing his loins.

'You get away from me. You disgusting—' she said, his breath, the astringent reek of his deodorant washing over her.

'I wouldn't hurt you in any way. You're a lovely woman, but your husband is working for Jews. Hush, hush, now, I just want to give you something to remember our little moment by.'

His arms encircled her waist, locking hand-on-wrist in the small of her back, tightening until she thought her rib cage would snap. He bent her backwards, smothering her body with his, then pushed his tongue deep inside her mouth. He held her a long moment, and as he did, he clenched her left kidney with one hand, like a machinist's vise fastening on a green walnut, and squeezed until yellow and red patterns danced behind her eyes and she felt urine running from her shorts.

She sat cross-legged and weeping against the wall, her face buried in her hands as he started his red convertible in the drive, tuned his radio, and backed out into the dirt road, the dappled sunlight spangling on the waxed finish of his car.

chapter seven

There was no record of a Will Buchalter with the New Iberia city police or the sheriff's department or with the state police in Baton Rouge. No parish or city agency in New Orleans had a record of him, either, nor did the National Crime Information Center in Washington, D.C. Nor could Bootsie identify him from any of the mug shots at the Iberia Parish sheriff's office.

Our fingerprint man lifted almost perfect sets of prints from the water glass used by the man who called himself Will Buchalter, from the record jackets he'd touched, and from the box of candy he'd left behind. But without a suspect in custody or corresponding prints on file, they were virtually worthless.

There was another problem, too, one that many victims of a sexual assault discover. Sexual crimes, as they are defined by our legal system, often fall into arbitrary categories that have nothing to do with the actual degree of physical pain, humiliation, and emotional injury perpetrated on the victim. At best we would probably only be able to charge the man who called himself Will Buchalter with misdemeanor battery, committed under circumstances that would probably make a venal defense lawyer lick his teeth.

I called Hippo Bimstine early the next morning, then drove to New Orleans and met him at his house in the Carrollton district by the levee. He sat in a stuffed red velvet chair by the front window, which reached from the floor to the ceiling, and kept fooling with a cellophane-wrapped cigar that was the diameter of a twenty-five-cent piece. His hair was wet and freshly combed, parted as neatly as a ruled line down the center of his head. His lower stomach bulged like a pillow under his slacks. Hanging on the wall above the mantel was a gilt-framed photograph of Hippo and his wife and their nine children, all of whom resembled him.

'How about sitting down, Dave?' he said. 'I don't feel too comfortable with a guy who acts like he was shot out of a cannon five minutes ago.'

'He knew you.'

'So do a lot of people. That doesn't mean I know them.'

'Who is he, Hippo?'

'A guy who obviously doesn't like Jews. What else can I tell you?'

'You'd better stop jerking me around.'

'How about a Dr Pepper or something to eat? Look, you think I rat-fuck my friends? That's what you're telling me, I set you up for some lowlife to come in your house and molest your wife?'

'He said you were raising money for Israel.'

'Then he's full of shit. I'm an American businessman. The big word there is *American*. I care about this city, I care about this nation. You bring me that Nazi fuck and I'll clip him for you.'

'How do you know he's a Nazi?'

'I took a wild guess.'

'What's in that sub?'

'Seawater and dead krauts. Jesus Christ, how do I know what's in there? Like I've been down in German submarines?' He looked at me a long moment, started to unwrap his cigar, then dropped it on the coffee table and stared out the window at a solitary moss-strung oak in his front yard. 'I'm sorry what this guy did to your wife. I don't know who he is, though. But maybe there're more

63

of these kinds of guys around than you want to believe, Dave. Come on in back.'

I followed him deep into his house, which had been built in the 1870s, with oak floors, spiral staircases, high ceilings, and enormous windows that were domed at the top with stained glass. Then we crossed his tree-shaded, brick-walled backyard, past a swimming pool in which islands of dead oak leaves floated on the chemical green surface, to a small white stucco office with a blue tile roof that was almost completely encased by banana trees. He used a key on a ring to unlock the door.

The furniture inside was stacked with boxes of documents and files, the corkboards on the walls layered with thumbtacked sheets of paper, newspaper clippings, yellowed photographs with curled edges, computer printouts of people's names, telephone numbers, home and business addresses. The room was almost frigid from the air-conditioning unit in the window.

I stared at an eight-by-ten photograph in the middle of a cork-board. In it a group of children, perhaps between the ages of five and eight, had rolled up their coat sleeves from their right forearms to show the serial numbers that had been tattooed across their skin.

'Those kids look like they're part of a hoax, Dave?' he said.

'What's going on, partner?'

He didn't answer. He sat down at his desk, his massive buttocks splaying across the chair, his huge head sinking into his shoulders like a pumpkin, and clicked on his computer and viewing screen. I watched him type the name 'Buchalter' on the keyboard, then enter it into the computer. A second later a file leaped into the blue viewing screen. Hippo tapped on a key that rolled the screen like film being pulled through a projector while his eyes narrowed and studied each entry.

'Take a look,' he said. 'I've got a half dozen Buchalters here, but none of them seem to be your man. These guys are too old or they're in jail or dead.'

'What is all this?'

'I belong to a group of people who have a network. We keep tabs on the guys who'd like to see more ovens and searchlights and guard towers in the world – the Klan, the American Nazi party, the Aryan Nation, skinheads out on the coast, a bunch of buttwipes called Christian Identity at Hayden Lake, Idaho. They don't just spit Red Man anymore, Dave. They're organized, they all know each other, they've got one agenda – they'd like to make bars of soap out of people they disagree with. Not just Jews. People like you'd qualify, too.'

'Try another spelling,' I said.

'No, I think we've got the right spelling, just the wrong generation. I'll give you a history lesson. Look at this.' He tapped the key again that rolled the screen, then stopped at the name *Buchalter, Jon Matthew*. 'You ever hear of the American-German Bund?'

'Yeah, it was a fascist movement back in the nineteen thirties. They held rallies in Madison Square Garden.'

'That's right. And an offshoot of the Bund was a group called the Silver Shirts. One of their founders was this guy Jon Matthew Buchalter. He went to federal prison for treason and got out in nineteen fifty-six, just in time to die of liver cancer.'

'Okay?'

'He was from Grand Isle.'

'So maybe the guy who came to my house is related to him?'

He clicked off his computer and turned to face me in his chair. His head sank into his neck, and his jowls swelled out like the bottom of a deflated basketball. 'I've got no answers for you,' he said. 'Sometimes I wonder if I haven't gone around the bend. How many people keep a rat's nest of evil like this in their backyard?'

I looked into his eyes.

'I don't want to offend you, Hippo, but I don't think you've squared with me. Is there something about this submarine you haven't told me?'

'Hey, time for a flash, Dave. You told *me* about the sub, remember? You bargained with *me* about the finder's fee. You think I got secrets, I live in a private world? You bet your oysters I do. The bars on my house windows, the electronic security system, the rent-a-cops I pay to watch my kids, you think I got all that because I'm worried a bunch of coloreds from Magazine are gonna walk off with my lawn furniture? You're living in the New Jerusalem, Dave. It's the year zero; it's us against them. We either make it or we don't.'

'I'm not sure I get what you're saying, Hippo. I'm not sure I want to, either. It sounds a little messianic.'

His face was flushed, his collar wilted like damp tissue paper around his thick neck.

'Go on back to the worm business, Dave,' he said. 'That guy comes around your house again, do the earth a favor, screw a gun barrel in his mouth and blow his fucking head off. Leave me alone now, will you? I don't feel too good. I got blood pressure could blow gaskets out of a truck engine.'

He wiped at his mouth with his hand. His lips were purple in the refrigerated gloom of his office. He stared at a collection of thumbtacked news articles and photographs on his corkboard as though his eyes could penetrate the black-and-white grain of the paper, as though perhaps he himself had been pulled inside a photograph, into a world of freight cars grinding slowly to a stop by a barbed-wire gate that yawned open like a hungry mouth, while dogs barked in the eye-watering glare of searchlights and files of the newly arrived moved in silhouette toward buildings with conical chimneys that disappeared into their own smoke.

Or was I making a complexity out of a histrionic and disingenuous fat man whose self-manufactured drama had accidentally brought a stray misanthrope out of the woodwork?

It was hard to buy into the notion that somehow

World War II was still playing at the Bijou in New Orleans, Louisiana.

I left him in his office and walked outside into the light. The heat was like a match flame against my skin.

'It sounds deeply weird,' Clete said, biting into his po'-boy sandwich at a small grocery store up by Audubon Park, where the owner kept tables for working people to eat their lunch. 'But maybe we're just living in weird times. It's not like the old days.'

'You believe this American Bund stuff?'

'No, it's the way people think nowadays that bothers me. Like this vigilante gig and this Citizens Committee for a Better New Orleans. You knew Bimstine and Tommy Lonighan are both on it?'

'No. When did Lonighan become a Rotarian?'

'Law-and-order and well-run vice can get along real good together. Conventioneers looking for a blow job don't like getting rolled or ripped off by Murphy artists. Did you know that Lucinda Bergeron is NOPD's liaison person with the Committee?'

He chewed his food slowly, watching my face. Outside, the wind was blowing and denting the canopy of spreading oaks along St. Charles.

'Then this preacher whose head glows in the dark shows up at your dock and tells you he's part of the same bunch. You starting to see some patterns here, noble mon?' he said.

'I don't know what any of that has to do with the guy who hurt Bootsie.'

'Maybe it doesn't.' He watched the streetcar roll down the track on the neutral ground and stop on the corner. It was loaded with Japanese businessmen. In spite of the temperature they all wore dark blue suits, ties, and long-sleeve shirts. 'If I were a worrying man, you know what would worry me most? It's not the crack and the black punks in the projects. It's a feeling I've got about the normals, it's like they wouldn't mind trying it a different way for a while.'

'What do you mean?'

'Maybe I'm wrong, but if tomorrow morning I woke up and read in *The Times-Picayune* that an election had just been held and it was now legal to run the lowlifes through tree shredders, you know, the kind the park guys use to grind oak limbs into wood chips, it wouldn't be a big surprise.'

'Did you ever hear of anybody in the city who fits the description of this guy Buchalter?'

'Nope. I've got a theory, though; at least it's something we can check out. He's an out-of-towner. He went to your house to shake up your cookie bag. Right? There doesn't seem to be any obvious connection between our man and any particular local bucket of shit we might have had trouble with. Right? What does all that suggest to you, Streak?'

'One of the resident wise guys using out-of-town talent to send a message.'

'And whose Johnson did we just jerk on? It can't hurt to have a talk with Tommy Bobalouba again, can it?'

'I thought he was part of your meal ticket.'

'Not anymore. I don't like the way he acted in front of Martina. You take an Irish street prick out of the Channel, put him in an eight-hundred-thou house by Lake Pontchartrain, and you've got an Irish street prick in an eight-hundred-thou house by Lake Pontchartrain. How about we have a little party?'

'I'm on leave, and I'm out of my jurisdiction.'

'Who cares? If the guy's clean, it's no big deal. If he's not, fuck that procedural stuff. We scramble his eggs.'

The cashier cut his eyes toward us, then turned the floor fan so that our conversation was blown out the open door, away from the other customers.

'Let me call home first,' I said.

'No argument?'

I shrugged my shoulders. He watched my face.

'How much sleep did you get last night?' he asked.

'Enough.'

'You could fool me.'

'You want to go out to Lonighan's or not?'

There was a pause in his eyes, a fine bead of light. He made a round button with his lips and scratched at his cheek with one fingernail.

Lonighan lived a short distance from the yacht club in an imitation Tudor mansion that had been built by a New Orleans beer baron during the 1920s. The grounds were surrounded by a high brick wall, at the front of which was a piked security gate, with heavy clumps of banana trees on each side of it, and a winding driveway that led past a screened-in pool and clay tennis courts that were scattered with leaves. We parked my truck, and Clete pushed the button on the speaker box by the gate.

'Who is it?' a voice said through the box.

'Clete Purcel. Is Tommy home?'

'He's over at his gym. You want to come back later or leave a message?'

'Who are all those people in the pool?'

'Some guests. Just leave a message, Clete. I'll give it to him.'

'When'll he be home?'

'He comes, he goes, what do I know? Just leave a fucking message, will you?'

'Here's the message, Art. I don't like talking to a box.'

'I'm sorry, I'll be down. Hey, Clete, I'm just the hired help, all right?'

A moment later the man named Art walked down the drive with a pair of hedge clippers in his hand. He was bare-chested and sweaty and wore grass-stained white shorts and sandals that flopped on his feet.

'Open up,' Clete said.

'You're putting me in a bad place, man. Why'd you have to get Tommy upset?'

'I didn't do anything to Tommy.'

'Tell that to him. Christ, Clete, you know what kind of guy he is. How you think he feels when a broad tells him off in public?'

'You gonna open up?'

'No.'

'You're starting to piss me off, Art.'

'What can I say? Wait in your truck, I'll send you guys out some drinks and sandwiches. Give me a break, all right?'

He walked back toward the house. The swimmers were leaving the screened-in pool for a shady area in the trees, set with lawn chairs, a drinks table, and a smoking barbecue pit. The skin flexed around the corners of Clete's eyes.

'You still got your binoculars?' he asked.

'In the glove compartment.'

He went to the truck and returned to the gate. He focused my pair of World War II Japanese field glasses through the steel bars and studied the people in the shade.

'Check it out, mon,' he said, handing me the glasses.

One woman lay on a reclining chair with a newspaper over her face. A second, older, heavyset and big-breasted, her skin tanned almost the color of mahogany, stood on the lawn with her feet spread wide, touching each toe with a cross-handed motion, her ash blond hair cascading back and forth across her shoulders. A third woman, with dyed red hair, who could not have been over twenty or twenty-one, was bent forward over a pocket mirror, a short soda straw held to one nostril, the other nostril pinched shut with a forefinger. Seated on each side of her was a thick-bodied, sun-browned, middle-aged man with a neon bikini wrapped wetly around the genitals, the back and chest streaked with wisps of black and gray hair. The face of one man was flecked with fine patterns of scab tissue, as though he had walked through a reddish brown skein of cobweb.

'When did Tommy Blue Eyes hook up with the Caluccis?' Clete said. 'They always hated each other.'

'Business is business.'

'Yeah, but the micks always looked down on the greaseballs. They didn't socialize with them.' He took the glasses out of my hand and looked again through the bars. 'If you think Bobo and Max are geeks, check out the cat flopping steaks on the grill.'

A man who must have been six and one half feet tall had come out of the side entrance to the house with a tray of meat. He had a flat Indian face, a cheerless mouth, and wide-set, muddy eyes that didn't squint or blink in the smoke rising from the pit. His hair was jet black and freshly barbered and looked like a close-cropped wig glued on brownish red stone.

'All the guy needs are electrodes inset in his temples,' Clete said.

'I don't think this is going anywhere,' I said. 'I probably should head back to New Iberia.'

His green eyes roamed over my face. 'You don't think Bootsie can handle it?' he asked.

'How do I know, Clete? He humiliated her, he put his tongue in her mouth, he left bruises on her kidney like he'd taken a pair of pliers to her.'

He nodded and didn't speak for a moment. Then he said, 'That blonde doing the aerobics is Tommy's regular punch when his old lady's out of town. No, she's more than that, he got a real Jones for her. Believe me, Tommy and that clunk of radiator hose he's got for a schlong aren't far away. Dave, look at me. You got my word, I'm going to dig this guy Buchalter out of the woodwork. If you're not around, I'll give you a Polaroid, then you can burn it.'

He continued to stare into my face, then he said, 'You're troubling me, noble mon.'

'What's the problem?'

'You look wired to the eyes, that's the problem.'

'So what?'

'You have a way of throwing major monkey shit through the window fan, that's what.'

'*I* do?'

'Go down to the corner and call Bootsie. Then we'll give it another hour. If Tommy's not back by then, we'll hang it up.'

We waited in the truck for another hour, but Tommy Lonighan didn't return. The metal of my dashboard burned my hands when I touched it, and the air smelled of salt and dead water beetles in the rain gutters. I started the engine.

'Wait a minute. They're coming out. Let's not waste an opportunity, mon,' Clete said.

The electronic piked gate opened automatically, and the Calucci brothers, in a light blue Cadillac convertible, with the two younger women in the backseat, drove out of the shade into the sunlight. I started to block their exit with the truck, but it was unnecessary. Max Calucci, the driver, and one of the women in back were arguing furiously. Max stepped hard on the brakes, jolting everyone in the car forward, turned in his leather seat, and began jabbing his finger at the woman. The woman, the one who had been doing lines through a soda straw earlier, climbed out of the backseat in her shorts and spiked heels, raking a long, paint-curling scratch down the side of the Cadillac.

Max got out of the car and struck the woman full across the mouth with the flat of his hand. He hit her so hard that a barrette flew from her lacquered red hair. Then he slapped her across the ear. She pressed her palms into her face and began to weep.

None of them saw us until we had walked to within five feet of their car.

'Better ease up, Max. People might start to think you abuse women,' Clete said.

'What are *you* doing here?' Max said. He was bald down through the center of his head, and drops of sweat the size of BB's glistened in his thick, dark eyebrows. Up close, the scabs on his face and neck looked like curlicues of reddish brown, fine-linked chain.

'Art didn't let you know we were out here?' Clete said. 'That's why you didn't invite us in?'

'You blindsided me the other night, Purcel. It's not over between us. You better haul your fat ass out of here,' Max said.

'Y'all know a dude by the name of Will Buchalter? Streak here'd really like to talk to him,' Clete said.

'No, I don't know him. Now get out of here—' He stopped and raised his finger in the face of the woman with the dyed red hair. 'And *you*, get back in the car. You're gonna polish that scratch out if you have to do it with your twat. Did you hear me, move! You don't open that mouth again, either, unless I want to put something in it.'

He clamped his hand on the back of her neck, squeezed, and twisted her toward the car while tears ran from her eyes.

The shovel lay propped among some rosebushes against the brick wall. It had a long, work-worn wood handle with a wide, round-backed blade. Max Calucci did not see me pick it up. Nor did he see me swing it with both hands, from deep behind me, as I would a baseball bat, until he heard the blade ripping through the air. By then it was too late. The metal whanged off his elbow and thudded into his rib cage, bending him double, and I saw his mouth drop open and a level of pain leap into his eyes that he could not quite find words to express.

Then I reversed the shovel in my hands and swung the blade up into his face, as you would butt-stroke an adversary with a pugil stick. I saw him tumble backwards on the grass, his knees drawn up in front of him, his face bloodless with shock, his mouth a scarlet circle of disbelief. I heard feet running down the drive, Bobo Calucci blowing the car horn with both hands in desperation, then Clete was standing in front of me, pressing me back with his palms, his armpits drenched with perspiration, the strap of his nylon shoulder holster biting into one nipple.

'For Christ's sakes, back off, Dave, you're gonna kill the guy,' he was saying. 'You hear me? Let it slide, Streak. He's not the guy we care about.'

Then his big hands dropped to the handle of the shovel and twisted it from my grasp, his Irish pie-plate face two inches from mine, his eyes filled with pity and an undisguised and fearful love.

chapter eight

That night, as I lay next to Bootsie in our bed, I did not tell her about the incident with the Calucci brothers. Even though I had been in Alcoholics Anonymous a number of years, and to one degree or another had been through the twelve steps of recovery and had tried to incorporate them into my life, I had never achieved a great degree of self-knowledge, other than the fact that I was a drunk; nor had I ever been able to explain my behavior and the way I thought, or didn't think, to normal people.

I always wanted to believe that those moments of rage, which affected me almost like an alcoholic blackout, were due to a legitimate cause, that I or someone close to me had been seriously wronged, that the object of my anger and adrenaline had not swum coincidentally into my ken.

But I had known too many cops who thought the same way. Somehow there was always an available justification for the Taser dart, the jet of Mace straight into the eyes, the steel baton whipped across the shinbones or the backs of the thighs.

The temptation is to blame the job, the stressed-out adversarial daily routine that can begin like a rupturing peptic ulcer, the judges and parole boards who recycle psychopaths back on the street faster than you can shut their files. But sometimes in an honest moment an unpleasant conclusion works its way through all the rhetoric of the self-apologist, namely, that you are drawn to this world in the same way that some people are fascinated by the protean shape and texture of fire, to the extent that they need to slide their hands through its caress.

I remember an old-time gunbull at Angola who had spent forty-seven years of his life shepherding convicts under a double-barreled twelve-gauge out on the Mississippi levee. During that time he had killed four men and wounded a half dozen others. His liver had been eaten away with cirrhosis; the right side of his chest was caved in from the surgical removal of a cancerous lung. To my knowledge, he had no relatives with whom he kept contact, no women in his life except a prostitute in Opelousas. I asked him how he had come to be a career gunbull.

He thought about it a moment, then dipped the end of his cigar in his whiskey glass and put it in his mouth.

'It was me or them, I reckon,' he said.

'Beg your pardon?'

'I figured the kind of man I was, one way or another I was gonna be jailing. Better to do it up there on the horse than down there with a bunch of niggers chopping in the cane.'

I didn't tell Bootsie about the Caluccis, nor did I say anything to her about the smell of bourbon that she brought to bed with her that night. I fell asleep with my hand on her back. At about one in the morning I felt her weight leave the mattress. I heard her walk barefooted into the kitchen, open a cabinet without turning on the light, then clink a bottle against a glass. A moment later she was in the bathroom, brushing her teeth.

She seldom drank and had little physical tolerance for alcohol. The following morning she stayed in the shower for almost fifteen minutes, then ate an aspirin with her coffee and talked brightly at the breakfast table for a long time, until finally her face became wan and she put her forehead down on her palm.

I walked around behind her chair and rubbed her neck and shoulders.

'Sometimes it's hard to accept this, Boots, but there's no reason to feel shame when we're overcome by superior physical force,' I said. 'No more than a person should be ashamed of contracting the flu or being undone by the attack of a wild animal.'

'I keep smelling his odor and feeling his tongue in my mouth,' she said. 'I feel somehow that I allowed him to do it.'

'It's what all victims feel. We open our doors to the wrong person, then we think that somehow our expression of trust means we're weak and complicit. You didn't do anything wrong, Boots. You mustn't think that way anymore.'

But that kind of advice, under those kinds of circumstances, is similar to telling a person who has been stricken with a cerebral disease to rise from his sickbed and walk.

I turned off the grits on the stove, washed and put away our coffee cups and saucers, and took Bootsie to a restaurant on the Vermilion River in Lafayette for brunch. When I went to the men's room, she called the waiter back to the table and ordered a vodka collins. After we had eaten, we walked out on the deck that overlooked the water and watched some kids waterskiing. The sun was white and straight up in the sky, the air laced with the smell of diesel smoke from the trucks passing over the concrete bridge. Down below in the muddy current, a dead snow egret floated among an island of twigs and torn camellia leaves. The egret's wing had been broken, and above one eye was the coppery glint of an embedded BB in the feathers.

'Oh,' Bootsie said, and let out her breath. Then she turned away from the deck railing and said, 'Maybe we should go now, Dave. I'm going to listen to you and stay out of the sun. I've been terribly careless about it, I know. It's wrong to make other people worry about you, isn't it? I am not going to allow myself to be a careless person anymore, I promise.'

Her eyes were as bright and intent as if she were putting together a syllogism that in one way or another would solve a particular problem for all time. She walked back through the restaurant and out the front without waiting for me.

When we got home the phone was ringing in the kitchen. Bootsie went into the bedroom, turned on the window fan, and lay down on the bed with her arm across her eyes.

'Hello,' I said into the telephone receiver.

'This Mr. Robicheaux?'

'Yes.'

'How come you ain't he'ped my mama?'

'Excuse me?'

'She he'ped you, ain't she? How come you ain't he'ped her?'

'Who is this?'

'Zoot Bergeron.' But the tone of voice had become less aggressive and certain. 'My mama said Mr. Baxter's gonna get her fired if he can.'

'You're Lucinda's son?'

'Yes, suh.' Then he tried to deepen his voice. 'Yeah, that's right.'

'How old are you, podna?'

'Seventeen. I'm seventeen years old.' In the background I could hear echoes, like people shouting at each other in a public hall, and slapping sounds like leather hitting against leather.

'Does your mother know you're making this call?' I said.

'She tole you some stuff and you tole it back to Mr. Baxter. That ain't right she got to be in trouble 'cause you went and tole what you wasn't supposed to.'

Oh boy, I thought, *the business about the other homicide victims being mutilated.*

'I'll talk to your mother about it,' I said.

I could almost hear his breath click in his throat.

'That won't do no good. I can tell you who them vigilantes are. Then you and my mama can arrest them.'

'Oh? Why don't you just tell her?'

''Cause she don't believe me.'

'I see.'

'You coming down here?' he said.

'Where would that be?'

'The gym. Mr. Lonighan's Sport Center. You know where that's at?'

'What are you doing around Tommy Lonighan, partner?'

'I box here and I sweep up in the evening. You coming?'

'I'll think about it.'

I heard somebody begin to do a *rat-a-tat-tat* on a timing bag.

'You gonna tell her I called?'

'What's your name again?'

'Zoot.'

'That's a nifty name, Zoot. No, I'm not going to tell your mama that you called. But you listen to what I tell you, now. Don't be telling other people you know anything about vigilantes. Particularly around that gym. Okay?'

'Yes, suh. I mean, I got it. I'll be expecting you though. A deal's a deal, right? We got us a deal, ain't that right?'

'Wait a minute ...'

'My mama said you was a nice man, said for me not to be blaming her trouble with Mr. Baxter on you. She's right, ain't she? I be here this evening, I be here early in the morning.'

He hung up before I could answer.

At three that same afternoon I received a call from the

lawyer I had retained to represent Batist. He was the most successful criminal attorney in Lafayette. My five-minute conversation with him was another lesson in how the laws of finance apply to our legal system. The lawyer had confronted the prosecutor's office in New Orleans with the information given me by Lucinda Bergeron about the other murders; he also told them he could present a half dozen depositions to the effect that Batist was nowhere around New Orleans when they were committed. He also mentioned the possibility of civil suit against the city of New Orleans.

The homicide charge against Batist was to be dropped by tomorrow morning.

'That's it?' I said.

'That's it.'

'Did they bother to explain why he was ever charged in the first place?'

'They make mistakes like anybody else.'

'It sounds like they're pretty good at self-absolution.'

'I think we've done pretty well today.'

'How much do I owe you, Mr. Guidry?'

'There're no fees beyond what we originally agreed upon,' he said.

'You're telling me six thousand dollars for making some phone calls?'

'There was some investigative work involved as well.'

'Six thousand dollars without even going to trial?'

'I thought you'd be pleased to hear your friend was out of trouble.'

I was. I was also down eleven thousand dollars in attorney and bondsman's fees, which I would have to pay in monthly installments or with borrowed money.

That evening I took Bootsie and Alafair to a movie in New Iberia. It was raining when we got home, and the air smelled like fish left on the warm planks of a dock and wet trees and moldy pecan husks. Then, just when we were going to bed, Clete called from New Orleans and told me a strange story that had been passed on to him by a friend of his in the Coast Guard.

Two days ago, at sunset, out on the salt south of Cocodrie, a Coast Guard cutter had spotted a twenty-two-foot cabin cruiser anchored in the swells, the bow bouncing against the incoming tide. All week the cutter had been looking for a mother ship, perhaps a Panamanian tanker, that had been dumping air-sealed bales of reefer, with floating marker bottles, overboard for smaller, high-powered boats to fish out of the water and run through the bayous and canals to overland transporters who waited on high ground up in the wetlands.

There were two men in wet suits on board the cabin cruiser. They were lowering a cluster of underwater lights on a cable over the side when they saw the cutter approaching them. The Coast Guard skipper was sure he had found a pickup boat.

He lost any doubt when the men on the cabin cruiser pulled the cluster of lights clattering back over the rail, sawed loose the anchor rope with a bowie knife, and hit it full-bore for the coastline and shallower water, where there was a chance the cutter would go aground on a sandbar.

But when they made their turn the late sun must have been directly in their eyes. Or perhaps in their attempt at flight they simply did not care that they had left a diver overboard, a man in a wet suit, with air tanks, whose head was shaved as bald as a skinned onion. He popped through a swell at exactly the spot his friends had cut the anchor rope. He probably had no explanation for the fact that the rope had suddenly gone slack in his hands and the gulf's placid surface had churned to life with the cabin cruiser's screws and the dirty roar of exhaust pipes at the waterline.

Then through the humidity inside his mask, through the green chop against the glass, he must have realized that his worst fears as a diver – losing his electric light deep in the bowels of a sunken ship or perhaps being pulled down into a bottomless canyon by a mouthful of hooked teeth that snapped his bones as easily as sticks – were never legitimate fears at all, that the most terrible moment of his life was now being precipitated by his companions, for no reason that he could understand, in a way that made his screams, his waving arms, his last-second attempt to dive deep below the surface the impotent and futile gestures of a nightmare.

The cabin cruiser must have been hitting thirty-five knots when it plowed over him and the screws razored his body and left him floating like a rubber-wrapped tangle of mismatched parts in the boat's wake.

'Why were the guys on the boat running?' I said to Clete.

'They'd stolen it. Well, not exactly. It's owned by some millionaire yachtsman in Baltimore, but this alcoholic skipper keeps it for him in Biloxi. So the drunk thought he'd make a few bucks by renting it to these three guys. But at the last minute the three guys decided they didn't need to pay him the money after all, so instead they just stomped the shit out of him. They told him if he made a beef about it they'd catch him later and kick one of his own whiskey bottles up his ass.'

'Who were the guys?'

'The two in custody are just a couple of Biloxi beach farts who've been in and out of Parchman on nickel-and-dime B and E's. But dig this, the guy who got run through the propeller had some beautiful Nazi artwork on both arms – swastikas and SS lightning bolts.'

'So do most cons in the Aryan Brotherhood,' I said.

'But here's the kicker, mon. This guy was not home-grown. The Coast Guard found his passport on the cabin cruiser. He was from Berlin.'

'Do the guys in custody say what they were after?'

'They were hired by the German guy, but they claim the German guy wouldn't tell them what was down there. They thought maybe it was a scuttled boat with a lot of dope on it. Here's the real laugh, though. The

Coast Guard says there's no boat down at that spot. What the beach farts and the skinhead probably saw on their sonar was an oil rig that sank there in a hurricane about twenty years ago.'

'Thanks for the information, Clete.'

'You want to talk to the guys in custody?'

'Maybe.'

'I'd do it soon. The rummy in Biloxi isn't filing charges, and the kraut's death is going down as accidental. I don't guess anybody's going to lose sleep over a skinhead getting turned into potted meat out on the salt.'

'Thanks again, Clete.'

'You think they were after that sub?'

'Who knows?'

'Hippo Bimstine does. I want in on this, mon. When Streak operates in the Big Sleazy, he needs his old podjo to cover his back. Am I right?'

'Right. Good night, Cletus.'

I heard him pop the cap on a bottle and pour it into a glass.

'Bless my soul, I love that old-time rock 'n' roll, when the Bobbsey Twins from Homicide made their puds shrivel up and hide,' he said.

My palms felt stiff with fatigue, hard to fold closed, and my eyes burned as though there were sand behind the lids. Clete was still talking, rattling fresh ice into his glass, when I said good night a final time and eased the receiver down into the telephone cradle.

Tommy Lonighan's Sport Center was located on the edge of downtown New Orleans, in a late-nineteenth-century two-story brick building that had originally been a firehouse, then an automotive dealership in the 1920s, and finally a training gym for club boxers who fought for five dollars a fight during the Depression.

The interior smelled of sweat and leather and moldy towels; the canary yellow paint on the walls was blistered and peeling above the old iron radiators; the buckled and broken spaces in the original oak flooring had been patched over with plywood and linoleum. The body-building equipment was all out of another era – dumb-bells and weight-lifting benches, curling bars, even a washtub of bricks hung on a cable for pull downs. The canvas on the four rings had been turned almost black from scuff marks, body and hair grease, and kicked-over spit buckets.

But it was still the most famous boxing gym in New Orleans, and probably more Golden Gloves champions had come out of it than out of any other boxing center in the South. In the sunlight that poured down through the high windows, black, Latin, Vietnamese kids and a few whites sparred in headgear and kidney guards, clanked barbells up and down on a wide rubber pad, skipped rope with the grace of tap dancers, and turned timing bags into flying, leathery blurs.

A small, elderly white man, with a thick ear and a flat, toylike face, who was pulling the laces out of a box full of old gloves, pointed out Zoot to me.

'That tall kid about to break his nose on the timing bag,' he said. 'While you're over there, tell him he ain't carried the trash out to the Dumpster yet.'

The boy had his mother's elongated turquoise eyes and clear, light-brown skin. But he was unnaturally tall for his age, over six feet, and as slim and narrow-shouldered as if his skin had been stretched on wire. The elastic top of his trunks was sopping with the sweat that streamed in rivulets down his hairless chest. Each time his fist missed the timing bag, he would glance nervously a few feet away at another kid who had turned *his* timing bag into an explosion of sound and movement. Then Zoot would smash the bag with a right cross, snapping it back on the chain, try to connect with a left, miss, swing again with his right, and miss again.

'Try not to hit harder with one hand than the other,' I said. 'You have to create a kind of circular momentum.'

'A what?'

Great choice of words, I told myself.

'You called my house yesterday,' I said.

'You Mr. Robicheaux?'

'Yes.'

'Oh, yeah, well – I be with you in a minute, okay? They waiting for me over at the ring. I'm gonna go three with that white boy putting on his kidney guard.'

'You said you had some pretty important things to tell me, Zoot.'

His eyes flicked sideways, then came back on my face again.

'I gotta go my three. This ain't an easy place to talk, you know what I mean?'

'Yeah, I guess so.' I looked at the white kid who was climbing up in the corner of one of the rings. His skin had the alabaster iridescence of someone who seldom went out in the sunlight, but his stomach, which was tattooed with a red-and-green dragon, was a washboard, and the muscles in his arms looked like pieces of pig iron. 'Who is he?' I asked.

'Ummm, he fights in Miami and Houston a lot.'

'He's a pro?'

'Yes, suh.'

'You sure you want to do this, partner?'

He licked his lips and tried to hide the shine of fear in his eyes.

'He's a good guy. He's been up against some big names. He don't do this for just anybody,' Zoot said. 'I'll be right back. You ain't got to watch if you don't want. There's a Coca-Cola machine back in the dressing room.'

'I'll just take a seat over here.'

'Yes, suh. I'll be right back.'

I don't think I ever saw anyone box quite as badly as Zoot. Either he would hold both gloves in front of his face so that he was unable to see his opponent or he would drop his guard suddenly and float his face up like a balloon, right into a rain of blows. His stance was wrong-footed, he led with his right hand, he used his left

85

like a flipper, he took shot after shot in the mouth and
eyes because he didn't know how to tuck in his chin and
raise his shoulder against a right cross.

Fortunately the white kid went easy on him, except in
the third round when Zoot swung at the white kid's head
coming out of a clench. The white kid stepped inside
Zoot's long reach and hooked a hard chop into his nose.
Zoot went down on his butt in the middle of the canvas,
his long legs splayed out in front of him, his mouth-piece
lying wet in his lap, his eyes glazed as though someone
had popped a flashbulb in his face.

Twenty minutes later he came out of the dressing room
in his street clothes, combing his wet hair along the sides
of his head. His nose had stopped bleeding, but his left
eye had started to discolor and puff shut at the corner.
We walked across the street to a café that sold pizza by
the slice and sat at a table in back under a rotating
electric fan.

'Have you been boxing long?' I said.

'Since school let out.'

'You trying for the Golden Gloves?'

'I just do it for fun. I don't think about the Gloves or
any of that stuff.'

'Let me make a suggestion, Zoot. Keep your left
shoulder up and don't lead with your right unless you go
in for a body attack. Then get under the other guy's
guard and hook him hard in the rib cage, right under the
heart.'

He fed a long slice of pizza into his mouth and looked
at me while he chewed.

'You been a fighter?' he said.

'A little bit, in high school.'

'You think maybe I could try for the Gloves?'

'I guess that'd be up to you.'

He smiled and lowered his eyes.

'You don't think I'm too good, do you?' he said.

'You just went three rounds against a pro. That's not
bad.'

'I know what you're really thinking, though. You ain't got to make me feel good. Like I say, I do it for fun.' He touched at the corner of his puffed eye with one fingernail.

'You said you were going to tell me something about the vigilante murders,' I said.

'It's gang bangers. They fighting over who's gonna deal tar in the projects. Tar's real big again, Mr. Robicheaux. Lot of people don't want to mess with crack anymore.'

'How do you know it's the gangs, Zoot?'

'I get around. I got friends in the projects – the St. Thomas, the Iberville, the Desire. They all say there ain't no vigilante.'

'Is there a particular murder you have information about?'

He thought for a moment. 'Yeah, last spring,' he said. 'A dealer got thrown off the roof acrost from our school. The gang bangers said he was working the wrong neighborhood.'

He watched my face expectantly.

'Are there any names you want to give me?' I said.

'I'm just telling you what my friends say. I ain't got no names.'

'You come from a good home, Zoot. You think you should be hanging around gang bangers?'

'I got the friends I want. People don't tell me who I hang with.'

'I see. Well, thanks for the information.' I stood up to leave.'

'Ain't you gonna he'p out?'

'I'm afraid I don't have a lot to work with here.'

'Mr. Robicheaux, my mama's gonna lose her job.'

I sat back down. 'Where's your dad?'

His eyes became unfocused, then he looked over at the jukebox as though he had just noticed it.

'I ain't got one. Why you ax that?' he said.

'No reason. Your mother's a tough lady. Stop worrying about her.'

'Easy for you to say. You ain't there when she come home, always telling me—'

'Telling you what?'

'I ain't nothing but a big drink of water, I gotta be a *man*, I gotta stop slouching around like somebody pulled my backbone outta my skin.' He rolled up a paper napkin in his palm and dropped it in his plate. 'It ain't her fault. They get on her case where she works, then she just *got* to get on mine. But I'm tired of it.'

For the first time I noticed how long and narrow his hands were. Even his nails were long, almost like a girl's.

'You feel like putting your trunks back on?' I said.

'What for?'

'Take a walk with me to the drugstore, then we'll head back to the gym and talk about clocks and bombsights.'

'What?'

'Come on, I'm over the hill. You'll dump me on my butt, Zoot.'

We went into the drugstore on the corner, and I bought a rubber ball, just a little smaller than the palm of my hand, and dropped it in the pocket of my slacks. Then we crossed the street to the gym, and Zoot put on his trunks again and met me in an alcove with padded mats on the floor and a huge ventilator fan bolted into the wire-mesh windows. I hung my shirt on a rack of dumbbells and slipped on a pair of sixteen-ounce gloves that were almost as big as couch pillows.

Advice is always cheap, and the cheapest kind is the sort we offer people who have to enter dangerous situations for which they are seriously unprepared or ill-equipped. I probably knew a hundred one-liners that a cut-man or a trainer had told me in the corner of a Golden Gloves ring while he worked my mouthpiece from my teeth and squeezed a sponge into my eyes ('Swallow your blood, kid. Don't never let him see you're hurt … He butts you again in the clench, thumb him in the eye … He's telegraphing. When he drops his right shoulder, click off his light').

But very few people appreciate the amount of courage that it takes to stand toe-to-toe with a superior opponent who systematically goes about breaking the cartilage in your nose, splitting your eyebrows against the bone, and turning your mouth into something that looks like a torn tomato, while the audience stands on chairs and roars its approval of your pain and humiliation.

'Let's try to keep two simple concepts in mind,' I said. 'Move in a circle with the clock. You got that? Circle him till he thinks you're a shark. Always to the left, just like you're moving with the clock.'

'All right ...' He started circling with me, his gym shoes shuffling on the canvas pad, the skin around his temples taut with expectation, his eyes watching my fists.

'Then you look him right in the eye. Except in your mind you're seeing his face in a bombsight ... Don't look at my hands, look at my face. His face is right in the crosshairs, you understand me, because you know it's just a matter of time till you bust him open with your left, maybe make him duck and come up without his guard, and then pull the trigger and bust him with your right.'

He circled and squinted at me above his gloves with his puffed left eye.

'Hit me,' I said.

His jabs were like spastic jerks, ill-timed, fearful, almost pathetic.

'I said hit me, Zoot!'

His left came out and socked into my gloves.

'Hit *me*, not the glove,' I said. 'You're starting to piss me off.'

'What?'

'I said you're pissing me off. Do you have some problem with your hearing?' I could see the verbal injury in his eyes. I flipped a left jab at his head and drove my right straight into his guard. Then I did it again. His head snapped back with the weight of the blow, then he caught his balance and hunched his shoulders again. I saw him lower his right slightly and a glint form in one eye like a rifleman peering down iron sights.

His left missed me and scraped past my ear, but he had forced me to duck sideways, and when he unloaded his right he snapped his shoulder into it, the sweat leaping off his face, and caught me squarely across the jaw.

I lowered my gloves and grinned at him.

'That one was a beaut,' I said, and started pulling off my gloves.

'You quitting?'

'I told you, I'm over the hill for it. Besides, I have to get back to New Iberia.'

'Go three with me.'

I reached in my slacks, took out the rubber ball I had bought at the drugstore, and tossed it to him.

'Squeeze that in each hand five hundred times a day. Do *that*, and keep working on that right cross, and you'll be able to tear off your opponent's head and spit in it, Zoot.'

When I walked toward the exit, I looked back and saw him shadowboxing in front of the ventilator fan, his right hand working the rubber ball, his head ducking and weaving in front of the spinning fan blades. Advice might be cheap, but there is nothing facile about the faith of those to whom we give it. I wished Zoot lots of luck. He was probably going to need a pile of it.

chapter nine

I was almost out the front door of the gym when Tommy Lonighan came out of his office and shook my hand like a greeter at a casino. His muscular thighs bulged out of a pair of cut-off gray sweat trunks. His light blue eyes and pink face were radiant with goodwill.

'I saw you working out with Zoot,' he said.

'He's a good kid. I hope he does all right here, Tommy.'

'I'm a bad influence?'

'He shouldn't be going up against pros.'

'He got in the ring with that white kid, the one with the dragon tattooed on his belly?'

'Yes.'

'No kidding? That's not bad for a kid whose mother was probably knocked up by a marshmallow.'

'You know how to say it, Tommy.'

'Step into my office,' he answered, smiling. 'I want to talk.'

'I'm on my way out of town.'

'I'll buy you a beer. You want a pastrami sandwich? I got your pastrami sandwich. Forget about the other night. I had too much to drink. Come on, don't be a hard-ass.'

'What's on your mind?'

'On *my* mind? Somebody hurts your wife, and the next thing I know you're beating up people in my fucking driveway. Hey, it's all right. The Caluccis are scum. I just want to talk.'

I went inside his glassed-in office and sat down in front of his desk. The walls were covered with old prizefight posters and newspaper clippings about fighters that Lonighan had owned or managed. Above a shelf filled with boxing trophies was an autographed photograph of President Reagan, with two crossed American flags tucked behind the frame.

'How did you know about my wife, Tommy?' I said.

'Because Clete Purcel's been all over town, threatening to jam a chain saw up the butt of anybody with information who doesn't pass it on.' He took a long-necked bottle of beer out of a cooler by his feet, wiped off the ice, set the cap on the edge of his desk, and popped it off with the heel of his hand. He offered it to me.

'No, thanks.'

He poured it into a schooner, took a deep drink, and wiped the corners of his mouth with the back of his wrist.

'Let me cut to it, Tommy,' I said. 'You're right, a man came to our house and harmed my wife. It was right after you tried to discourage me from working for Hippo Bimstine.'

'I got a hard time believing this, Dave. You think that's how I operate, I got to send degenerates around to hurt the wives of people I respect?'

'You tell me.' I looked directly into his eyes. The cast in them reminded me of light trapped inside blue water. They remained locked on mine, as though wheels were turning over in his brain. Then he looked out the window with a self-amused expression on his face and picked up a sandwich from a paper plate in front of him.

'Is there a private joke you want to share with me, Tommy?'

'Dave, you insulted me at your table, in front of people, then you beat the shit out of a guy with a shovel in my driveway. Then you come to my place of business and tell me I'm sending perverts over to New Iberia to

92

bother your family. What did I do to deserve this? I offered you a fucking business situation. You don't see the humor in that?'

'I remember a line a journalist for *The Picayune* used about you once, Tommy. I never forgot it.'

'Yeah?'

'You're a mean man in a knife fight.'

'Oh yeah, I always liked that one.' He leaned forward on his elbows. His curly white hair hung across his forehead. 'I want that fucking sub. Anything the mockie's paying you, I'll double.'

'See you around, Tommy.'

'I don't get you. You act like I got jock odor or something. But it doesn't bother you to do business with a fanatic who gets people fired from their jobs.'

'I don't follow you.'

'Your buddy, bubble butt ... *Bimstine*, Dave. He belongs to the Jewish Defense Organization. They don't like somebody, they rat-fuck him where he works.'

'I wouldn't know. I don't like the way you talk about him, though.'

'Excuse me?'

'You take cheap shots, Tommy.'

'Like maybe I'm un-American, an anti-Semite or something?'

'Read it like you want.'

'I was sixteen years old at Heartbreak Ridge. I love this country. You saying I don't—' He stopped and smiled. 'You and me might have to forget we're mature people.'

'You don't know anybody named Will Buchalter?'

'This the guy hurt your wife?'

I didn't answer and stared straight into his face. He set his sandwich on his plate, removed a wisp of lettuce from his lip, then took a sip of beer from his schooner and brought his eyes back to mine.

'What can I say? I'm fighting with cancer of the prostate,' he said. 'You want to know what's on my mind? Dying. You know what else is on my mind? Dying broke. I don't know any guy named Buchalter.'

'I'm sorry to hear about your health problem, Tommy.'

'Save it. That sweaty pile of gorilla shit you call a friend is trying to break me. We get casino gambling in New Orleans, he's gonna own it all. I got to take a piss. Which I do with my eyes closed because half the time there's blood in the bowl. You want a beer, they're in the cooler.'

He opened a small closet that had a toilet inside and, without closing the door, began urinating loudly into the water while he flexed his knees and passed gas like it was a visceral art form.

How do you read a man like Tommy Lonighan?

Heartbreak Ridge, Irish bigotry, right-wing patriotism, morbidity that he used like a weapon, speech and mood patterns that had the volatility of tinfoil baking in a microwave.

The day a person like Lonighan makes sense to you is probably the day you should seriously reexamine your relationship to the rest of the human gene pool.

And on that note I waved good-bye and left before he had finished shaking himself and thumbing his gray sweat trunks back over his genitalia.

I stopped by Clete's office on St. Ann to see if he had found out anything about the man who called himself Will Buchalter.

'If the guy's local, he's low-profile,' Clete said. 'Like below street level. I think I talked to every dirtbag and right-wing crazoid in town. Have you ever been to any of these survivalist shops? I think we ought to round up some of their clientele while there's still time.'

He started to take a cigarette out of a pack on his desk; instead, he put a mint on his tongue and smiled at me with his eyes.

'How about hookers?' I said.

'The ones I know say he doesn't sound like any of their johns. I don't think he's from around here, Streak. A guy like this earns people's attention.'

'Thanks for trying, Clete.'

'Hang on. You've got two messages,' he said, taking his feet off his desk and looking at two memo slips by his telephone. 'That black sergeant, Ben Motley, you remember him, he always had his fly unzipped when he was in Vice, he wants you to call him about some dude who electrocuted himself in custody last night—'

'What?'

'Hang on, mon. I got a similar message from this character Reverend Oswald Flat. Isn't that the guy who was out at your bait shop? He's got a voice like somebody twanging on a bobby pin.'

'That's the guy.'

'Well, he called Bootsie and she told him to call here. NOPD picked up some wild man in the Garden District, can you dig this, a forty-year-old guy with tattoos on his head, wearing black leather in August. The autopsy showed he'd been shooting up with speed and paint thinner. How about that for a new combo?'

'What's the connection?'

'He had a silenced .22 Ruger automatic on him and Hippo Bimstine's address in his pocket. We'd better go talk to Motley and this guy with a mouthful of collard greens.'

'*We?*'

'Let's be serious a minute, Dave. I think you're fucking with some very bad guys. I don't know who they are, why they're interested in this submarine, or what the connections are between this citizens committee and dope dealers in the projects having their hearts cut out. But I'll bet my ass politics doesn't have diddle-shit to do with it.'

'I think this time it might.'

'Anyway, I'm backing your action, Jackson, whether you like it or not.' He leaned back in his swivel chair, grinned, and drummed on his stomach with his knuckles like a zoo creature at play.

I called Motley and told him that Clete and I would meet him at his office.

'You don't need to bring Purcel,' he said.

'Yeah, I do.'

'Suit yourself. I remember now, you always did drink down.'

'Thanks, Motley.'

Then I called the Reverend Oswald Flat and asked what I could do for him.

'Hit's about this man killed hisself in custody,' he said.

'Why would you call me?'

'Because you cain't seem to keep your tallywhacker out of the hay baler.'

'I beg your pardon?'

'You disturb me. I think there's people fixing to do you some harm, but you have a way of not hearing me. Is there a cinder block up there between your ears?'

'Reverend, I'd appreciate it if you'd—'

'All right, son, I'll try not to offend you anymore. Now, get your nose out of the air and listen to me a minute. I do counseling with prisoners. I bring 'em my Faith Made Easy tapes. I tried to counsel this crazy man they brought in there with tattoos on his head and a stink you'd have to carry on the end of a dung fork—' He stopped, as though his words had outpaced his thoughts.

'What is it?' I said.

'Hit wasn't a good moment. No, sir, hit surely wasn't. I looked into his eyes, and if that man had a soul, I believe demons had already claimed hit.'

'He was shooting up with speed and paint thinner, Reverend.'

'That may be. Your kind always got a scientific explanation. Anyway, I taped what he said. I want you to hear hit.'

I asked him to meet Clete and me down at Motley's

office. He said he'd be there, but he didn't reply when I said good-bye and started to hang up.

'Is there something else?' I said.

'No, not really. Maybe like you say, he was just a man who filled his veins with chemicals. I just never had a fellow, not even the worst of them, claw at my eyes and spit in my face before.'

Oswald Flat was wearing a rain-spotted seersucker suit, a clip-on bow tie, white athletic socks with black shoes, and his cork sun helmet when he came through the squad room at district headquarters and sat on a wood bench next to me and Clete. He carried a small black plastic tape recorder in his hand. He blew out his breath and wiped his rimless glasses on his coat sleeve.

At the other end of the room we could see Motley through the glass of Nate Baxter's office. Motley was standing; he and Baxter were arguing.

'You want to hear hit?' Oswald Flat said, resting the recorder on his thigh. The side of his face wrinkled, as though he were reluctant to go ahead with his own purpose.

'That'd be fine, Reverend,' I said.

When he pushed the Play button I could hear all the noises that are endemic to jailhouses everywhere: steel doors clanging, radios blaring, a water bucket being scraped along a concrete floor, cacophonous and sometimes deranged voices echoing through long corridors. Then I heard the man's voice – like words being released from an emotional knot, the syntax incoherent, the rage and hateful obsession like a quivering, heated wire.

'You got mud people coming out of your sewer grates, you got—' he was saying when Motley came out of Baxter's office and Oswald Flat clicked off the recorder.

'Movie time,' Motley said, scratching at the side of his mustache.

'What's Nate Baxter on the rag about?' Clete said.

'What do you think, Purcel? He's just real glad to see you guys down here again,' Motley said.

'Get him transferred back to Vice. At least he could get laid once in a while,' Clete said. He looked at the expression on my face. 'You think I'm kidding? The transvestites in the Quarter really dug the guy.'

The four of us went inside Motley's office. He closed the door behind us and inserted a videocassette into a VCR unit.

'The guy's name was Jack Pelley,' Motley said. 'He had a dishonorable discharge from the Crotch for rolling queers in San Diego, priors in New Orleans for statutory rape and possession of child pornography. One federal beef for possession of stolen explosives. From what we can tell, he became an addict in the joint, muled tar for both the Aryan Brotherhood and the Mexican Mafia while he was inside, then jumped his parole about three years ago.'

'How'd he get picked up?' I said.

'He locked himself in a filling station rest room on Carrollton and wouldn't let anybody else in. When the owner opened the door, Pelley had his leathers down over his knees and was shooting into his thigh with a spike made out of an eyedropper. The Ruger was sitting on top of the toilet tank.'

'How far away was he from Hippo Bimstine's house?' I said.

'About two blocks,' Motley said. 'His pockets were full of rainbows, blues, purple hearts, leapers, you name it. I think somebody gave him the whole candy store to fuck up Bimstine's day.' He glanced at Oswald Flat. 'Sorry, Reverend.'

'Get on with hit,' Flat said.

Motley dropped the blinds on his office glass, turned off the overhead light, and started the VCR.

'The arresting officers put him in the tank,' Motley said. 'In five minutes half the guys in there were yelling through the bars at the booking room officer to move him to a holding cell. The guy had five-alarm gorilla armpit odor. Anyway, we messed up. We should have transferred him to a psychiatric unit.'

The film, made without sound by a security camera, was in black and white and of low grade, the images stark in their contrast, like those in booking room photography. But the tortured travail of a driven man, flailing above a self-created abyss, was clearly obvious. Like those of most speed addicts, his body was wasted, the skin of his face drawn back tightly over the bone, the eyes sunken into skeletal sockets. His head looked like it had been razor-shaved and the hair had grown out in a thin gray patina, the color of rat's fur, below a wide bald area. Beginning at the crown of his skull, right across the pate, was a tattoo of a sword, flanged by lightning bolts.

He paced about maniacally, urinated all over the toilet stool, banged with his fists on the bars, whipped at the walls with his leather jacket, then began slamming the iron bunk up and down on its suspension chains.

'This is where we blew it big-time,' Motley said. 'That cell should have been shook down when the last guy went out of it.'

The man in custody, Jack Pelley, raised the bunk one final time and crashed it down on its chains, then stared down at a piece of electrical cord that had fallen out on the concrete floor. He picked it up in both hands, stared at it, then began idly picking at the tape and wire coil that were wrapped on the end of it.

'What do you call them things?' Flat said.

'A stinger,' Motley said. He paused the VCR. 'It's like a home-made hot plate. Except our man here has got other plans for it. You sure you want to watch this, Reverend?'

'You got something on that tape worse than Saipan?' Flat answered.

Motley took a Baby Ruth out of his desk drawer, started the film again, sat on the corner of his desk, and peeled the wrapper off his candy bar while he watched the television screen.

Jack Pelley splashed water from the toilet bowl onto the cement floor of the cell, peeled off his leather trousers, flattened his skinny buttocks into the middle of the puddle, inserted the stinger's coil into his mouth, sank one hand into the toilet, then calmly fitted the other end of the stinger into a wall socket.

His head snapped back once, as though he had just mainlined a hot shot; his eyes widened, one arm trembled slightly inside the toilet bowl; his lips seemed to curl back momentarily from his clenched teeth, then his jaw fell open like that of someone experiencing an unexpected moment of ecstasy. Then he slumped against the stool, his head on his chest, as though he had tired of a wearisome journey and had simply gone to sleep.

'The ME said the shock shouldn't have killed him by itself,' Motley said. 'But he'd probably hyped eight or nine times in the twenty-four hours before he got busted. The ME said his heart looked like a muskmelon.'

'Have you got any registration on the Ruger?' I asked.

'The serial numbers are burned off,' Motley said.

'Sounds like the greaseballs,' Clete said.

'The greaseballs don't send speed freaks on a hit,' Motley said.

'How about ties to the AB?' I said.

'Maybe. But these guys don't have much organization outside the joint. Most of them are more worried about their cock than politics, anyway,' Motley said. 'Reverend, why don't you go ahead and play your tape?'

Flat snapped the Play button down on his recorder, then set the recorder on the desktop. Once again, I heard the heated voice of Jack Pelley, like a disembodied hiss rising with gathering intensity out of the din of jailhouse noise.

'You got mud people coming out of your sewer grates, you got 'em eating dogs out of the city parks, fucking like minks in the projects, queers spreading AIDS in the blood banks, you think I'm kidding, you ever heard of Queer Nation, it ain't an accident half of them got kike names, how about that mud person over there in New Iberia thinks he's gonna deliver up the gift to a Jew, you think we come this far to let that happen, the sword ain't gonna allow it, no way, motherfucker, tell the screw to send down some toilet paper, they didn't leave none when they fed me, hey, you put that on that tape, what the fuck you think you doing, man—'

The recording ended with a brittle, clattering sound.

'That's when he knocked hit out of my hand,' Flat said. 'I never saw a man in so much torment.'

'Run it again,' Clete said.

We listened once more. I saw Clete put a breath mint on his tongue, then crack it between his molars and stare thoughtfully into space. When the tape ended he smiled in order to hide whatever thought had been in his eyes.

'How's it feel to be a mud person, Streak?' he said.

'We talked to the feds and a couple of snitches in the AB about any group that might call itself "The Sword." They never heard of it,' Motley said.

'Who's "we"?' I said.

'Me.'

'Baxter's blowing it off?' I said.

'What do I know?' Motley said.

Clete, Oswald Flat, and I walked out into the squad room. Clete and Flat went ahead of me. I stepped back into Motley's office.

'I appreciate what you've done, Motley,' I said.

'Tell me straight, Robicheaux, what's "the gift" this guy was talking about?'

'I don't have the slightest idea.'

'Somebody thinks you do.'

'Maybe he was talking about somebody else.'

'Yeah, probably the archbishop. A thought you might take with you – if they're using meltdowns like Jack Pelley, you can bet they've got a shit pile of them in reserve. Purcel's a cracker, but sometimes he's got his point of view, you know what I mean?'

'Not really.'

'People tend to fuck with him only once. There's never any paperwork around later, either.'

'Bad advice from a cop, Motley.'

'I got a flash for you, Robicheaux. I made a copy of the preacher's tape and gave it to Baxter. Ten minutes later I saw him erase it and throw it in the trash.'

He bit down on his Baby Ruth and stared at me reflectively.

chapter ten

Outside, I shook hands with Oswald Flat and thanked him for his help, then I drove Clete back toward his office in the French Quarter. It was raining, and the thick canopy of oaks over St. Charles looked gray in the blowing mist. The streetcar rattled past us on the neutral ground, its windows down to let in the cool air.

'You were a little quiet in there,' I said.

'Why argue with Motley? I think he pissed his brains out his pecker on beer and hookers a long time ago.'

'What are you saying?'

'Come on, Dave. Have you ever seen a hit done with a silenced twenty-two that wasn't a mob contract? It's their trademark – one round in the back of the head, one through the temples, one in the mouth.'

'They use pros, not guys like this Pelley character.'

'It's Pelley that convinces me even more that I'm right. Think about it. Where's a brain-fried hype like that going to come up with a silenced Ruger, one with burned serial numbers?'

'You're thinking about Lonighan?'

'Maybe. Or maybe Lonighan *and* the greaseballs. Look, Dave, you stomped the shit out of Max Calucci in front of his chippies. Max is a special kind of guy. When he was up at Angola he found out his punk was getting it on with another con. The kid begged all over the joint to go into lockdown. Nobody'd listen to him. A couple of days later somebody broke off a shank made from window glass in his throat.'

'They don't hit cops, Clete.'

'But what if it's not a regular contract? What if Max and Bobo Calucci just pointed the meltdown in your direction and gave him the Ruger, or had somebody give it to him? Nobody's going to make it for a greaseball hit, right? Motley didn't.'

'You've got more reason to worry about the Caluccis than I do.'

We drove out of the tunnel of oaks on St. Charles into Lee Circle. Clete took off his porkpie hat and readjusted it on his brow.

'You're wrong there, noble mon,' he said. 'I was never big on rules. They know that.'

I looked at him.

'But you are. They know that, too,' he said. 'They feel a whole lot safer when they go up against guys who play by the rules.'

'Stay away from them, Clete.'

'You've been out of New Orleans too long, Dave. All the old understandings are gone. It's an open city, like Miami, anybody's fuck. There's only one way to operate in New Orleans today – you keep reminding the other side they're one breath away from being grease spots in the cement.'

It was raining much harder now, and people were turning on their car lights. I looked at Clete's hulking profile in silhouette against the rain. His face was cheerless, his green eyes staring straight ahead, his mouth a tight seam.

After I dropped him at his office, I made one final stop in New Orleans – at Hippo Bimstine's house, down by the Mississippi levee. The rain had almost quit, and he was in his backyard, dipping leaves out of his swimming pool with a long pole. He wore wraparound black sunglasses, plaid Bermuda shorts, and a Hawaiian shirt printed with brown-skinned girls dancing in grass skirts. The fatty rings in his neck were bright with sweat.

'Yeah, that colored cop Motley told me all about it,' he said. 'This tattooed guy sounds like some kind of zomboid, though. I don't think we're talking the first team here.'

'I had to learn a hard lesson a long time ago, Hippo. The guy who blows out your candle is the one who's at your throat before you ever expect it.'

'A guy with a sword tattooed on his head, shooting dope in his crotch with an eyedropper? Dave, give me a break. I got serious enemies. I don't lose sleep over guys who get arrested in filling station rest rooms.'

'You have a very copacetic attitude, Hippo.'

'You're trying to insult me? That's what we're doing here?'

'I don't think you want me asking you hard questions.'

He set down the pole on a stone bench, removed his sunglasses, and wiped his face on his sleeve. The air was hot and muggy, and raindrops dripped from the trees into the pool.

'I got no secrets. Everybody in New Orleans knows my politics,' he said.

'What's the Jewish Defense Organization?'

'It's the network I belong to. There's no mystery here. We got a project called Operation Klan Kick. We find out who these cocksuckers are, where they work, and we make some phone calls. You got a problem with that, Dave?'

'Do you know why this guy Pelley might talk about "a gift" or a group called The Sword?'

'What are you talking about *gift* and *sword*? Listen, you know why Tommy Lonighan wants that sub? Because I bother him. Everything I do bothers him. You know why I bother him? Because he's got a guilty conscience, like a big, black tumor always eating on his brain.'

'Over what?'

'He killed my little brother.'

'He did what?'

'He didn't bother to tell you that, huh? We grew up across the street from each other in the Channel. We were all playing in a homemade cart, you know, made out of crates and planks with some roller skates nailed on the bottom. Tommy wheeled my little brother out from behind a car right into an ice truck. To this day, that sonofabitch has never said he was sorry.'

'I didn't know that, Hippo.'

'Maybe there's some other stuff you don't know, either, Dave. Come in my office.'

'What for?'

'Because you don't like the way me and my friends do business. Because you think these shitheads should have their day in court. Indulge me, blow five minutes of your day.'

We went inside the stucco cottage he used as an office. He began clattering through a box of videocassette tapes. He took one out and read the taped label on it.

'Some friends of mine got this off a bunch of guys who were watching it for entertainment,' he said. 'In a cinder-block house, up in a piney woods, just north of Pascagoula. When my friends got finished with them, they weren't interested in watching old newsreels any-more. So they really didn't mind giving up their cassette.'

'Who are your friends?'

'Some guys who could be great baseball players, you know what I mean? Terrific guys with a bat.'

'You think it's a victory to become like the other side?'

'Dave, you're a laugh a minute. That's why I like you. You already ate lunch, didn't you? Because this film seems to fuck up people's appetite for some reason.'

He started the tape in the VCR under his television set. The video was composed of a series of newsreels, Nazi propaganda footage, and still photographs spliced together in a collage that was almost like watching distilled evil: the profiles of Jews being superimposed upon those of rats, Heinrich Himmler reviewing concentration camp inmates in striped uniforms behind barbed wire, columns of children with bundles, their faces distorted with terror, marching between rows of black-helmeted SS; and finally a scene that was the most cruel I had ever seen on film – nude Polish women, deep in a forest, their arms gathered over their breasts and pubic hair, lining up to be shot in the back of the neck and flung into an open trench.

'On your worst day in Vietnam, you ever see anything like that, Dave?'

'No.'

'It's back. On an international level. You don't buy it, do you?'

'Maybe. But it doesn't change anything with us, Hippo. I think my family and I are swimming into somebody else's field of fire. I think you're responsible, too.'

He looked down at his hands, which were folded between his thighs. He looked at them a long time.

'Hippo?'

His sleek, football-shaped face was morose when he looked back up at me.

'Who can plan how things turn out?' he said. 'What I do or don't do no longer matters. There're people, I'm talking about cretins like that pervert at your house, who believe you can find that sub. It's what they *believe* that counts, Dave.'

'Why's it important to them?'

'Why does a tumblebug like to roll in shit?'

'Cut the Little Orphan Annie routine, Hippo. I'm getting tired of it.'

'They like shrines.'

'Not good enough.'

'I don't want you killed. Forget about the sub. I'll find it on my own or I won't. Don't come around here anymore. I'm going to put out the word that you're a waste of time, you couldn't find your butt with both hands. Maybe they'll believe it.'

'It's too late for contrition, Hippo. This guy Buchalter has left my wife a memory that she'll never quite get rid of.'

'You can put out a hit in this town for five hundred bucks. Did you know that, Dave? For a hundred, you can have a guy remodeled with a ball peen hammer and Polaroids left for you in a bar on Claiborne. You want a phone number? Or you want to keep hanging your ass out in the breeze and blaming me for your troubles?'

'I didn't know you and Tommy Bobalouba grew up together, Hippo. It explains a lot.'

'No kidding?'

'No kidding.'

'Sounds real clever.'

'Not really. You're both full of shit.'

'I wish I had a wit like that,' he said, then held up the videocassette in his hand. 'Then I could explain how there're people can watch stuff like this for fun in my own country and nobody cares. Hey, Dave, if they ever fire up the ovens again, I'll probably be one of the first bars of soap off the conveyor belt. But you and your kind won't be far behind. You don't mind letting yourself out, do you?'

I drove back toward New Iberia, through Baton Rouge, across the wide yellow sweep of the Mississippi into the western sun and the Atchafalaya marsh. I noticed a wallet stuck down in the crack of the passenger's seat. It was Clete's and must have slipped out of his back pocket before I dropped him off at his office. When I got off I-10 at Breaux Bridge I stopped at a convenience store and called him on a pay phone, then headed down the back road through St. Martinville, past the old French church and the spreading oaks on Bayou Teche where Evangeline and her lover are buried, and through the cooling afternoon and waving fields of green sugarcane into New Iberia.

I pulled into the dirt drive and parked under the oaks at the foot of my property. The house was deep in shadow, my neighbor's cane field and the woods that bordered it silhouetted against a blazing sunset. Bootsie's car was parked by the side of the house, the trunk open and sacked groceries still inside. The front rooms of the house were dark, the rose-print curtains fluttering in the windows, but the light was on in the kitchen. Batist was out on the dock, pushing pools of rainwater out of the folds in the awning with a broom handle.

'You need any help closing up?' I called.

'Ain't much bidness this afternoon. The rain brung in everybody early,' he said.

'Is Alafair down there?'

'She gone to the show wit' some ot'er children.'

I waved at him and walked up the slope toward my house, lifted two sacks of groceries out of Bootsie's car trunk, and walked around to the back door. Fireflies had started to light in the trees, and the dome of lavender sky overhead reverberated with the drone of cicadas. The house was still; no sound came from the radio on the kitchen windowsill, which Bootsie almost always listened to while she fixed supper.

I hefted the grocery sacks in my arms, opened the back screen with my shoe, and let it slam behind me. The wood planks of the back porch were littered with pet bowls and dry cat food. Through the doorway all the surfaces in the kitchen looked bright and clean, but I could smell okra burning and hear water hissing through a kettle top and scorching in the fire.

'Bootsie?' I said.

Out front, the tin roof on the gallery pinged in the cooling air.

'Bootsie?' I said again, hitching the sacks up against my chest.

I walked into the kitchen and started to set the sacks

on the drain board; I saw her sitting at the breakfast table, motionless, her posture rigid, her eyes straight ahead, one hand resting on top of the other.

'Bootsie, what's wrong?' I said.

Then I saw the film of perspiration on her brow and upper lip, the flutter in her throat, the rise and fall of her breasts. Her mouth opened stiffly, and her eyes broke and fastened on mine; they were charged with a light I had never seen in them before.

'Get out, Dave. Run! Please!' she said, her voice seeming to crack and rise from a great depth at the same time.

But it was too late. The blond man with a neck like a tree stump, with hands that had the power of vise grips, stepped out of the hallway into the light. He wore a Panama hat with a flowered band tilted on his head and a boyish, lopsided smile. His pleated white slacks, tropical shirt printed with green and yellow parrots, and shined, tasseled loafers gave him the appearance of a health enthusiast you might see on a morning television show, perhaps with a beach at his back. In the shadow of his hat brim you could hardly see the spray of blackheads that fanned back from his eyes like cat's whiskers.

'Come on in, Dave. I'm glad you're here. We weren't sure when you'd be back. We're going to work this thing out. Hey, I was listening to your records. I love them,' he said.

Behind him, seated on a chair turned backwards in the hallway, was a small man with defective eyes and a head shaped like a tomato. There was even a furrow in his scalp, with a twist of hair in it, like the indentation and stem of a tomato freshly torn from the vine. In his hands was a military-issue crossbow, the kind sometimes used in special operations, with a steel-flanged arrow mounted on the bowstring. The small man's elbows were propped on the back of the chair, and his eyes, which were crossed, one locking intermittently by the bridge of his nose, were sighted in their peculiar way along the arrow's shaft at the side of Bootsie's face.

chapter eleven

They had drawn the blinds on the windows now, and the small man with crossed eyes was drinking from a bottle of milk at the breakfast table and spitting pistachio shells into a paper bag. After he had locked my wrists behind me with the handcuffs he'd found on my dresser he bound Bootsie's forearms to her chair with electrician's tape, then crisscrossed it through her breasts and wrapped it around the back of the chair. The man named Buchalter watched with a small .25 caliber Beretta in the palm of his hand, a torn smile like that of Will Rogers at the corner of his mouth.

'You remember me?' he said.

'No.'

'You saw me in the helicopter. Out on the gulf,' he said.

'This is of no value to you, or your cause, or whatever it is you're after,' I said. 'You've got the wrong people.'

He pulled up a chair and sat between me and Bootsie. He pushed his hat back on his head. A strand of fine blond hair fell in his eyes.

'Are you mad at me? Because of what I did to Mrs. Robicheaux?' he said.

I stared at his face, his unblinking, inquisitive eyes, and didn't answer. I could feel the handcuffs biting into my wrists, cutting off the blood, swelling the veins.

'We don't know why you've come here. You have

nothing to gain by being here. Don't you understand that?' Bootsie said.

'I wouldn't say that. There're always possibilities in every situation. That's what I like to believe, anyway,' he said, and reached out, touched my cheek with his hand, and let his glance rove lazily over my face.

I saw tears well in Bootsie's eyes.

'Try to hear this, Buchalter,' I said. 'I'm a police officer. I work with people who'll square this one way or another. No matter what happens here tonight, they'll find you and blow up your shit, I guarantee it.'

He made shushing noises with his lips, and again his hand reached up and touched my face and brushed gingerly around the corners of my mouth. I could feel the grain of his skin against mine and smell an odor on it like hair oil and the inside of a leather glove.

'You take your hands off him, you degenerate, you vile animal—' Bootsie said. Her eyes were hot and receded, her face as gray as cardboard.

Buchalter nodded to the small man with crossed eyes. He spat a pistachio shell into the paper sack, then walked behind Bootsie's chair and wound the electrician's tape across her mouth, wrapping it around and around the thick swirls of her hair at the back of her head, tightening it across her mouth each time he made a revolution. She leaned forward and gagged on her tongue.

I could feel my heart thundering against my rib cage, hear the blood roaring in my ears like wind in a seashell.

'I don't know where the sub is,' I said. 'I'd tell you if I did. I don't even known why you guys want it. Why would I keep the information from you?'

'Because you work for Jews, my friend,' he said. 'Because I think you lie.'

'It's got air trapped in the hull. It floats right above the gulf's floor. It probably drifts in a pattern with the Gulf Stream,' I said. 'Hire some salvage people who understand those things. New Orleans and Miami are full of them.'

'But evidently you've found it twice. That means you know something other people don't.'

'There may be more than one sub down there,' I said. 'The Navy nailed three or four of them during nineteen forty-two. Maybe I saw two different subs.'

He took a nautical chart from his pocket, unfolded it, and spread it flat on the table in front of me. It showed the Louisiana coast, all its bays and soundings, and the northern gradations of the gulf. He stood behind my chair and fitted his huge hands over my shoulders, inserted his thumbs in the back of my neck.

'Our business can end here tonight in a couple of ways,' he said. 'I believe you understand me.'

'After you know where the sub is, you'll just go away?'

'Why not?' he said. His fingers tightened on my shoulder tendons.

'Because you're in over your head.'

He lowered his mouth to my ear. 'It isn't a time to be clever, Dave,' he said. 'You want me to make you trace the drift pattern with your nose?'

I tried to lean forward, away from the steady beat of his breath on my skin. Then he cupped one hand under my chin, the other on the back of my neck, like a man about to do a trick shot with a basketball.

'Would you like me to snap it?' he said. 'I can turn your body into a slug's from the neck down. I'm not exaggerating, Dave. I've done it twice before. Ask Chuck there.'

Think, think, think.

I tried to avoid swallowing, tried to keep my voice empty of fear. I closed and opened my eyes, and blinked the sweat out of them. Bootsie's hair had fallen in her face; the black tape that cut across her mouth was slick with saliva, and her eyes were red and liquid with terror at what she was about to witness.

'There're two things that aren't going to happen here tonight, Buchalter,' I said. 'I'm not going to give you information I don't have, and nobody here is going to kiss your butt. You're a piece of shit. Nothing you can do here will ever change that fact.'

He was quiet a moment. I felt his fingers move, but they were uncertain now, the pressure against my chin and neck temporarily in abeyance.

'You want to say that again?' he asked.

'Guys like you are cruel because you got fucked up in toilet training. That's how it works. Go to a psychologist and check it out. It's better than living with skid marks in your underwear.'

The man with crossed eyes started to laugh, then looked at Buchalter's face.

Buchalter was breathing heavily now. His hands were moist with perspiration, poised on my chin and neck. But the indecision, the physical pause, was still there, the means of resolving the insult not quite yet in place.

Then the man with crossed eyes turned in his chair and stared at the side window, whose blinds were drawn. He raised one hand in the air.

'Will, there's somebody outside,' he said.

Buchalter's hands slid away from me. He took the Beretta from his pocket while the man called Chuck peeked out the side of the blinds.

'It's a delivery guy,' he said.

'What do you mean "a delivery guy"?' Buchalter said.

'A fucking delivery guy. With a clipboard and a flashlight. He's coming to the back door.'

'Let him give you what he's got, then get rid of him.'

'Me?'

'Yes, you.'

The man called Chuck went out on the back porch, beyond my angle of vision. Buchalter rested one hand on my shoulder and placed the barrel of the Beretta behind my ear.

'UPS. I got a box for Dave Robicheaux. I guess your doorbell's broke,' a voice said out in the darkness.

I saw Bootsie's eyes fasten on mine.

'Put it on the gallery,' Chuck said.

'It's COD.'

'How much?'

'Eight fifty.'

'Wait a minute.'

The man named Chuck came back into the kitchen, his face filled with consternation.

'I ain't got any money, Will,' he said.

'Here,' Buchalter said, and handed him a twenty-dollar bill.

'What if I got to sign for it?'

'Just scribble on the board. Now, get out there and do it.'

Chuck went back out on the porch. I could see his shadow moving about under the bug-crusted light.

'All right, thanks a lot,' I heard him say. 'Just set it on the gallery. I'll carry it in later.'

'I'll bring it around. It's no trouble.'

'No, man. You don't need to do that.'

'It's going to rain. We're responsible for water damage.'

Chuck came back into the kitchen, the skin around one eye twitching with anxiety.

'Calm down,' Buchalter said. 'Go out front and help the man. Just keep him away from the back.'

'I'm cool, I'm cool.'

'I can see that, all right.'

'I don't need you on my case, Will. This one gets fucked up, I'm going down on a habitual.'

'It's better you not talk anymore, Chuck.'

'You don't get it. I been down four times. I don't need this kind of shit in my life. Now there's this fucking weird guy for UPS. I'm telling you, I don't need this kind of shit, man. I ain't up for it.'

'You're under a strain, Chuck. Wait a minute, what do you mean "weird guy"?'

'He looks like an ape with a UPS cap on its head. Wearing fucking Budweiser shorts. You don't call that weird?'

Buchalter's hand pinched at his mouth. I could feel the heat from his body, smell the mixture of sweat and deodorant secreting under his arms.

'Go out the front door, Chuck,' he said. 'You talk to the man out front. You keep him there. That's your assignment. You understand me?'

'Why me? I don't like this, Will. You want to 'front the guy, you 'front the fucking guy.' Then the skin of Chuck's face drew tight against the bone, stretching his eyebrows like penciled grease marks.

'The sonofabitch is coming around the side again,' he said.

'I'll handle it. You keep these two quiet,' Buchalter said.

'You wouldn't listen to me, man. Now it's turning to shit. I can feel it.'

'Shut up, Chuck. If it goes sour, you make sure Mr. and Mrs. Robicheaux catch the bus,' Buchalter said. 'If he doesn't work for us, he doesn't work for the Jews, either.'

'You want to clip a cop? With our prints all over the place? Are you out of your goddamn mind?'

Buchalter raised his fingers for the cross-eyed man to be silent, then dropped the Beretta into his pants pocket and walked out onto the back porch, with a smile at the corner of his mouth that looked like an elongated keyhole.

Chuck picked up his crossbow and leveled it at my throat. His hands looked round and white and small against the bow's dark metal surfaces. He breathed loudly through his nose and shook a fly out of his face. Large, solitary drops of rain began hitting in the trees outside.

I heard Buchalter open the screen door out on the porch.

'Okay? Is that everything now?' he said.

'I need you to sign.'

'All right.'

'You got a pen? Mine must have fallen off my clipboard.'

'No, I don't. And I'm rather busy right now.'

'Maybe it's in my pocket—'

'Now listen, my friend—'

'Hands on your head, down on your knees, mother-fucker! Do it! Now! Don't think about it!'

I heard the weight of two large bodies crash against the wood slats and rake across the tangle of garden tools on the porch; then Buchalter and Clete Purcel fell into the kitchen, and Clete's blue-black .38 revolver skittered across the linoleum.

Buchalter got to his feet first, his flat buttocks pinched together, the change jangling in his slacks, his triangular back rigid with muscle, and drove his right fist into the center of Clete's face. Clete's head snapped sideways with the force of the blow, blood whipping from his nose across his cheek. But he grabbed Buchalter around the legs, locked his wrists behind Buchalter's thighs, and smashed him against the doorjamb.

'Chuck!' Buchalter yelled out, as he tried to get his hand into his pants pocket.

But Chuck had taken his crossbow and gone through the hallway and out the front door like a shot.

Buchalter began swinging both his fists into the top of Clete's head. He wore a large Mexican ring on his right hand, one with a raised, knurled design on it, and each time he swung his right fist down, he twisted the ring with the blow, and I could see gashes bursting like tiny purple flowers in Clete's scalp.

But Clete Purcel was not one who gave up or went down easily. With rivulets of blood draining out of his hair into his eyes, he reached behind him, grasped a three-pronged dirt tiller by the wood handle, and jerked the sharpened tines upward into Buchalter's scrotum.

Buchalter's face went white, his mouth opening wide with a roar that seemed to rise like a rupturing bubble from the bottom of his viscera, as though bone and linkage were being sawed apart inside him. He stumbled sideways, lifting his knees into Clete's face, and crashed through the screen door into the backyard. Then I heard his feet running into the darkness.

Clete pulled himself up by the doorknob and walked like a drunk man into the kitchen, soaked a dish towel under the faucet, and pressed it to the top of his head. He kept widening his eyes and breathing hard through his mouth. His knees were barked, and one sock was pulled down over his ankle.

'Pick up your piece,' I said.

He wiped at his nose and eyes with the towel, then leaned over heavily, holding the towel to his scalp, and closed his hand around his .38.

'The handcuff key is on the dresser in the bedroom,' I said.

He went into the bedroom, came back with the key, and began unlocking the handcuffs. I could feel water dripping out of his hair onto my neck. The handcuffs clattered to the floor. My hands were purple, bloated with lack of circulation, the skin dead to the touch. I opened my pocketknife, cut through the electrician's tape at the back of Bootsie's head, eased it out of her mouth, then began sawing loose the tape on her arms.

'Oh God, Dave,' she said. Her breath came in gasps, as though she had been held underwater for a long time and her lungs were aching for air. 'Oh Lord, God. Oh God, he was going—'

'It's over,' I said.

'He was going to cripple you. He was going to deliberately cripple you,' she said, then squeezed her eyes shut against the tears that coursed down her cheeks. I held her face against my chest and kissed the top of her head. I could smell the heat in her hair.

'Your phone's dead. They must have cut it outside,' Clete said.

'Give me your piece,' I said.

'Where's yours?'

'In the glove compartment of the truck.'

'Man, I can't see straight. That guy's got fists like chunks of concrete.'

'Take Boots down to the bait shop and call the sheriff's office from there,' I said.

'Where are you going, Dave?' Bootsie said, her eyes clearing with a new sense of alarm.

'They probably parked their car farther up the road,' I said.

'No,' she said. 'Let somebody else handle it this time.'

'He's a fanatic and a psychopath, Boots. If we don't nail him now, he'll be back.'

I looked away from the expression on her face. I started out the door with the revolver in my hand.

'Hey, Dave—' Clete said.

He followed me onto the back porch.

'Forget the rules on this one,' he said. 'You get the chance, close this cocksucker's file.'

'Tell the sheriff to call the bridge tender and have him raise the drawbridge,' I said.

'Listen to me—' he began, his face stretching with impatience. Then he stopped and lowered his voice. 'This kind of guy sits in a jail cell and thinks for a long time about things to do to people. Don't live with regret later, Streak. Buchalter is as bad as they get.' He pointed a finger at my face, then wiped a smear of blood off his nose on his wrist.

The moon had risen in the east from behind a bank of black clouds, and a steady, warm rain was dancing on the duck pond at the foot of my property and clicking on the tall stalks of sugarcane in my neighbor's field. When I had returned from New Orleans I hadn't seen any vehicles parked on the dirt road by the bayou, and I guessed that Buchalter and the man with crossed eyes had driven past my house, parked on the far side of it, and cut back through a pecan orchard by the four corners, over a wooded knoll, and through my neighbor's cane field.

Beyond the duck pond, right by the remnant of my

collapsed barn, I saw two fresh sets of footprints glistening in the mud, leading through the barbed-wire fence into the field. I lifted up the top strand of barbed wire and stepped into the cane. It grew so thick that the earth was still dry inside the rows. The sound of the rain on the leaves was like marbles striking dry sheets of newspaper. I saw a bolt of lightning splinter the sky and pop in the woods, and when the thunder echoed off the trees, my neighbor's cattle began lowing in terror at the bottom of the coulee.

There was no wind inside the cane, and the air was heated and alive with insects. Ahead, I could see a winding pattern, like a faint serpentine tunnel, through the rows where somebody had either wedged the stalks sideways or cracked them at the base with his shoe. I knelt in the row and listened. At first I heard only the sound of the rain clicking on the leaves overhead, then there was a voice, one man calling out to another, just as lightning burst in a white tree all over the southern horizon and thunder rumbled across the fields.

They must have gotten all the way to the wooded knoll, almost to the pecan orchard and the four corners down the bayou road, I thought. I stepped back outside the sugarcane and began running toward the far side of the field, toward the elevated grove of oak trees whose leaves were flickering with a silver light in the wind off the marsh.

Long ago Clete Purcel had made his separate peace with the system of rules that govern the justifiable taking of human life. I never questioned the validity of Clete's moral vision, no more than I would have questioned his loyalty and courage and his selfless devotion to me during the worst periods in my life. In truth, I often envied the clarity of line that he used to distinguish between right and wrong. I had also harbored fears since I first became a street patrolman in New Orleans that I would one day wrongly exercise the power of life and death over an individual, through accident or perhaps fearful impetuosity or maybe even by self-righteous design.

But Buchalter was not an ordinary player. Most of the psychological mutants with whom a police officer comes in contact daily are bumbling, ineffectual losers who sneak through life on side streets and who often seek out authority and self-validation through their adversarial relationship with police and parole officers, since in normal society they possess about the same worth as discarded banana peels.

Psychopaths like Ted Bundy and Gary Gilmore have a way of committing their crimes in states which practice capital punishment. Then they turn their trials and executions into televised theater of world-class proportions.

The Will Buchalters have no such plan for themselves. They don't leave paperwork behind; they stay out of the computer. When they do get nailed, they make bond and terrify witnesses into perjuring themselves; they convince psychologists that they have multiple personalities that cannot be simultaneously put on trial; their fall partners either do their time or are murdered in custody. No one is ever sure of how many people they actually kill.

Will Buchalter belonged to that special group of people who live in our nightmares.

I could still smell his odor; it was like animal musk, like lotions that were at war with his glands, like someone who has just had sex. I could still feel the grain and oil of his skin on mine.

I pressed my hand tighter around the butt of the .38. The hand-worn walnut grips felt smooth and hard against my palm.

As I neared the end of the cane field I heard a strand of fence wire twang against a post, heard someone curse, as though he were in pain or had fallen to the ground. I swung wide of the field to broaden my angle of vision; then I saw two silhouettes against the veiled moon – one man on his buttocks, holding his ankle, the other man bent over him, trying to lift him up, and I remembered the old fence that my neighbor had crushed flat with his tractor so his livestock could drink at the coulee.

They saw me, too. Before I could squat into a shooting position and yell at them to put their hands on their heads, a small-caliber pistol popped in the darkness, then popped again, just like a firecracker. I ran for the lee of the sugarcane, out of their line of vision, and squatted close into the stalks away from the moon's glow, which streaked the rain with a light like quicksilver.

I heard someone burrow into the cane, thrash through several rows, then stop.

Were there one or two men inside the field now? I couldn't tell. There was no sound except the rain hitting on the leaves over my head.

I worked my way down a furrow, deeper into the cane. I could smell something dead in the trapped air, a coon or possum, an odor like that of a rat that has crawled inside a wall and died. My eyes stung with salt, and the dirt cut into my knuckles and knees like pieces of flint. I saw a wood rabbit bolt across the rows, stop and look at me, his ears flattened on his head, then begin running again in a zigzag pattern. He crashed loudly through the edge of the cane and was gone.

Not twenty feet from me a man rose from his knees in the midst of the cane, his body almost totally obscured by the thickly spaced stalks and long festoons of leaves around him. He tried to ease quietly through the rows to the far side of the field, which opened onto a flat space and the wooded knoll and the pecan orchard.

I pulled my shirt up and wiped my face on it, then aimed as best I could at the man's slowly moving silhouette. I cocked the hammer on the .38 and brought the sight just below an imaginary line that traversed his shoulder blades.

Now! I thought.

'Throw your weapon away! Down on your face with your hands out in front of you!' I yelled.

But he wanted another season to run.

He tore through the sugarcane, flailing his arms at the stalks, stumbling across the rows. I was crouched on one knee when I began shooting. I believe the first shot went high, because I heard a distant sound in a tree, like a rock skipping off of bark and falling through limbs. And he kept plowing forward through the cane, trying to hack an opening with his left hand, shielding a weapon with his right.

But the second shot went home. I know it did; I heard the impact, like a cleated shoe connecting with a football, heard the wind go out of his lungs as he was driven forward through the cane.

But he was still standing, with a metallic object in his right hand, its flat surfaces blue with moonlight, and he was turning on one foot toward me, just as a scarecrow might if it had been spun in a violent wind.

Clete had loaded only five rounds in the cylinder and had set the hammer on an empty chamber. I let off all three remaining rounds as fast as I could pull the trigger. Sparks and fine splinters of lead flew from the sides of the cylinder into the darkness.

His left arm flipped sideways, as if jerked by a wire, his stomach buckled, then his chin snapped back on his shoulder as if he had been struck by an invisible club.

The hammer snapped dryly on the empty sixth chamber. Then something happened that I didn't understand. As he crumpled sideways to the earth, breaking the stalks of cane down around him, he yelled out in pain for the first time.

I walked across the rows to where he lay on his back, his crossed eyes opening and closing with shock. He kept trying to expel a bloody clot from his mouth with the tip of his tongue. My last round had hit him in the chin and exited just above the jawbone. His left arm was twisted in the sleeve like a piece of discarded rope. He had taken another round in the side, with no exit wound that I could see, and blood was leaking out of his shirt into the dirt. Then I saw his right hand quivering uncontrollably above the feathered shaft of the aluminum arrow that had discharged from his crossbow when he fell. The flanged point had sliced down into the thigh and emerged gleaming and red through the kneecap.

I knelt beside him, loosened his belt, and brushed the dirt out of his eyes with my fingers.

'Where's Buchalter?' I said.

He swallowed with a clicking sound and tried to speak, but his tongue stuck to the roof of his mouth. I turned his head with my hands so his mouth could drain.

'Where did Buchalter go, Chuck?' I said. 'Don't try to protect this guy. He deserted you.'

'I don't know,' he said. His voice was weak and devoid of all defense. 'Get the arrow out.'

'I can't do it. You might hemorrhage. I'm going to call an ambulance.'

His crossed eyes tried to focus on mine. They were luminous and black with pain and fear. His tongue came out of his mouth and went back in again.

'What is it?' I said.

'I need a priest. I ain't gonna make it.'

'We'll get you one.'

'You gotta listen, man ...'

'Say it.'

'I didn't have nothing against y'all. I done it for the money.'

'For the money?' I said as much to myself as to him.

'Tell your old lady I'm sorry. It wasn't personal. Oh God, I ain't gonna make it.'

'Give me Buchalter, Chuck.'

But his eyes had already focused inward on a vision whose intensity and dimension probably only he could appreciate. In the distance I heard someone start a high-powered automobile engine and roar southward, away from the drawbridge, down the bayou road in the rain.

chapter twelve

The next morning I went down to the sheriff's office and got my badge back.

Chuck, whose full name was Charles Arthur Sitwell, made it through the night and was in the intensive care unit at Iberia General, his body wired to machines, an oxygen tube taped to his nose, an IV needle inserted in a swollen vein inside his right forearm. The lower half of his face was swathed in bandages and plaster, with only a small hole, the size of a quarter, for his mouth. I pulled a chair close to his bed while Clete stood behind me.

'Did Father Melancon visit you, Chuck?' I said.

He didn't answer. His eyelids were blue and had a metallic shine to them.

'Didn't a priest come see you?' I asked.

He blinked his eyes.

'Look, partner, if you got on the square with the Man Upstairs, why not get on the square with us?' I said.

Still, he didn't answer.

'You've been down four times, Chuck,' I said. 'Your jacket shows you were always a solid con. But Buchalter's not stand-up, Chuck. He's letting you take his fall.'

'You're standing on third base,' Clete said behind me.

I turned in the chair and looked into Clete's face. But Clete only stepped closer to the bed.

'Chuck was in max at Leavenworth, he was a big stripe at Angola. He wants it straight,' he said to me. 'Right,

Chuck? Buchalter'll piss on your grave. Don't take the bounce for a guy like that.'

Chuck's defective eyes looked as small as a bird's. They seemed to focus on Clete; then they looked past him at the swinging door to the intensive care unit, which had opened briefly and was now flapping back and forth.

His mouth began moving inside the hole in the bandages. I leaned my ear close to his face. His breath was sour with bile.

'I already told the priest everything. I ain't saying no more,' he whispered. 'Tell everybody that. I ain't saying no more.'

'I don't want to be hard on you, partner, but why not do some good while you have the chance?' I said.

He turned his face away from me on the pillow.

'If that's the way you want it,' I said, and stood up to go. 'If you change your mind, ask for the cop at the door.'

Out in the corridor, Clete put an unlit cigarette in his mouth.

'I never get used to the way these fuckers think. The sonofabitch is on the edge of eternity and he's scared he'll be made for a snitch,' he said, then noticed a Catholic nun with a basket of fruit two feet from him. 'Excuse me, Sister,' he said.

She was dressed in a white skirt and lavender blouse, but she wore a black veil with white edging on her head. Her hair was a reddish gold and was tapered on her neck.

'How is he doing?' she said.

'Who?' I said.

'That poor man who was shot last night,' she said.

'Not very well,' I said.

'Will he live?' she said.

'You never know, I guess,' I said.

'Were you one of the officers who—'

'Yes?'

'I was going to ask if you were one of the officers who arrested him.'

'I'm the officer who shot him, Sister,' I said. But my attempt at directness was short-lived, and involuntarily my eyes broke contact with hers.

'Is he going to die?' she said. Her eyes became clouded in a peculiar way, like dark smoke infused in green glass.

'You should probably ask the doctor that,' I said.

'I see,' she said. Then she smiled politely. 'I'm sorry. I didn't mean to sound rude. I'm Marie Guilbeaux. It's nice meeting you.'

'I'm Dave Robicheaux. This is Clete Purcel. It's nice meeting you, too, Sister,' I said. 'You're not from New Iberia, are you?'

'No, I live in Lafayette.'

'Well, see you around,' I said.

'Yes, good-bye,' she said, and smiled again.

Clete and I walked out into the sunlight and drove back toward my house. It was the beginning of the Labor Day weekend, and the convenience stores were filled with people buying beer and ice and charcoal for barbecues.

'Why didn't the nuns look like that when I was in grade school?' Clete said. 'The ones I remember had faces like boiled hams ... What are you brooding about?'

'Something you said. Why's Chuck Sitwell stonewalling us?'

'He wants to go out a mainline, stand-up con.'

'No, you said it earlier. He's scared. But if he's scared Buchalter will be back to pull his plug, why doesn't he just give him up?'

Clete looked out into the hot glare of the day from under the brim of his porkpie hat and puffed on his cigarette. His face was pink in the heat.

'You're a good guy, Streak, but you don't always think straight about yourself,' he said.

'What's that supposed to mean?'

'You parked four rounds in the guy.'

I looked at him.

'Come on, Dave, be honest,' he said. 'You only stopped popping caps when you ran out of bullets. You were trying to blow him all over that cane field. You don't think the guy knows that? What if he or Buchalter tell you what they had planned for you and Bootsie, Bootsie in particular, maybe even Alafair if she walked in on it? I'd be scared of you, too, mon.'

He glanced sideways at me, then sucked once on his cigarette and flipped it in a spray of sparks against the side of a red stop sign.

The weekend was hot and dry and uneventful. A guard remained on duty twenty-four hours at the door of Charles Arthur Sitwell's hospital room. Sitwell kept his promise; he refused to answer questions about anything.

I got up Tuesday morning at dawn, helped Batist open the bait shop, then walked up the slope through the trees to have breakfast with Bootsie before going to the office. The house was still cool from the attic and window fans that had run all night, and the grass in the backyard was thick with mockingbirds who were feeding on bread crumbs that Bootsie had thrown out the screen door.

'A deputy will be parked out front again today,' I said.

'How long do you plan to keep one here, Dave?' Bootsie said. She sat across from me, her shoulders straight, her fingers resting on the sides of her coffee cup. She had put aside her piece of toast after having eaten only half of it.

'It gives the guy something to do,' I said.

'We can't live the rest of our lives with a deputy parked out front.'

'We won't have to.'

She had just washed her face, but her eyes looked tired, still not quite separated from the sleep that came to her with certainty only at first light.

'I want to buy a gun,' she said.

'That's never been your way.'

'What kind of pistol is best for a woman? I mean size or whatever you call it.'

'A thirty-two, or maybe a thirty-eight or nine millimeter. It depends on what a person wants it for.'

'I want to do that this evening, Dave.'

'All right.'

'Will you show me how to use it?'

'Sure.' I watched her face. Her eyes were flat with unspoken thoughts. 'We'll take the boat down the bayou and pop some tin cans.'

'I think we ought to teach Alafair how to shoot, too,' she said.

I waited a moment before I spoke. 'You can teach kids how to shoot a pistol, Boots, but you can't teach them when to leave it in a drawer and when to take it out. I vote no on this one.'

She gazed out the back screen at the birds feeding in the grass under the mimosa tree.

Then she said, 'Do you think he's coming back?'

'I don't know.'

Her eyes went deep into mine.

'If I get to him first, he'll never have the chance,' I said.

'I didn't mean that,' she said.

'I did.'

I felt her eyes follow me into the hallway. I changed into a pair of seersucker slacks, loafers, a brown sports shirt, and a white knit tie, then went back into the kitchen, leaned over Bootsie's chair, hugged her across the chest, and kissed her hair.

'Boots, real courage is when you put away all thought about your own welfare and worry about the fate of another,' I said. 'That was my wife the other night. A fuckhead like Buchalter can't touch that kind of courage.'

She stroked the side of my face with her fingers without looking up.

The phone rang on the wall above the drain board.

'I hear you're back on the clock,' a voice with a black New Orleans accent said.

'Motley?'

'Do you mind me calling you at your house?'

'No, not at all. How'd you know I was back on duty?'

'We're coordinating with your department on this guy Sitwell. Did you know he and the space-o speed freak who electrocuted himself were cell mates at Angola?'

'No.'

'They were both in a rock 'n' roll band in the Block. So if they did everything else together, maybe they both muled dope for the AB.'

'I already talked to the warden. Sitwell didn't have any politics; there're no racial beefs in his jacket. He was always a loner, a walk-in bank robber and a smash-and-grab jewel thief.'

'I think you should come to New Orleans this morning.'

'What for?'

'There's a shooting gallery up by Terpsichore and Baronne. The main man there is a bucket of shit who goes by the name of Camel Benoit. You know who I'm talking about?'

'He used to pimp down by Magazine sometimes?'

'That's the guy. We've been trying to shut down that place for six months. We bust it, we nail a couple of sixteen-year-olds with their brains running out their noses, a week later Camel's got Mexican tar all up and down Martin Luther King Drive. Except at about five this morning, when everybody was nodding out, some sono-fabitch broke the door out of the jamb and pasted people all over the wall with an E-tool.'

'With an *entrenching tool*?'

'You heard me. Sharpened on the edges with a file. After he broke a few heads, he went after our man Camel. I would have bought tickets for that one.'

'What happened?'

'I don't know, we're still finding out.'

'Come on, Motley, you're not making sense.'

'There used to be adult education classes in that building. The guy who busted down the door evidently chased Camel through a bunch of rooms upstairs with a flagstaff. At least that's what we think.'

'I don't understand what you're saying. Where's Camel Benoit?'

He made a whistling sound in exasperation.

'I'm trying to tell you, Robicheaux. We don't know for sure. We think he's inside the wall: Anyway, there's blood seeping through the mortar. You know any mice that are big enough to bleed through a brick wall?'

The two-story building had been the home of a Creole slave trader and cotton dealer in the 1850s. But now the twin brick chimneys were partially collapsed, the iron grillwork on the balconies was torn loose from its fastenings, and the ventilated wood shutters hung at odd angles on the windows. An air compressor for a jackhammer was wheezing and pumping in front of the entrance. I held up my badge for a uniformed patrolman to look at as I threaded my way between two police cars and an ambulance into the entrance of the building.

At the back of a dark corridor covered with spray-can graffiti, a workman in gloves and a hard hat was thudding the jackhammer into the wall while Motley and two white plainclothes watched. Motley was eating an ice cream cone. The floor was powdered with mortar and brick dust. I tried to talk above the noise and gave it up. Motley motioned me into a side room and closed the door behind us. The room was strewn with burnt newspaper, beer cans, wine bottles, ten-dollar coke vials, and discarded rubbers.

'We should have already been through the wall, but it looks like somebody poured cement inside it when the foundation settled,' he said. He brushed a smear of ice cream out of his thick mustache.

'What was this about a flagstaff?'

'A couple of noddies say there was an American flag on a staff in the corner with a bunch of trash. The wild man grabbed it and ran Camel Benoit upstairs with it, then stuffed him through a hole in the wall. For all we know, he's still alive in there.' He took a bite of his ice cream and leaned forward so it wouldn't drip on his tie.

'What have you got on the wild man?'

'Not much. He had on a Halloween mask and wore brown leather gloves.'

'Was he white or black?'

'Nobody seems to remember. It was five in the morning. These guys were on the downside of smoking rock and bazooka and hyping all night.' He used his shoe to nudge a rubber that was curled on top of a piece of burnt newspaper like a flattened gray slug. 'You think these cocksuckers worry about safe sex? They get free rubbers from the family planning clinic and use them to carry brown scag in.'

'Motley, I think you might be a closet Republican.'

'I'm not big on humor this morning, Robicheaux.'

'Why did you want me down here?'

'Because I want to take this guy off the board. Because I'm not feeling a lot of support from Nate Baxter, or from anybody else, for that matter. If it hasn't occurred to you, nobody's exactly on the rag because a few black dealers are getting taken out.'

'Maybe Camel's operation is being hit on by another dealer.'

'You mean by another *black* dealer, don't you?' He bit into the cone of his ice cream, then flipped it away into a pile of trash. 'Come on, they've quit out there. Let's go see the show.'

'I didn't mean to offend you, partner.'

'Get off of it, Robicheaux. As far as the department is concerned, this is still nigger town. On a scale of priority of one to ten, it rates a minus eight.'

The air in the hallway was now gray with stone dust. Two workmen used crowbars to rake the bricks from the wall and the chunks of concrete inside onto the hallway floor. The gash in the wall looked like a torn mouth that they kept elongating and deepening until it almost reached the floor. One of the workmen paused, pushed his goggles up on his forehead, and leaned into the dark interior.

He brought his head back out and scratched his cheek.

'I can see a guy about three feet to the left. I'm not sure about what else I see, though,' he said.

'Look out,' Motley said, pushed the workman aside, and shined a flashlight into the hole. He pointed the light back into the recess for what seemed a long time. Then he clicked off the light and stood erect. 'Well, he always told everybody he was a war veteran. Maybe Camel'd appreciate a patriotic touch.'

I took the flashlight from Motley's hand and leaned inside the hole. The air was cool and smelled of damp earth and rats and old brick.

The flashlight beam danced over Camel's body, his copper-bright skin, his hair shaved into dagger points and corn-rolled ridges, his dead eye that looked like a frosted blue-white marble. He was wedged in a reclining position between the bricks and a pile of broken cinder blocks. The workmen had entered the wall at the wrong location because Camel's blood had drained down a cement mound into a bowllike depression at the bottom of the wall.

The wound was like none I had ever seen in my years as a homicide detective. Someone had driven the winged, brass-sheathed end of a broken flagstaff through Camel's back, all the way through the heart cavity, until the staff had emerged below the nipple. The remnant of an American flag, long since faded almost colorless and partially burned by vandals, was streaked bright red and glued tightly against the staff by the pressure of the wound.

'Get the rest of the wall down,' Motley said to the workmen. Then he motioned me to follow him up the stairwell to the second floor. We stood on a landing outside a closed door. The building shook with the thudding of the jackhammer. 'What do you think?'

'I don't know,' I said. 'I thought the vigilante special-
ized in heart removal.'

'So he modified his technique.'

'I thought he usually left flowers behind.'

'Maybe he didn't have time.'

'Did the killer take anything? Money or drugs?'

'He seemed to be too busy breaking heads. At least
according to our witnesses.'

'Where are they?'

'Either in the hospital or in a holding cell at the district
... Except one.'

'Oh?'

'Yeah,' he said. 'You want to check him out?'

He opened the door on a room that was stacked with
school desks. Sitting on the floor, under a portable
blackboard with holes the size of bowling balls knocked
in the slate, was Zoot Bergeron, his knees drawn up
before him, his eyes red-rimmed with fatigue. There was
a puddle of what looked like urine in the corner.

'He walked in the back door about five minutes after
two patrolmen got here,' Motley said. 'Bad luck for
Lucinda's boy.'

Zoot looked at me, then dropped his eyes to his tennis
shoes. He had made fists of both his hands, with his
thumbs tucked inside his palms. Motley kicked him in the
sole of the shoe.

'Look at me,' he said.

'Yes, suh,' Zoot said.

'Tell Detective Robicheaux what you told me.'

'I was picking up a friend. That's all. I don't know
nothing about what goes on here.'

'Do you think all big people are dumb, Zoot? Do I
look like a big, dumb, fat man to you?' Motley asked.

'I ain't said that, Sergeant Motley. My friend ax me to
pick him up here and carry him to work.'

'Maybe we ought to take you down to the detox and
get you UA-ed,' Motley said. 'You ever been there? You

got to watch out for some of those old-time hypes in the shower, though. They'll try to take your cherry.'

'I don't care you UA me or not. I don't care you try to scare me with that kind of talk, either. I ain't used no dope, Sergeant Motley.'

'What do you know about Camel Benoit?' I said.

'Everybody up Magazine know Camel. He's a pimp.'

'He was a drug dealer, too, Zoot,' I said.

He fastened his eyes on his shoes again.

'Do you know who killed him?' I said.

'Sergeant Motley just said it. I wasn't here.'

He locked his hands on his knees, then rested his forehead on the back of his wrist. His eyelashes were as long as a girl's.

'You trying to fuck your mother?' Motley said.

'Suh?' Zoot said, raising his head. His face was the color of dead ash.

'You heard me, fuck your mother. Because that's what you're doing, you stupid little shit.'

Zoot tried to return Motley's stare, but his left eye began to tremble and water.

'Get out of here,' Motley said.

'Suh?'

'You got earplugs on? Get out of here. If I catch you around a crack house again, I'm going to kick your skinny ass all up and down Martin Luther King Drive.'

Zoot got to his feet uncertainly. He flinched when he straightened his back. Motley opened the door and leaned over the stair railing.

'There's a kid coming out. Let him go. He doesn't know anything,' he called to the detectives below. Then he walked back to Zoot and punched him in the breastbone with his forefinger.

'Don't ever give me reason to get mad at you. Do you understand me?' he said.

'Yes, suh. I ain't.'

'You tell anybody I cut you loose, I'll kick your ass anyway.'

'Yes, suh.'

'Get out!'

After Zoot was gone, I looked at Motley. He was lighting a cigar. His whiskers were jet black inside the grain of his cheeks.

'You're all right, Motley.'

'Tell me that five years from now. That kid's going to end up facedown on a sidewalk.'

'Why?'

'Because he's like half the black kids in New Orleans. Every day he's got to prove he doesn't have his mama's pink finger up his butt. Come on, I'll buy you a beignet. This place is depressing me.'

I spent the next two hours in the library, or morgue, as it's called, of *The Times-Picayune*. I could find almost nothing on German U-boat activity in the Gulf of Mexico that had been printed during the war years, since all military news was censored from late 1941 until after V-J Day. There was one exception, however: a headline story which ran for three days concerning four Nazi saboteurs who had been apprehended by the FBI south of Baton Rouge in a truck loaded with explosives.

A page one photograph showed them in fedoras and baggy suits, locked to a wrist chain, staring out at the camera with pale, rectangular faces and buckshot eyes. The cutline below said they had planned to blow up the Standard Oil refinery on the banks of the Mississippi at Baton Rouge. The last article in the series dealt with the arrest of an American accomplice, a retired oil man in Grand Isle by the name of Jon Matthew Buchalter, who had been a founder of the American Silver Shirts.

I jumped the microfilm ahead to the year 1956 and found the name of Jon Matthew Buchalter once again. It was in a twenty-inch feature story in the regional section, written with the detached tone one might use in examining an anthropological curiosity, about the oil man who had betrayed his country, flashed a signal one night through the mist at a U-boat south of Grand Isle, and helped bring ashore four men who, had they succeeded in their mission, would have dried up the flow of fuel to American and English forces for at least two weeks.

At the bottom of the page was a 1935 wire-service photograph of Buchalter with Adolf Hitler and Hermann Goering. Buchalter was a barrel-chested, vigorous-looking man, resplendent in white riding breeches, silver shirt, polished Sam Browne belt, black tie, and red-and-black armband. His right hand clasped Hitler's; he was smiling with the confidence of a man who knew that he had stepped into history.

After he was arrested in Grand Isle, a drunken mob of shrimpers tried to break him out of jail. They fled when sheriff's deputies began firing shotguns in the air. They left behind a thirty-foot spool of chain and a five-gallon can of gasoline.

He did his fourteen years of federal time in isolation, despised by both his warders and his fellow prisoners, eating food delivered through a slit by a trusty who in all probability spat in it first.

His wife and children had long ago moved out of state; his property had been confiscated for taxes. He weighed eighty pounds when his liver finally failed and he died in a public ward at Charity Hospital in New Orleans. There was no marker placed on his grave in potter's field other than a stamped tin number pressed into the sod.

I wondered what importance he would give the fact that the old potter's field in Orleans Parish was not segregated, like other cemeteries during that historical period, and that he would sow his teeth and bones among those of Negroes and perhaps even Jews.

Later that afternoon I parked in front of Lucinda Bergeron's house off Magazine. Just as I was turning off the engine, an open Jeep with oversized tires and four black kids inside pulled to the curb in front of me. The rap music playing on the stereo was deafening, like an electronic assault on the sensibilities. Zoot got out of the Jeep and went inside his house, his eyes straight ahead, as though I were not there. The three other boys did leg stretches on the lawn while they waited for him. All three were dressed in an almost paramilitary fashion – baggy black trousers like paratroopers might wear, gold neck chains, Air Jordan tennis shoes, black T-shirts with scrolled white death's-heads on them. Their hair was shaved to the scalp on the sides, with only a coarse, squared pad on the crown of the skull. Zoot came back out the front door and gave each of them a can of Pepsi-Cola.

When they drove away, the rap music from their stereo echoed off housefronts all the way down the street.

'You get an eyeful?' Zoot said.

'You run the PX for these characters?'

'The what?'

'Sergeant Motley's worried about you.'

He looked at me, waiting to see what new kind of trap was being constructed around him.

'He thinks you're going to get cooled out one of these days,' I said.

'Cooled … what?'

'He thinks you're cruising for a big fall.'

'Why y'all on my case? I ain't done nothing.'

'Did you tell your mother about what happened this morning?'

His eyes flicked sideways toward the house. He sucked in his cheeks and tried not to swallow.

'I remember something a guy told me once,' I said. 'He said it's as dishonorable to let yourself be used as it is to use someone else.'

'What you mean?'

'Your friends impress me as shitheads.'

'I don't care what you say. We stand by each ot'er. They're my friends in all kinds of ways.'

'Zoot, I didn't see one of those guys say thank you

when you handed him a soft drink. Who's kidding who, podna?'

I found his mother on her knees in the backyard, spading out a hole for a pot of chrysanthemums. The Saint Augustine grass was thick and spongy underfoot, and the beds along her weathered wood fences were bursting with azaleas, banana trees, elephant ears, flaming hibiscus, and pink and blue hydrangeas. She was barefoot and wore a pair of white shorts and a purple blouse with green flowers on it. Her hair was on her shoulders, and her face was hot with her work. For the first time I saw a prettiness in her. I sat on a wood box next to her and turned on the garden hose and let it sluice into the fresh hole while she fitted the plant in and troweled dirt over the roots.

'How'd you know I was home?' she said.

'Your office told me you're working nights now.'

'What were you talking to Zoot about out there?' she said, without looking up.

'Not too much … His friends.'

'You don't approve of them?'

'People sure know when they're around.'

'Well, I guess you're glad you don't have to be around them very long, aren't you?'

'A boy can gravitate to certain kids for a reason.'

'Oh?' she said, and rested her rump on her heels. As she looked at me she tilted her head in feigned deference.

'I don't know why you think it's funny. He's a good boy,' I said. 'Why don't you stop treating him like a douche bag?'

She made a sound like she had swallowed bile. 'I can't believe you just said that,' she said.

'Why don't you give the kid some credit? He's got a lot of courage. Did he tell you he went three rounds against a professional fighter who could have turned his brains into mush?'

'Where do you get off telling me how to raise my child?'

'*That's* it, Lucinda. He's not a child.'

Then she made the same sound again, as though she couldn't remove a vile taste from her throat. 'Please spare me this, would you?' she said. 'Go away somewhere, find a nice white neighborhood, find a white lady digging in her garden, and please give her your advice about the correct way to raise children. Can you do that for me, please?'

'We've got another dead dealer, a guy named Camel Benoit down on Terpsichore and Baronne.'

The heat went out of her eyes.

'Did you know him?' I said.

She brushed the dirt off her palms. 'He used to work some girls out of this neighborhood,' she said.

'Somebody drove an American flag through his heart.' I saw the question mark in her face. I told her about the man in gloves and a Halloween mask who had torn up the shooting gallery, about the body in the wall and the force that must have been required to drive the brass-winged staff through the heart cavity. All the while she continued to sit with her rump on her heels and look reflectively at the flower bed in front of her.

'Who's in charge of the investigation?' she said.

'Motley.'

'He'll do his best with it.'

'Somebody else won't?'

'The department has its problems.'

'Is Nate Baxter one of them?' I said.

She smoothed the wet dirt around the base of the chrysanthemum plant with her garden trowel.

'Is there another problem, too?' I asked. 'Like this citizens committee that doesn't seem too upset over a bunch of black lowlifes being canceled out?'

'You think the Citizens Committee for a Better New Orleans is involved with murder?' But her tone did not quite reflect the outrageousness of the idea.

'Some funny people keep showing up on it. Tommy

Blue Eyes, Hippo Bimstine … you as the liaison person for NOPD. That's a peculiar combo, don't you think?'

'Lots of people want New Orleans to be like it was thirty years ago. For different reasons, maybe.'

'What's your own feeling? You think maybe the times are such that we should just whack out a few of the bad guys? Create our own free-fire zone and make up the rules later?'

'I don't think I like what you're saying.'

'I heard you went up to Angola to watch a man electrocuted.'

'That bothers you?'

'I had to witness an execution once. I had dreams about it for a long time.'

'Let me clarify something for you. I didn't go *once*. I do it in every capital conviction I'm involved with. The people who can't be there, the ones these guys sodomize and mutilate and murder, have worse problems than bad dreams.'

'You're a tough-minded lady.'

'Save the hand job for somebody else.'

I stood up and turned off the hose. The iron handle squeaked in my hand.

'The bad thing about vigilantes is that eventually they're not selective,' I said.

'Is that supposed to mean something to me?'

'I'm going to violate a confidence. If Zoot had walked into that crack house a little earlier this morning, he might have had his head opened up with that E-tool like some of the others. He's not a good listener, either, Lucinda.'

Her lips parted silently. I could not look at the recognition of loss spreading through her face.

It was hot that night, with an angry whalebone moon high above the marsh. The rumble of dry thunder woke me at three in the morning. I found Bootsie in the kitchen, sitting in the dark at the breakfast table, her bare feet in a square of moonlight. Her shoulders were rounded; her breasts sagged inside her nightgown.

'It's the lightning,' she said. 'It was popping out in the marsh. I saw a tree burning.'

I walked her back to the bed and lay beside her. In a little while the rain began ticking in the trees; then it fell harder, drumming on the eaves and the tin roof of the gallery. She fell asleep with her head on my arm and slept through a thunderstorm that broke across the marsh at daybreak and flooded the yard and blew a fine, cool mist through the screens.

At eight o'clock the sheriff called and told me to go directly to Iberia General rather than to the office. Charles Sitwell, our only link to Will Buchalter, would never be accused of ratting out on his friends.

chapter thirteen

The window blinds in Sitwell's hospital room were up, and the walls and the sheets on his bed were bright with sunlight. A nurse was emptying Sitwell's bedpan in the toilet, and the deputy who had stood guard on the door was chewing on a toothpick and staring up at a talk show on a television set whose sound was turned off.

'I can't tell you with any certainty when he died,' the doctor said. 'I'd say it was in the last two or three hours, but that's a guess. Actually, I thought he was going to make it.'

Sitwell's head was tilted back on the pillow. His mouth and eyes were open. A yellow liquid had drained out of the plaster and bandages on his face into the whiskers on his throat.

'You want to guess at what caused his death?' I said.

The doctor was a powerfully built, sandy-haired man, a tanned, habitual golf player, who wore greens and protective plastic bags over his feet.

'Look at his right hand,' he said. 'It's clutching the sheet like he was either afraid of something or he was experiencing a painful spasm of some kind.'

'Yes?'

'That's not unusual in itself, so maybe I'm just too imaginative.'

'You're going to have to be a little more exact for me, Doctor.'

He flipped out his rimless glasses, fitted them on his nose, then bent over Sitwell's body.

'Take at look at this,' he said, rotating Sitwell's chin sideways with his thumb. 'You see that red spot in his whiskers, like a big mosquito bite? Come around in the light. Here, right by the jugular.'

'What about it?'

'Look closely.' He used his thumb to brush back the whiskers. 'The skin's torn above the original puncture. You want to know what I think, or had you rather I stay out of your business?'

'Go ahead, Doc, you're doing just fine.'

'I think maybe somebody shoved a hypodermic needle in his throat.'

I rubbed back Sitwell's whiskers with the tips of my fingers. His blood had already drained to the lowest parts of his body, and his skin was cold and rubbery to the touch. The area right above the puncture looked like it had been ripped with an upward motion, like a wood splinter being torn loose from the grain of the skin.

'If someone did put a needle in him, what do you think it might have been loaded with?' I said.

'Air would do it. A bubble can stop up an artery like a cork in a pipe.'

I turned toward the deputy, who was sitting in a chair now, still staring up at the silent talk show on television. His name was Expidee Chatlin, and he had spent most of his years with the department either as a crossing guard at parish elementary schools or escorting prisoners from the drunk tank to guilty court.

'Were you here all night, Expidee?' I asked.

'Sure, what you t'ink, Dave?' He had narrow shoulders and wide hips, a thin mustache, and stiff, black hair that no amount of grease seemed capable of flattening on his skull.

'Who came in the room during the night?' I asked.

'Hospital people. They's some ot'er kind working here?'

'What kind of hospital people, Expidee?'

'Nurses, doctors, all the reg'lar people they got working here.' He took a fresh toothpick from his shirt pocket and inserted it in the corner of his mouth. His eyes drifted back up to the television set. The doctor went out into the hall. The nurse began untaping the IV needle from Sitwell's arm. I reached up and punched off the television set.

'Did you leave the door at all, Expidee?' I said.

'I got to go to the bat'room sometimes.'

'Why didn't you want to use the one in the room?'

'I didn't want to wake the guy up.'

'Did you go anyplace else?'

He took the toothpick out of his mouth and put it back in his pocket. His hands were cupped on the arms of the chair.

'Being stuck out there on a wooden chair for twelve hours isn't the best kind of assignment, partner,' I said.

'Come on, Dave …' His eyes cut sideways at the nurse.

'Ma'am, could you leave us alone a minute?' I said.

She walked out of the room and closed the door behind her.

'What about it, podna?' I said.

He was quiet a moment, then he said, 'About six o'clock I went to the cafeteria and had me some eggs. I ax the nurse up at the counter not to let nobody in the room.'

'How long were you gone?'

'Fifteen minutes, maybe. I just didn't t'ink it was gonna be no big deal.'

'Who was the nurse, Expidee?'

'That one just went out … Dave, you gonna put this in my jacket?'

I didn't answer.

'My wife ain't working,' he said. 'I can't get no ot'er job, neither.'

'We've got a dead man on our hands, Expidee.'

'I'm sorry I messed up. What else I'm gonna say?'

There was nothing for it. And I wasn't sure of the cause of death, anyway, or if the deputy's temporary negligence was even a factor.

'If you weren't at the door when you should have been, it was because you went down the hall to use the men's room,' I said.

'T'anks, Dave. I ain't gonna forget it.'

'Don't do something like this again, Expidee.'

'I ain't. I promise. Hey, Dave, you called up the church for that guy?'

'Why do you ask?'

'A man like that try to hurt your family and you call the church for him, that's all right. Yes, suh, that's all right.'

I asked the nurse to come back in. She was in her fifties and had bluish gray hair and a figure like a pigeon's. I asked her if anyone had entered Sitwell's room while Expidee was away from the door.

'I wouldn't know,' she said.

'Did you see anyone?'

'You gentlemen have such an interesting attitude about accountability,' she said. 'Let me see, what exact moment did you have in mind? Do you mean while Expidee was asleep in his chair or wandering the halls?'

'I see. Thank you for your time,' I said.

She flipped the sheet over Chuck Sitwell's face as though she were closing a fly trap, released the blinds, and dropped the room into darkness.

I went to the office and began opening my mail behind my desk. Through the window I could see the fronds on the palm trees by the sidewalk lifting and clattering in the breeze; across the street a black man who sold barbecue lunches was building a fire in an open pit, and the smoke from the green wood spun in the cones of sunlight shining through the oak branches overhead. It wasn't quite yet fall, but the grass was already turning a paler green, the sky a harder, deeper blue, like porcelain, with only a few white clouds on the horizon.

But I couldn't concentrate on either my mail or the beautiful day outside. Regardless whether the autopsy showed that Charles Sitwell had died of complications from gunshot wounds or a hypodermic needle thrust into his throat, Will Buchalter was out there somewhere, with no conduit to him, outside the computer, running free, full-bore, supercharged by his own sexual cruelty.

What was there to go on, I asked myself.

Virtually nothing.

No, music.

He knew something about historical jazz. He even knew how to hold rare seventy-eights and to place them in the record rack with the opening in their dustcovers turned toward the wall.

Could a sadist love music that had its origins in Island hymns and the three-hundred-year spiritual struggle of a race to survive legal and economic servitude?

I doubted it. Cruelty and sentimentality are almost always companion characteristics in an individual but never cruelty and love.

Buchalter was one of those whose life was invested in the imposition of control and power over others. Like the self-serving academic who enjoys the possession of an esoteric knowledge for the feeling of superiority it gives him over others, or the pseudojournalist who is drawn to the profession because it allows him access to a world of power and wealth that he secretly envies and fears, the collector such as Buchalter reduces the beauty of butter-flies to pinned insects on a mounting board, a daily reminder that creation is always subject to his murderous hand.

The phone on my desk rang.

'Detective Robicheaux?' a woman said.

'Yes?'

'This is Marie Guilbeaux. I hope I'm not bothering you.'

'I'm sorry, who?'

'The nun you met at the hospital. Outside Mr. Sitwell's room.'

'Oh yes, how are you, Sister?'

'I wanted to apologize.'

'What for?'

'I heard about Mr. Sitwell's death this morning, and I remembered how judgmental I must have sounded the other day. That wasn't my intention, but I wanted to apologize to you anyway.'

'There's no need to. It's good of you to call, though.'

I could hear a hum in the telephone, as though the call was long-distance.

'You've been very nice,' she said.

'Not at all ... Is there something else on your mind, Sister?'

'No, not really. I think I take myself too seriously sometimes.'

'Well, thanks for calling.'

'I hope to see you again sometime.'

'Me too. Good-bye, Sister.'

'Good-bye.'

The musical community in southern Louisiana is a large and old one. Where do you begin if you want to find a person who's interested in or collects historical jazz?

There was certainly nothing picturesque about the geographic origins of the form. If it was born in one spot, it was Storyville at the turn of the century, a thirty-eight-block red-light district in New Orleans, named for an alderman who wanted to contain all the city's prostitution inside a single neighborhood. *Jazz* meant to fornicate; songs like 'Easy Rider' and 'House of the Rising Sun' were literal dirges about the morphine addiction and suicidal despair of the prostitutes who lived out their lives in the brothels of Perdido Street.

When I walked down Bourbon that evening, not far from Basin, one of the old borders of Storyville, the air was filled with a purple haze, lit with neon, warmly redolent of the smell of beer and whiskey in paper cups, the sky overhead intersected by a solitary pink cloud off Lake Pontchartrain. The street, which was closed to automobile traffic, was congested with people, their faces happy and flushed in the din of rockabilly and Dixieland bands. Spielers in straw boaters and candy-striped vests were working the trade in front of the strip joints; black kids danced and clattered their clip-on steel taps on the concrete for the tourists; an all-black street band, with tambourines ringing and horns blaring, belted out 'Millersburg' on the corner at Conti; and a half block farther up, in a less hedonistic mood, a group of religious fanatics, with signs containing apocalyptical warnings, tried to buttonhole anyone who would listen to their desperate message.

I talked to an elderly black clarinetist at Preservation Hall, a sax man at the Famous Door who used to work for Marcia Ball, a three-hundred-pound white woman with flaming hair and a sequined dress that sparkled like ice water, who played blues piano in a hole-in-the-wall on Dumaine. None of them knew of a Will Buchalter or a jazz enthusiast or collector who fit his description.

I walked over on Ursulines to a dilapidated book and record store run by two men named Jimmie Ryan and Count Carbonna, who was also known sometimes as Baron Belladonna. Jimmie was a florid, rotund man with a red mustache who looked like a nineteenth-century bartender. But the insides of both his forearms were laced with the flattened veins and gray scar tissue of an old-time addict. Before he had gotten off the needle, he had been known as Jimmie the Dime, because with a phone call he could connect you with any kind of illegal activity in New Orleans.

His business partner, the Count, was another matter. He had blitzed his brain years ago with purple acid, wore a black vampire's cape and slouch hat, and maintained that the soul of Olivia Newton-John lived under the waters of Lake Pontchartrain. His angular body could have been fashioned from wire; his long, narrow head and pinched face looked like they had been slammed in a door. Periodically he shaved off his eyebrows so his brain could absorb more oxygen.

'How do you like being out of the life, Jimmie?' I asked.

As always, my conversation with Jim would prove to be a rare linguistic experience.

'The book business ain't bad stuff to be in these days,' he said. He wore suspenders and a purple-striped long-sleeve shirt with sweat rings under the arms. 'There's a lot of special kinds of readers out there, if you understand what I'm saying, Streak. New Orleans is being overrun by crazoids and people who was probably cloned from dog turds, and the government won't do anything about it. But it's a crazy world out there, and am I my brother's keeper, that's what I'm asking, a buck's a buck, and who am I to judge? So I've got a bin here for your vampire literature, I got your books on ectoplasm, your books on ufology and teleportation, I got your studies on tarot cards and Eckankar, you want to read about your Venusian cannibals living among us, I got your book on that, too.'

'I'm looking for a guy named Will Buchalter, Jimmie. He might be a collector of old jazz records.'

His mustache tilted and the corners of his eyes wrinkled quizzically.

'What's this guy look like?' he asked.

I told him while he rolled a matchstick in his mouth. The Count was cleaning bookshelves with a feather duster, his eyes as intense as obsidian chips in his white face.

'He's got blackheads fanning back from his eyes like cat's whiskers?' Jimmie said.

'Something like that,' I said.

'Maybe I can give him a job here. Hey, is this guy mixed up with this Nazi submarine stuff?'

'How do you know about the sub, Jimmie?'

'The whole fucking town knows about it. I tell you, though, Streak, I wouldn't mess with nobody that was connected with these tin shirts or whatever they used to call these World War II commonists.'

'Wait a minute, Jim. Not everybody knows about the Silver Shirts.'

'I'm Irish, right, so I don't talk about my own people, there's enough others to do that, like you ever hear this one, you put four Irish Catholics together and you always got a fifth, but I got to say you cross a mick with a squarehead, you come up with a pretty unnatural combo, if you're getting my drift, mainly that wearing a star-spangled jockstrap outside your slacks ain't proof you're one-hunnerd-percent American.'

'You've truly lost me, Jimmie.'

'I lived right down the street from his family.'

'*Who?*'

'Tommy Bobalouba. Sometimes you're hard to get things across to, Streak. I mean, like, we got jet planes going by overhead or something?'

'Tommy Lonighan's family was mixed up with Nazis?'

'His mother was from Germany. She was in the, what-do-you-call-'em, the metal shirts. That's why Tommy was always fighting with people. Nobody in the Channel wanted anything to do with his family … Hey, Count, we got a customer named Will Buchalter?'

Count Carbonna began humming to himself in a loud, flat, nasal drone.

'Hey, Count, I'm talking here,' Jimmie said. 'Hey, you got stock in the Excedrin company … Count, knock off the noise!'

But it was no use. The Count was on a roll, suddenly dusting the records with a manic energy, filling the store with his incessant, grinding drone.

Jimmie looked at me and shrugged his shoulders.

'Listen, Jim, this guy Buchalter is bad news,' I said. 'If he should come in your store, don't let on that you know me, don't try to detain him or drop the dime on him while he's here. Just get ahold of me or Clete Purcel after he leaves.'

'What's this guy done?'

I told him.

'I'm not showing offense here,' he said, 'but I'm a little shocked, you understand what I'm saying, you think a geek like that would be coming into my store. We're talking about the kind of guy hangs in skin shops, beats up on hookers, gets a bone-on hurting people, this ain't Jimmie Ryan just blowing you a lot of gas, Streak, this kind of guy don't like music, he likes to hear somebody scream.'

He leaned on his arms and bit down on his matchstick so that it arched upward into his mustache.

But my conversation with Jimmie was not quite over. A half hour later he called Clete Purcel's apartment, just before I was about to head back to New Iberia.

'I'm glad I got you,' he said. 'Something's wrong here.'

'What's happened?'

'It's the Count. After we close the shop, he always goes upstairs to his room and eats a can of potted meat and watches Pat Robertson on TV. Except tonight he kept droning and humming and walking in circles and cleaning the shelves till the place looked like a dust storm, then for no reason he goes crashing up the stairs and throws everything in a suitcase and flies out the back door with his cape flapping in the breeze.'

'You're saying Buchalter *was* in your store? Maybe when the Count was by himself?'

'You tell me. Hey, when a guy who talks to Olivia Newton-John through the hole in the lavatory is scared out of town by sickos, I'm wondering maybe I should move to Iraq or one of them places where all you got to worry about is your nose falling off from the BO.'

In the morning I got the autopsy report on Charles Sitwell. He didn't die of an air bubble being injected into his bloodstream. The syringe had been loaded with a mixture of water and roach paste.

It was time to talk to Tommy Lonighan about his knowledge of German U-boats and Silver Shirts, preferably in an official situation, in custody, outside of his own environment. I called Ben Motley and asked about the chances of rousting him from his house or gym and bringing him down to an interrogation room.

'On what basis?' he said.

'He's lying about the reasons for his interest in this U-boat.'

'So he didn't want to tell you his mother was a Nazi. It's not the kind of stuff anybody likes to hang on the family tree.'

'It's too much for coincidence, Motley. He's connected with Buchalter. He's got to be.'

'You want me to get a warrant on a guy, in a homicide investigation, because of something his mother did fifty years ago?'

'We just bring him in for questioning. Tommy likes to think of himself as respectable these days. So we step on his cookie bag.'

'I wonder why the words *civil suit* keep floating in front of my eyes. It probably has something to do with my lens prescription.'

'Don't give this guy a free pass. He's dirty, Motley. You know it.'

'Give me a call if you come up with something more. Until then, I don't think it helps to be flogging our rods over the wastebasket.'

'Listen to me, Ben—'

'Get real, Robicheaux. NOPD doesn't roust people, not even Tommy Blue Eyes, when they live on lakefront property. Keep it in your pants, my man.'

I worked late that evening on two other cases, one involving a stabbing in a black nightclub, the other, the possible suffocation of an infant by his foster parents.

The sky was the color of scorched pewter when I drove along the dirt road by the bayou toward my house. The wind was dry blowing across the marsh, and the willows were coated with dust and filled with the red tracings of fireflies. The deputy on guard at the house started his car engine, waved at me as he passed, and disappeared down the long corridor of oak trees.

Bootsie was washing dishes at the sink when I came in. She wore a pair of grass-stained white dungarees and a rumpled yellow blouse that was too small for her and exposed her midsection.

'Where's Alafair?' I said, and kissed her on the cheek. I could smell cigarette smoke in her clothes and hair.

'In the living room. Doing her homework,' she said. She kept her face turned toward the open window when she spoke.

'Where'd you go today?' I said.

'What does it matter?'

'Beg your pardon?'

'What does it matter where we go?'

'I don't understand, Boots.'

'It doesn't matter where we go. He's going to be there.'

'You mean Buchalter?'

'He called.'

'Here? When?'

'This afternoon.'

'Why didn't you call me at the office?'

'And tell you what?'

I put my hands lightly on her shoulders and turned her toward me. She breathed through her nose and kept her face at an angle to me.

'What did he say, Boots?'

'Nothing. I could hear music, like the kind you hear in a supermarket or an elevator. And then a man breathing. His breath going in and out, like he was waiting for something.'

'Maybe it was somebody else, maybe just a crank.'

'He did something else. He scratched a fingernail back

and forth on the receiver. The way a cat paws at the door.'

Her mouth parted, and she looked up into my face. Her breath smelled like bourbon-scented orange slices.

'We'll get an unlisted number in the morning,' I said.

'It *was* Buchalter, wasn't it?'

'Maybe. But what we have to remember, Boots, is that when these guys try to scare people with telephone calls, they're running on the rims. They don't have anything else going.'

Her eyes went back and forth, searching inside mine.

'We've got a computer sketch of the guy all over town,' I said. 'I don't think he'll come back.'

'Then who killed the man in the hospital?'

'I don't know.'

'He's out there, Dave. I know he is.'

Her experience with Buchalter had been even worse than mine, and I knew that my words could not take the unrelieved sense of vulnerability out of her face. I held her against me, then walked her into the bedroom, turned on the shower, waited while she got inside the stall, locked the house, then said Alafair's prayers with her. The moon was down, the pecan and oak trees were motionless and black outside the screens, and the only sound I could hear besides the suck of the attic fan was Tripod running up and down on his chain and wire clothesline.

I poured a glass of milk, fixed a ham and onion sandwich, and ate it at the kitchen table. When the phone on the wall rang, I knew who I would be talking to.

His voice sounded as though he were waking from sleep, or as though he had been disturbed during copulation. It was in slow motion, with a *click* to it, deep in his throat, that was both phlegmy and dry at the same time.

'It doesn't have to be bad between us.'

'What doesn't?'

'You, me, your wife. Y'all could be part of us.'

'Buchalter, you've got to understand this. I can't wave a wand over the gulf and bring up a depth-charged sub. I think you're a sick man. But if I get you in my sights, I'm going to take you off at the neck.'

Again, I heard a wet, clicking sound, like his tongue sticking to the insides of his cheeks.

'I like you,' he said.

'You *like* me?'

'Yes. A great deal.'

I waited before I spoke again.

'What do you think is going to happen the next time I see you?' I said.

'Nothing.'

'Nothing?'

'You'll come around to our way. It's a matter of time.'

My palm was squeezed damply on the receiver.

'Listen, every cop in Iberia Parish knows what you look like. They know what you've done, they're not big on procedure. Don't make the mistake of coming back here. I'm telling you this as a favor.'

'We can give you power.'

You're learning nothing. Change the subject.

'I know where you've been in New Orleans,' I said. 'You talked too much about music. You left a trail, Buchalter.'

'I could have hurt you the other night, in ways you can't dream about, but I didn't,' he said. 'Do you want to hear how they reach a point where they beg, what they sound like when they beg?'

'Will you meet with me?'

I heard him drinking from a glass, deeply, swallowing like a man who had walked out of a great, dry heat.

'Because I'm different, you shouldn't treat me as though I'm psychotic. I'm not. Good night,' he said. 'Tell your wife I remember our moment with fondness. She's a beautiful specimen of her gender.'

He hung up the receiver as gently as a man completing a yawn.

My heart was racing inside my chest. My pistol was still clipped to my belt. I unsnapped the holster, slipped the .45 out of the leather, which I had rubbed with saddle soap, and ran my fingers along the coolness of the metal. The balls of my fingers left delicate prints in the thin sheen of oil. I released the magazine from the butt, rubbed my thumb over the brass casing of the top round, pulled the slide back and forth, then shoved the magazine back into the butt. The grips felt hard and stiff inside my hand.

I looked through the window into the dark. I wanted Buchalter to be out there, perhaps parking his car behind a grove of trees, working his way across the fields, confident that this time he could pull it off, could invade my house and life with impunity. And this time—

I put the .45 on the nightstand in our bedroom and undressed in the dark. My own skin felt as dry and hot as a heated lamp shade. Bootsie was still asleep when I moved on top of her, between her legs, without invitation or consent, a rough beast who could have been hewn out of desert stone.

I made love to her as a starving man might. I put my tongue deep in her mouth and tasted the whiskey and candied cherries and sliced oranges deep in her wet recesses. I plummeted into her fecund warmth, I inhaled the alcohol out of her breath, I robbed her of the golden and liquid heat that had been aged in oak and presented mistakenly as a gift to her heart's blood rather than to mine.

chapter fourteen

The early sun looked like a sliver of pink ice, just above the horizon's misty rim, when I stopped my truck at the locked entrance to Tommy Lonighan's driveway. I got out of the truck and pushed the button on the speaker box.

'Who is it?' the voice of the man named Art said.

'Detective Dave Robicheaux. I'm here to see Tommy.'

'He's busy.'

'No, he's not.'

'The last time you were here you were busting up people with a shovel.'

'Yesterday's box score, Art.'

'It's seven o'clock in the fucking morning. How about some slack?'

'Are you going to open up or not? If not, I can come back with a warrant that has your name on it.'

'Is Purcel with you?'

'No.'

'You sure?'

'Last chance, Art.'

'Okay, take it easy, I'm buzzing you in. Tommy's out back. I'll tell him you're here. Hey, can you do me a favor?'

'What?'

'It's a nice day. The Indian and me are serving breakfast for Tommy and his guests out on the terrace.

Let's keep it a nice day. Okay, man? Shit don't go good with grits and eggs.'

A minute later I parked my truck at the end of Lonighan's drive. The interior of the compound was the architectural and landscaped antithesis of everything in the Irish Channel neighborhood where Tommy had grown up. His imitation Tudor house was surrounded by citrus and pine and oak trees; steam rose from the turquoise surface of his screened-in pool and his coral goldfish ponds; the Saint Augustine grass was thick and wet from soak hoses, shining with dew in the hazy light. Beyond his protective brick walls, I could hear canvas sails flapping and swelling with wind on the lake.

He was behind the house, in an orange bikini swimsuit and a pair of black high-top ring shoes, thudding his taped fists into what looked like a six-foot stack of sandbags. His pale body, which rippled with sweat, was the color and texture of gristle. A tubular, red scar, with tiny pink stitch holes on each side, wound in a serpentine line from his right kidney up to his shoulder blade.

He stopped hitting the bags when he saw me, and wiped his meringue hair and armpits with a towel. His flushed face smiled broadly.

'You're just in time to eat,' he said, pulling the adhesive tape off his hands. 'How about this weather? I think we got ourselves an early fall.' He flipped his towel on top of an azalea bush. His knuckles were round and hard and protruded from his skin as though he were holding a roll of quarters in each hand.

'You work out on sandbags, Tommy?'

'Cement. If you don't bust your hand or jam your wrist on a cement bag, you sure ain't gonna do it on a guy's face. What's up, Dave?'

'I've got a big problem with this guy Buchalter. He can't seem to stay out of my life.'

'If I can help, let me know.' He worked a blue jumper over his head as we walked down a gravel path toward a glass-topped table on his patio, where an ash blond woman in a terry-cloth robe was drinking coffee and reading the paper. 'I don't want a guy like this around, either. He gives the city a bad reputation.'

'I didn't say he was from New Orleans, Tommy.'

'You wouldn't be here unless you thought he was. Sit down and eat. You're too serious. Charlotte, this is Dave Robicheaux.'

She lowered her paper and looked at me with eyes that had the bright, blue tint of colored contact lenses, that were neither rude nor friendly, curious or wary. I suspected that she read news accounts of airline disasters with the same level of interest as the weather report. Her freckled, sun-browned skin had the smooth folds in it of soft tallow.

Her mouth was red and wet when she took it away from the coffee cup and acknowledged me.

'The gentleman who performs so well with a shovel,' she said.

'Sometimes it's better to use visual aids when you're talking to the Calucci brothers,' I said.

'Fucking A,' Tommy said. 'Neither one of those dagos could give himself a hand job without a diagram. But when you got to do business with the oilcans, you got to do business with the oilcans, right?'

'What kind of deals do you have with the Caluccis, Tommy?' I said.

'Are you kidding? Restaurant linen, valet parking, food delivery, carpenters and electricians working on my casino, you deal with the greaseballs or you get a picket line in front of everything you own.'

His house servant came out the back door with a huge, rope-handled wood tray between his hands and began setting silver-topped containers of scrambled eggs, grits, sausage links, bacon, and peeled oranges and grapefruit in front of us. The servant was the same enormous man I had seen on my earlier visit. His Indian face was as expressionless and flat as a cake pan, his brown, skillet-sized hands veined with scar tissue like tiny bits of white string.

'You're staring, Mr. Robicheaux,' Charlotte said.

'Excuse me?'

'At Manuel. It's rude to stare at people,' she said.

'He didn't mean anything,' Tommy said. 'Dave's a gentleman. He's got a college degree. In English literature, right, Dave? We're talking fucking class guy here.'

He winked at me as he spread his napkin.

The house servant named Manuel brushed against me when he poured my coffee. I could smell chemical fertilizer and garden dirt in his clothes. He never spoke, but after he went back inside the house, I saw his face look back at me from a kitchen window.

'Dig this,' Tommy said. 'Manny looks like he just got up out of a grave in *Night of the Living Dead*, but actually he's a fruit. He's gonna be in a music video called 'She's a Swinging Stud.' Hey, y'all quit looking at me like that. You think I could make up something like that? They show these kinds of videos in those homo joints on Dauphine.'

'Your mother was in the American-German Bund, Tommy,' I said.

'What?' His face looked as though ice water had been poured on it.

'I guess it's common knowledge in the Channel. That's why you know what's in that sub, isn't it, partner?' I smiled at him.

'You're sitting at my breakfast table …' He cleared his throat and tried to regain his words. 'Right here at my table, at my own house, you're making insults about my mother?'

'That's not my intention.'

'Then clean the fucking mashed potatoes out of your mouth.'

The woman named Charlotte put her hand in his lap.

'It's one way or the other, Tommy,' I said.

'What is?'

'You either know something about the sub through your mother, or you've got a serious personal problem with Hippo Bimstine that you're not talking about.'

His tangled, white eyebrows were damp with perspiration against his red face. I saw the woman named Charlotte biting her lip, kneading her hand in his lap.

'What problem you talking about?' he said.

'You want it right down the pipe?'

'Yeah, I do.' But his face looked like stretched rubber, like that of a man about to receive a spear through the breastbone.

'He says you killed his little brother.'

His breath went in and out of his mouth. His eyes looked unfocused, impaired, as though he had been staring at a welder's electric arc. He pinched his nose and breathed hard through his nostrils, rolled his head on his neck.

But it was the woman who spoke.

'You filthy bastard,' she said.

'You want a free shot, Tommy?' I said.

'If I want to take a shot, you won't know what hit you,' he said. But his voice was suddenly hoarse and somehow separate from himself.

'Maybe it was a rough thing to say. But Will Buchalter is doing a number on my wife,' I said. 'It has to stop, Tommy. You understand what I'm saying to you? When you create a free-fire zone, it works both ways. We're not operating on the old rules here.'

'Where you get off talking free-fire zone? I had a Chinese bayonet unzip my insides when you were still fucking your fist.'

'You want one of my Purple Hearts?'

'You're a sonofabitch, Robicheaux,' he said.

'You don't make a convincing victim, Tommy.'

'We were all kids. It was an accident. What's the matter with you, what kind of guy you think I am? Why you doing this?'

'Are you going to help me out?'

'Get off my property.'

'All right,' I said, and stood up to go. Then I saw Zoot Bergeron jogging up the drive in black gym shorts, a red bandanna tied around his forehead. I looked down at Tommy Lonighan.

'I've got a deal for you,' I said. 'You put Buchalter in my custody, you'll probably never see me again. But if he comes back around my house, I'm going to punch your ticket.'

'Yeah?' he said, the rims of his nostrils whitening. 'That's what you're gonna do? You can't bust the right people, you can't protect your own wife, you need somebody to wipe your ass for you, you come around making threats, telling me I killed a child, I'm about to take your fucking head off, Dave, you got that?'

'We'll see who walks out of the smoke, Tommy,' I said, and walked across the sun-spangled, blue-green lawn toward my truck. I didn't look back.

Zoot slowed from his jog, his sleek chest rising and falling, his sweat-soaked gym shorts twisted around his loins.

'What are you doing here, partner?' I asked.

'Mr. Tommy give me a job around his yard, let me work out wit' him.'

'You're staying here?'

'I did last night.'

'Why?' He didn't answer, and I said it again, 'Why's that, Zoot?'

'She got a man at the house.' His eyes avoided mine. 'A white man she goes out wit' sometimes. I come over here and Mr. Tommy let me stay.'

'I don't want to tell you what to do, Zoot, but I think Tommy Lonighan is a gangster and a racist prick who you ought to avoid like anthrax.'

Then, too late, I saw the alarm in Zoot's eyes as they focused on something behind me.

Tommy Lonighan was moving fast when he hit me between the shoulder blades and drove me into the side of my truck. Before I could turn, he had ripped my .45 loose from my belt holster. He clenched it at an upward angle in front of me, his neck corded with veins, his nostrils flaring, and pulled back the slide, feeding a hollow-point round into the chamber. I could hear the gravel crunch under the soles of his shoes.

'Don't be a dumb guy, Tommy,' I said.

'You think you can punch my buttons, make me ashamed of myself in front of people?'

'Give me the piece, Tommy.'

'You want it? Then you got it, cocksucker.'

He jammed the butt into my palm, but he didn't let go. He wrapped both his hands around mine, tightening his fingers until they were white with bone, and pointed the .45's barrel into his sternum. His blue eyes were round and threaded with light; his breath stank of the pieces of meat wedged in his teeth.

'You talk war record, you talk Purple Hearts, you got the balls for this?' he said.

The hammer was cocked, the safety off, but I was able to keep my fingers frozen outside the trigger housing.

'Step back, Tommy.'

His breath labored in his chest; there was a knot of color like a red rose in his throat.

'I didn't kill no kid back there in the Channel,' he said. 'It was an accident. Everybody knows it but that mockie. He won't let go of it.'

For just a moment the focus in his eyes seemed to turn inward, and his words seemed directed almost at himself rather than at me. I felt the power go out of his grip.

I flipped up the safety on the slide, jerked the .45 loose from his grasp, and whipped the barrel across his nose. He stood flat-footed, his fists balled at his sides, his eyes the same color as the sky, a solitary string of blood dripping from his right nostril. I started to hit him again.

But his face broke, just like a lamp shade being burned in the center by a heat source from within. One eye seemed to knot, as though someone had put a finger in it;

his mouth became a crimped, tight line, downturned at the corners, and the flesh in one cheek suddenly filled with wrinkles and began to tremble. He turned and walked into his house, his back straight, his arms dead at his sides, his eyes hidden from view.

I stared openmouthed after him, my weapon hanging loosely from my hand like an object of shame.

chapter fifteen

I had always wanted to believe that I had brought the violence in my life with me when I came back from Vietnam. But one of the most violent moments in my life, or at least the most indefensible, came at the end of my first marriage and not because I was a police officer or a war veteran.

My first wife was a beautiful, dark-haired girl from Martinique who loved thoroughbred horses and race-track betting as much as I, but she also developed a love for clubhouse society and men who didn't daily mortgage their tomorrows with Beam straight up and a Jax draft on the side.

We were at an afternoon lawn party on Lake Pontchartrain. The sky was storm-streaked, the water out on the lake slate green and capping, the sailboats from the yacht club dipping hard in the swells. I remember standing at the drinks table, next to my wife, while a black waiter in a white butler's jacket was shaking a silver drink mixer. Then my wife's current lover, a geologist from Houston, was next to her, chatting with her, idly stroking the down on her forearm as though I were not there.

I could hear the palm fronds rattling overhead, a jazz combo playing on the terrace, the words of my wife and her lover disappearing like bubbles in the wind. He was an athlete and mountain climber and had the profile and rugged good looks of a gladiator. Then I remember a sound like Popsicle sticks breaking and a wave of red-black color erupting behind my eyes.

When they pulled me off him, he was strangling on his own tongue.

Later, I pretended that he had deserved it, and that my wife had deserved to be shamed and humiliated in front of her friends. But I was deceiving myself, as was my way in those days when I sincerely believed that I could experience no worse fate in this world than to be deprived of charcoal-filtered whiskey and the amber radiance with which it animated and filled my life. I had simply made my wife and her lover pay for events that had occurred many years earlier.

My father, whose name was Aldous, who was also called Big Al in the oil field, where he worked as a derrick man up on the monkey board, was a huge, dark, grinning Cajun with fists the size of cantaloupes. He loved to fight in bars, sometimes taking on three or four adversaries at once. Oil field roughnecks would break their hands on his head; bouncers would splinter chairs across his back; but no one ever hurt Big Al except my mother, who worked in a laundry with Negro women to support us while he was in the parish jail.

When he went back to Marsh Island for the muskrat season, a man named Mack, a bouree dealer from Morgan City who wore a fedora, zoot slacks, suspenders, French cuffs, and two-tone shoes, began to come by the house and take her for rides in his Ford coupe.

One day in late fall I came home early from school. There was no sound in the house. Then I walked past my parents' bedroom door. My mother was naked, on all fours, pointed toward the head of the bed, and Mack was about to mount her. He had a thin, white face, oiled black hair parted in the center, and a pencil mustache. He looked at me with the momentary interest that he might show a hangnail, then entered my mother.

I sat on a sawhorse in the barn until it was almost dusk. The air was raw, and leaves were blowing across the dirt yard. Then Mack was standing in the barn door, his silhouette etched with the sun's last red light, a bottle of beer in his left hand. I heard him tilt it up and drink from it.

'What you t'ink you seen?' he said.

I looked at my shoes.

'I ax you a question. Don't be pretend you ain't heard me,' he said.

'I didn't see anything.'

'You was where you didn't have no bidness. What we gonna do 'bout that?' He held out his right hand. I thought he was going to place it on my shoulder. Instead, he put the backs of his fingers under my nose. 'You smell that? Me and yo' mama been fuckin', boy. It ain't the first time, neither.'

My eyes were full of water, my face hot and small under his stare.

'You can tell yo' daddy 'bout this if you want, but you gotta tell on her, too.' He drank out of the beer bottle again and waited. 'What's you gonna do, you? Sit there and cry?'

'I'm not going to do anything.'

'That's good,' he said. ''Cause you do, I'm gonna be back.'

Then he was gone, out of the red light, and down the dirt lane to his car. The pecan and oak trees around the house were black-green and coated with dust; the dry coldness of the air felt like a windburn against the skin. I hid when my mother called me from the back porch. Behind the barn, I sat in the weeds and watched our two roosters peck a blind hen to death. They mounted her with their talons, their wings aflutter with triumph, and drove their beaks deep into her pinioned neck. I watched them do it for a long time, until my mother found me and took me back inside the kitchen and, while she fixed our supper, told me that Mack had helped her find a good job as a waitress at a beer garden in Morgan City.

* * *

The day after my trouble with Tommy Lonighan, I received a phone call from Clete Purcel at my office.

'I hear you pistol-whipped Tommy Bobalouba,' he said.

'Who told you that?'

'A couple of the Caluccis' lowlifes were talking about it in the Golden Star this morning.'

'Ah, the Caluccis again.'

'That's what I was trying to tell you, mon. They're going across tribal lines.'

'Who were these two guys?'

'Nickel-and-dime gumballs. Were you trying to sweat Tommy about that sub?'

'Yeah, but I didn't get anywhere.'

'Dave, maybe there's another way to get Buchalter out of the woodwork. What if you *can* find that sub again, you mark it, then you tell *The Times-Picayune* and every salvage company in town about it?'

'It's a thought.'

'By the way, congratulations on getting Lonighan's attention. Somebody should have mopped up the floor with that guy a long time ago ... Why the silence?'

'I shouldn't have hit him.'

'Why not?'

'He's a tormented man. The guy's got a furnace in his head.'

'I'm weeping on my desk, Dave. Oh, that's great, mon. Tommy Lonighan, the tormented man ...' He was laughing loudly now. 'Did you see the body of the guy Tommy drowned with the fire hose? It looked like the Michelin Man. Tommy shoved the nozzle down the guy's mouth. Tommy, the tormented man, oh Dave, that's beautiful ...'

I went home early that evening, with plans to take Bootsie and Alafair to Mulate's in Breaux Bridge for crawfish. When the deputy who was on guard by the drive saw my truck approaching, he started his engine and headed back toward New Iberia. At the head of the drive, close by the house, was a two-door white Toyota that I didn't recognize.

I walked down to the end of the dock, where Alafair was skipping stones across the water into a cypress stump.

'Want to go eat some crawfish, Alf?' I said.

'I don't care,' she said. Her face was sullen. She whipped another stone across the bayou.

'What's wrong, little guy?'

'I told you I don't like 'little guy' anymore, Dave.'

'All right. Now, what's wrong, Alf?'

'Nothing. Bootsie says she's sick. That's all.'

'"Says" she's sick?'

'She's been in her room all afternoon. With the door shut. She says she's sick. I told you.' She propped one hand against a post and brushed dried fish scales off the planks into the water with her tennis shoe.

'Tell me the rest of it, Alf.'

Her eyes followed a cottonmouth moccasin that was swimming across the bayou into a flooded cane brake.

'She put an empty whiskey bottle in the garbage can out back,' she said. 'She wrapped it up in a paper bag so nobody would see it. Then the sister went and got her some beer.'

'What?'

'There's a sister up there. She went down to the four corners and bought Bootsie a six-pack of beer. Why didn't Bootsie just get it out of the bait shop if she wanted some beer?'

'Let's go find out.'

'I don't want to.'

'You want to go to Mulate's later?'

'No. I don't like the way Bootsie is. I don't like that sister, either. What's she doing here, Dave?'

I rubbed the top of her head and walked up the slope through the deep shade of the trees and the drone of the cicadas. There was no sound or movement in the front of the house, and the door to Bootsie's and my bedroom was closed. I went on through the hallway into the kitchen. Sister Marie Guilbeaux was rinsing glasses and two plates in the sink.

'Oh!' she said, her shoulders twitching suddenly when she heard me behind her. She turned, and her face colored. 'Oh, my heavens, you gave me a start.'

I continued to stare at her.

'Oh, this is embarrassing,' she said. 'I hope you understand what's, why I—'

'I'm afraid I don't.'

'Of course … you couldn't. I called earlier, but you weren't here.'

'I *was* at my office.'

'I tried there. You had already left.'

'No, I was there until a half hour ago.' I could see a half dozen empty beer cans in the yellow trash basket. 'No one called.'

'*I* did. A man, a dispatcher, took a message.'

'I see. Where's Bootsie, Sister?'

'Asleep. She's not feeling well.' Her face was filled with perplexity. 'I know this looks peculiar.'

'A little.'

'I teach part-time at an elementary school in Lafayette. We're having a program on safety. You were so courteous at the hospital and over the phone I thought you might be willing to visit our class.'

'I'm a little tied up right now.'

'Yes, Bootsie told me.'

'Can you tell me why you bought beer for my wife, Sister?'

Her face was pink. 'Mr. Robicheaux, I wandered into somebody's personal situation and I've obviously mishandled it.'

'Just tell me what's happened here, please.'

'Your wife was going to drive to the store for some beer. I didn't think she should be driving. I told her I'd go for her.'

'Why didn't you just get it from the bait shop? We own it.'

'She didn't want me to.'

'I see. Is there anything else I can help you with?'

'No ... I apologize. I don't know what else to say. I'll go now. Please excuse my coming here.'

Then she was out the back door, walking fast toward her car, her green eyes shiny with embarrassment. I caught up with her just as she was opening her car door.

'Sister, there's something going on here you don't understand,' I said. 'My wife has a problem because of some events that occurred at our house. But when a person is drunk or has had too much to drink and wants you to give him more, you don't do it.'

'Then I guess I've learned a lesson today.'

'Come see us again.'

'That's kind of you.' My hand was resting on the windowsill. She placed hers lightly on top of mine and looked directly into my eyes. A shaft of sunlight fell through the tree on her reddish gold hair. I removed my hand from under hers and walked back into the house.

I opened the bedroom door and looked in on Bootsie. The blinds were drawn, and she was sleeping with her clothes on and her head under the pillow. While I fixed supper I tried to concentrate on Alafair's conversation from the table about something that Tripod had done, but my thoughts were like birds clattering about in a cage, and I found myself absently touching the top of my right hand.

You're imagining it, I thought. *It was an innocent gesture. Some of them are just socially inept.*

But my energies were too dissipated to worry about Sister Marie Guilbeaux. I knew that beyond our closed bedroom door, my wife had taken up residence in that special piece of geography where the snakes hang in fat loops from the trees and a tiger with electrified stripes lights your way to his lair.

* * *

It rained that night, and through the screen window I could smell the trees and an odor from the marsh like fish spawning. As I fell asleep, I wondered again about the Nazi submarine and Buchalter's obsession with it. When I was a child in Catholic school, we were taught that evil eventually consumes itself, like fire that must destroy its own source. Was the submarine an underwater mausoleum or historical shrine from which Buchalter and his kind believed they could renew and empower their demented and misanthropic vision? Did they hate the present-day world so much that they would seek the company of drowned men who had reveled in setting afire the seas, in machine-gunning clusters of oil-streaked merchant sailors who had bobbed like helpless corks in the swell?

It rained all night. The air in the bedroom was cool and damp, and in my sleep I thought I could smell salt in the wind. I dreamed of black-clad submariners, their white skin layered with deodorant, their unkempt beards like charcoal smeared on their faces. They guided a long, gleaming torpedo into a waiting tube, touching its hard sides like a farewell caress. The torpedo burst from beneath the bow, its propeller spinning, its steel skin rippling with moonlight just below the surface. The men in black dungarees stood motionless in the battery-lighted interior of their ship, their eyes lifted expectantly, their breasts aching with an unspoken and collective wish that made them wet their lips and nudge their groins against the cool, cylindrical side of another torpedo.

The explosion against the hull of the freighter on the horizon, the screech of girders and rent metal, the avalanche of salt water into the hold, the secondary explosion of boilers that blew the bridge into sticks and heated the hatches into searing iron rectangles that would scorch a human hand into a stump, even the final geysering descent beneath the waves and the grinding of the keel against the sand – it all filtered through the darkness outside the sub with the softness of an old Vienna waltz swelling and dissipating in the mist.

It must have been two or three in the morning when I felt the coldness in the room. In my sleep I reached for the bedspread at the foot of the bed and pulled it up over Bootsie and me. I thought wind was blowing through the house, when there should have been none, then I realized that my pillow was damp from the mist that was blowing through the window fan, which was turned off.

I sat up in bed. The doors to both the closet and the bathroom were open, and the night-light in the bathroom had either burned out or been turned off. From the back porch I could hear the screen door puffing open and falling back upon the jamb in the wind. I reached under the bed and picked up the .45.

I didn't have far to go before I knew he had been there. As I walked past the closet I felt water under my bare feet. I turned on every light in the house. The screen was slit on the back porch door, the deadbolt prized out of the jamb on the door to the kitchen.

'What is it, Dave?' Bootsie said, blinking her eyes against the light.

I stared at the floor area in front of the closet. There were two stenciled shoe prints on the boards, surrounded by a ring of water that had dripped off his coat. Then she saw what I was looking at.

'Oh God, I can't take this, Dave,' she said.

'Take it easy. He's gone now.'

'He was here. Watching us sleep.' She sat up and pressed her hands to her stomach. 'I think I'm going to be sick.'

'Use the other bathroom.'

'What?'

'Don't go in our bathroom.'

'Why? Wh—'

'He might have left evidence in there, Boots, that's all.'

When she was gone, I clicked off the light in our bathroom, closed the door, and turned the lock, but not before having to look again at the words that he had lipsticked brightly across the wall: *DAVE, YOU MUST BECOME ONE WITH THE SWORD. I'LL LOVE YOU IN A WAY THAT NO WOMAN CAN, W.B.*

chapter sixteen

The next morning I tried to concentrate on the daily routine at the office. But it was no use. I stared out the window at the rain.

What drove the engines of a man like Will Buchalter?

The conclusion I came to wasn't a pleasant one. He was a sadist, pure and simple, and, like all sadists, he developed erotic fixations about the people and animals he planned to hurt in a methodical way. The pain he imposed upon his victim was intended to humiliate and degrade and was always administered personally, by his hand, only a breath away from the victim's face. As with all of his kind he had found an ideological purpose that justified his perversity, but in reality the cries with which he could fill a room made his back teeth grind softly together while his loins tingled like a swarm of bees.

The phone on my desk rang. It was Lucinda Bergeron.

'Your friend over here is becoming a pain in the ass to a lot of people,' she said.

'Who?'

'Cletus Purcel.'

'What's wrong with Clete?'

'What's right with him?'

'Give it a break, Lucinda.'

'He tried to turn somebody into a human bell clapper. Do you know a character by the name of Dogshit Dolowitz?'

'No Duh Dolowitz, the merry prankster?'

'Yeah, I guess he's called that, too. Your friend crammed a garbage can over his head, then pounded the can all over an alley with a baseball bat.'

'What for?'

'Ask him ... Wait a minute.' She set the phone down and closed a door. 'Listen, Detective, Nate Baxter would like to put your buddy's ham hocks in a skillet. I'd have a serious talk with him.'

'Is Zoot back home yet?'

'I don't *believe* you. I think you must come from outer space.'

'You're telling me he should be living over at Tommy Lonighan's?'

'I thought I was doing a favor for your friend.'

'I appreciate it.'

I heard her make a sound like she was digesting a thumbtack.

'Take it easy,' I said.

'God, I hate talking to you!' Then she caught her breath and started again. 'Listen, your buddy hasn't been arraigned yet, but my guess is his bond will be around two thousand dollars. You want me to give him a message?'

'No Duh pressed charges?'

'No, Nate Baxter did. Disturbing the peace and resisting arrest. Good-bye, Detective Robicheaux. In all honesty I don't think I'm up to many more conversations with you.'

She hung up the phone.

I called her back.

'Look, I can't take off work just to bail a friend out of the slam. Why'd Clete knock Dolowitz around?'

'It has something to do with the Calucci brothers.'

'What about them?'

'I don't know,' she said, the exasperation rising in her voice. 'Nate Baxter's handling it. What's that tell you,

Robicheaux, besides the fact he's got a major hard-on for Purcel?'

'I'm not sure.'

'He's on a pad.'

'For the Calucci brothers?'

'Who else?'

'You can prove that?'

'Who to? Who cares? The city's broke. *That*'s what's on people's minds.'

'I'll try to get over there. It's a bad day, though.'

'What's wrong?'

I told her about Buchalter's visit of the night before.

'Why didn't you tell me that?' she said.

'You've got your own problems.'

She paused a moment. 'You saw Zoot over at Tommy Lonighan's?' she said.

'Yeah, for just a few minutes.'

'Did he say—' She let out her breath in the receiver and didn't finish.

'I think you mean a lot to him, Lucinda. I'd bring him back home. I'm sorry if I sound intrusive sometimes.'

I called Bootsie at the house, then signed out of the office. It was still raining when I got to NOPD headquarters in the Garden District. Lucinda Bergeron was out of the office, but Benjamin Motley told me that the Reverend Oswald Flat had gotten Clete released in his custody without having to post bail and they were waiting for me at a café up on St. Charles by the Pontchartrain Hotel.

It was a working man's place that served rib-eye steaks, deep-fried catfish, and biscuits with sausage gravy that you could stoke boilers with. It was also the café where the Calucci brothers ate lunch every day.

I parked my truck around the corner, then ran back in the rain under the dripping overhang of the oak trees on St. Charles. The inside of the restaurant was warm and crowded and loud. Clete and the preacher were at a checker-cloth-covered table in front. In the center of the table was a solitary, green-stemmed purple rose set in a dime-store glass vase. Between the preacher's feet I could see a worn-edged, black guitar case with the words *The Great Speckled Bird* hand-lettered on the side.

I let my eyes rove over the people at the tables; then I saw Max and Bobo Calucci and a half dozen of their entourage eating at a long table against the back wall, three feet from an old jukebox, whose maroon and orange plastic casing rippled with light.

I sat down with Clete and the preacher.

'You ought to get you an umbrella, son. You look like a hedgehog somebody drowned in a rain barrel,' Oswald Flat said.

'Thank you, Reverend,' I said.

'Sorry to get you down here for no reason, Streak,' Clete said. 'I tried to catch you after Brother Oswald here got me out of the bag, but you were already down the road.' He grinned while he chewed on a bread stick.

'What are you doing beating up on a guy like No Duh Dolowitz?' I said.

'Yeah, I always dug ole No Duh myself,' Clete said, then turned to the preacher. 'You see, this guy No Duh – sometimes they call him Dogshit because that's what he put in some sandwiches once at a Teamsters convention in Miami – he used to be a second-story creep till a night watchman bonged a big dent in his forehead with a ball peen hammer. But instead of turning into a mush brain, he developed a genius for playing pranks. The mob knows talent when it sees it.

'If they want to take over an apartment building or a bunch of duplexes at fire-sale prices, they send in Dolowitz. He pours cement mix down all the drains, puts Limburger cheese in the air vents, tapes bait fish under the furniture, maybe has a landscape service pour a dump truck load of cow manure in the swimming pool. This contractor built some real class condos in Jefferson Parish, then he finds out too late that he doesn't have clear title to the land and that part of it is owned by the

Giacano family. So while he's trying to hold off the Giacanos in court, they send in No Duh, who makes keys to all the doors, stops up the toilets, stocks the cabinets with Thunderbird and Boone's Farm, then buses in about twenty winos from skid row and tells them to have a good time. I heard the cleaning crews had to scrape the carpets up with shovels.'

He laughed, pushed his porkpie hat up on his head, and put a cigarette in the corner of his mouth. His hand looked huge on his Zippo lighter. I noticed that his eyes never looked in the Caluccis' direction.

'Why the beef with a guy like that, Clete?' I said.

The humor drained out of his face, and his eyes drifted toward the rear of the restaurant.

'I gave Martina the two grand to pay off the Caluccis. Guess what? They told her that's just the back payment on the vig. She still owes another two large. Last night we came back from the show and there's Dolowitz hiding in the shrubs by the side of Martina's garage. So I ask him what the hell he thinks he's doing there.

'He tells me he lives two blocks away, up by Audubon Park, and he's been walking his dog. I say, "That's funny, I don't see any dog." He says, "No duh, Purcel. Because my dog run away." "Oh, I see. That's why you're in the shrubs," I say. "No duh, my fast-thinking man," he says.

'I say, "I got another problem here, No Duh. People like you don't live by Audubon Park. Not unless the neighborhood has recently been rezoned for meltdowns and toxic waste. If I remember right, you live in a shithole by the Industrial Canal. So why are you hiding here by Martina's garage, and if you give me one more wiseass answer, I'm going to stuff your dented head up the tailpipe of my car."

'So he puts his fingers in the corners of his mouth and stretches out his lips like a jack-o'-lantern. Can you believe this guy? I say, "No Duh, your mother must have defecated you into the world," and I shake him down against the wall, and what do we find, our man's got a bottle of muriatic acid in his pants pocket.'

'I don't get it. Dolowitz isn't an enforcer,' I said.

'I didn't get it, either. Also, dispensation time for dimwits was starting to run out. I go, "What do you think you're doing with this, fuckhead?" Suddenly he's like a guy who just sobered up. He goes, "It's just a prank, Purcel. I don't hurt people." That's when I screwed the trash can down on his head and got a ball bat out of my car and bounced him around the alley. Finally he's yelling inside the can, "I was going to put it in her gas tank! I wasn't going to have nothing to do with the rest of it!"

'You want to know what "the rest of it" was?' Clete mashed out his cigarette in the ashtray. His eyes cut sideways toward the rear of the café. 'Martina goes on shift cocktail-waitressing at a club in Gretna at ten P.M. Dolowitz was going to mess up her car so it'd kill somewhere between her house and work. A guy was going to be following her. You want to hear how No Duh put it? "Max and Bobo Calucci got some kind of geek working for them, not no ordinary button guy, either, Purcel, a guy who can fuck up people real bad, in ways nobody ever thought about."'

Clete propped his elbow on the table and inserted a thumbnail in his teeth.

'You think I was too hard on ole Dogshit?' he said.

'Sir, could you watch your language?' the manager, who had come out from behind the cash register, said quietly.

'Yeah, yeah, yeah,' Clete said, flipping his hand at the air.

'You think it could be Buchalter?' I said.

'Maybe. But I don't know how he'd tie in with the greaseballs back there in the booth.'

'Maybe he's connected with Tommy Lonighan's interest in the Nazi sub, and now Lonighan's mixed up with the Caluccis. Anyway, he was in my house last night,' I said.

'He was *what*?'

'Standing in our closet, watching us while we slept.'

'Jesus Christ, Dave.'

'He cut the back screen, prized out the deadbolt, walked around in the house, and I never heard him.'

Clete sat back in his chair.

'This guy's a new combo, mon,' he said. 'I thought if he ever came back, it'd be to cool you out.'

'You think the real problem is y'all don't have no idea of what you're dealing with?' Oswald Flat said.

We both looked at him. His clip-on bow tie was askew on his denim shirt. His pale eyes looked as big as an owl's behind his glasses.

'You cain't find that fellow 'cause maybe he ain't human,' he said. 'Maybe y'all been dealing with a demon. You ever consider that?'

'I can't say that I have,' I said.

'It's the end of the millennium,' he said.

'Yes?' I said.

'Son, I don't want to be unkind to you. But when the brains was passed out, did you grab a handful of pig flop by mistake?'

He paused to let his statement sink in.

'The prophesy is in Nostradamus. The Beast and his followers are going to be loosed on the earth,' he said. 'Call me a fool. But you're a policeman, and the best you got ain't worth horse pucky on a rock, is hit?'

I looked back at him silently. His short, dun-colored hair was combed neatly and parted almost in the center of his scalp. His washed-out eyes never blinked and seemed wide with a knowledge that was lost on others.

The waiter set plates of deep-fried pork chops, greens, and dirty rice in front of him and Clete.

'You're not going to eat?' Oswald Flat said.

'No, thanks.'

'I offended you?'

'Not at all,' I said.

Clete lowered his fork onto his plate and looked toward the rear of the restaurant again.

'It looks like the Vitalis twins are about to finish their lunch. I don't know if they should slide out of here that easily,' he said.

'Let it go,' I said.

'Trust me.'

'I mean it, Clete. Baxter's got you in his bombsights. Don't play his game.'

'You worry too much, big mon. It's time to check out the jukebox and the ole hippy-dippy from Mississippi, yes indeed, Mr. Jimmy Reed. I'll be right back.'

Clete strolled to the rear of the restaurant, past the Caluccis' table, his eyes never registering their presence. He dropped a quarter into the jukebox and punched off 'Big Boss Man,' then began snapping his fingers and slapping his right palm on top of his left fist while he scanned the other titles. The back of his neck looked as thick as a fire hydrant.

The preacher's gaze moved back and forth from Clete to the Caluccis. His false teeth were stiff and white in his mouth.

'He'll be all right, Reverend. Clete just likes to let people know he's in the neighborhood,' I said.

But Oswald Flat didn't answer. There were pools of color in his cheeks, nests of wrinkles at the edges of his eyes.

'You play guitar?' I said.

'I played with Reno and Smiley, I played with Jimmy Martin and the Sunny Mountain Boys. Hit don't get no better than that,' he said. But his eyes were riveted on the Caluccis when he spoke.

Clete sat back down, his green eyes dancing with light, while Jimmy Reed sang in the background.

The Caluccis were watching him now. Clete made a frame of his hands, with his thumbs joined together, tilting the frame back and forth, sighting through it at

Max and Bobo, the way a movie director might if he were envisioning a dramatic scene. Then he began pointing his finger at them, grinning, tapping it in time to 'Big Boss Man's' driving rhythm.

'Knock it off, Clete,' I said.

'They need to know they've been ratted out, mon. You never let a shit bag forget he's a shit bag. You got to keep them buttoned down under the sewer grates, big mon.'

'You're both good fellows, but one is as wrongheaded as the other,' Oswald Flat said.

'Excuse me?' Clete said.

'You don't outwit evil. You don't outthink hit, you don't joke with hit, no more than you tease or control fire by sticking your hand in hit.'

'You all right, Reverend?' I said.

'No, I ain't.'

His sun-browned, liver-spotted hands were flat on the table-cloth. His nails looked like hooked tortoiseshell.

'What's the trouble, partner?' I said.

'They took my boy.'

'Who?' Clete said.

'He come back from Vietnam with needle scars on his arm. Wasn't no he'p for hit, either. Federal hospitals, jails, drug programs, he could always get all the dope he needed from them kind yonder. Till he killed hisself with hit.'

The music on the jukebox ended. Clete looked at me and raised his eyebrows. Oswald Flat slipped the purple rose out of the dimestore vase in the center of the table and sliced off the green stem with his thumbnail.

'Hey, hold on, Brother. Where you going?' Clete said.

Oswald Flat walked toward the rear of the restaurant. He moved like a crab, his shoulders slanted to one side, the rose hanging from his right hand. The Caluccis were finishing their coffee and dessert and at first did not pay attention to the man with the clip-on bow tie standing above them.

Then Max stopped talking to a woman with lacquered

blond hair next to him and flicked his eyes up at Oswald Flat.

'What?' he said. When Flat made no reply, Max said it again. 'What?'

Then Bobo was looking at the preacher, too.

'Hey, he's talking to you. You got a problem?' he said.

The people at nearby tables had stopped talking now.

'Hey, what's with you? You can't find the men's room or something?' Max said.

The blond woman next to him started to laugh, then looked at Oswald Flat's face and dropped her eyes.

'Y'all think you're different from them colored dope dealers? Y'all think hit cain't happen to you?' the preacher said.

'What? What can happen?' Max said.

'Your skin's white but your heart's black, just like them that's had hit cut out of their chests.'

The restaurant was almost completely silent now. In the kitchen someone stopped scraping a dish into a garbage can.

'Listen, you four-eyed fuck, if Purcel and that cop sent you over here—' Max began.

Oswald flipped the purple rose into Max Calucci's face.

'You're a lost, stupid man,' he said. 'If I was you, I'd drink all the ice water I could while I had opportunity. Hell's hot and it's got damn little shade.'

The Reverend Oswald Flat picked up his guitar case, fitted his cork sun helmet on his head, and walked out the front door into a vortex of rain.

As I crossed the wide, brown sweep of the Mississippi at Baton Rouge and headed across the Atchafalaya Basin toward home, I thought about Oswald Flat's speculation on the elusiveness of Will Buchalter.

It seemed the stuff of an Appalachian tent revival where the reborn dipped their arms into boxes filled with poisonous snakes.

But the preacher's conclusion that we were dealing with a demonic incarnation was neither eccentric nor very original and, as with some other cases I've worked, was as good an explanation about aberrant human behavior as any.

Ten years ago, when Clete and I worked Homicide at NOPD, we investigated a case that even today no one can satisfactorily explain.

A thirty-five-year-old small contractor was hired to build a sun-porch on a home in an old residential neighborhood off Canal. He was well thought of, nice-looking, married only once, attended church weekly with his wife and son, and had never been in trouble of any kind. At least that we knew of.

The family who had contracted him to build the addition on their house were Rumanian gypsies who had grown wealthy as slum-lords in the black districts off Magazine. Their late-Victorian home had polished oak floors, ceiling-high windows, small balconies dripping with orange passion vine, a pool, and a game room with a sunken hot tub.

They thought well enough of the contractor to leave him alone with their fifteen- and twelve-year-old daughters.

The father should have been gone for the day, checking out his rental property miles away. Instead, he came home unexpectedly for lunch. Someone waited for him behind the living room door, then fired a .22 Magnum round into his ear. The bullet exited his opposite cheek and embedded in the far wall.

No one heard the shot. Around one in the afternoon neighbors saw the contractor drive away in the father's Buick. Three hours later the mother returned from shopping and found both her daughters drowned in the hot tub. They were bound ankle and wrist with electrician's tape; both had been raped.

The contractor pawned his tools, his watch, and his wedding ring at three different stops between New

Orleans and Pensacola, Florida, where he was arrested after a call he made to his wife was traced to a motel there. Clete Purcel and I transported him back to New Orleans from the Pensacola city jail.

He was likable; there was nothing of the con artist about him; he was well-mannered and didn't use profanity; he never complained about riding handcuffed to a D-ring in the backseat.

At his trial he maintained that he'd had a blackout, that he had no memory of the events that took place in the house off Canal, but a sense of terror, with no apparent source, had caused him to flee across I–10 to the Florida panhandle.

Prosecution lawyers, state psychologists, and news reporters came up with every script possible to explain the contractor's behavior: He was a clandestine user of LSD; he had been a marine door gunner in Vietnam; he was badly in debt and teetering on a nervous breakdown. Or, more disturbingly, he had once been seen at a shopping mall with a high school girl from his neighborhood whose strangled and decomposed body was found nude in a swamp north of Lake Pontchartrain. On her ankle was a tattoo of a pentagram.

All the evidence against him was circumstantial. None of his fingerprints were in the game room where the girls died, nor on the electrician's tape that was used to bind them. Also the tape was not the same brand that he always bought from a wholesale outlet. There were no skin particles under the dead girls' fingernails.

He probably would have walked if he could have afforded a better lawyer. But the jury convicted him of second-degree murder, perhaps less out of certainty of his guilt than fear that he was guilty and would kill or rape again if set free.

His friends and family were numb with disbelief. The pastor from his church raised money to begin an appeal of the verdict. His parishioners put together twenty thousand dollars for the conviction of the real killer. Two attorneys from the ACLU took over the contractor's case.

Clete and I went back over the crime scene a dozen times. We must have interviewed a hundred people. We decided that if we couldn't prove this man conclusively guilty, then we would prove him innocent.

We did neither. All we ever determined was that there was a two-year gap in the contractor's younger life during which he had left behind no paperwork or record of any kind, as though he had eased sideways into another dimension. We also concluded, with a reasonable degree of certainty, at least to ourselves, that no else entered or left that house, besides the father, from the time the contractor showed up to work and the time he fled the crime scene in the Buick.

It became the kind of case that eventually you close the file on and hope the right man is in jail. Clete and I were both glad when we heard that the lower court's decision had been overturned and that a new trial date was to be set soon. Maybe someone else could prove or disprove what we could not.

Three days later, a psychotic inmate at Angola, a big stripe, attacked the contractor with a cane knife and severed his spinal cord with one blow across the back of the neck. The body was lying in state at a funeral home in Metairie when the mother and aunts of the murdered girls burst into the room, screaming hysterically like Shakespearean hags, and flung bags of urine on the corpse.

For a long time I had a recurrent dream about the contractor. He awoke in the blackness of his coffin, then realized that tons of earth had been bulldozed and packed down on top of him. He couldn't move his shoulders or twist his body against the hard, sculpted silk contours of the coffin; his screams went no farther than the coffin's lid, which hovered an inch from his mouth.

As time passed and his nails and eyebrows and hair grew long and filled the air cavity around him, and he realized that his death was to be prolonged in ways that no mortal thought imaginable, he began to plan ways that he could burn himself even more deeply, more painfully, into our memory.

He would reveal to the rest of us a secret about his soul that would forever make us think differently about our common origins. With nails that were yellow and sharp as talons he cut his confession into the silk liner above him, his mouth red with gloat as he wounded us once more with a dark knowledge about ourselves.

But those are simply images born of my dreams. Maybe the contractor was innocent. Or maybe in the murder house he began to enact a fantasy, tried to lure one of the girls into a seduction, and found himself involved in a kaleidoscopic nightmare whose consequences filled him with terror and from which he couldn't extricate himself.

I don't know. Ten months on the firing line in Vietnam, twenty years in law enforcement, and a long excursion into a nocturnal world of neon-streaked rain and whiskey-soaked roses have made me no wiser about human nature than I had been at age eighteen.

But Brother Oswald had made another remark that forced me to reexamine a basic syllogism that I had been operating on: 'You think the real problem is y'all don't have no idea of what you're dealing with?'

I had not been able to find any record anywhere on a man named Will Buchalter.

Why? Perhaps because that was not his name.

I had assumed from the beginning that Buchalter was not an alias, that the man who had violated my wife and home was a relative of Jon Matthew Buchalter, a founder of the Silver Shirts. It was a natural assumption to make. Would someone choose the name of Hitler or Mussolini as an alias if he wished to avoid drawing attention to himself?

Maybe the man who called himself Will Buchalter had thrown me a real slider and I had swung on it.

It was time to have a talk with Hippo Bimstine again.

But I didn't get the chance. At seven the next morning I went to an Al-Anon meeting to get some help for Bootsie that I wasn't capable of providing myself, then two minutes after I walked into my office Lucinda Bergeron called from New Orleans.

'Hey, Lucinda. What's up?' I said.

'The East Baton Rouge Parish Sheriff's Department just nailed a mule with a suitcase full of Mexican tar in his trunk. This'll be his fourth time down. He says he'll do anybody he can for some slack.'

'So?'

'The dope drop's in New Orleans. That's why Baton Rouge called us. This guy says the tar's going into the projects.'

'I'm still not with you.'

'He says the Calucci brothers are dealing the tar. It looks like they're making a move on the projects. Anyway, the guy says he can do them.'

'I doubt it.'

'Why?'

'Max and Bobo always have three or four intermediaries between themselves and whatever they're in.'

'I had the impression you thought they were connected with Lonighan and that Lonighan was mixed up with this psychopath who keeps coming around your house.'

'That's right.'

'So do you have a better lead?'

'Not really.'

'Good. I'll meet you at the jail in two hours. Also, I'm a little pissed with you this morning, Mr. Robicheaux.'

'Oh?'

'You can't seem to stay out of other people's business.'

'What is it now?'

'I'll tell you when I see you,' she said, and hung up.

Lucinda really knew how to set the hook. All the way across the Atchafalaya Basin, on a beautiful, wind-kissed fall day when I should have been looking at the bays and canals and flooded cypress and willow trees along I-10, I kept wondering what new bagful of spiders she would like to fit over my head.

She met me in the parking lot at the lockup. She wore a pair of white slacks and a purple-flowered blouse, and her hair was brushed out full on her shoulders. She had one hand on her hip and a pout on her face. She looked at the tiny gold watch on her wrist.

'Did you stop for a late breakfast?' she said.

'No, I didn't. I came straight from the office. Get off it, Lucinda.'

'Get *off* it?'

'Yeah, I'm not up to being somebody's pincushion today.'

'My son is back home. He told me you made some inquiries about the company I keep.'

'No, I didn't.'

'He said you seemed to take an interest in the fact that I had a white man at my house.'

'Kids get things turned around. He volunteered that information on his own.'

'Do you think it should be of some concern to you, sir?'

'No. But one troubling thought did occur to me.'

'Yes?'

'Was it Nate Baxter?'

She looked like a wave of nausea had just swept through her system.

'Do you stay up all night thinking of things like this to say to people?' she said.

'I've known him for twenty years. He'll try to coerce a woman in any way he can. If he hasn't done it to you yet, he will later. He's a sonofabitch and you know it.'

'That doesn't mean I'd allow him in my house.'

'Okay, Lucinda, I apologize. But I know what he did to some women in the First District.'

'I'll buy you a cup of coffee later and tell you about Nate Baxter. In the meantime, our man is waiting on us.'

His name was Waylon Rhodes, from Mount Olive, Alabama; he had skin the color of putty, hands dotted with jailhouse art, a narrow, misshapen head, and a wide slit of a mouth, whose lips on one side looked like they had been pressed flat by a hot iron. His premature gray hair was grizzled and brushed back into faint ducktails; his eyes jittered like a speed addict's. Inside his left arm was a long, blue tattoo of a bayonet or perhaps a sword.

Lucinda and I sat across the wood table from him in the interrogation room. He smoked one cigarette after another, crumpling up an empty pack, ripping the cellophane off a fresh one. The backs of his fingers were yellow with nicotine; his breath was like an ashtray.

'There's no reason to be nervous, partner,' I said.

'Y'all want me to do the Caluccis. That ain't reason to be nervous?' he said.

'You don't have to do anybody. Not for us, anyway. Your beef's with the locals,' I said.

'Don't tell me that, man. Y'all got a two-by-four up my ass.'

'Watch your language, please,' I said.

He smoked with his elbow propped on the table, taking one puff after another, like he was hitting on a reefer, sometimes pressing a yellow thumb anxiously against his bottom lip and teeth.

'They're dangerous people, man,' he said. 'They tied a guy down on a table once and cut thirty pounds of meat out of him while he was still alive.'

'Here's the only deal you're getting today,' Lucinda said. 'We can pull the plug on this interview any time you want. You say the word and we're gone. Then you can have visitors from two to four every Sunday afternoon.'

'What she means, Waylon, is we made a special effort to see you. If this is all a waste of time, tell us now.'

He mashed out his cigarette and began clenching one

hand on top of the other. *Make him talk about something else*, I thought.

'Where'd you get the tattoo of the sword?' I said.

'It's a bayonet. I was in the Airborne. Hunnerd and first.'

'Your jacket says you were in the Navy and did time at Portsmouth brig.'

'Then it's wrong.'

'What can you give us on Max and Bobo?' Lucinda said.

'They're dealing.'

'They're going to be at the drop?' I said.

'Are you kidding?' he said.

'Then how are you going to do them, Waylon?' I said.

He began to chew on the flattened corner of his mouth. His eyes jittered as if they were being fed by an electrical current.

'A whack's going down. A big one,' he said.

'Yeah?' I said.

'Yeah.'

'Who's getting clipped, Waylon?'

'A couple of guineas were talking in Mobile when I picked up the dope.'

'You're not being helpful, Waylon,' Lucinda said.

'There's nig ... There's black people mixed up in it. New Orleans is a weird fucking town. What do I know?'

'You'd better know something, partner, or your next jolt's going to be in the decades,' I said.

'They're going to clip some guy that ain't supposed to be clipped. That's what these dagos were saying. That's all I know, man.'

'When you think of something else, give us a call,' I said.

He ran his hand through his grizzled hair. His palm was shiny with sweat.

'I'm sick. I got to go to a hospital,' he said.

'What's the sword on your arm mean?' I said.

He put his face in his hands. 'I ain't saying no more,' he said. 'I'm sick. I got to have some medication.'

'How many times a day do you fix, Waylon?' I said.

'I got it down to three. Look, get me into a hospital and maybe I can he'p y'all a whole lot better.'

'It doesn't work that way, partner,' I said, and slipped my business card under the flat of his arm. 'Give us a call when your memory clears up.'

A half hour later Lucinda and I took coffee and pastry from a bakery downtown and sat on a stone bench in a small green park by the capitol building. It was a blue-gold day, with a breeze off the Mississippi, and the grass in the park looked pale green in the sunlight.

'Why'd you keep asking him about a sword?' Lucinda said.

'I think it's the name or the logo of a group of neo-Nazis or Aryan supremacists of some kind.'

'The tattoo looked like a bayonet to me.'

'Maybe. But he's a speed addict, too, just like the guy who electrocuted himself in y'all's custody. Buchalter called me once during what sounded like the downside of a drug bender. Maybe like Hippo Bimstine says, we're talking about speed-fried Nazi zomboids.'

'You think Waylon Rhodes will give us anybody?'

'He'll try to, when he starts to come apart. But by that time you won't be able to trust anything he tells you.'

'I believe him about the hit. When they lie, they're not vague.'

I took a bite out of my pastry and drank from my paper cup.

'Why the silence?' she asked.

'No reason. What were you going to tell me about Nate Baxter?'

'I don't think he has designs on me, that's all.'

I nodded.

'A white supervisor trying to get into a black female officer's pants doesn't make his kind of racial remarks,' she said.

'You don't have to tell me anything about Nate Baxter, Lucinda.'

'He said Ben Motley got where he is by spitting watermelon seeds and giving whitey a lot of "yas-suhs." He said I'd never have to do that, because I'm smart and I have a nice ass. How do you like that for charm?'

'Nate's a special kind of guy.'

'I don't think so. Not for a black woman, anyway.'

'Don't underestimate him, Lucinda. He raped and sodomized a hooker in the Quarter. Then he ran her out of town before anybody from Internal Affairs could talk to her.'

She stopped eating and looked across the grass at some children running through the camellia bushes. Then she set the pastry down on a napkin in her lap and brushed the powdered sugar off her fingers.

'I was raised by my aunt,' she said. 'She was a prostitute. A white man tried to rape her behind a bar on Calliope. She shot him to death. What do you think about that?'

'Did she go up the road for it?'

'Yes.'

'So even in death he raped her. Drop the dime on Baxter if he gets near you or makes another off-color remark.'

She stood up and walked cooly to a trash can, dropped her paper cup and unfinished pastry in it, and sat back down on the stone bench. Her flowered blouse puffed with air in the breeze.

'Don't try to stonewall me about this contract stuff,' she said. 'Who is it the greaseballs don't clip?'

'Politicians.'

'Who else?'

'Ordinary people who are on the square. Particularly influential ones.'

'Come on, Robicheaux.'

'Would you not call me by my last name, please? It reminds me of the army.'

'Who else?'

'They don't do made guys without the commission's consent.'

'That's it?'

'Cops,' I said.

She looked me evenly in the eyes, biting down softly on the corner of her lip.

That night I dreamed of a desolate coastline that looked like layered white clay. On it was a solitary tree whose curled, dead leaves were frozen against an electrical blue sky. The ocean should have been teeming with fish, but it, like the land, had been stricken, its chemical green depths empty of all life except the crew of a German submarine, who burst to the surface with emergency air tanks on their backs, their bone-hard, white faces bright with oil. They gathered under the tree on the beach, looking over their new estate, and I realised then that they had the jowls and mucus-clotted snouts of animals.

They waited for their leader, who would come, as they had, from the sea, his visage crackling with salt and light, and, like Proteus, forever changing his form to make himself one of us.

A psychologist would smile at the dream and call it a world destruction fantasy, the apocalyptic fear that a drunk such as myself carries around in his unconscious or that you see on the faces of religious fundamentalists at televised revivals.

But when I woke from the dream I sat in the dark and thought about the preacher's words, about things coming apart at the center, about blood-dimmed tides and mackerel-crowded seas that could wrinkle from continent to continent with the reverberating brass gong of the millennium, and I did not sleep again until the trees outside were black and stiff with the coming of the gray dawn.

chapter seventeen

Two days later, at five-thirty on Saturday morning, Bootsie heard a car turn into our driveway. She stood at the window in her nightgown and looked through the curtain.

'It's somebody in a pink Cadillac,' she said.

'Maybe he's just turning around,' I said from the bed. There was mist in the trees outside and a cool smell blowing through the window.

'No, they're just sitting there. Two people.'

'Batist probably hasn't opened the shop yet. I'll go down,' I said.

'Dave—'

'It's all right. Bad guys don't park in your drive at sunrise.'

I dressed in a pair of khakis, old loafers, and a denim shirt, and walked out on the gallery. The light was on in the bait shop. The Cadillac was parked in the shadows under the trees, but I could see two figures in the front seat. The air smelled like flowers and damp earth. I walked across the yard toward the car. To my right I could hear Tripod scratching against the screen on his hutch.

Tommy Bobalouba got out on the driver's side, dressed in striped, dark brown slacks, tasseled loafers, and a form-fitting canary-yellow polo shirt. Across the bridge of his nose was a thick, crusted scab where I had pistol-whipped him. He was smiling. He put his finger to his lips and motioned me away from the automobile.

'Charlotte's sleeping,' he whispered. 'She ain't used to being up this early.'

'What are you doing at my house, Tommy?'

'It's the weekend. Sometimes I like a drive in the country. Maybe I can rent a boat, you can take us out.'

He combed his white hair while he gazed approvingly at the surroundings.

'You didn't come here to square a beef, did you, partner?' I said.

'You got a cup of coffee?'

'We can walk down to the bait shop.'

'The bait shop? What is this, the white trash treatment I get?'

'My wife's not dressed yet.'

'I want a favor from you.'

'Tommy, I'm having a hard time with your presence here.'

'What? I'm a germ?'

'I'm the guy who hit you across the face with a forty-five. Now you're at my house.'

'I don't hold a grudge.'

'Good. Then you won't be offended when I recommend that you give me a call during business hours at the office.'

'You made some remarks at my house. About stuff that's maybe on my conscience. So maybe I'm gonna try to set it right. You don't want to help me, then run it up your hole.'

'I'd appreciate it if you'd watch what you say around my house.'

The door on the passenger's side opened, and the ash blond lady named Charlotte got out and stretched sleepily.

'Oh, Mr. Robicheaux, our favorite daytime nightmare,' she said.

'We're gonna have some coffee. Down at his shop,' Tommy said.

'Breakfast among the worms. How could a girl ask for more?' she said.

'His wife ain't up yet,' Tommy said. Then with his back to the woman, he moved his lips silently so I could read the words *Give me some fucking help, man*.

I took a quiet breath and put my hands in my back pockets.

'I apologize for not inviting y'all in,' I said. 'But Batist has some doughnuts and some ham-and-egg sandwiches that I can heat up.'

'Boy, that sounds good. I could go for that,' Tommy said. He hit me hard on the arm with the flat of his hand.

The three of us walked down the slope to the dock. I couldn't begin to explain Tommy Blue Eyes' mercurial behavior. He walked on the balls of his feet, talking incessantly, his shoulders rolling, his eyes flicking from the bayou to the outboards leaving the dock to a flight of black geese dissecting the early sun.

He and the woman named Charlotte sat at a spool table under the canvas awning while I went inside and brought out coffee and doughnuts on a tray.

'Call Hippo for me,' Tommy said.

'What for?'

'Maybe I don't want to be enemies anymore. Maybe we ought to work together.'

'Call him yourself,' I said.

'I get three words out and he hangs up.'

'Write him a letter.'

'What I look like, St. Valentine or something?' He glanced at his wristwatch, then shook it close to his ear. 'You got the time?'

'It's ten to six,' I said.

'Look, why should Hippo and me be always cutting a piece out of each other? We're both in the casino business. Hippo's a good businessman, he'd be a good partner, he doesn't steal from people. I want you to tell him I said that.'

'I think you got some damn nerve, Tommy.'

He took his coffee cup away from his mouth and pointed four stiffened fingers into his chest. 'You come out to my house, you give me a lecture on conscience and responsibility, you hit me in the face with a gun, now I get another lecture?'

'Is there anything else you want to tell me? I have some work to do.'

He pushed a knuckle against his teeth, then clamped his hand across my forearm when I attempted to rise. He took it away and made a placating gesture.

'It's not easy for me to talk to Hippo,' he said. I saw his blue eyes fill with a pained, pinched light. 'He just doesn't listen, he sees it one way, it's always been like that, he'd just walk off when I tried to say I was sorry about his little brother. I tried a whole bunch of times.'

'When?'

'When we were growing up.'

'It's between you and him, Tommy. But why don't you say it to him once more, as honestly as you can, then let it go?'

'*He*'s not. He sees me on the street, he looks at me like I was butt crust.'

'So long, Tommy. About the other day, I didn't want to hit you. I'm sorry it happened.' I nodded to the woman as I got up to go.

He wiped part of a doughnut off his mouth with his wrist.

'We're gonna rent a boat and some gear, do some fishing,' he said. 'If you're around later, we'll buy you lunch.'

'I'm tied up. Thanks, anyway,' I said, and walked up the dock toward my house just as Alafair was coming down the slope, with Tripod on his chain, to get me for breakfast.

At noontime Batist and I were outside in the cool lee of

the bait shop, serving our customers barbecue chickens from our split-barrel pit, when I saw Tommy and the woman named Charlotte coming up the bayou in one of our boat rentals. The engine was out of the water, and Tommy was paddling against the current, his face heated and knotted with frustration as the boat veered from side to side. It had rained hard at midmorning, then had stopped abruptly. The woman's hair and sundress were soaked. She looked disgusted.

A few minutes later they came into the bait shop. Without asking permission the woman went around behind the counter and unrolled a huge wad of paper towels to dry her hair.

'I owe you some money. I ran the motor over a log or something,' Tommy said.

'It's in the overhead,' I said.

He hit on the surface of his watch with his fingers.

'What time is it?' he said.

I pointed at the big electric clock on the wall.

'Twelve-fifteen. Boy, we were out there a long time,' he said. 'A snake ate my fish, too. It came right up to the boat and sucked it off my stringer. Are they supposed to do that?'

'Take an ice chest next time.'

'That's a good idea.' He opened two long-necked beers from the cooler and gave one to the woman, who sat in a chair by a table, rubbing the towels back over her long hair. 'I guess we better hit the road. I didn't know it was already afternoon.'

They went out the screen door, then I saw Tommy stop in the shade, tap one fist on top of another, turn in a circle, then stop again. He looked back through the screen at me and raised his fists momentarily in a boxer's position, as though he wanted to spar. He reminded me of a mental patient spinning about in a bare room.

I walked outside. It was breezy and cool in the shade, and the sun was bright, like yellow needles, on the water.

'What's on your mind, podna?' I said.

He craned a crick out of his neck and pumped his shoulders. The cords in his neck flexed like snakes. Then he shook my hand without speaking. His palm felt like the hide on a roughened baseball.

'You got to understand something, Dave. You mind if I call you Dave?'

'You always have, Tommy.'

'I go by the rules. I don't break rules, not the big ones, anyway. The greaseballs got theirs, cops got 'em, guys like me, micks who've made good from the Channel I'm talking about, we got ours, too. So when somebody breaks the rules, I got no comment. But I don't want to get hurt by it, either. You understand what I'm saying here?'

'No.'

'I never hurt anybody who didn't try to do a Roto-Rooter on me first.'

'A hit's going down that you don't like?'

'I said that? Must be a ventriloquist around here.'

'What's the game, Tommy?'

'No game. I got to do certain things to survive. You hold that against me? But that doesn't mean I wasn't on the square about Hippo. He was once my friend. I ain't trying to job you on that one.'

I watched him walk up the dock toward his car, his head turned sideways into the breeze, the red scab on his nose like an angry flag, his blue eyes hard as a carrion bird's, as though hidden adversaries waited for him on the wind.

I decided that it would take a cryptographer to understand the nuances of Tommy Lonighan.

I walked around the side of the house to the backyard and turned on the soak hose in my vegetable garden. The bamboo and periwinkles along the coulee ruffled in the breeze. Beyond my duck pond, the sugarcane in my neighbor's field flickered with a cool purple and gold light.

Bootsie had gone shopping in New Iberia, and Alafair was fixing sandwiches at the drain board when I walked into the kitchen. From the front of the house I heard the flat, tinny tones of a 1920s jazz orchestra, then the unmistakable bell-like sound of Bunk Johnson's coronet rising out of the mire of C-melody saxophones.

'What's going on, Alf?' I said.

She turned from the counter and looked at me quizzically. I could see the outlines of her training bra under her yellow T-shirt.

'Who put one of my old seventy-eights on the machine?' I said.

'I thought you did,' she said.

The record ended, then the mechanical arm swung back automatically and started again. I walked quickly into the living room. The front door was open, and the curtains were swelling with wind. I opened the screen door and went out on the gallery. The yard and drive were empty and blown with dead leaves. Out on the dirt road black kids on bicycles, with fishing gear propped across their handlebars, were pedaling past the dock. I went back inside, lifted the arm off the record, and turned off the machine. The paper jacket for the record lay on the couch. The record itself was free from any finger smudges; it had been placed on the spindle with professional care.

'Alf, it's all right if you wanted to play the record,' I said in the kitchen. 'But it's important you tell me whether or not you did it.'

'I already told you, Dave.'

'You're sure?'

'You think I'm lying?'

'No, I didn't mean that. How long has it been playing?'

'I don't know. I was outside.'

'Did Bootsie put it on before she left?'

'Bootsie doesn't play your old records, Dave. Nobody does.'

'Bootsie hasn't been herself, Alf.'

204

She turned back to the counter and began spreading mustard on her sandwich bread, her face empty, the way it always became when she knew something was wrong in the house. Her pink tennis shoes were untied, and her elastic-waisted jeans were stained with grass at the knees from weeding in the garden.

I saw her hand with the butter knife slow, then stop, as a thought worked its way into her face.

'Dave, I heard the front screen slam about fifteen minutes ago. Was that you?'

'I was at the dock, Alf. Maybe it was Bootsie.'

'Bootsie left an hour ago.'

'Maybe she came back for something.'

'She would have said something. Was it that bad man, Dave?'

I picked her up and sat her on top of the drain board, like she was still a small child, and began tying her tennis shoes.

'Was it that bad man?' she said again.

'I don't know, Alf. I truly don't.' My fingers were like a tangle of sticks when I tried to tie the bow on her shoe.

That evening, at dusk, the clouds in the western sky were marbled with orange light, and fireflies spun their wispy red circles in the darkening trees. Bootsie had taken Alafair to the video-rental store in town, and the house was empty and creaking with the cooling of the day. I called Clete at his apartment in the French Quarter.

'Buchalter was here,' I repeated. 'No one else would have put that record on. The guy went in and out of my house in broad daylight and nobody saw him.'

'I don't like what I'm hearing you say, Streak.'

'I don't either.'

'I don't mean that. The Bobbsey Twins from Homicide don't rattle.'

'The guy seems to float on the air, like smoke or something. What am I supposed to say?'

'That's what he wants you to think.'

'Then tell me how he got in and out of my house today?'

'That's part of how he operates. He wants you to feel like you've been molested, like he can reach out and touch you anytime he wants. It's like you don't own your life anymore.'

I could hear my own breath echoing off the receiver.

'My ex's first husband tried to do a mind fuck on her the same way,' he said. 'He hired a PI to take zoom-lens pictures of her on the toilet and mail them to her boss, then he got in her bedroom while she was asleep and slashed up all her underwear with a razor ... Hey, lighten up, Dave. Buchalter is flesh and blood. He just hasn't moved across the right pair of iron sights yet.'

'Clete, I've got every cop in Iberia Parish looking for this guy. How—'

'You *think* he was there today. You didn't see him. Listen, big mon, we're going to turn it around on this guy. They all go down, it's just a matter of time ... Are you listening?'

'Yes.'

'Your problem is you think too much.'

'Okay, Clete, I've got your drift.'

'I thought you were calling me about Nate Baxter.'

'Why would I call you about *him*?'

'Nate almost got deep-fried in his own grease early this morning. Evidently he gets it on in Algiers sometimes with this biker broad who used to be his snitch in the First District. But he wakes up this morning, the broad is gone, and the dump she lives in is burning down. Except she's got French doors that are locked across both handles with Nate's handcuffs. He wrapped his head in a wet sheet and curled up in the bathtub or he wouldn't have made it.'

'Where's he now?'

'At Southern Baptist, up on Napoleon. Why?'

'Is he pressing any charges?'

'Not according to the cop who told me about it. I guess

getting set on fire just goes with the territory when Nate tries to get laid.'

'Who's the woman?'

'Pearly Blue Ridel, you remember her, she used to work in a couple of the Giacanos' massage parlors, then she got off the spike and hooked up with some born-again bikers or something. Too bad Baxter's still got her by the umbilical cord.'

'Pearly Blue's no killer, Clete. She starts every day with a nervous breakdown.'

'Tell that to Nate.'

'I think it's a hit. A heroin mule in Baton Rouge sheriff's custody told me and Lucinda Bergeron that the Calucci brothers were going to take somebody out, somebody they weren't supposed to touch. Then this morning Tommy Lonighan showed up at my dock and made a point of establishing his whereabouts from six to noon or so.'

'Let them whack each other out. Who cares? If Baxter had caught the bus, half of NOPD would be plastered right now.'

'Would you like Lonighan setting you up for his alibi?'

'Keep it simple, Streak. Buchalter's the target. These other guys are predictable. Your man is not.'

Your man? I thought, after he had hung up. For some reason the possessive pronoun brought back the same sense of visceral revulsion and personal shame and violation that I had felt when Mack, on that raw, late-fall afternoon in the barn, had extended the backs of his fingers to my face and made me an accomplice in the sexual degradation of my mother.

Why?

Because as the object of someone else's perverse sexual obsession, you feel not only that you are alone, and I mean absolutely alone, but that there is something defective in you that either attracts or warrants the bent attentions of your persecutor.

Ask anybody who has ever been there. Even a cop.

* * *

207

I knew Pearly Blue Ridel on another level besides the one that Clete had mentioned over the telephone, but the principles of Alcoholics Anonymous prevented me from acknowledging to an outsider that she was a member of our fellowship.

Bootsie, Alafair, and I went to an early Mass at St. Peter's in New Iberia the next morning, then I dropped them off at my cousin Tutta's in town and headed back for New Orleans.

Pearly Blue's AA group was not a conventional one. It was made up of low-bottom drunks and outlaw bikers across the river in Algiers, and it was called the Work the Steps or Die, Motherfucker group. Because most of the members rode chopped-down Harleys, often had shaved heads, were covered with outrageous tattoos, and were generally ferocious in their appearance, they couldn't rent a meeting hall anywhere except in a warehouse that adjoined a biker bar where many of them used to get drunk. I parked in the alley behind the warehouse and used the rest room in the back of the bar before I went into the noon meeting.

On the condom machine someone had written in felt pen, *Gee, this gum tastes funny*. Written in the same hand on the dispenser for toilet-seat covers were the words *Puerto Rican Place Mats*.

The AA meeting area in the warehouse was gray with cigarette smoke, dense with the smell of sweaty leather, engine grease rubbed into denim, expectorated snuff, and unwashed hair. I stood against the wall by the doorway until Pearly Blue would look at me. She wore Levi's that were too large for her narrow hips, no bra, and a tie-dyed shirt that showed the small bumps she had for breasts. Her hair was colorless, stuck together on the ends, and the circles under her eyes seemed to indicate as much about the hopelessness of her life as about her emotional and physical fatigue. You did not have to be around Pearly Blue long to realize that she was one of those haunted souls who waited with certainty at each dawn for an invisible hand to wrap a cobweb of fear and anxiety around her heart.

My stare was unrelenting, and finally she got up from the table and walked with me out into the alley. She leaned against my truck fender, put a cigarette in her mouth, and lit it with both hands, although there was no wind between the buildings. She huffed the smoke out at an upward angle, her chin pointed away from me.

As with most of her kind, Pearly Blue's toughness was a sad illusion, and her breaking point was always right beneath the skin.

'You want to tell me what happened with Nate Baxter?' I said.

She looked down at the end of the alley, where a clump of untrimmed banana trees grew by a rack of garbage cans and traffic was passing on the street. She took another hit on her cigarette.

'Pearly Blue, as far as I'm concerned, we're still inside the meeting. Which means anything you tell me doesn't go any farther.'

'I went down to the store to buy some eggs to make his breakfast,' she said. She had a peckerwood accent and a peculiar way of moving her lips silently before she spoke. 'He always wants an omelette when he gets up in the morning. When I came back, fire was popping the glass out of all the windows.'

'Who handcuffed the doors together?'

'I don't know. I didn't.' She looked up at the telephone wires, an attempted pout on her mouth, like a put-upon adolescent girl.

'Why are you still hanging around with a guy like Baxter, Pearly Blue?'

'I wrote a couple of bad checks. He said he'll tell my P.O.'

'I see.'

'I wasn't hanging paper. It was just an overdraft. But with the jacket I already got—'

She made a clicking sound with her tongue and tried to

look self-possessed and cool, but the color had risen in her throat, and her pulse was fluttering like an injured moth.

'Who torched the place?' I said.

'I don't know, Streak. Everything I owned was burned up. What am I supposed to tell you?' Her eyes were wet now. She opened and closed them and looked emptily at the graffiti-scrolled wall of a garage apartment.

'Were the Calucci brothers behind it?'

'Don't be telling people that. Don't be using my name when you go talking about them kind of people.'

'I won't let you get hurt, Pearly Blue. Just tell me what happened.'

'Some guy called, it was like he knew everything about me, about my kid getting taken away from me, about where I work, about some stuff, you know, not very good stuff, I did at the massage parlour, he said, "Get out of your place by six, have yourself a nice walk, when you come back you won't have to be this guy's fuck no more."'

'You don't know who it was?'

'You think I want to know something like that? You remember what happened to my roommate in the Quarter when she told a vice cop she'd testify against one of the Giacano family? They soaked her in gasoline. They—'

'You're out of it, Pearly Blue. Forget about Baxter, forget about the Calucci brothers. Where are you living now?'

'At my sister's. I just want to go to meetings, work at my job, and get my little boy back. My P.O.'s a hard ass, he hears about the checks, calls from the wise guys, stuff like that, I'm going down again. It's full of bull dykes in there, Streak. I just can't do no more time.'

'You won't, not if I have anything to do with it.'

'Baxter's gonna find me. He's gonna make me ball him again. It's sickening.'

I took a business card out of my wallet, pressed it into

her palm, and closed her fingers on it. Her hand was small and moist in mine.

'Believe me when I tell you this,' I said. 'If Nate Baxter ever bothers you again, call me, and he'll wish his parents had taken up celibacy.'

Her face became confused.

'He'll wish his father'd had his equipment sawed off,' I said.

The corner of her mouth wrinkled with a smile, exposing a line of tiny, silver-capped teeth.

Nate Baxter's room was as utilitarian and plain and devoid of cheer as his life. It contained no flowers, greeting cards, clusters of balloons, and certainly no visitors, unless you counted the uniformed cop on duty at the door.

'You don't look too bad, Nate,' I said. Which wasn't true. His face was wan, the reddish gold beard along his jawline was matted with some kind of salve, and stubble had grown out on his cheeks.

He didn't speak; his eyes regarded me carefully.

'I talked with an arson inspector. He said somebody put a fire-bomb under your bed, probably gasoline and paraffin,' I said.

'You're making that your business, along with everything else in Orleans Parish?'

'I've got a special interest in Max and Bobo Calucci. I think you do, too, Nate.'

'What's that mean?'

'You're on a pad.'

'I remember once when you smelled like an unflushed toilet with whiskey poured in it. Maybe that's why IA busted you out of the department. Maybe that's why you can't ever get that hard out of your pants. But I'm not up to trading insults with you. Do me a favor today, go back home.'

He turned his head on the pillow to reach a drinking

211

glass filled with Coca-Cola. I could see a tubular, raw-edged lump behind his right ear.

'I think you tried to up the juice on the Caluccis, Nate. Then they decided to factor you out of the overhead.'

'It's always the same problem with you, Robicheaux. It's not what you don't know, it's what you think you know that makes you a fuckup. No matter where you go, you leave shit prints on the walls.'

'You were asleep, maybe you still had a half a bag on, Pearly Blue went to the store, somebody sapped you across the head, then he really lit up your morning.'

'I was in her apartment because she's still my snitch. You want to give it some other interpretation, nobody's going to be listening. Why? Because you don't work here anymore. For some reason, you can't seem to accept that simple fact.' His hand moved toward the cord and call button that would bring a nurse or the guard at the door.

'You know what denial is, Nate?'

'I breathed a lot of smoke yesterday. I'm not interested in wetbrain vocabulary right now. Every one of you AA guys thinks you deserve the Audie Murphy award because you got sober. Here's the news flash on that. The rest of us have been sober all along. It's not a big deal in the normal world.'

'A heroin mule in Baton Rouge custody knew about the hit. So did some greaseballs in Mobile. So did Tommy Lonighan. They're talking about you like you're already off the board.'

'Get out of here before I place you under arrest.' His hand went toward the call button again. I moved it out of his reach.

'You're a bad cop, Nate. Somebody should have clicked off your switch a long time ago.'

I pushed back my seersucker coat and removed my .45 from my belt holster. His eyes were riveted on mine now.

'You're bad not because you're on a pad; you're bad because you don't understand that we're supposed to protect the weak,' I said. 'Instead, when you sense weakness in people, you exploit it, you bully and humiliate them, you've even sodomized and raped them.'

'You've got a terminal case of assholeitis, Robicheaux, but you're not crazy. So get off it.' He tried to keep the conviction in his voice, his eyes from dropping to the pistol in my hand.

'I know an AA bunch called the Work the Steps or Die, Motherfucker group. Some of them are bad dudes, guys who've been on Camp J up at Angola. They say you've been hitting on Pearly Blue for a long time. They wanted to do something about it.' I pulled back the slide on the .45 and eased a round from the magazine into the chamber. 'But I told them I'd take care of it.'

'That gun-threat bullshit is an old ruse of yours. You're firing in the well. Get out of my room.'

I sat on the edge of his bed.

'You're right, it is,' I said. 'That's why I was going to shove it down your mouth and let you work toward that conclusion while you swallowed some of your own blood, Nate ... But there's no need.'

'What are you—'

I released the magazine, ejected the round from the chamber, and dropped it clinking into his drinking glass.

'She found out this week she's HIV positive,' I said. 'I'd get some tests as long as I was already in the hospital. But no matter how you cut it, Nate, Pearly Blue is out of your life. We're clear on that, aren't we?'

His lips looked gray and cracked, the texture of snakeskin that has dried in the sun, and the whites of his eyes were laced with pink blood vessels. The light through the blinds seemed to reflect like a liquid yellow presence in his incredulous glare. I heard his drinking glass crash to the floor and the call button clicking rapidly in his fist as I walked toward the door.

That evening I had to go far down the bayou in a boat to tow back a rental whose engine one of our customers had plowed across a sandbar. It was dark before I finally locked up the bait shop and walked to the house. Bootsie was asleep, but as soon as I entered the bedroom I knew how she had spent the last three hours. Her breathing had filled the room with a thick, sweet odor like flowers soaked overnight in cream sherry.

I sat on the edge of the bed in my skivvies and looked at the smooth white curve of her hip in the moonlight. I rubbed my hand along her rump and thigh; her skin felt heated, flushed, as though she were experiencing an erotic dream, but it was also insensitive to my touch.

I put my fingers in the thick curls of her hair, kissed her back, and felt like a fifty-five-year-old adolescent impotently contending with his own throbbing erection.

I had been saved from my alcoholism by AA. Why did it have to befall her?

But I already knew the answer. The best way to become a drunk is to live with one.

What are we going to do, Boots? I thought. Bring the dirty boogie full tilt into our lives, then do a pit stop five years down the road and see if the trade-off was worth it?

But somebody else was already working on an answer for me. At 2:00 A.M. I heard the door on my father's old tractor shed, which was always padlocked, knocking against the jamb in the wind, then I heard music, a song that was a generation out-of-date, that seemed to float across wine-dark seas crowded with ships in a time when the lights almost went out all over the world.

I slipped on my khakis and loafers, took my .45 from under the bed, and walked with a flashlight along the edge of the coulee to the shed. I bounced the beam ahead of me on the willows and the weathered gray sides of the shed, the open door that drifted back and forth on two rusty hinges, the hasp and padlock that had been splintered loose from the wood.

Then I clearly heard the words to 'Harbor Lights.'

I clicked off the safety on the .45, flipped back the door with my foot, and shined the light inside the shed.

In front of my father's old tractor was a butcher block where we used to dress game. Someone had covered it with white linen that was almost iridescent in the moonlight burning through the spaces in the slats. On the tablecloth was a cassette player, a clean china plate with a blue, long-stemmed rose laid across it, a freshly uncorked bottle of Jack Daniel's, a glass tumbler filled with four inches of bourbon, and a sweat-beaded uncapped bottle of Dixie beer on the side. A crystal goblet of burgundy that was half empty stood in a shaft of moonlight on the far side of the butcher block. On the rim of the glass was the perfect lipsticked impression of a woman's mouth.

chapter eighteen

Before he had been elected to office, the sheriff had owned a dry-cleaning business and had been president of the local Rotary Club, or perhaps it was the Lions, I don't recall which, but it was one of those businessmen's groups which manage to do a fair amount of civic good in spite of their unprofessed and real objective.

He was watering his window plants with a hand-painted flowered teapot while I told him of my 2:00 A.M. visitor. He had a round, cleft chin, soft cheeks veined with tiny blue and red lines, and a stomach that pouched over his gunbelt, but his posture was always so erect, his shirt tucked in so tightly, that he gave you the impression of a man who was both younger and in better physical condition than he actually was.

But even though the Rotary or Lions Club still held strong claim on the sheriff's soul, he often surprised me with a hard-edged viewpoint that I suspected had its origins in his experience at the Chosin Reservoir during the Korean War, which he refused, under any circumstances, to discuss with anyone.

'Well, you didn't drink any of it. That's what seems most important, if you ask me.'

'Some people might call that a pretty cavalier attitude,' I said.

'It's your call. Write it up, Dave. Bring our fingerprint man in on it. I don't know what else to say.'

He sat down in his swivel chair behind his desk. He pushed at his stomach with his stiffened fingers. Then he had another running start at it.

'Dave, what's it going to sound like when you tell people that somebody, maybe a woman, did a B and E on you so she could cover your butcher block with a tablecloth and set it with burgundy, cold beer, and expensive whiskey?'

'It's Buchalter, Sheriff. Or somebody working with him.'

'What was the motive for his house call last night?'

'He doesn't need one. He's a psychopath.'

'That's no help.' He began picking a series of bent paper clips out of a glass container and throwing them at the waste can. 'Before you came to the department, we had a particularly nasty homicide case.' *Ping.* 'Maybe you remember it. A lowlife degenerate named Jerry Dipple raped and then hanged a four-year-old child.' *Ping.* 'We thought we had him dead bang. His prints were all over the murder scene, there was a torn theater ticket in his shirt pocket from the show where he'd abducted the child, the rope he used was in the bottom of his closet.' *Ping.* 'Guess what? The lamebrain handling the investigation went into Dipple's house and seized the evidence without a warrant. Then when he realized he'd screwed up, he put the evidence back and let his partner find it later.' *Ping.*

'Guess what again? I learned about it and didn't say a thing. But Dipple's lawyer was a smart greasebag from Lafayette, you know him, the same guy who was fronting points for a PCB-incinerator outfit last year, and he found out what the lamebrain and his partner had done.' *Ping.* 'Our case was down the drain and we were about to turn loose a child killer who had done it before and would do it again. Bad day for the good guys, Dave.

'Except six months earlier we had raided a trick pad on the St. Martin line. One of the girls had some photographs of our lawyer-friend from Lafayette, I'm talking about real Tijuana specials, you know what I mean? So I invited our friend in and let him have a look. If he wanted to investigate our practices, we'd let some people in the state bar association have a peek at his.' *Ping, ping, ping.*

'Dipple fried. I thought it might bother me. But the night he rode the bolt I took my grandchildren to the movies and then went home and slept like a stone.'

'I don't know if I get your point.'

'I'll be honest with you, I don't know what we're dealing with here. Whatever it is, it's not part of the normal ebb and flow.' He stopped, ran his fingers through his hair, and kneaded the back of his neck. 'Look, I think Buchalter is trying to hit you where you're weakest.'

'Where's that?'

'Booze.'

'A guy like that can't make me drink, Sheriff.'

'I'm not talking about you.' He rubbed one hand on top of the other, then folded them on the desk blotter and looked me in the face. 'This guy's trying to mess up your family and I think he's doing a good job of it.'

'That's not a very cool thing to say, Sheriff.'

'Bootsie almost had a DWI yesterday afternoon.'

I felt something sink in my chest.

'Fortunately the right deputy stopped her and let the other lady drive,' the sheriff said.

The room seemed filled with white sound. I took my sunglasses out of their leather case, then slipped them back in again. I opened my mouth behind my fist to clear my ears and looked out the window. Then I said, 'What other lady?'

'I don't know. Whoever she was with.'

'I'll finish my report now and put it in your box.'

'Don't. The newspaper'll get ahold of it for sure. It's just what this character wants. Walk outside with me.'

It was warm in the parking lot, and the wind was flattening the leaves in the oak grove across the street. The sheriff unlocked the trunk of his car, took out a stiff, blanket-wrapped object, and walked to my truck with it. He laid the object across the seat of my truck and flipped the blanket open.

'Some people might tell you to wire up a shotgun to your back door,' he said. 'The problem is, you'd probably kill an innocent person first or only wound the sonofabitch breaking into your house, then he'd sue you and take your property. You know what this is, don't you?'

'An AR-15, the semiauto model of the M-16.'

'It's got a thirty-round magazine in it. Jerry Dipple's in a prison cemetery and children around here are a lot safer because of it. Nobody cares how the box score gets written, just as long as the right numbers are in it.' He tapped down the lock button on the door with the flat of his fist, closed the door, and looked at his watch. 'Time for coffee and a doughnut, podna,' he said, and laid his arm across my shoulders.

Back in my office I tore my unfinished report in half and dropped it in the wastebasket. There were two ways to think about the sheriff's behavior, neither of which was consoling:

1. *Semper fi*, Mac, you're on your own.

Which was too severe an indictment of the sheriff. But—

2. No application of force or firepower has so far been successful. Since we've concluded that we don't understand what we're dealing with, use more force and firepower.

Yes, that was more like it. It was old and familiar logic. If you feel like a reviled and excoriated white sojourner in a slum area, break the bones of a drunk black motorist with steel batons. If you cannot deal with the indigenous population of a Third World country, turn their rain forests into smoking gray wasteland with napalm and Agent Orange.

But my cynicism was cheap, born out of the same impotence in trying to deal with evil that had caused the sheriff to make me a present of his Colt Industries urban-Americana meatcutter.

My desk was covered with fax sheets from the National Crime Information Center in Washington, D.C., and photocopied files from NOPD that had been sent to me by Ben Motley. The people in those combined pages could have been players in almost any city in the United States. They were uniquely American, ingrained in our economy, constantly threading their way in and out of lives, always floating about on the periphery of our vision. But nothing that we've attempted so far has been successful in dealing with them. In fact, I'm not even sure how to define them.

1. Max and Bobo Calucci: In popular literature their kind are portrayed as twentieth-century Chaucerian buffoons, venial and humorous con men whose greatest moral offense is their mismatched wardrobe, or charismatic representatives of wealthy New York crime families whose palatial compounds are always alive with wedding receptions and garden parties. The familial code of the last group is sawed out of medieval romance, their dalliance with evil of Faustian and tragic proportions.

Maybe they are indeed these things. But the ones I have known, with one or two exceptions, all possessed a single common characteristic that is unforgettable. Their eyes are dead. No, that's not quite correct. There's a light there, like a wet lucifer match flaring behind black glass, but no matter how hard you try to interpret the thought working behind it, you cannot be sure if the person is thinking about taking your life or having his car washed.

I once spent three hours interviewing a celebrity mafioso who lives today in the federal witness protection program. Two-thirds of his stomach had been surgically removed because of ulcers, and his flesh was like wrinkled putty on his bones, his breath rancid from the saliva-soaked cigar that rarely left his mouth. But his recall of his five decades inside the Outfit was encyclopedic. As he endlessly recounted conversations with other members of the mob, the subject was always the same – money: how much had been made from a score, how much had been pieced off to whom, how much laundered, how much delivered in a suitcase for a labor official's life.

Thirty years ago, in the living room of a friend, he had wrapped piano wire around the throat of an informer and pulled until he virtually razored the man's head off his shoulders.

Then I said something that my situation or job did not require.

'The man you killed, he had once been your friend, hadn't he?'

'Yeah, that's right.'

'Did that bother you?'

'It's just one of them things. What're you gonna do?' He shrugged his shoulders and arched his eyebrows as though an impossible situation had been arbitrarily imposed upon him.

Then I posed one more question to him, one that elicited a nonresponse that has always stayed with me.

'You've told the feds everything about your life, Vince. Did you ever feel like indicating to God you regret some of this bullshit, that you'd like it out of your life?'

His eyes cut sideways at me for only a moment. Through the cigar smoke they looked made from splinters of green and black glass, watery, red-rimmed as a lizard's, lighted with an old secret, or perhaps fear, that would never shake loose from his throat.

I clicked off my recorder, said good-bye, and walked out of the room. Later, he told an FBI agent that he never wanted me in his presence again.

2. Tommy Bobalouba: Like Max and Bobo, he operated on the edges of the respectable world and constantly tried to identify himself with an ethnic heritage that somehow was supposed to give his illegal enterprises the mantle of cultural and moral legitimacy. The reality was that Tommy and the Caluccis both represented a mind-

numbing level of public vulgarity that sickened and embarrassed most other Irish and Italians in New Orleans.

Tommy had been kicked out of his yacht club for copulating in the swimming pool at 4:00 A.M. with a cocktail waitress. At the Rex Ball during Mardi Gras he told the mayor's wife that his radiation treatments for prostate cancer caused his phallus to glow in the dark. After wheedling an invitation to a dinner for the New Orleans Historical Association, he politely refused the asparagus by saying to the hostess, 'Thank you, anyway, ma'am, but it always makes my urine smell.'

3. We'll call the third player Malcolm, a composite of any number of black male kids raised in New Orleans's welfare projects. Caseworkers and sociologists have written reams on Malcolm. Racist demagogues love Malcolm because he's the means by which they inculcate fear into the electorate. Liberals are far more compassionate and ascribe his problems to his environment. They're probably correct in their assessment. The problem, however, is that Malcolm is dangerous. He's often immensely unlikable, too.

A full-blown crack addict has the future of a lighted candle affixed to the surface of a woodstove. Within a short period of time he will be consumed by the unbanked fires burning inside him or those that lick daily at his skin from the outside. In the meantime he drifts into a world of moral psychosis where shooting a British tourist in the face for her purse or accidentally killing a neighborhood child has the significance of biting off a hangnail.

I knew a kid from New Iberia whose name *was* Malcolm. He had an arm like a black whip and could field a ball in deep center and fire it on one hop into home plate with the mean, flat trajectory of a BB. At age seventeen he moved with his mother into the Desire Project in New Orleans, a complex of welfare apartments where the steady din is unrelieved, like the twenty-four-hour noise in a city prison – toilets flushing, plumbing pipes vibrating in walls, irrational people yelling at each other, radios and television sets blaring behind broken windows. The laws of ordinary society seem the stuff of comic books. Instead, what amounts to the failure of all charity, joy, and decency becomes the surrogate for normalcy: gang rape, child molestation, incest, terrorization of the elderly, beatings and knifings that turn the victims into bloody facsimiles of human beings, fourteen-year-old girls who'll wink at you and proudly say, 'I be sellin' out of my pants, baby,' or perhaps a high school sophomore who clicks his MAC-10 on up to heavy-metal rock 'n' roll and shreds his peers into dog food.

In a year's time Malcolm smoked, hyped, snorted, bonged, dropped, or huffed the whole street dealer's menu – bazooka, Afghan skunk, rock, crank, brown scag, and angel dust. His mother brought him back to New Iberia for a Christmas visit. Malcolm borrowed a car and went to a convenience store for some eggnog. Then he changed his mind and decided he didn't need any eggnog. Instead, he sodomized and executed the eighteen-year-old college girl who ran the night register. He maintained at his trial that he was loaded on speed and angel dust and had no memory of even entering the convenience store. I was a witness at his electrocution, and I'm convinced to this day that even while they strapped and buckled his arms and legs to the oak chair, fitted the leather gag across his mouth, and dropped the black cloth over his face, even up to the moment the electrician closed the circuits and arched a bolt of lightning through his body that cooked his brains and exploded his insides, Malcolm did not believe these people, whom he had never seen before or harmed in any way, would actually take his life for a crime which he believed himself incapable of committing.

That evening I sat at the kitchen table with a nautical chart of the Louisiana coast spread out before me.

Through the open bedroom door I heard Bootsie turn on the shower water. Recently she had made a regular habit of taking long showers in the afternoon, washing the cigarette smoke from a lounge out of her hair, holding her face in the spray until her skin was ruddy and the appearance of clarity came back into her eyes. I had not spoken to her yet about the DWI she had almost received the previous day.

I flattened and smoothed the nautical chart with my hand and penciled X's at the locations where I had sighted the German U-boat when I was in college and on my boat with Batist. Then I made a third X where Hippo Bimstine's friend, the charter-boat skipper, had pinged it with his sonar. The three X's were all within two miles of each other, on a rough southwest-northeastwardly drift line that could coincide with the influences of both the tide and the currents of the Mississippi's alluvial fan. If there was a trench along that line, tilting downward with the bevel of the continental shelf, then the movements of the sub had a certain degree of predictability.

But I couldn't concentrate on the chart. I stared out the back window at the tractor shed by the edge of the coulee. The door yawned open, and the late sun's red light shone like streaks of fire through the cracks in the far wall. I called Clete at his apartment in New Orleans and told him about the break-in of last night, the linen-covered butcher block, the offering of bourbon, the crystal goblet half-filled with burgundy and rimmed with lipstick and moonlight.

'So?' he said when I had finished.

'It's not your ordinary B and E, Clete.'

'It's Buchalter or his trained buttwipes, Streak.'

'Why the blue rose on a china plate?'

'To mess up your head.'

'You don't think it has anything to do with the vigilante?'

'Everybody in New Orleans knows the vigilante's MO now. Why should Buchalter be any different?'

'Why a woman's lipstick on the glass?'

'He's probably got a broad working with him. Sometimes they dig leather and swastikas.'

I blew out my breath and looked wanly through the screen at the fireflies lighting in the purple haze above the coulee.

'You got framed once on a murder beef, Dave. But you turned it around on them, with nobody to help you,' Clete said. 'I've got a feeling something else is bothering you besides some guy with rut for brains opening bottles in your tractor shed.'

I could still hear the shower water running in the bathroom.

'Dave?'

'Yes.'

'You want me to come over there?'

'No, that's all right. Thanks for your time, Clete. I'll call you in a couple of days.'

'Before you go, there's something I wanted to mention. It sounds a little zonk, though.'

'*Zonk?*'

'Yeah, deeply strange. Brother Oswald told me he was in the merch when World War II broke out.' He paused a moment. 'Maybe it's just coincidence.'

'Come on, Clete, get the peanut brittle out of your mouth.'

'He says he was a seventeen-year-old seaman on an oil tanker sailing out of New Orleans in nineteen forty-two. Guess what? A pigboat nailed them just south of Grand Isle.'

A solitary drop of perspiration slid down the side of my rib cage. Through the back screen I could see black storm clouds, like thick curds of smoke, twisting from the earth's rim against the molten red ball of setting sun.

'He says while the tanker was burning, the sub came to the surface and rammed and machine-gunned the lifeboats. He was floating around in the waves for a couple of days before a shrimper fished him out ... It's kind of weird, isn't it, I mean the guy showing up about the same time as Buchalter?'

'Yeah, it is.'

'Probably doesn't mean anything, though, does it? I mean … What do you think?'

'Like somebody told me yesterday, I'm firing in the hole on this one, Clete.'

After I hung up I walked into the bedroom. Through the shower door I could see Bootsie rinsing herself under the flow of water. She held her hair behind her neck with both hands and turned in a slow circle, her buttocks brushing against the steamed glass, while the water streamed down her breasts and sides. I wanted to close the curtains and latch the bedroom door, rub her dry with a towel, walk her to our bed, put her nipples in my mouth, kiss her lean, supple stomach, then feel my own quivering energies enter and lose themselves in hers, as though my desperate love could overcome the asp that she had taken to her breast.

Then I heard her open the medicine cabinet and unsnap the cap on a plastic vial. Her face jumped when she saw me in the mirror.

'Oh, Dave, you almost gave me a coronary,' she said. Her hand closed on the vial. I took it from her and read the typed words on the label.

'Where'd you get these, Boots?'

'Dr. Bienville,' she said.

'Dr. Bienville is a script doctor and should be in prison.'

'It's just a sedative. Don't make a big thing out of it.'

'They're downers. If you drink with them, they can kill you.' I shook the pills into the toilet bowl, then cracked the vial in the palm of my hand and dropped it in the wastebasket. Her eyes were blinking rapidly as she watched me push down the handle on the toilet. She started to speak, but I didn't let her.

'I'm not going to lose you, Boots,' I said, wrapped her terry-cloth robe around her, and walked her to our bed.

We sat down on the side of the mattress together, and I blotted her hair with a towel, then laid her back on the pillow. Her face looked pale and fatigued in the gloom. I remained in a sitting position and picked up one of her hands in mine.

'The sheriff told me about your almost getting a DWI,' I said. 'If a person commits himself to an alcoholic life, he or she is going to drive drunk. Then eventually that person gets a DWI or maybe he kills somebody. It's that simple.'

Her eyes started to water; she looked sideways at the window and the curtains that were lifting in the breeze.

'The sheriff's a good guy,' I said. 'He knows we're having problems. He wants to help. Everybody does, Boots. That's why I want you to go to a meeting with me in the morning.'

Her eyes tried to avoid mine. Then she said, 'It's gone that far?'

'An AA meeting isn't the worst fate in the world.'

'Do you think I'm an alcoholic?'

'Booze is starting to hurt you. That fact's not going to go away.'

She turned her head sideways on the pillow and rested the back of her wrist on her temple.

'Why did this come into our lives?' she said.

'Because I let Hippo Bimstine take me over the hurdles.'

'It goes deeper than that, though, doesn't it? This man … Buchalter … he's evil in a way I don't know how to describe. It's as if he has the power to steal the air out of a room. If I think about him, I can't breathe. It's like I'm drowning.'

'The only power he has is what we allow our fear to give to him.'

But I was falling prey to that old self-serving notion that well-intended rhetoric can remove a stone bruise from the soul.

I pulled the sheet over her and didn't say anything for

what seemed a long time. Then I said, to change the subject, 'Who was the woman with you when you got stopped?'

'Sister Marie.'

'Who?'

'Marie Guilbeaux, the nun from Lafayette.'

'What were you doing with *her*?'

'She was bringing some potted chrysanthemums out to the house. Then she saw me coming out of the convenience store, and I asked her to go with me to the drive-in for a beer. She's a nice person, Dave. She felt bad about her last visit here. What's wrong?'

'I don't want her around here anymore.'

'I don't understand your attitude.'

'She keeps showing up at peculiar times.'

'I don't think you should blame Sister Marie for my behavior, Dave.'

'We'll address our own problems, Boots. We don't need anybody else aboard. That's not an unreasonable attitude, is it?'

'I guess not. But she is nice.'

'I'll fix supper now. Why don't you take a short nap?'

'All right,' she said, and touched my forearm. 'I'm sorry about all this. I want to go to a meeting with you. First thing tomorrow morning. I won't break my promise, either.'

'You're the best.'

'You too, kiddo.'

Later, I strung an entire spool of baling wire, six inches off the ground, hung with tin cans, through the oak and pecan trees in the front and side yards, around the back of the house, across the trunk of the chinaberry tree and the back wall of the tractor shed, over the coulee, and back to Tripod's hutch, where I notched it tightly around an oak trunk. Then I put the sheriff's AR-15 on the top shelf of the bedroom closet, my .45 under the mattress, and got under the sheet next to Bootsie. Her body was warm with sleep, her mouth parted on the pillow with her breathing. The muscles in her back and shoulders and the curve of her hip were as smooth as water sliding over stone. Deep inside a troubling dream she began to speak incoherently, and I pressed myself against her, pulled the contours of her body into mine, breathed the strawberry smell of her hair, and, like a bent atavistic creature from an earlier time, his loins caught between desire and fear, waited for the tinkling of cans on a wire or the soft, milky glow of a predictable dawn.

After work the next afternoon, just as I pulled into the drive, I saw Zoot Bergeron sitting on top of a piling at the end of my dock, flipping pea gravel at the water. I parked my truck under the trees and walked back down the slope toward him. He jumped from the piling, straightened his back, and flung the rest of the gravel into the canebrake. His skin was dusty and his pullover sweater stained with food. In the lobe of his left ear was a tiny green stone, like a bright insect, on a gold pin.

'What's happening, Zoot?' I said.

'I need a job. I thought maybe you could put me on here. I done this kind of boat work before. Lot of it.'

'How'd you get here?'

'Rode the bus to New Iberia. Then walked.'

'You walked fifteen miles?'

'That man yonder give me a ride the last two miles.' He pointed up the road to a parked, mud-caked van where a man in coveralls was working under the front end with a wrench. 'I'll work hard for you, Mr. Dave. I won't get in no trouble, either.'

'What about school, partner?'

'I ain't going back there. I need to train, get in shape, maybe get on a card. You don't need school for that. Mr. Tommy tole me he quit school when he was sixteen.'

'That's part of the reason he's a moral imbecile, Zoot.'

'A wha—'

'What's your mom say about all this?'

He didn't answer.

'Does she know where you are?' I said.

'What she care? She told me this morning I ain't gonna be no better than my daddy. How can I be like my daddy when I never even seen my daddy? I want to join the Marine Corps but she won't sign for me. She say all they'll use me for is cleaning their toilets. She called up the sergeant at the recruiting center and tole him that. That's what she done.'

'Let me be up-front with you, partner. I've got a mess of grief around here right now. I can't help you out, at least not in the way you want me to.'

'Mr. Dave—'

'Sorry, Zoot.'

The air was cool, and red and gold leaves tumbled out of the sunlight into the water. He looked down the road at the shadows among the oak trees, as though they held an answer to his situation.

'I'll find you a place to stay tonight, then I'll drive you to the bus depot in the morning,' I said.

I saw the flicker of injury in his face.

'There've been some bad people around my house, Zoot. I don't want you getting mixed up in it,' I said. 'Look, maybe you should give your mom another chance. Maybe she's scared. In her mind, you're all she's got. That makes her possessive and probably a little selfish. But it's not because she doesn't respect you.'

'It don't make what she say right. You ain't got to find a place for me. That fellow yonder's from New Orleans. He say when he get his van fixed, I can ride back wit' him.'

'You want me to call your mom for you?'

'I ain't going back home. Mr. Tommy'll he'p me out. Y'all can say what you want about him, he ain't a bad white man. He don't get on my case and run me down, he don't tell me he got a mess of grief and don't got time for his friends.'

'I'm sorry you feel that way.'

'You a cop, Mr. Dave.'

'What's that mean?'

'You talk different, you ain't mean like Mr. Baxter, you're smart and educated, too, but you a cop, just like my mama. When it come down to it, you ain't gonna go against the rule, you're on the side got the power. Don't tell me it ain't so, neither.'

He walked down the road through the tunnel of oak trees. His tennis shoes and the bottoms of his jeans were gray with dust, and one elbow poked through the sleeve of his sweater. He squatted in a clump of four-o'clocks and watched the man in coveralls work on his van. In the waning afternoon light his black skin seemed lit with an almost purple sheen.

I went in the house, and Bootsie, Alafair, and I had supper at the kitchen table. Later, Alafair and I fed Tripod and put him in his hutch so he wouldn't make noise in the dead leaves during the night, then I checked the baling wire and tin cans that I had strung the day before and locked up the house. Just after Bootsie and Alafair went to bed, someone knocked on the front screen door.

It was Zoot. He was yawning when I opened the door, and his hair was mussed with pieces of leaves under the yellow porch light.

'Can you come he'p the man wit' the van?' he said.

'I thought you didn't want any favors, Zoot.'

'I didn't ax for one. The man did. He got the tire rod fixed. His batt'ry dead, though.'

'Oh, I see, that's different. Zoot, you're becoming a pain in the butt.'

'He tole me to ax. You don't want to he'p, I can walk down to the fo' corners.'

I locked the door behind me, and we got in my truck. Zoot rubbed the sleep out of his face. Then he said, 'I ain't meant to be rude, Mr. Dave. I just had a lot of stuff on my mind today. I don't see no answer for it, either.'

'You really want to join the Corps?'

'Sure.'

'Let me talk to your mom about it.'

'You'll do that?'

'Why not, partner?'

We drove down the road toward the parked van. The moon was yellow, veiled with a rain ring, low over the cypress trees in the marsh. A few raindrops began hitting on the bayou's surface. In the headlights I could see the man in coveralls bent down into the van's engine, his back pocket swollen with chrome wrenches. But behind the van's shadow I also saw a parked pickup truck, its lights off.

'It looks like your friend's already found some help,' I said.

'That guy come by earlier but he don't have no cables,' Zoot said.

I left my lights and engine on, got out in the road, and unlocked the lid of the equipment box that was welded to the floor of my truck bed. I looped the jumper cables over my shoulder and walked toward the man in coveralls. His face was as pointed as an ax blade, his jaws covered with a fine silver beard that grew to a point on his chin. His smile was like a wrinkled red line inside his beard.

'Thanks for coming out, Mr. Robicheaux,' he said.

'I don't think I know you,' I said.

'You don't. The boy told me your name.'

'I see.' I glanced at his face again in the slanting rain. His eyes were as bright as a pixie's. 'Well, clamp the red cable on your positive terminal and the black on your negative and we'll get you started.' I handed him the ends of the cables and turned to pop my hood. As I did I saw Zoot step backwards toward my truck, his mouth open, his stare suddenly disjointed.

I turned back toward the man in coveralls and saw the Luger in his hand. His smile was wet, his eyes dancing with light.

'That's the way it goes,' he said. 'I wouldn't feel bad about it. It took me a half day and Son of Sambo here to work this scam.'

'What's going on, Mr. Dave?' Zoot said.

'Who you working for, podjo?' I said.

'Podjo? I dig it. I heard you were a cute motherfucker,' he said, still smiling, and moved past me to my open truck door, the Luger aimed at my chest, and switched off the ignition and headlights.

'Cut the kid loose. He's not a player,' I said.

'Nits makes lice. Stamp 'em out when you get the chance. That's what some people say.'

'I think you're standing in your own shit, buddy,' I said. 'You pop a cap on this road and you won't get back across the drawbridge.'

But even while I was talking I saw a shadow, a large one, moving from the parked pickup truck, along the side of the van, and I knew that I had not yet confronted my real adversary that night.

A scorched-black bank of thunderclouds over the marsh pulsed and flickered with veins of lightning, and in the white glow through the canopy of trees I saw Will Buchalter step out in front of the van, his Panama hat pushed back on his head, his lopsided Will Rogers grin as affectionate as that of an old friend.

He reached out with his hand to feel my face, just as a blind man might. My head jerked back from the sour smell of his palm.

'I'm sorry to do this to you, Dave, but you don't ride the beef easy,' he said, stepped close to me, his thighs widening, and clamped both his forearms on each side of my neck.

'Yeah, ride the beef, man. Ride that motherfucker down,' the other man said, and began giggling.

Then Buchalter's forearms flexed as tight as iron and squeezed into the sides of my neck like machinery breaking bird bone. I could feel his body trembling with strain, his breath quivering like a feather against my ear, then I felt the arteries to the brain shut down, and my knees buckled as though the tendons had been severed. A wave of nausea and red-black color slid across my eyes, and I was tumbling into a dark, cool place where the rain bounced off the skin as dryly as paper flowers and the distant thunder over the gulf was only the harmless echo of ships' guns that had long since been muted with moss and the lazy, dull drift of sand and time.

chapter nineteen

Pain can be a bucket of gasoline-smelling water hurled into the face, the concrete floor that bites into the knees, the hemp knotted into the wrists behind the squared wood post, the wrenched muscles in the arms, the Nazi flag coming back into focus against a urine yellow cinderblock wall, then once again the gears turning dully on a hand-crank generator, gaining speed now, starting to hum now, whining louder through the metal casing as the current strikes my genitals just like an iron fist, soaring upward into the loins, mashing the kidneys, seizing an area deep in the colon like electric pliers.

I was sure the voice coming out of my mouth was not my own. It was a savage sound, ripped out of the viscera, loud as cymbals clapped on the ears, degrading, eventually weak and plaintive, the descending tremolo like that of an animal with its leg in a steel trap.

A redheaded, crew-cut, porcine man in a black Grateful Dead T-shirt, with white skin, a furrowed neck, and deep-set, lime green eyes, sat forward on a folding chair, pumping his chubby arms furiously on the handles of the generator. Then he stopped and stared at one of his palms.

'I got a blister on me hand,' he said.

'Ease it up, Will. You're gonna lose him again,' the man with the silver beard said.

'It ain't Will's fault. All the sod's got to do is flap 'is fouking 'ole for us,' the man at the generator said.

'Electricity's funny, Will. It settles in a place like water. Maybe it's his heart next,' the man with the beard said.

Will Buchalter was shirtless, booted in hobnails. His upper torso tapered down inside his olive, military-style dungarees like the carved trunk of a hardwood tree. His armpits were shaved and powdered, and, just above his rib cage, there were strips of sinew that wrinkled and fanned back like pieces of knotted cord from the sides of his breasts. He sat with one muscular buttock propped on a battered desk, his legs crossed, his face bemused, lost in thought under the brim of his Panama hat.

'What about it, Dave?' he asked.

My head hung forward, the sweat and water streaming out of my hair.

'Answer the man, you dumb fouk,' the porcine man in the black T-shirt said, and lifted my chin erect with a wood baton. His skin was as white as milk.

'Don't hurt his face again, Freddy,' Buchalter said.

'I say leave off with the technology, Will,' the man called Freddy answered. 'I say consider 'is nails. I could play a lovely tune with 'em.'

Will Buchalter squatted down in front of me and pushed his hat to the back of his head. A bright line of gold hair grew out of his pants into his navel.

'You've got stainless-steel *cojones*, Dave,' he said. 'But you're going through all this pain to prevent us from having what's ours. That makes no sense for anybody.'

He slipped a folded white handkerchief out of his back pocket and blotted my nose and mouth with it. Then he motioned the other two men out of the room. When they opened the door I smelled grease, engine oil, the musty odor of rubber tires.

'Freddy and Hatch aren't the sharpest guys on the block, Dave. But armies and revolutions get built out of what's available,' Buchalter said. His eyes glanced down at my loosened trousers. He picked up one of the generator's wires and sucked wistfully on a canine tooth. 'I promise you you'll walk out of it. We have nothing to gain by hurting you anymore or killing you. Not if you give us what we want.'

A bloody clot dripped off the end of my tongue onto my chin.

'Go ahead, Dave,' he said.

But the words wouldn't come.

'You're worried about the Negro?' he said. 'We'll let him go, too. I promise I won't let Freddy get out of control like that again, either. He's just a little peculiar sometimes. When he was a kid some wogs took a liking to him in the back room of a pub, you know what I mean?'

He placed his palm across my forehead, as though he were gauging my temperature, then pressed my head gently back into the post. His eyes studied mine.

'It's almost light outside,' he said. 'You can have a shower and hot food, you can sleep, you can have China white to get rid of the pain, you can have a man's love, too, Dave.'

He brought his face closer to mine and smiled lopsidedly.

'It's all a matter of personal inclination, Dave. I don't mean to offend,' he said. He looked at the smear of blood and saliva across his squared handkerchief, folded it, and slipped it back into his pocket. Then the light in his eyes refocused, as though he were capturing an elusive thought. 'We're going to take back our cities. We're driving the rodents back into the sewers. It's a new beginning, Dave, a second American Revolution. You can be proud of your race and country again. It's going to be a wonderful era.'

He shifted his weight and settled himself more comfortably on one knee, like a football coach about to address his players. He grinned.

'Come on, admit it, wouldn't you like to get rid of them all, blow them off the streets, chase them back into their holes, paint their whole end of town with roach paste?' he said. He winked and poked one finger playfully in my ribs.

'I apologize, it's a bad time for jokes,' he said. 'Before we go on, though, I need to tell you something. In your house you said some ugly things to me. I was angry at the time, but I realize you were afraid and your only recourse was to try to hurt and manipulate me. But it's all right now. It makes our bond stronger. It's pain that fuses men's souls together. We're brothers-in-arms, Dave, whether you choose to think so or not.'

He got to his feet, went to the desk, and returned with a nautical chart of the Louisiana coast unrolled between his hands. He squatted in front of me again. In the shadow of his hat the spray of blackheads at the corners of his eyes looked like dried scale.

'Dave, the sub we want had the number U-138 on the conning tower. It also had a wreathed sword and a swastika on the tower,' he said. 'Is that the one you found? Can you tell me that much?'

A floor fan vibrated in the silence. I saw him try to suppress the twitch of anger that invaded his face. He put his thumb on a spot south of Grand Isle.

'Is this the last place you saw it?' he asked.

The red, black, and white flag puffed and ruffled against the cinder-block wall in the breeze from the fan.

His hand slipped over the top of my skull like a bowl. I could feel the sweat and water oozing from under his palm.

'You going to be a hard tail on me? Are the Jews and Negroes worth all this?' he said. He slowly oscillated my head, his mouth open, his expression pensive, then wiped his palm on the front of my shirt. 'Do you want me to let Hatch and Freddy play with your hands?'

He waited, then said, rising to his feet, 'Well, let's have one more spin with army surplus, then it's on to Plan B. Freddy and Hatch don't turn out watchmakers, Dave.'

He walked past the corner of my vision and opened the door.

'It's going to be daylight. I need to get 'ome to me mum, Will,' Freddy said.

'He's right. We're spending too much time on these guys,' the man named Hatch said. 'Look at my pants. The burrhead was swallowing the rag I put in his mouth. When I tried to fix it for him, he kicked me. A boon putting his goddamn foot on a white man.'

'We're not here to fight with the cannibals, Hatch,' Buchalter said. 'Dave's voted for another try at electro-shock therapy. So let's be busy bees and get this behind us.'

I hear the rotary gears gain momentum, then the current surges into my loins again, vibrating, binding the kidneys, lighting the entrails, but this time the pain knows its channels and territory, offers no surprises, and nestles into familiar pockets like an old friend. The hum becomes the steady thropping of helicopter blades, the vibrations nothing more than the predictable shudder of engine noise through the ship's frame. The foreheads of the wounded men piled around me are painted with Mercurochromed M's to indicate the morphine that laces their hearts and nerve endings; in their clothes is the raw odor of blood and feces. The medic is a sweaty Italian kid from Staten Island; his pot is festooned with rubber spiders, a crucifix, a peace symbol, a bottle of mosquito dope. My cheek touches the slick hardness of his stomach as he props me in his arms and says, 'Say good-bye to Shitsville, Lieutenant. You're going home alive in 'sixty-five. Hey, don't make me tie your hands. It's a mess down there, Loot.'

But I'm not worried about the steel teeth embedded in my side and thighs. My comrades and I are in the arms of God and Morpheus and a nineteen-year-old warrant officer from Galveston, Texas, who flew the dust-off in through a curtain of automatic weapons fire that sounded like ball peen hammers whanging against the fuselage, and now, with the windows pocked and spiderwebbed, the floor yawing, the hot wind sucking through the doors, the squares of flooded rice plain flashing by like mirrors far below, we can see green waves sliding toward us like a wet embrace and a soft pink sun that rises without thunder from the South China Sea.

Oh, fond thoughts. Until I hear the bucket filling again under a cast-iron tap and the water that stinks of gasoline explodes in my face.

'Time I had a go at 'im, Will,' Freddy said.

Then the door opened again, and I could hear leather soles on the concrete floor. The three men's faces were all fixed on someone behind me.

'Give me another hour and we'll have it resolved,' Buchalter said.

''E's a tight-ass fouker,' Freddy said. 'We give him a reg'lar grapefruit down there.'

'It's all getting to be more trouble than it's worth, if you ask me,' Hatch said. 'Maybe we should wipe the slate clean.'

The person behind me lit a cigarette with a lighter. The smoke drifted out on the periphery of my vision.

'You want to call it?' Buchalter said.

'All I ask is ten fouking minutes, one for each finger,' Freddy said. 'It'll come out of 'im loud enough to peel the paint off the stone.'

'I've had a little problem in controlling some people's enthusiasms,' Buchalter said to the person behind me.

'You've got a problem with acting like a bleeding sod sometimes,' Freddy began.

'You're not calling me a sodomist, are you, Freddy?'

'We're doing a piece of work. You shouldn't let your emotions get mixed up in it, Will. That's all I'm trying to get across 'ere,' Freddy said.

I heard the person behind me scrape up a steel ruler that had been lying on a workbench. Then the person touched the crown of my skull with it, idly teased it along my scalp and down the back of my neck.

'I think Dave'll come around,' Buchalter said. 'He just needs to work out some things inside himself first.'

Whoever was behind me bounced the ruler reflectively on my shoulder and pushed a sharp corner into my cheek.

Buchalter kept staring at the person's face, then he said, reading an expression there, 'If that's the way you want it. But I still think Dave can grow.'

I heard the cigarette drop to the floor, a shoe mash it out methodically against the cement; then the door opened and shut again.

Freddy smiled at Hatch. His skin was so white it almost glowed. He shook a pair of pliers loose from a toolbox. Hatch was smiling now, too. They both looked down at me, expectant.

Will Buchalter bit a piece of skin off the ball of his thumb. He crouched down in front of me, removed his Panama hat, and rested it on one knee. His blond hair was as fine as a baby's and grew outward from a bald spot the size of a half-dollar in the center of his scalp. He lifted up my chin gently with the wood baton.

'Last chance. Don't make me turn it over to them,' he said.

I lifted my eyes to his and felt my lips part dryly.

'What is it, Dave? Say it,' Buchalter said.

My lips felt like bruised rubber; the words were clotted with membrane in my throat.

'It's all right, take your time,' Buchalter said. 'You've had a hard night ... Get him a drink of water.'

A moment later Buchalter held a tin cup gingerly to my lips. The water sluiced over my chin and down my throat; I gagged on my chest.

'Dave, I understand your pain. It's the pain of a soldier and a brave man. Just whisper to me. That's all it takes,' Buchalter said.

Hatch was bent down toward me, too, his hands on his knees, his face elfish and merry. Buchalter leaned his ear toward my mouth, waiting. I could see the oil and grain in his skin, the glistening convolutions inside his ear.

I pushed the words out of my chest, felt my lips moving, my eyes blinking with each syllable.

A paleness like the color of bone came into Buchalter's face. One hobnailed boot scratched against the cement as he rose to his feet.

'What'd 'e say?' Freddy asked.

'He said Will was a cunt,' Hatch answered, his grin scissoring through his beard. He and Freddy rocked on the balls of their feet, hardly able to keep their mirth down inside themselves.

Then Hatch said, 'Sorry, Will. We're just laughing at the guy. He hasn't figured out yet who's on his side.'

'That's right, Will,' Freddy said. ''E's a stupid fouk for sure. Go have breakfast. Me and Hatch'll finish it up here.'

But the insult had passed out of Buchalter's face now. He began pulling on a pair of abbreviated gray leather gloves, the kind a race driver might wear, with holes that allowed the ends of the fingers to extend above the webbing. He dried each of his armpits with a towel, then positioned himself in front of me.

'Stand him up,' he said.

'Maybe that's not a good idea, Will,' Freddy said. 'Unless you've given up. Remember what happened out in Idaho. Like an egg breaking, it was.'

'I say tear up his ticket, Will,' Hatch said. 'He's in with Hippo Bimstine. You're gonna trust what he tells you? Rip his ass.'

Then, as though he had given permission for his own anger to feed and stoke and fan itself, Hatch's hands began to shake, his teeth glittered inside his beard, and he wrenched me under one arm and tried to tug me upward against the wood post, his breath whistling in his nostrils.

'You know what's lower than a Jew?' he said. 'An Aryan who works for one. You think you're stand-up,

242

motherfucker? A punk like you couldn't cut a week on Camp J. See how you like the way Will swings.'

Freddy grabbed my other arm, and they raked me upward against the post like a sack of feed. I could feel splinters biting into my forearms, my ankles twisting sideways with my weight.

'Get your fouking head up,' Freddy said.

'Strap his belt around his neck,' Hatch said.

'Step back, both of you,' Buchalter said.

Strands of hair were glued in my eyes, and a foul odor rose from my lap. I heard Buchalter's boots scrape on the cement as he set himself.

'I'm going to hit you only three times, Dave, then we'll talk again,' Buchalter said. 'If you want to stop before then, you just have to tell me.'

'Your juices are about to fly, Mr. Robicheaux,' Freddy said.

Then the three men froze. The Nazi flag rippled along the cinder blocks with pockets of air from the floor fan.

'It's glass breaking,' Freddy said.

'I thought you said the Negro was tucked away,' Buchalter said.

''E was, Will. I locked 'im in the paint closet,' Freddy said.

'The paint closet? It's made of plywood. You retard, there're upholstery knives in there,' Buchalter said.

'Hatch didn't tell me *that*. Nobody told me *that*. You quit reaming me, Will,' Freddy said.

But Buchalter wasn't listening now. He ripped Hatch's Luger from a holster that hung above the workbench and moved quickly toward the door behind the post where I was tied, the muscles in his upper torso knotting like rope. But even before he flung the metal door back against the cinder blocks, I heard more glass breaking, cascading in splintered panes to the cement, as though someone were raking it out of window frames with a crowbar; then an electric burglar alarm went off, one with a horn that built to a crescendo like an air-raid siren, followed by more glass breaking, this time a more congealed, grating sound, like automobile windows pocking and folding out of the molding, while automobile alarms bleated and pealed off the cement and corrugated tin roof.

'He's out the door!' Buchalter said.

'The guy who owns this place uses a security service. They're probably already rolling on that alarm,' Hatch said.

'Y'all had a fucking security service into a place where you meet?' Buchalter said.

'How'd anybody know you'd want to use it for an interrogation? I told you to pop the burrhead last night, anyway.'

'Get out there and stop that noise,' Buchalter said.

'The shit's frying in the fire, it is. Time to say cheery-bye and haul it down the road, Will,' Freddy said.

'Can't you rip a wire out of a mechanism? Do I have to do everything myself?' Buchalter said.

'No, I can drive very nicely by meself, thank you. Since that's me van out there, I'll be toggling to me mum's now. I think you've made a bloody fouking mess of it, Will. I think you'd better get your fouking act together,' Freddy said.

The Luger dripped like a toy from Buchalter's huge hand. The smooth, taut skin of his chest was beaded with pinpoints of sweat; his eyes raced with thought.

Freddy unbolted a door at the far end of the room and stepped out into the gray dawn.

'Fuck it, I'm gone, too, Will,' Hatch said. 'Snap one into this guy's brainpan and clean him out of your head … All right, I'm not gonna say anything else. Don't point my own piece at me, man. It ain't my place to tell you what to do.'

Hatch backed away from Buchalter, then paused, chewing on his beard, his eyes trying to measure the psychodrama in Buchalter's face. He unhooked the Nazi flag from the wall and draped it over his arm.

'I'm taking the colors with me,' he said. 'Will, all this stuff tonight don't mean anything. It goes on, man. We're eternal. You know where you can find me and Freddy later. Hey, if you decide to smoke him, lose my piece, okay?'

Then he, too, was gone into the brief slice of gray light between the door and jamb.

Buchalter's thumb moved back and forth along the tip of the Luger's knurled grip. His tongue licked against the back of his teeth; then it made a circle inside his lips. As though he had stepped across a line in his own mind, he slipped the Luger into the top of his trousers and bent his face three inches from mine. He twisted his fingers into my hair and pulled my head back against the post.

'I'm stronger inside than you are, Dave. You can never get away from me, never undo me,' he said. 'I gave Bootsie a gift to remember me by. Now one for you.'

He tilted his head sideways, his eyes closing like a lover's, his mouth approaching mine. The Luger was hard and stiff against his corded stomach. In the next room the burglar and car alarms screamed against the walls and tin roof.

I sucked all the spittle and blood out of my cheeks and spat it full into his face.

His face went white, then snapped and twitched as though he had been slapped. His skin stretched against his skull and made his brow suddenly simian, his eye sockets like buckshot. He wiped a strand of pink spittle on his hand and stared at his palm stupidly.

But he didn't touch me again. He straightened to his full height with a level of hate and cruelty and portent in his eyes that I had never seen in a human being before, then, working his tropical shirt over one arm, snugging the Luger down tight in his belt, one eye fixed on me like a fist, he went out the door into the gray mist. But I believed I had now seen the face that inmates at Bergen-Belsen and Treblinka and Dachau had looked into.

Five minutes later Zoot Bergeron, his face swollen like

a bruised plum, sawed loose the rope and leather straps that bound my wrists, and in the wail of the approaching St. Mary Parish sheriff's cars, we slammed the door back on its hinges and stumbled out into the wet light, into the glistening kiss of a new dawn, into an industrial-rural landscape of fish-packing houses, junkyards, shrimp boats rocking in their berths, S.P. railway tracks, stacks of crisscrossed ties, a red-painted Salvation Army transient shelter among a clump of blue-green pine trees, oil-blackened sandspits, gulls gliding over the copper-colored roll of the bay, two hoboes running breathlessly over the gravel to catch a passing boxcar, the smells of diesel and salt-water, creosote, fish blood dried on a dock, nets stiff with kelp and dead Portuguese men-of-war, flares burning on offshore rigs, freshly poured tar on natural gas pipe, the hot, clean stench of electrical sparks fountaining from an arc welder's torch.

And in the distance, glowing like a chemical flame in the fog, was Morgan City, filled with palm-dotted skid-row streets, sawdust bars, hot pillow joints, roustabouts, hookers, rounders, bouree gamblers, and midnight ramblers. Zoot helped me stand erect, and I wiped my eyes on my sleeve and looked again at the two hoboes who had belly flopped onto the floor of the boxcar and were now rolling smokes as the freight creaked and wobbled down the old Southern Pacific railroad bed. Their toothless, seamed faces were lifted into the salt breeze with an expression of optimism and promise that made me think that perhaps the spirits of Joe Hill, Woody Guthrie, and Jack Kerouac were still riding those pinging rails. But the scene needed no songwriter or poet to make it real. It was a poem by itself, a softly muted, jaded, heartbreakingly beautiful piece of the country that was forever America and that you knew you could never be without.

chapter twenty

At home the next day, I sat in the cool shade of the gallery and listened to Clete Purcel talk about his latest encounter with the Calucci brothers. The cane along the bayou's banks looked dry and yellow in the wind, and hawks were gliding high above the marsh against a ceramic blue sky. I had the same peculiar sense of removal that I had experienced after I was wounded seriously in Vietnam. I felt that the world was moving past me at its own pace, with its own design, one that had little to do with me, and that now I was a spectator who listened to interesting stories told by other people.

'You remember how we used to do it when the greaseballs thought they could take us over the hurdles, I mean when they got the mistaken idea they were equal members of the human race and not something that should have run down their mother's leg?' he said. 'We'd show up in the middle of their lawn parties, have their limos towed in, roust them on nickel-and-dime beefs in public, flush their broads out of town, use a snitch to rat-fuck 'em with the Chicago Outfit, hey, you remember the time we blew up Julio Segura's shit in the backseat of his car? They had to wash him out with a hose, what a day that was.'

Clete ripped the tab on a can of beer, drank the foam, and smiled at me. His face was pink with a fresh sunburn, and the corners of his eyes crinkled with white lines.

'So that's what I did, big mon,' he said. 'I started following Max and Bobo all over town. Bars, restaurants, a couple of massage parlors they own, three fuck pads, black slum property, dig this, they've actually got a guy fronting a bail bonds office for them in Metairie, an escort service, a PCB incinerator out on the river. Dave, these two guys get up in the morning and go across Jefferson and Orleans parishes like a disease, it's impressive.

'The problem is, I've got a convertible now, and it's a little hard to be inconspicuous. After a while Max and Bobo are doing big yawns when they see me and I'm starting to feel like part of the scenery while the neighbourhood dogs hose down my tires. So yesterday, when the Caluccis and all their gumballs go to lunch at Mama Lido's, I decide it's time to shift it on up into overdrive and I get a table out on the terrace, three feet behind one of Max's broads.

'It was perfect timing, the ultimate New Orleans lowlife geek-out. Guess who shows up first? Tommy Blue Eyes and his main punch, what's her name, Charlotte, with her ta-tas sticking out of her sundress like a couple of muskmelons, and of course the Caluccis' hired help are winking at each other and squeezing their floppers under the table while Tommy's trying to act big-shit and order Italian dishes like he knows what he's doing, except he sounds like he's got Q-tips shoved up his nose.

'Then Tommy's Indian zombie pulls up in front of the restaurant with Mrs. Lonighan in the passenger's seat. Have you ever seen her? Think of a fire hydrant with bow legs. She charges out onto the terrace, her glasses on crooked, spittle flying from her mouth, shouting about Tommy and the punch leaving a used rubber under her bed, and when the maître d' tries to calm her down, she squirts a bottle of seltzer water in his face.

'Naturally, the Caluccis and the other greaseballs and

their broads are loving all this. Tommy's face is getting redder and redder, his punch is using a little brush to powder her ta-tas, and the Indian is standing there like a lobotomy case who needs a spear in his hand and a bone in his nose. Then Mrs. Lonighan storms out of the place, gets in her car without the Indian, and drives across the curb into a bunch of garbage cans down the street.

'So Tommy tries to blow it all off by talking about how the Jews are taking over legalized gambling in Louisiana. Then he starts telling these anti-Semitic jokes that have got people at the other tables staring with their mouths open, you know, stuff like "This Nazi officer told these Jewish concentration camps inmates, 'I got good news and bad news for you guys. The good news is you're going to Paris. The bad news is you're going as soap.'"'

'Anyway, the greaseballs are roaring at Tommy's jokes, and I'm wondering why I'm letting these guys act like I've used up my potential and I'm not a factor in their day anymore. So I lean over and tap Tommy on the shoulder with a celery stick and say, "Hey, Tommy, too bad you left your peter cheater lying around for Miz Bobalouba to step on. You ought to get you a fuck pad in the Pontalba like Max and Bobo here."

'The whole place goes quiet except for the sound of the Indian slurping up his squids. I'm thinking, *Ah, show time*. Wrong. Bobo calls the maître d' and has me thrown out. Can you dig it? Here's a collection of people that would turn the stomach of a proctologist, but I get eighty-sixed out on the street, right in front of a busload of Japanese tourists who are on their way back from the battleground at Chalmette.

'I'm thinking. What's wrong with this picture? I was humping it outside Chu Lai while Max and Bobo were boosting cars and doing hundred-buck hits for the Giacano family. Plus I look back at the terrace and the maître d' is picking up my silverware and changing the tablecloth like some guy with herpes on his hands had been eating there.

'I look down the street and some guys are taking a break from pouring a concrete foundation for a house. You remember that story you told me about how this mob guy in Panama City got even with his wife for giving a blow job to a judge behind a nightclub?

'The guy in charge of the cement truck is a union deadbeat and a part-time bouncer in the Quarter I went bail for about two years ago. I say, "Mitch, you mind if I drive your truck around the block, play a joke on a friend?" He says, "Yeah, we were just going to have a beer and a shot across the street if somebody'd stand the first round." I say, "Why don't you let me do that, Mitch? I think I have a tab there." He goes, "I was just telling my friends here you're that kind of guy, Purcel."

'I pull the truck right up to Max's Caddy convertible. It's gleaming with a new wax job, the top's down, the dashboard's made of mahogany, the seats are purple leather and soft as warm butter. I get out of the truck, clank that feeder chute over the driver's door, and let 'er rip. Streak, it was beautiful. The cement splatters all over the dashboard and the windows, covers the floors, oozes up over the seats, and hangs in big gray curtains over the doors. Even with the mixer roaring I could hear people yelling and going crazy out on the terrace. In the meantime, the Japanese have piled back off the bus in these navy blue business suits that look like umpire uniforms, laughing and applauding and snapping their Nikons because they think a movie is being made and this is all part of the tour, and while Max and Bobo are trying to fight their way through the crowd, the springs on the Caddy collapse, the tires pop off the rims, the cement breaks out the front windows and crushes the hood down on the engine. You remember that character called "The Heap" in the comic books? That's what the Caddy looked like, two headlights staring out of this big, gray pile of wet cement.'

'Have you lost your mind?' I said.

'What's wrong?'

'You're going to end up in the bag or get your P.I. license pulled. Why do you keep clowning around with these guys? It doesn't get the score changed.'

'They loan-sharked the Caddy out of a builder in Baton Rouge. The last thing Max wants is a police report filed on it. Lighten up, noble mon. You've been around the local Rotary too much.'

Then I saw his eyes look into mine and his expression change. I looked away.

'You really spit in Buchalter's face?' he said.

'It wasn't a verbal moment.'

'I'm proud of you, mon.'

His eyes kept wandering over my face.

'Will you cut it out, Clete?'

'What?'

'Staring at me. I'm all right. Both the guys with Buchalter are fuckups and aren't going to be hard to find. Particularly the cockney. We've got the feds in on it now, too.'

He made tiny prints with the ball of his index finger in the moisture and salt on top of his beer can.

'You think Buchalter's some kind of Nazi superman?' I said. 'He's not. He's a psychotic freak, just like dozens of others we sent up the road.'

'NOPD and the sheriff's office in Lafourche Parish probably haven't gotten hold of your boss yet. But they will.'

'What are you talking about?'

'You're right. Those two were fuckups. That's why they're off the board now.'

The sunlight seemed to harden and grow cold on the garden.

As best as I could reconstruct it, this is how Clete (and later a Lafourche sheriff's deputy) told me the story:

The previous night, out in a wetlands area southwest of New Orleans, a man who had been gigging frogs emerged terrified from the woods, his face whipped by branches and undergrowth, and waved down a parish sheriff's car with his shirt. It had started to rain, and ground fog was blowing out of the trees

'They's a man got some other men tied up on the mudflat. Somebody got to get down there. He's fixin' to—' he said.

'Slow down, podna. It's gonna be all right. He's fixin' to what?' the deputy said.

'He's got one of them lil chain saws. Back yonder, right by the marsh.'

The deputy was young and only eight months with his department. He radioed his dispatcher, then made a U-turn in the middle of the highway and bounced down an abandoned board road that wound through thickly spaced trees and mounds of briar bushes webbed with dead morning glory vines. Sheets of stagnant water and mud splashed across his windshield, and an old road plank splintered under one wheel and *whanged* and clattered against his oil pan. But in the distance, through the blowing mist and the black silhouette of tree trunks, he could see a brilliant white chemical flame burning against the darkness. Then he heard the surge of a chain saw, and a second later, even louder than the erratic, laboring throb and shriek of the saw and the roar of his car engine, the sustained and unrelieved scream of a man that rose into the sky like fingernails scraping on slate.

The deputy snapped a tie-rod and spun out into a tangle of willow and cypress trees fifty yards before the road dead-ended at the marsh. He pulled his twelve-gauge Remington shotgun, sawed off at the pump and loaded with double-ought buckshot, from the clip on the dashboard and began running with it at port arms through the undergrowth.

In a clearing by the swamp's edge, next to a parked pickup truck with a camper shell in the bed, a Coleman lantern hissed on the ground like a phosphorous flare. The deputy could see the shadow of a huge man moving about on the far side of the truck. On the ground, partly obscured by the truck's tires, were the shapes of two prone men, their arms pinioned behind them, their faces bloodless and iridescent in the soft rain and the hissing light of the lantern.

The chain saw was idling on a piece of cardboard now. Then the deputy saw the large man bending over the shapes on the ground, a bouquet of roses scattered about his booted feet, pulling, working at something with his hands. The water and trees in the swamp were black, the shadows in the clearing changing constantly with the frenetic movements of the man, whose hands the deputy now knew were laboring at something tribal and dark, far beyond the moral ken of a youthful law officer, a glimpse into a time before the creation of light in the world, hands as broad as skillets, popping with cartilage, scarlet to the wrist, the fingers wet with the lump of heart muscle that they lifted from a man's chest cavity.

The deputy vomited on a tree, then tried to step into the clearing with his shotgun aimed at the man who had suddenly raised erect, a rain hat tied under his chin, a disjointed and maniacal stare in his eyes.

He wanted to yell *Down on your face, hands on your head*, or any other of the dramatic verbal commands that always reduce television criminals to instant prisoners, but the words hung like pieces of wet newspaper in his throat and died in the heavy air, and he tripped over a tangle of morning glory vines as though he were stumbling about in a dream.

Then the large man was running into the marsh, his legs ripping through islands of lily pads, water splashing to his waist, his shoulders humped, when the deputy let off the first round and sent a shower of sparks out into the dark. At first the deputy thought he had missed, had fired high, and he jacked another shell into the chamber, aimed at the base of the running man's spine, and pulled the trigger. Then he fired twice more and saw the man's shirt jump, heard the slugs *whunk* into his back.

But the running man crashed and tunneled through the flooded cypress and willows and was gone. The deputy's

253

fifth shot peeled away through the trees like marbles rattling down a long wooden chute. He would swear later that he saw a half dozen rents in the shirt of the fleeing man. He would also get off duty that night and get so drunk in a Lockport bar that his own sheriff would have to drive him home.

'The pickup truck was boosted in Lafitte that morning,' Clete said. 'The guy with the silver beard was Jody Hatcher. He was a four-time loser, including one time down as an accessory in the rape of a child. The guy named Freddy is a blank. The feds think he might be a guy who dynamited a synagogue in Portland, but they're not sure ... Streak, look at the bright side. There're two less of these guys on the planet. I tell you something else. They made a real balloon payment when they checked out. The M.E. said there was a look frozen in their eyes even he had trouble dealing with.'

Batist was cranking an engine out on the bayou. The wind was wrinkling the water and ruffling the cane in the sunlight.

'None of it makes any sense,' I said.

'It does to me. Buchalter doesn't leave loose ends.'

'Why does he go to the trouble of using the vigilante's MO?'

'Maybe he likes roses. Maybe he has shit for brains.'

'Maybe we're not dealing with Buchalter, either. What's this stuff about the deputy planting double-ought bucks in his back?'

'Maybe the guy doesn't want to admit he was so scared he couldn't hit a billboard with bird shot.'

I stood up to go inside. A pain spread out of my loins into my abdomen.

'You beat Buchalter, Streak. That's all that counts,' Clete said. 'I don't think I could have cut it. I'd have rolled over.'

'No, you wouldn't.'

He crushed his empty beer can in his hand.

'Let me take y'all to supper tonight,' he said.

'That sounds very copacetic,' I said.

'My second day in Vietnam a hard-nosed gunny gave me some advice about fear and memory and all that stuff: "Never think about it before you do it, never think about it after it's over." '

'No kidding?' I said, with the screen half opened.

'I tried,' he answered, and held up his palms and made half-moons of his eyebrows.

chapter twenty-one

On Saturday morning, when I walked down to the dock, I noticed a pickup truck with a David Duke sticker parked by the shell boat ramp. Inside the bait shop, Alafair and Batist were working behind the counter and two fishermen were eating chilli dogs with forks and drinking bottled beer at one of the tables. Batist did little more than nod when I said good morning.

'What's wrong with him?' I asked Alafair while we were pulling the canvas awning out on the wires over the spool tables.

'Batist made a mistake with those men's change,' she answered. 'One man said, the one with the big face, he said, "Louisiana's got fifteen percent unemployment, and this place hires something like that to run the cash register." '

I went back through the screen door. The two men, both dressed in the khaki clothes of heavy equipment operators, were sharing a smoked sausage now and drinking their beer. I picked up the cash register receipt from their table, flattened it on the counter, added up the price of the beer and sausage and sales tax, rang open the cash drawer, and placed four one-dollar bills and thirty-six cents in coins on their table.

'This table's closed,' I said, and picked up their beer bottles and the paper shell with the sliced sausage in it.

'What the hell do you think you're doing?' the larger of

the two men said. His head looked like granite, and his closely cropped hair was lightly oiled and shaved neatly on his neck.

'You were rude to my employee. I don't want your business.'

'Just hold on a minute, there.'

'End of discussion, gentlemen.'

'Well then ... well ... well then ... Fuck you, then.'

After they were gone, I wiped off their table. Then, before I realized it, Batist had walked down the dock, gotten into his truck, and driven south toward the four corners and his house.

Oh boy.

'Watch the store, Alf. I'll be back in about twenty minutes,' I said.

'Why'd Batist leave?'

'He has his own way of doing things.'

He lived in a rambling, paintless house that had been built on to randomly by three generations of his family. The tin roof was orange with rust, the dirt yard strewn with chicken coops, tractor and car parts. On the sagging gallery were stacks of collapsible crab traps and an old washing machine that he had turned into a barbecue pit. His small farm had once been part of a plantation where Federal and Confederate troops had fought a furious battle during General Banks's invasion of southwestern Louisiana. Through the pines on the far side of the coulee which bordered Batist's property, you could see the broken shell and old brick pillars and chimneys of a burned-out antebellum home that the Federals first looted and then fired as they pushed a retreating contingent of Louisiana's boys in butternut brown northward into New Iberia. Every spring, when Batist cracked apart the matted soil in his truck patch with a singletree plow, minie balls, shards of broken china, and rusted pieces of canister would peel loose from the earth and slide back off the polished point of the share like the contents of a fecund and moldy envelope mailed from the year 1863.

I found him in his backyard, raking leaves onto a compost pile that was enclosed with chicken wire. The dappled sunlight through the oak branches overhead slid back and forth across his body like a network of yellow dimes.

'If you're going to take off early, I'd appreciate your telling me first,' I said.

'When I tole you you gotta t'row people out the shop 'cause of me?'

'Those were low-rent white people, Batist. I don't want them on my dock. That's my choice.'

'If a white man got to look out for a black man, then ain't nothin' changed.'

'This is what you're not understanding, partner. We don't let those kind of people insult Alafair, Bootsie, you, or me. It doesn't have anything to do with your race.'

He stopped work and propped his hands on the wood shaft of the rake. His wash-faded denim shirt was split like cheesecloth in back.

'Who you tellin' this to? Somebody just got off the train from up Nort'?' he said.

'Next time I'll keep my hand out of it. How's that?'

'Get mad if you want. T'rowin' them white men out ain't solvin' nothin'. It's about money, Dave. It's always about money. The white man need the nigger to work cheap. That ain't no mystery to black people. It's white folk don't figure it out, no.'

'I need you to help close up tonight,' I said.

'I'm gonna be there. Hey, you runnin' round in circles lookin' for this man been killin' dope dealers, this man who hurt you so bad the ot'er day, it don't have nothin' to do with no vigilante. When somebody killin' black people, it don't matter if up in a tree, or breakin' in a jail and hangin' a man on a beam, they can say it's 'cause he raped a white woman, or he killed a white man, or he done some ot'er t'ing. But it's over money. It means the black man stay down at the bottom of the pile. The dumbest nigger in Lou'sana know that.'

His eyes lingered indulgently on mine. He squeezed the rake handle, and his callused palm made a soft grating sound like leather rubbing against wood.

Monday morning I returned to work. The first telephone call I received was from Lucinda Bergeron.

'Fart, Barf, and Itch are no help on Will Buchalter,' she said. 'I don't understand it. Is the guy made out of air?'

'He didn't seem like it to me.'

'Then why doesn't he show up in the system?'

'You can't throw an electronic net over every psychopath in the country.'

'Somebody has to know who this guy is. Being around him must be like getting up in the morning and biting into a shit sandwich for breakfast.'

Too much time around squad rooms, Lucinda, I thought.

'How's Zoot doing?' I said.

'He's fine, thank you.'

'What's the problem?'

'He said you thought he should join "the Crotch." That's swinging-dick talk, isn't it? Quite a vocabulary you guys have.'

'How about your own?' I said.

'I'm not the one encouraging a seventeen-year-old boy to drop out of school.'

'He wanted me to talk to you about joining the Corps. He can get a GED there. I don't think it's the worst alternative in the world.'

'He can forget about it.'

'You do him a disservice. Why'd you call, Lucinda?'

Her anger seemed almost to rise from the perforations in the telephone receiver.

'That's a good question. When I figure it out, I'll tell you.' Then she made that sound again, like she had just broken a fingernail. A moment later, she said, 'We're operating a sting out of a motel dump by Ursulines and Claiborne. You want in on it?'

'What for?'

'We're going to roll over some dealers from the Iberville Project.'

'You think they're going to tell you something about the vigilante?'

'They're the bunch most likely to undergo open-heart surgery these days.'

'You think this will lead you back to Buchalter?'

'Who knows? Maybe there's more than one guy killing black dope dealers.'

'Lucinda, listen to me on this one. Buchalter doesn't have any interest in you or Zoot. Don't make it personal. Don't bring this guy into your life.'

'That sounds strange coming from you.'

'Read it any way you want. Zoot and I were lucky. The time to go home is after you hit the daily double.'

'You want in on the sting or not?'

'What's the address?'

I talked with the sheriff, arranged to have a deputy stay at the house until I returned sometime that evening, then signed out of the office and went home to change into street clothes. Bootsie's car was gone, and Alafair was at school. I used the Memo button on our telephone answering machine to leave Bootsie a recorded message. I gave her both Lucinda Bergeron's and Ben Motley's extension numbers, and, in case she couldn't reach me any other way, I left the name and address of the motel off Claiborne where the sting was being set up.

It seemed a simple enough plan.

On the way back down the dirt road, on the other side of the drawbridge, I saw the flatbed truck, with the conical loudspeakers welded on the roof, of the Reverend Oswald Flat, banging in the ruts and coming toward me in a cloud of dust. Crates of machinery or equipment of some kind were boomed down on the truck bed.

Oswald Flat recognized my pickup and clanked to a halt in the middle of the road. His pale eyes, which had the strange, nondescript color of water running over a pebbled streambed, stared at me from behind his large, rimless glasses. His wife sat next to him, eating pork rinds out of a brown bag.

'Where you running off to now?' he said.

'To New Orleans. I'm in a bit of a hurry, too.'

'Yeah, I can tell you're about to spot your drawers over something.'

'Today's not the day for it, Reverend.'

'Oh, I know that. I wouldn't want to hold you back from the next mess you're about to get yourself into. But my conscience requires that I talk to you, whether you like hit or not. Evidently you got the thinking powers of a turnip, son. Now, just stop wee-weeing in your britches a minute and pull onto the side of the road.'

'Os, I told you to stop talking to the man like he's a *mo*-ron,' his wife said, dabbing at the rings of fat under her chin with a handkerchief.

I parked in a wide spot and walked back toward his truck. Through the slats in one of the crates fastened to the flatbed with boomer chains I could see the round brass helmet, with glass windows and wing nuts, and the rubber and canvas folds of an ancient diving suit.

'I hate even to ask what you're doing with that,' I said.

'Bought hit at a shipyard outside Lake Charles – air hoses, compressor, weighted shoes, cutting torch, stuff I don't even know the name of. Now I got to get aholt of a boat.'

'You're going to try to find that sub?'

He smiled and didn't answer.

'Do you know what's in it?' I asked.

'I'd bet on a lot of Nazis ready for a breath of fresh air.'

'I think you're going to get hurt.'

'Hit's something they want. So I'll do everything I can to make sure they don't get hit.'

'Don't do this, sir.'

'I cain't fault you. You mean well. But you still don't get hit. You ain't chasing one man, or even a bunch of men. Hit's something wants to take over the earth and blot out the sun. Hit's evil on a scale the likes of ordinary people cain't imagine.'

His eyes searched in mine like those of a man who would never find words to adequately explain the enigmas that to him had the bright, clear shape of a dream.

'You lost your son to forces you couldn't control, Reverend,' I said. 'I lost my wife Annie in a similar way. I was full of anger, and after a while I came to believe the whole earth was a dark place.'

He was already shaking his head before I could finish.

'I was on a tanker got torpedoed. Right out yonder,' he said, and pointed toward the southern horizon. 'There ain't no way to describe hit for somebody ain't been there. Holding on to the life jacket of a man whose face is burnt off ... Boilers blowing apart under the water ... Men crawling around on the hull like ants just before she slips to the bottom ... Somebody screaming out there inside an island of flaming oil. You don't never want to hear a sound like that, Mr. Robicheaux.'

'Sometimes you have to let things go, partner.'

'They got to make people afraid. That's the plan. Make 'em afraid of the coloreds, the dope addicts, the homeless, the homosexuals, hit don't matter. When they got enough people afraid, that's when they'll move.'

'Who?'

'The Book of Revelation says the Beast will come from the sea. In the Bible the sea means politics.'

'I think you're a decent man. But don't go down after that sub with this junk.'

'Just leave things alone ... Don't be messin' ... Let the law handle hit ... You put me in mind of a woodpecker tapping away on a metal light pole.' He pursed his lips and began to whistle, then opened the door to the truck cab and reached behind the seat. 'Tell me what you make of this?'

'An iron rose.'

'Hit was probably tore off a tomb or a gate. But this morning hit was on my front porch. The stem was stuck through the heart on a valentine card.'

It was heavy in my palm, the iron black with age, the edges of the petals thin and serrated with rust.

'Have you given somebody reason to be upset with you?' I said.

'I been working down in the Desire Project for the last week.'

'You know how to pick them.'

'Jesus didn't spend a lot of time with bankers and the fellows at the Chamber of Commerce.'

I placed the iron rose back in his hand.

'Good luck to you, Reverend. Call me if I can help with anything,' I said.

I left him there, a good man out of sync with the world, the era, even the vocabulary of his countrymen. But I doubted if anyone would ever be able to accuse the Reverend Oswald Flat of mediocrity. His kind ended on crosses, forever the excoriated enemies of the obsequious. To him my words of caution bordered on insult and my most reasoned argument had the viability of a moth attempting to mold and shape a flame.

A narcotics sting sounds interesting. It's not. It usually involves what's called rolling over the most marginal players in the street trade – hypes, hookers, and part-time mules, and any of their demented friends and terrified family members who are unlucky enough to get nailed with them. As a rule, the mules, or couriers, are dumb and inept and spend lifetimes seeking out authority figures in the form of probation officers and social workers. In the normal world most of them couldn't make sandwiches without an instruction manual. They are almost always users themselves, dress as though they're color-blind, speak in slow motion, and wonder why cops can easily pick them out of a crowd at a shopping mall.

They scheme and labor on a daily basis at the bottom of the food chain. When they're busted in a sting, their choices are immediate and severe – they either roll over and give up somebody else, or they go straight to jail, sweat out withdrawal over a toilet bowl in a holding cell, then meditate upon their mistakes while hoeing soybeans for several years at Angola.

Shitsville in the street trade is when you're spiking six balloons a day and suddenly you're in custody and the Man can snap his fingers and turn you into a Judas Iscariot or a trembling bowl of Jell-O.

'You telling me you want to ride the beef, Albert?' the plainclothes says to the frightened black man, who sits on the edge of the motel bed, his wrists handcuffed behind him, his thin forearms lined with the infected tracks and gray scar tissue of his addiction.

'If I give you Bobby, he'll fuck me up, man,' Albert answers. 'Cat's got a blade. He did a guy in Houston with it.'

The plainclothes, a heavy, choleric man in a sweaty, long-sleeve white shirt, reaches out and taps Albert sharply on the cheek with his hand.

'Are you stupid, Albert?' he says. 'You're already fucked up. You're taking Bobby's fall. Bobby has kicked a two-by-four up your ass. Look at me, you stupid shit. Bobby told me your old lady whores for lepers. He laughs at both of you behind your back. He's got you copping his joint and you're too fucking dumb to know it.'

'He told you my old—'

'You want to go back to Angola? You want to get turned out again, made into a galboy, that's what you're telling me, Albert? You like those swinging dicks to turn you out? I heard they tore up your insides last time.'

'You gotta he'p me on this. I cain't go down again, man.'

'Get him out of my sight,' the plainclothes says to another cop.

'You gotta keep my name out of it, okay? The cat tole me to meet him in a pizza joint out in Metairie. He's gonna be there in an hour.'

'You got to make him take you to his stash, Albert. That's the only deal you get. Bobby goes down, you walk. Otherwise, your next high is going to be on nutmeg and coffee. Is it true that stuff can give you a hard-on like a chunk of radiator pipe?'

Albert trembles like a dog trying to pass broken glass; Albert vomits in his lap; Albert makes the plainclothes turn away in disgust.

What's it all worth?

You've got me.

The people at the top usually skate. They buy defense attorneys who used to be prosecutors for the U.S. Justice Department. A million-dollar bond is simply factored into the overhead.

Albert goes to jail, or into a diversion program, or into the graveyard. And nobody, except Albert, particularly cares which one, since Albert doesn't even qualify as a footnote.

In an adjoining room Lucinda and I questioned seven individuals – five of them black, two white – about the vigilante. But these were people who long ago had accepted the sleepy embrace of the succubus or incubus that had insinuated itself into their lives through a tied-off, swollen vein. Their concept of mortality did not extend past the next five minutes of their day. They shot up with one another's syringes, used the public health clinic as a temporary means to knock their venereal diseases into remission, looked upon AIDS as just another way of dying, and daily accepted the knowledge that a vengeful supplier could give them a hot shot that would transform their hearts into kettledrums.

Their beef was with the narcs. Their angst was centered on their own metabolism and the fact that they were about to rat out their friends. Why bargain with a couple of homicide investigators who could offer them nothing? They turned to stone.

Then one of those terrible moments happened, the kind that you dream about, that you hope will never occur in your career, that will always somehow be the misfortune of someone else. Later, you'll attribute it to bad judgment, callousness, inhumanity, bad luck, or simple stupidity, like a safety-minded fool righteously padlocking fire exits, but it remains forever as the moment that left you with the mark of Cain.

The plainclothes who had been interrogating Albert decided to tighten and tamp down the dials a little more and whipped Albert repeatedly across his nappy head with a fedora, yelling at him simultaneously, until another cop stopped it and walked him outside for a cigarette. When they came back in, the plainclothes's face was still flushed and his armpits were gray with sweat. The thermostat switch was broken, and the room was hot and dry with the electric heat from the wall panels. The plainclothes ripped off his tie, kneaded the thick folds in the back of his neck, then hung his shoulder holster on the back of a wood chair.

Albert was shirtless, his lap soiled with vomit, his face wringing wet. His shoulders trembled, and his teeth clicked in his mouth. He begged to go to the toilet.

The plainclothes walked him into the bathroom, unlocked one cuff, then snipped it on a water pipe and closed the door.

Albert was strung out, delusional, popping loose seam and joint. His body was foul with its own fluids; his pitiful attempt at integrity had been robbed from him; his new identity was that of snitch and street rat. With luck he'd be out of town before his friend Bobby made bail.

But Albert was jail-wise and had been underestimated.

He feverishly lathered his wrist with soap and pulled his thin hand through the cuff like it was bread dough. The plainclothes stared with disbelief as Albert came through the bathroom door and tore the .38 out of the shoulder holster that hung on the chair back, his hand shaking, his eyes blood-flecked and bulging with fear, sweat streaming down his chest.

The plainclothes's face looked like a large, round, white clock that had run out of time.

'Put it down, Albert!' Lucinda shouted, pointing her nickel-plated .357 Magnum straight out with both hands from the doorway.

The plainclothes's chest was heaving; he clutched at his left breast, and his breath rose from his throat like bubbles bursting from an underwater air hose. Lucinda's feet were spread, her midriff winking above her Clorox-faded Levi's. Albert's eyes were half-dollars, his clenched right hand trembling as though it were painted with electricity.

'You don't want to do this, Albert,' she said, fitted her thumb over the knurled spur of the hammer, and cocked it back. The notched grooves and the cylinder locked into place with a sound like a dry stick snapping. 'We can all walk out of this. You'll go downtown. Nobody'll hurt you. I give you my word. Lower the gun, Albert ... Wait ... Don't do it, don't let those thoughts get in your head ... Albert!'

But it was too late. A facsimile of a man, with the soft bones of a child and muscles like jelly, with lint in his navel and a snake feeding at his heart, was imploding inside and looking for his executioner. He gripped the pistol with both hands, squeezed his eyes shut, turned toward Lucinda, and lowered his head between his extended arms as he tightened his finger inside the trigger housing.

She fired only once. The round caught him in the crown of the skull and knocked him back against the wall as though he had been struck by an automobile.

The air was bitter with the smell of gunpowder, dry heat, and a hint of nicotine and copulation in the bed clothing. My ears were ringing from the explosion, then I saw the plainclothes pointing at the red horsetails on the wallpaper while he giggled and wheezed uncontrollably, his left hand clawing at his collar as though it were a garrote about his neck.

Three hours later, after the paperwork, the questions, the suspension from active duty, the surrender of her weapon to Nate Baxter, I drove her home. Or almost home.

'Stop at the corner,' she said.

'What for?'

'I want a drink.'

'Bad day to feed the dragon,' I said.

'Drop me off and I can walk.'

'Lucinda, this is what happens. Tonight, you'll finally fall asleep. You'll have troubling dreams, but not exactly about the shooting. It's like your soul has a headache and can't allow itself to remember something. Then you'll wake up in the morning, and for a few moments it'll all be gone. Then, boom, it'll wash over you like the sun just died in the sky. But each day it gets better, and eventually you come to understand there's no way it could have worked out differently.'

Her eyes had the unnatural sheen of an exhausted person who just bit into some black speed.

'Are you coming in or not?' she said when I pulled to the curb in front of an old wood-front bar with a colonnade on Magazine.

'I guess not.'

'See you around, sport,' she said as she slammed the door and walked into the bar, the tip of a white handkerchief sticking out of the back pocket of her Levi's, her bare ankles chafing against the tops of her dusty tennis shoes.

Bad situation in which to leave a distraught lady, I thought, and followed her inside.

It was dark and cool inside and smelled of the green sawdust on the floor and a caldron of shrimp the black bartender was boiling on a gas stove behind the counter. I used a pay phone by the empty pool table to call home. It was the second time I had called that afternoon and gotten no answer. I left another message.

Lucinda drank a whiskey sour in two swallows. Her eyes widened, then she let out her breath slowly, almost erotically, and ordered another.

'Join me?' she asked.

'No thanks.'

She drank from the glass.

'How many times has it happened to you?' she said.

'Who cares?'

'I don't know if I can go back out there again.'

'When they deal the play and refuse the alternatives, you shut down their game.'

'How many times did you do it? Can't you answer a simple question?' she said.

'Five.'

'God.'

I felt a constriction, like a fish bone, in my throat.

'Who'd you rather have out there, people who do the best they can or a lot of cops cloned from somebody like Nate Baxter or that blimp in the motel room?'

She finished her drink and motioned to the bartender, who refilled her glass from a chrome shaker fogged with moisture. She flattened her hands on the bar top and stared at the tops of her fingers.

'I busted Albert four years ago,' she said. 'For stealing a can of Vienna sausage out of a Winn-Dixie. He lived in the Iberville Project with his grandmother. He cried when I put him in the holding cell. His P.O. sent him up the road.'

'A lot of people wrote that guy's script, but you weren't one of them, Lucinda. Sometimes we just end up being the punctuation mark,' I said, slid the whiskey glass away from the ends of her fingers, and turned her toward the door and the mauve-colored dusk that was gathering outside in the trees.

I drove her to her house and walked with her up on the gallery. The latticework was thick and dark with trumpet vine, and fireflies were lighting in the shadows. The lightbulb above our heads swarmed with bugs in the cool air. She paused with her keys in her hand.

'Do you want me to call later?' I said.

'I'll be all right.'

'Is Zoot here?'

'He plays basketball tonight.'

'It might be good if you ask somebody to come over.'

Her face looked up into mine. Her mouth was red; her breath was soft with the smell of bourbon.

'I'll call when I get back to New Iberia,' I said.

Her face looked wan, empty, her gaze already starting to focus inward on a memory that would hang in the unconscious like a sleeping bat.

'It's going to be all right,' I said, and placed one hand on her shoulder. I could feel the bone through the cloth of her blouse.

But nothing was going to be all right. She lowered her head and exhaled. Then I realized what she was looking at. On the tip of her tennis shoe was a red curlicue of dried blood.

'Why did it have to be a pathetic and frightened little man like Albert?' she said. She swayed slightly on her feet, and her eyes closed, and I saw the tears squeeze out from under the lashes.

I put my arms around her shoulders and patted her softly on the back. Her forehead was pressed against my chest; I could feel the thickness of her hair against my cheek, the thin and fragile quality of her body inside my arms, the brush of her stomach against my loins. On the neighbor's lawn the iron head of a broken garden sprinkler was rearing erratically with the hose's pressure and dripping water into the grass.

I took the door key from her fingers. It felt stiff and hard in my hand.

'I have to go back home now, Lucinda,' I said. 'Where can we get hold of Zoot?'

Then I turned and saw the car parked at the curb, a

two-door white Toyota. The car of Sister Marie Guil-beaux, whose small hands were as white as porcelain and resting patiently on the steering wheel. In the passenger seat sat Bootsie, her face disbelieving, stunned, hurt in a way that no one can mask, as though all the certainties in her life had proved to be as transitory as a photographic negative from one's youth dissolving on top of a hot coal.

chapter twenty-two

Bootsie looked straight ahead as we followed I-10 past the sand flats and dead cypress on the northern tip of Lake Pontchartrain. My mind was racing. None of the day's events seemed to have any coherence.

'I left Motley's and Lucinda's extensions on the answering machine, I left the address of the motel. I didn't imagine it,' I said.

'It wasn't there, Dave.'

'Was there a power failure?'

'How would I know if I wasn't home? It wouldn't have affected the recording, anyway.'

'There's something wrong here, Boots.'

'You're right. Sometimes you worry about other people more than you do your own family.'

'That's a rotten thing to say.'

'Goddamn it, he called while you were out of town looking after this Bergeron woman.'

'Buchalter?'

'Who else?'

'How could he? We just changed the number.'

'It was Buchalter. Do you think I could forget that voice? He even talked about what he did to me.'

I turned and looked at her. Her eyes were shiny in the green glow from the dashboard. A semi passed, and the inside of the pickup was loud with the roar of the exhaust.

'What else did he say?'

'That he'd always be with us. Wherever we were. His voice sounded like he had wet sand in his throat. It was obscene.'

'I think he's a hype. He calls when he's loaded.'

'Why does this woman have to drag you into her investigation?'

'It's my investigation, too, Bootsie. But you're right, I shouldn't have gone. We were firing in the well.'

'I just don't understand this commitment you have to others while a psychopath tries to destroy us.'

'Look, something's out of sync here. Don't you see it? How did the nun, what's her name, get involved in this?'

'She dropped by, that's all.'

'Then what happened?'

'Nothing. What do you mean?'

'Come on, think about it. What *happened* after she came by?'

'She used the phone. To call somebody at the hospital, I think.'

'When did Buchalter call?'

'A little later. I tried to get you at your office. That's when the sheriff told me there'd been a shooting. I couldn't just stay at home and wonder what happened to you and wait for Buchalter to call again. Marie and I took Alafair to Batist's, then drove to New Orleans. What else was I supposed to do?'

'Whose idea was it to go to New Orleans?'

'Mine ... Both of us, I guess ... She saw my anxiety, she was trying to be a friend.'

'How many nuns do you know who gravitate toward trouble, who are always around when it happens?' I said.

She was looking at me now.

'Did you check the machine when you first came in the house?' I asked.

'No.'

'Our new number is written down by the side of the phone, isn't it?'

'Yes.'

'It's time to check out Sister Guilbeaux, Boots.'

'You think she erased your message and called Buc – That's crazy, Dave. She's a good person.'

'Buchalter's flesh and blood. I think somebody close to us is helping him. How many candidates are there?'

Her eyes became fixed on the tunnel of trees ahead. I could see her chest rising and falling as she touched her fingers to her mouth.

The next morning, in my office, I sorted through all the case notes, crime scene photographs, autopsy reports, computer printouts, voice cassettes, rap sheets, convict prison records, and Xeroxes and faxes from other law-enforcement agencies that had anything to do with the vigilante killings, Tommy Lonighan, the Calucci brothers, and Will Buchalter and his followers.

I also called the office of the Catholic diocese in Lafayette. Both the bishop and his assistant were out. The secretary said one of them would return my call later. She was new to the job and was not sure if she knew a Sister Marie Guilbeaux.

I read every document on my desk twice. The more I read, the more ill-defined and confusing the case became.

Clete Purcel had always been a good cop because he kept the lines simple. I took a yellow legal pad and a felt pen from my desk drawer and tried to do the same. It wasn't easy.

The owner of the car repair shop where Zoot and I had been taken by Buchalter had turned out to be an alcoholic right-wing simpleton who had already fled the state on a bigamy charge. It seemed that anyone who might lead us to Buchalter had a way of disappearing or going off-planet.

Tommy Bobalouba's mother had emigrated from Germany and perhaps had been a member of the Silver Shirts. Tommy wanted to salvage the Nazi U-boat before Hippo Bimstine got to it, and his rhetoric was often anti-

Semitic. But in reality Tommy had never had any ideology except making money. He prided himself on his military record and blue-collar patriotism, and didn't seem to have any physical connection with Buchalter.

Why did Buchalter (if indeed it was Buchalter) attempt to ascribe the murder of his followers, the men called Freddy and Hatch, to the vigilante?

Was he involved with the ritualistic killings of black dope dealers in the projects? If not, how many psychological mutants of his potential did New Orleans contain?

Why had Lonighan crossed an old New Orleans ethnic line and gotten mixed up with the Calucci brothers, and did it have anything to do with the vigilante killings?

If you have ever been in psychoanalysis or analytically oriented therapy, you're aware that the exploration of one's own unconscious can be an intriguing pursuit. It is also self-inflating, grandiose, and endless, and often has the same practical value as meditating upon one's genitalia.

The inductive and deductive processes of police work offer the same temptation. You can drown in it. The truth is that most people, with the exception of the psychotic, commit crimes for predictable reasons.

Question: Why steal?

Answer: It's usually easier than working.

Question: Why rape and brutalize? Why rob people of their identity by terrorizing and degrading them at gunpoint, by reducing them to pitiful creatures who will never respect themselves again?

Answer: You don't have to admit that you're a born loser and in all probability were despised inside your mother's womb.

Batist's perception, like Clete's, was not obscured by self-manufactured complexities. He had grown up in Louisiana during the pre-Civil Rights era, and he knew that no one systematically killed people of color for reasons of justice. The vigilante's victims were people whom no one cared about, nickel-and-dime dealers whose presence or absence would never have any appreciable influence on the immense volume of the New Orleans drug trade.

The vigilante, like the plainclothes detective in the motel who was determined to emotionally twist and break Albert on the rack, was selective about his sacrificial offerings, and his purpose had nothing to do with ending the problem they were associated with.

But the preacher had said something on the dirt road by my house that would not go away, that hung on the edge of my consciousness like an impacted tooth that throbs dully in your sleep.

What if, instead of a particular crime, we were dealing with people, or forces, who wished to engineer a situation that would allow political criminality, despotism masked as law and order, to become a way of life?

Was it that hard to envision? The elements to pull it off seemed readily at hand.

Financial insecurity. Lack of faith in traditional government and institutions. Fear and suspicion of minorities, irritability and guilt at the visibility of the homeless and the mentally ill who wandered the streets of every city in the nation, the brooding, angry sense that things were pulling apart at the center, that armed and sadistic gangs could hunt down, rape, brutally beat, and kill the innocent at will. Or, more easily put, the general feeling that it was time to create examples, to wink at the Constitution, and perhaps once again to decorate the streetlamps and trees with strange fruit.

Hitler had to set fire to the Reichstag and place the blame on a Communist student in order to gain power.

The sight of Los Angeles burning, of motorists being torn apart with tire irons on live television, might serve just as well.

I was out of the office three hours that afternoon on a shooting in a black juke joint south of town. The wounded man, who was shot in the thumb, refused to identify the shooter, walked out of the emergency room at Iberia General without being treated, then drove out in the parish with a kerosene-soaked rag wrapped around his hand and tried to run down his common-law wife's brother in the middle of a sugarcane field. The brother refused to press charges. Bottom line: big waste of time.

It rained that afternoon, then the sun came out again and the air was bright and cool and the palm and oak trees along the street had a green-gold cast to them. Just as I was signing out of the office at five, Wally, the dispatcher, whose great bulk made his breath wheeze even when he was seated, looked up from a message that he was writing on a piece of memo paper.

'Oh hi, Dave. I didn't know you were still here,' he said. 'The monsignor called from the bishop's office in Lafayette. His message was—' He squinted at his own handwriting. 'Yes, he knows Sister Guilbeaux and he wants to know is she in any kind of trouble.'

'Did he say anything else?'

'No, not really. He seemed to wonder why the sheriff's office is interested in a nun. What's going on? A big bingo raid coming down?' His round face beamed at his own humor.

'You're up at the hospital sometimes. Did you ever see a nun there with reddish gold hair, about thirty or thirty-five years old?'

'I don't place her. What's the deal, the nuns been rapping the patients on the knuckles?' He smiled again.

'How about giving it a break, Wally?'

Then Wally raised himself from his chair, just far enough to stick his head out the dispatcher's window and look both ways down the hall. His face was ruddy from hypertension, and his shirt pocket bulged with fat, cellophane-wrapped cigars.

'Can I tell you something serious, Dave?' he said. 'All that stuff going on over in New Orleans, leave it alone. It's blacks killing blacks. Ain't we got enough problems here? Let them people clean up their own shit.'

'Thanks for taking the message, Wally.'

'Hey, don't walk out of here mad. People round here care about you, Dave. This Nazi guy been causing all this grief, he gets caught in the right situation, it's gonna get squared, you'd better believe it, yeah. You ain't got no doubt about what I mean, either, podna.'

He peeled the cellophane off a cigar, rolled it wetly in the center of his mouth, and scratched a kitchen match across the bottom of his desk drawer.

That night I couldn't sleep. At one-thirty in the morning I heard the *tink* of a tin can on the baling wire I had strung around the house. I took the AR-15 with the thirty-round magazine from the top of the closet, slid a shell into the chamber, and walked outside with it. It was windy in the trees, and the sky was full of moonlight. There was nobody in the yard or down by the bait shop. Tripod had gotten out of his hutch and was digging in an armadillo's hole by the tractor shed. I picked him up in my arms, refilled his food and water bowls, and put him back inside his hutch. Then I sat down on an upended bucket, under the darkness of an oak tree, the AR-15 propped against the trunk, and waited ten minutes to make sure that the noise I had heard earlier had been caused by Tripod.

The moonlight was the color of pewter on the dead cypress in the marsh. My neighbor had been burning the sugarcane stubble in the field behind my house, and the air was hazy with smoke and dense with a smell like burnt cinnamon. In the quietness of the moment, in the wind that blew through the leaves overhead, in the ruffling of the moonlight on the bayou's surface, and in the perfect black silhouette of my cypress and oak house against the handkerchiefs of flame that twisted and flickered out of the scorched dirt in my neighbor's field, I felt almost as if I had stepped into a discarded film negative from my childhood, in another time, another era.

In the wind I thought I could hear the fiddle and accordion music and the words to 'La Jolie Blonde.' For some reason I remembered a scene clipped out of the year 1945. It was V-J Day, and my parents had taken me with them to a blue-collar bar with a colonnade and a high sidewalk in front and big, green-painted, collapsible shutters that folded flush with the walls. My mother wore a plum-colored pillbox hat with a white veil pinned up on top, and a purple sundress printed with green and red flowers. My father, Aldous, had just been paid, and he was buying beers for the bar and dancing with my mother, while the jukebox played:

Jolie blonde, gardez donc c'est t'as fait.
Ta m'as quit-té pour t'en aller,
Pour t'en aller avec un autre que moi.

The doors on the bar were all open to let in the cool air after the rain, and the evening shadows and the sun's afterglow had the soft purple-and-gold tone of sugarcane right before the harvest. The streets were filled with people, some of them in uniform, some of them a little drunk, all of them happy because the lights were about to go on again all over the world.

Then my mother picked me up and balanced me on her hip while my father grinned and set his battered fedora on my head. My mother smelled like milk and bath powder, like the mint leaves and bourbon-scented cherries from the bottom of her whiskey glass. It was a happy time, one that I was sure would never end.

But both my parents were dead and so was the world in which I had grown up.

Then another image floated behind my eyes, a fearful and perhaps solipsistic projection of what it might be like if the Will Buchalters of the world were ever allowed to have their way. In my mind's eye I saw a city like New Orleans at nighttime, an avenue like St. Charles, except, as in the paintings of Bavarian villages by Adolf Hitler, there were no people. The sky was a black ink wash, the mosshung oaks along the sidewalks as motionless as stone; the houses had become prisons that radiated fear, and the empty streets were lighted with the obscene hues of sodium lamps that allowed no shadows or places to hide. It was a place where the glands had replaced the heart and the booted and head-shaved lout had been made caretaker of the sun.

The next morning I called the bishop's office again. This time I was told the bishop had gone to Washington and the monsignor was in Opelousas and would not be back until that afternoon. I left my number.

At noon I got a phone call from Tommy Bobalouba.

'I'll treat you to some étouffée,' he said.

'I'm working right now.'

'I drove all the way over here to talk. How about getting your nose out of the air for a little while?'

'The last time you were over here, you set me up as your alibi while somebody tried to clip Nate Baxter.'

'So you lost money? It don't mean I don't respect you.'

'What do you want?'

'I want to *talk*. I got a heavy fucking problem, man. It's something I can't talk to nobody else about. You don't got thirty minutes, then fuck you, Dave.'

'Where are you?' I said.

I drove up to the seafood restaurant on the back road to St. Martinville and found him inside, seated on a tall stool at the bar, eating raw oysters from a tray. He had covered each oyster with Tabasco sauce, and sweat was trickling out of his meringue hair. I recognized three of his crew at one of the tables, dour-faced Irish hoods with the mental capabilities of curb buttons, who had always run saloons or upstairs crap games for Tommy or shut down the competition when it tried to establish itself in areas Tommy had staked out for himself.

But Tommy had never used bodyguards and, always desirous of social acceptance by New Orleans's upper classes, did not associate openly with his employees.

'What are you looking at?' he said.

'Your crew seem to be enjoying their meal,' I said.

'I can't bring my boys to your town for a lunch?'

'What's up, partner?'

'I got some personal trouble.' He wiped his mouth with his hand and looked at it.

I waited.

He looked around, closed and opened his eyes, his face flexing like rubber, then stared disjointedly out into space. Then he tried to smile, all in seconds.

'Hey, Dave, you went to Catholic school, you boxed in Golden Gloves,' he said. 'You ever have a mick priest for a coach, guy who'd have all the fighters say a Hail Mary in the dressing room, then tell them to get out there and nail the other guys in the mush?'

'It sounds familiar, Tommy.'

'It was good coming up like that, wasn't it? Them was good days back then.'

'They weren't bad. Are you going to tell me what's on your mind?'

'I tried to get out of this prostate operation. The doc said it might leave me wearing a diaper. So we tried other stuff. Three days ago the doc tells me it's spread. Like a big worm eating its way through my insides. I ain't got to worry about an operation anymore. You understand what I'm saying? It's a funny feeling. It's like you're looking at a clock somebody just snapped the hands off.'

Then I saw it in his face, the grayness and the pinched quality around the mouth, the remoteness in the eyes, the knowledge that he had entered a piece of psychological moonscape on which there was no traveling companion.

'I'm sorry, Tommy,' I said.

He used a folded paper napkin to blot the perspiration around his hairline. He glanced through the big plate glass window at the back of the restaurant. Outside was a small, dark lake, and dead leaves were falling into the water.

'You still go to Mass?' he said.

'Yes.'

'I mean, for real, not just to make your old lady happy or something like that?'

'What can I do for you?'

'Look, if a guy maybe knows about something, maybe about even some people being clipped, people maybe even that's got it coming, but he don't do it himself, like it's out of his hands, you know what I mean, then it ain't on his soul, right?'

I tried to assimilate what he had said, but that was like trying to make ethical or theological sense out of Sanskrit read backwards.

'You want to float that one by me again?' I said.

'Look, I took out one guy in my life, I mean besides Korea. That was the guy I did with the fire hose. This guy was such a bum even the judge said he ought to be dug up again and electrocuted. I don't go around killing people, Dave. But what if I knew what was going on, maybe like there was other people doing it, and I figure it's their choice, I don't make people do what they got to do, I just hold on to my ass and walk through the smoke, it's a rough fucking town to keep a piece of, the hair ends up on the wallpaper, that's the way it shakes out sometimes, right?'

'I'm a police officer, Tommy. Maybe you'd better give some thought to what you're telling me.'

'I'm standing on third base here. You gonna come to the bone yard to arrest me? What if I made a contribution to the church? Maybe you know a priest don't go through everything with a garden rake. It ain't easy for me to figure all this stuff out, talk about it with people I don't know. I get a headache.'

His knuckles and eyebrows were half-mooned with scar tissue; his blue eyes had a bright sheen like silk. What do you say to an uneducated, confused, superstitious, angry man, with a frightened child inside him, as he tries to plea-bargain his sins and cop to a fine before he catches the bus?

'I can introduce you to a priest, a friend of mine,' I said. 'Just tell him what you told me. I wouldn't get into the area of contributions at that point, though.'

'What? It sound like bribery?'

'You might say that.'

'Oh.'

'Tommy, do you know something about the vigilante killings? Is that what we're talking about here?'

He wiped at the tip of his nose with one knuckle.

'If that's the case, why not come clean on it, get it out of the way?' I said.

His eyes bulged, and he poked me in the chest with his stiffened finger.

'Hey, I don't dime, I don't rat-fuck, you saying I do, Dave, you and me are about to remodel this place.'

'Adios,' I said.

'Hey, don't be like that,' he said, and grabbed my coat. Then he released it and smoothed the cloth with his hand. 'I'm sorry, I got a Coke bottle up my butt. I don't know how to act sometimes. Look, me and the Calucci brothers are quits. They welsh, they lie, they got no class, they'll blindside you and take you off at the neck. You do business with shit bags and greaseballs, you invite a load of grief into your life.

'I can't change what's already happened, I mean, maybe some stuff I'm part responsible for, but maybe I can make up for it a little bit. Your buddy Purcel ... Hey, I got your attention.'

'What about him?'

'He filled up Max and Bobo's Caddy with cement while about a hundred people were laughing and clapping and grabbing themselves. Even the cops were making jokes about it over their radios.'

'What are you saying, partner?'

'You know how many guys in New Orleans would like to take Purcel down? How many guys he's sent up the road or run through glass windows or stuck their heads in toilet bowls? It's an open contract, fifteen large, Dave, he's anybody's fuck. That ain't all, either. There's a ten large bonus if it's in pieces. You know, with Polaroids or a videocassette.'

He squeezed a lemon slice on an oyster, then lifted the shell and sucked the muscle into his mouth. But instead of swallowing it, he lowered his head, emptied his mouth into a napkin.

'I can't eat no more. I feel sick,' he said. His eyes wandered to the table where the three men from his crew were eating.

'Maybe in New Orleans you're lucky if you get to die from cancer these days,' he said.

'Is there a contract on you, too, Tommy?'

'You're a lot like Purcel. You think the Caluccis are clowns because you busted them up with a shovel and they didn't try to do anything about it. I got news for you, Dave. These guys eat their pain and wait. One time a button guy from the Cardo family was porking Bobo's broad. They waited three years, till everything was forgotten, till the broad had disappeared, till Bobo had a half dozen other bimbos hanging around him, then they asked the button guy out on their boat. They wined and dined him, made fun about the broad, like they were all great buddies and she was just some pork chops they passed around, then they held a gun to the guy's head and made him cut off his own cock.'

He ran his hand through his hair, wiped the perspiration on his shirt, blew out his breath, and ordered a double Scotch straight up. The corners of his mouth looked as gray as fish scale.

By five that afternoon I still had not heard back from the monsignor in Lafayette. Before signing out of the office, I called again.

'His mother's been quite ill. Can he call you at home, Detective Robicheaux? I know he'll want to,' the secretary said.

'Yes, I'd appreciate it if he would,' I said, and gave her our number.

Bootsie and I had planned to go to a seven o'clock AA step meeting in town, and I had told her not to prepare supper. On the way home I picked up some po'-boy sandwiches and dirty rice at a take-out place by City Park. As I drove down the dirt road along the bayou, smoke was drifting across the sun from a scorched sugarcane field, and the air smelled like burning leaves and late-blooming flowers. It was raining in the south, and you could see a gray squall line, splintered with lightning, moving inland from the gulf. The wind was already up, straightening the moss in the cypress trees out in the marsh, and most of the fishermen who had been out for saca-lait had turned their boats toward the dock.

The deputy who still guarded the house during the day waved at me and headed for town. I parked in the drive and went inside with the paper sack of po'-boys and dirty rice. The windows were all open, and the curtains were billowing with wind.

'Who's home?' I said.

But the house was quiet. I walked into the kitchen and set the sack of sandwiches on the table. Then I saw the empty sherry bottle and three beer cans half buried in a tangle of wet newspapers and coffee grounds in the plastic trash container. I rubbed my hand in my face, then opened the icebox to get a Dr Pepper, changed my mind for no reason, and slammed the door, rattling everything inside.

The phone rang on the counter.

'Detective Robicheaux?'

'Yes.'

'This is Monsignor DeBlanc. I'm sorry I didn't get back to you earlier. You called about Sister Marie?'

'Yes, Marie Guilbeaux.'

'Right. Is something wrong?'

'I'm not sure, really. I'm working a strange case now

285

... Sister Guilbeaux keeps showing up around here at odd times.'

'I'm sorry, I'm confused. What do you mean "showing up"?'

'Just *that*. She seems to take an inordinate interest in things that aren't her affair.'

'You mean she's been in New Iberia recently?'

'Yes.'

'I don't understand. Marie went back home to Napoleonville three months ago. She's had some severe problems with her health.'

I paused a moment. 'What does this lady look like, Monsignor?'

'Good for her age, I guess, but, well, time has its way with all of us.'

'Her age?'

'She's almost seventy years old. How old do you think she is?'

After I hung up I sat at the kitchen table and stared out the back screen at the orange wafer of sun descending into the smoke from the smoldering cane stubble. Why hadn't I seen it? She had been outside the intensive care unit when Clete and I had interviewed Charles Arthur Sitwell, who later was launched into the next world with an injection of water and roach paste. Even Alafair had felt there was something wrong about her, that she was a harbinger of trouble and discord.

I looked again at the empty sherry bottle and cans in the trash. When the bedroom door opened in the hallway I didn't even bother to turn around. There was no point in trying to go to a step meeting tonight. Bootsie's fears and anxieties had obviously sent her into a relapse; maybe tomorrow we'd give it another try. Or maybe I simply had to let go of her for a while, turn her over to my Higher Power, and let her bottom out. How could I demand more of her than had ever been demanded of me? But regardless of what I chose to do, anger would serve no purpose, and would only reinforce her determination to stay drunk.

I smelled the alcohol and the odor of cigarettes even before I felt the warm breath against my cheek, the touch of fingernails in my hair and on my scalp, the soft caress of a woman's breasts against the back of my neck. Then I felt the mouth and tongue in my ear, the tapered hand that slid down my chest toward my loins, and I turned and looked up into the face of the woman who called herself Marie Guilbeaux.

chapter twenty-three

'Tough day when they take the scales from your eyes?' she said. Her hand reached out to touch my hair. I pushed it away.

'Where are Bootsie and Alafair?' I said.

'The wifey's passed out. Doesn't she send your daughter off with the black man when she decides to go on the grog?'

I walked into the hall and opened the bedroom door. Bootsie was asleep, half undressed, on top of the sheets, her face twisted into the pillow. The curtains popped in the silence.

The woman who called herself Marie Guilbeaux stood in the center of the kitchen, putting lipstick on in front of her compact mirror. She wore sun-faded jeans, sandals, a beige terry-cloth pullover with a dipping neckline, and a gold chain with a pearl around her throat.

'Did you know the little wife has something of a pill problem?' she said, her eyes still fastened on the mirror.

'Who are you?'

She crimped her lips together in the mirror and clicked the compact closed.

'Want to find out?' she said. She smiled. Her eyes seemed to darken, like charcoal-colored smoke gathering inside green glass. She unsnapped the top of her jeans, exposing the pink edge of her panties, then reached behind her back and unhooked her bra. 'Sit down in the chair, Dave. It's time someone does something nice for you.'

I dumped her purse on the breakfast table. In it were car keys, an empty aspirin tin, a roll of breath mints, a perfume spray bottle, and a doeskin wallet. In the wallet was over six hundred dollars, and a Social Security card and driver's license with the name Marie Guilbeaux on them. The address on the license was in uptown New Orleans, back toward the levee. There were no credit cards.

'Do you like everything to be so hard?' she said, and moved her tongue in a circle inside her lips.

She worked her bra out from under her pullover and laid it over the chair top, then clasped her hands around the back of my neck and pressed her stomach against me. 'I have a feeling the wifey hasn't been treating you right,' she said.

'Where's your automobile?'

'Down by the dock.'

'Is anyone with you?'

'No.' She flexed her loins against me.

'I'll tell the wrecker service not to scratch it up,' I said, turning her in a half circle.

'What?'

'The guy we contract to haul cars into the pound is careless sometimes.' I pulled her forearms behind her. Her wrists were narrow and pale, and the undersides were lined with thin green veins. I snipped the handcuffs on each wrist, then stuffed her bra in the back pocket of her jeans.

'The offer's still open. With handcuffs. Think about it, Dave. Ouu,' she said, and made a pout with her mouth. 'You might even like it better than climbing on top of a drunk sow.'

'Try it on our jailer, Marie,' I said. 'He's a three-hundred-pound black homosexual. Maybe you can turn him around.'

* * *

289

The next morning at the department I picked up a cup of coffee and a doughnut by the dispatcher's cage and called Clete at his office in the Quarter. The sun was shining, and there was dew on the grass and trees outside my window. I had called him twice the day before and hadn't gotten an answer.

'The tape on my machine's screwed up. What's happening?' he said.

I told him about my conversation in the restaurant with Tommy Lonighan.

'You sound mad,' he said.

'I am.'

'What's the big deal?'

'I warned you about provoking these guys.'

'Look, Dave, what's "open hit" actually mean? Nothing. It's something these greasebags like to mouth off about while they're stuffing linguine in their faces. A real whack is when they bring in a mechanic, a mainline button man, a full-time sociopath, from Miami or Houston, and this guy *knows* he either leaves meat on the sidewalk or he's the next guy for the cooling board.'

'Clete—'

'Drop it, mon. Max and Bobo are always blowing gas. It's time they both get their snouts stuck in the commode.'

'I just don't believe you. Why don't you go stand in the middle of the streetcar tracks?'

'Okay, big mon, you've warned me. Listen, has Motley called you yet?'

'No.'

'Dig this. Ole Mots stopped thinking about food and cooze and being black long enough to do some real detective work.'

'I think Motley's turned out to be a good guy.'

'That's what I was saying. Is there static on the line or something? Yesterday afternoon he got some chest waders from the fire department, and he and I splashed out into that swamp in Lafourche Parish. It took a while, but we found it.'

'Found what?'

'The armored vest. The guy who cut open the two lowlifes with the chain saw, we found where he got out of the water on a levee not far from Larose. There were depressions in the mud that Sasquatch could have left. Anyway, about two hundred yards back into the swamp he'd dumped the vest by a sandbar. There were a half-dozen pieces of buckshot in the plates.'

'Why would he be wearing a vest?'

He laughed, then took the receiver away from his mouth and laughed again.

'You want to let me in on it?' I asked.

'You're beautiful, Streak. There's a secret that everybody seems to know except my old podjo from the First. You're one of the most violent people I've ever known. Why do you think Buchalter would wear a vest? You've probably got him spotting his Jockeys.'

'Thanks for going out there, Clete.'

'Hold on a minute. There's something else. Maybe it's important, maybe not. There was some stenciling on the cloth. The vest was Toronto PD issue.'

'It's Canadian?'

'Maybe he got it at a surplus store. But it's a thread, right? Anyway, talk with Motley.'

'You remember the nun we saw at the hospital?'

'Yes, she need somebody to pound erasers for her?'

'Not unless you want to visit her in the parish jail.'

Then I told him about all the events involving the woman who called herself Marie Guilbeaux.

'Definitely a weird scam, mon,' he said.

'I'll bet she and Buchalter have their umbilical cords tied together.'

'What are you holding her on?'

'Not much.'

'Don't let them kick her. Give me the address that's on her driver's license.'

I read it to him off the arrest report.

'Salt the shaft if you have to. You know why everybody loves straight shooters? Because they usually lose,' he said.

'See you later, Cletus,' I said, and hung up the phone just as the sheriff tapped on my glass and motioned me toward his office at the other end of the hallway.

He drank from his bottle of ulcer medicine, then leaned back in his swivel chair, bouncing the heels of his hands on the padded arms, and gazed at the potted plants and hand-painted flowered tea-pot on his windowsill. His stomach wedged over his hand-tooled gunbelt like a partly deflated football. He poked at it with his stiffened fingers.

'You never had ulcers, did you?' he said.

'No.'

'I think I'm getting another one. I eat grits and baby food and get up in the morning with barbed wire in my stomach. Why's that?'

'You got me.'

'What are we supposed to do with that gal you locked up last night?'

'We try to keep her there till we find out who she is.'

'She's got no arrest record. Also the charge you've got against her is a joke.'

'Not to me it isn't.'

'At arraignment, what do we tell the judge?'

'The truth.'

'How's this sound? "Your Honor, this lady represented herself as a Catholic nun in order to get the wife of Detective Robicheaux drunk. Because everybody knows that's what nuns do in their spare time."'

I opened and closed my right hand on my thigh. I fixed my gaze on a place about three inches to the side of his face.

'I apologize, I shouldn't have said that,' he said. 'But at best all we've got is a misdemeanor.'

'I think she murdered Charles Sitwell in the hospital.'

'Put her there, in the hospital, in the room, in her nun's veil, around the time of death and we have something. Look, the driver's license and Social Security card are real. She says she never told you or your wife or anybody else she was a nun.'

'You talked to her?'

'I went to the jail early this morning. The jailer's got her in isolation. A couple of the dykes were getting stoked up.'

'They like her?'

'Are you kidding? They were scared shitless. One of them claims your gal threatened to put out a cigarette in her eye.'

'Look, Sheriff, there's no easier ID to get than a driver's license and Social Security. But she had no credit cards. That's because credit bureaus run a check on the applicants. She's dirty, I think she's mixed up with Buchalter, and if we let her walk, we lose the only thread we have.'

'I admit, she puts on quite a performance. If I didn't know better, I'd probably let her baby-sit my grandchildren.'

'What explanation did she give you for being in my house?'

'She says she used to be a part-time librarian and now she's trying to become a freelance magazine writer. According to her, she met Bootsie in a lounge and befriended her because she thought she was a sad lady. She's pretty eloquent, Dave.'

He looked at my face and glanced away.

'Librarian where?' I said.

'She got a little vague.'

'I bet.'

He propped his elbow on the desk blotter and

scratched at the hollow of his cheek with a pink fingernail.

'She's got a lawyer from Lafayette. He's already raising hell down at the prosecutor's office,' he said.

'You want to talk to Clete Purcel? He saw her outside Sitwell's hospital room.'

'Great witness, Dave. Purcel's got a rap sheet that few mainline cons have. It looks like something a computer virus printed by mistake.'

'I think he was right.'

'About what?'

'He told me to salt the shaft. He knew how it was going to go down.'

The sheriff stuck his pipe in his leather tobacco pouch and began filling the bowl. He didn't look up.

'I didn't hear you say that,' he said.

'It's one man's point of view.'

He didn't answer. I got up to leave the room.

'The Americans won the Revolution because they learned to fight from the Indians,' he said. 'They shot from behind the trees. I guess it sure beat marching across a field in white bandoliers and silver breastplates.'

'I was never fond of allegory.'

'All I said was I didn't hear Purcel's remark. The woman's purse is in Possessions. Who knows what the lab might find?' He raised his eyebrows.

'We've got to hold her as a murder suspect, Sheriff.'

'It's not going to happen, Dave. You going to the arraignment?'

'You'd better believe it.'

He nodded silently, lit his pipe, and looked out the window.

Back inside my office, I looked again at all the paperwork concerning Will Buchalter. What were the common denominators? What had I missed?

Buchalter was perverse and sadistic and possibly an addict.

He was obviously a psychopath.

His followers were recidivists.

He appeared to be con-wise, talked about 'riding the beef,' but had no criminal record that we could find.

Was he a sodomist, was he depraved, were his followers all addicts? Were they men whom he had turned out (raped) and reduced to a form of psychological slavery? Why not? It went on in every prison in the country.

Except Buchalter had never been up the road.

Maybe Clete had come up with the answer. Maybe we had been looking for Buchalter on the wrong side of the equation. Maybe he was a fireman who set fires. Maybe he was one of us.

I talked with Ben Motley at NOPD. The prints lifted from the armored vest that he and Clete had found in the marsh matched those that Buchalter had left all over my house. But there was no serial number on the fabric.

'I wouldn't spend too much time on it,' he said. 'These paramilitary groups come up with shitloads of this stuff. You know what's still the best way to nail this guy? Find one of his lowlifes, then plug his pud into a light socket.'

Thanks, Mots, I thought.

Then I put in a call to the robbery division of the Toronto Police Department and talked with a lieutenant named Rankin. No, he knew nothing about a stolen armored vest. No, he had no knowledge whether or not the department might have sold off some of its vests; no, he had never heard of a Will Buchalter and, after leaving me on hold for five minutes, he said their computer had no record of a Will Buchalter.

'This man's a Nazi?' he said.

'Among other things.'

'What do you mean?'

'He likes to torture people.'

He cleared his throat.

'About eight or nine years ago I remember a case ... no, it wasn't a case, really, it was a bad series of events that happened with a detective named Mervain. We had a recruit who bothered Mervain for some reason. He couldn't get this fellow out of his mind. It seems like the fellow was suspected of stealing some guns from us, who knows, maybe it was some vests, too.'

'What was the recruit's name?'

'I'm sorry, I don't remember everything that happened and I don't want to say the wrong thing and mislead you. Let me check with a couple of other people here and call you back.'

'I'd appreciate it very much, sir.'

Arraignment for the nun impersonator was at 11:00 A.M., and my best throw of the dice kept coming back boxcars, deuces, and treys. Clete called collect from a pay phone in Metairie.

'Dead end,' he said. 'Her address is in an apartment building that a wrecking ball went through six months ago.'

'Did you ask around the neighborhood about her?'

'I'm in a phone booth in front of a liquor store that has bullet holes in the windows. There's garbage all over the sidewalk. As I speak I'm looking at a collection of pukes who are looking back at me like I'm an albino ape. Guess what color these pukes are? Guess what color the whole neighborhood is.'

Judge Robert Dautrieve presided over morning court, that strange, ritualistic theater that features morose and repentant drunks who reek of jailhouse funk, welfare cheats, deranged drifters, game poachers, and wife abusers whose frightened wives, with blackened eyes, dragging strings of children, plead for their husbands' release. Almost all of them are on a first-name basis with the bailiffs, jail escorts, bondsmen, prosecutors, and court-assigned attorneys and social workers, who will remain the most important people they'll ever meet. And no matter what occurs on a particular day in morning court, almost all of them will be back.

Judge Dautrieve had silver hair and the profile of a Roman legionnaire. During World War II he had been a recipient of the Congressional Medal of Honor for his valor at Sword Beach, and he had also been a Democratic candidate for governor who had lost miserably, largely due to the fact that he was an honorable man.

The woman who called herself Marie Guilbeaux filed into court on the long wrist chain with the other defendants from the parish jail. Her clothes were rumpled and her face white and puffy from lack of sleep. On the back of her beige pullover was a damp, brown stain, as though she had leaned against a wall where someone had spit tobacco juice. When the jail escort unlocked her wrist from the chain, she straightened her shoulders, tilted her chin up, and brushed her reddish gold hair back over her forehead with her fingers. Her face became a study in composure and serenity, as if it had been transformed inside a movie camera's lens.

I sat three feet behind her, staring at the back of her neck. She turned slowly, as though she could feel my eyes on her skin.

'Tell Buchalter we've got his vest,' I said.

But she looked past me toward the rear of the courtroom, as though she had never visited one before, her gaze innocuous, bemused, perhaps a bit fearful of her plight. To any outside observer, it was obvious that this lady did not belong on a wrist chain, or in a jail, or in a morning court that processed miscreants whose ongoing culpability and failure were as visible on their persons as sackcloth and ashes.

Her lawyer had once been with the U.S. Justice Department. He now represented drug dealers and a PCB incinerator group. His bald head was razor-shaved and waxed, and he had humps of muscle in his shoulders and upper arms like a professional wrestler. His collar and tie always rode high up on his thick neck, which gave him a Humpty-Dumpty appearance.

'Tell Buchalter his prints were all over the vest,' I said

to the nun impersonator's back. 'That means he's going down on premeditated double homicide. Nasty stuff, Marie. Lethal injection, the big sleep, that kind of thing.'

She looked straight ahead, her face cool, almost regal, but her lawyer, who was talking to another man at the defense table, glanced up, then walked over to where I sat, his eyes locked on mine.

'What is it that makes you think legal procedure has no application to you?' he said. His body seemed to exude physical power and the clean athletic-club smells of deodorant and aftershave lotion.

'I was just asking your client to pass on a message to one of her associates,' I said. 'He cut open two guys with a chain saw. These were his friends. He's quite a guy.'

'You're harassing this woman, Detective. You're not going to get away with it, either.'

'It's always reassuring to know you're on the other side, Counselor.'

'You, sir, belong in a cage,' he said.

For thirty minutes I watched the judge go through the process of trying to heal cancer with Mercurochrome, his face sometimes paling, his eyes glazing over when a stressed-out defendant would launch into an incoherent soliloquy intended to turn his role into that of victim.

I went out for a drink of water, then took a seat not far from the prosecutor's table. Five minutes before the nun impersonator had to enter her plea, the prosecutor looked at me impatiently, then gathered up a file folder and walked back to where I sat. He was a rail of a man, with a tic in his gray face, who made his daily nest in the high-tension wires. He kept tapping the file folder on my knee.

'This isn't shit. What the hell have y'all been doing?' he said.

'Her address is phony. Does that help?'

'It's shit and you know it. You guys spend your time fucking your fist, then blame us when they walk.'

'How about kicking it down a couple of notches, Newt?'

'You want my job? You tell us we've got the bride of Dracula in the parish jail, but I'm supposed to walk in here with nothing but my dork in my hand. Dautrieve's not in the mood for it, believe me.'

'She had an empty aspirin tin in her purse. I sent it to the lab this morning. Maybe there's a residue that indicates she was in possession.'

'An empty aspirin container? That's the kind of evidence I'm supposed to work with here? Do you live in a plastic bubble?'

'She's hooked up with Nazis. I'd bet my butt on it, Newt.'

'I've got news for you. You are. She's talking about suit. She said you tried to get in her bread when you busted her. That was a smart touch, sticking her bra in her back pocket, Dave. She's also talking about deprivation of civil rights, slander, and sexual assault while in the bag. How's that sound? And in two minutes I get to stand up in front of the court and get buggered by that greasy shit hog she hired. Y'all really fill out my day.'

'Don't let her get out of here, partner.'

'Break my chops.'

Judge Dautrieve was fixing his glasses on his nose and trying to keep the ennui out of his face by the time the woman who called herself Marie Guilbeaux stood before him, her lawyer by her side. He listened attentively to the prosecutor, one finger propped against a silver eyebrow. Then his eyes went from the prosecutor to me and back to the woman.

'This isn't April Fools' Day, is it, gentlemen?' he said.

'Your Honor, we believe this lady to be a serious flight risk,' the prosecutor said. 'She has no ties to the community, we believe she's using an alias, and the address on her driver's license has proved to be a fraudulent one. She's also a potential suspect in a homicide case. We request maximum bail.'

'Your Honor, my client claims she was sexually molested by Detective Robicheaux,' the woman's lawyer said. 'She was humiliated, put in a holding unit with lesbians who tried to assault her, then verbally harassed by Detective Robicheaux in this very courtroom. There's nothing to substantiate the charge against her, except the word of Detective Robicheaux, who himself may face criminal charges.'

The judge suppressed a sigh, took off his glasses, and beckoned with both hands. When no one moved, he said, 'Approach, approach, approach. It's late, gentlemen. The Three Penny Opera here needs to conclude. That means you too, Detective Robicheaux.'

The two attorneys and I stood close to the bench. Judge Dautrieve leaned forward on his forearms and let his eyes rove over our faces.

'Would any of y'all care to explain what we're doing?' he said. 'Is this part of a Hollywood movie? Do I need a membership in the Screen Actors Guild? *What* homicide are you talking about, sir?'

'The ex-convict who was murdered at Iberia General, Your Honor,' the prosecutor said. 'He was part of a neo-Nazi group of some kind. The woman was seen at the hospital in a nun's veil, close by the man's room.'

'Seen by whom? When?' the judge said.

'Detective Robicheaux and others.'

'I don't see the *others*. You didn't answer all my questions, either. Seen when? At the time of death?'

'We're not sure.'

'Not sure? Wonderful,' the judge said.

'That has nothing to do with the charge against her now, anyway,' the defense attorney said.

'It means she has every reason not to come back here,' the prosecutor said.

Then the judge looked me evenly in the eyes.

'What motive would this lady have in coming to your house and telling you she's a nun, when, in fact, she's not?' he said.

'I believe she wanted to do my wife injury, Your Honor,' I said.

'In what fashion?'

I cleared my throat, then pulled at my collar.

'Sir?' he said.

'She's tried to encourage my wife to drink excessively, Your Honor.'

'That's a rather unique statement,' he said. 'To be honest, I don't think I've ever heard anything quite like it. You're telling me the presence of a nun somehow has led your wife into problems with alcohol?'

'I think humor at the expense of others is beneath the court's dignity, Your Honor,' I said.

I saw the prosecutor's eyes light with anger.

'You're badly mistaken if you think I see humor in any of this, Detective. Step back, all of you,' the judge said. When he folded his hands, his knuckles looked like white dimes. 'I don't like my courtroom used as a theater. I don't like sloppy presentations, I don't like sloppy investigative work, I don't like police officers and prosecutors trying to obtain a special consideration or privilege from the court at the defendant's expense. I hope my meaning is clear. Bail is set at three hundred dollars.'

He flicked his gavel down on a small oak block.

On the way out of the courtroom the prosecutor caught my arm.

'Don't give it a second thought, Dave. I always enjoy calling a witness who makes me look like I've got my ass on upside down. Why didn't you flip Dautrieve's tie in his face while you were at it?' he said.

I followed the woman and her attorney out to the attorney's maroon Lincoln. The day was bright and clear, and leaves were bouncing across the freshly mowed lawn.

'Don't talk to him,' the attorney said, opening his door.

'It's all right. We're old pals, really. He and I share a lot of family secrets. About the wifey and that sort of thing,' she said. She put on a pair of black sunglasses and began tying a flowered bandanna around her hair.

'You share a big common denominator with most scam artists, Marie. You're cunning but you're not smart,' I said.

'Oh, hurt me deep inside, Dave,' she said, and pursed her lips at me.

'You didn't understand what I told you in there. Buchalter is going to be charged with murdering two of his own people. Bad PR when you're leading a cause. Even his lamebrain followers read newspapers.'

She hooked her purse on her wrist, then placed her hand on her hip.

'I've got a problem. My tractor don't get no traction. Can you give me a few minutes, baby-pie?' she said.

'Marie, don't spend any more time on this man,' her attorney said.

'How about it, Dave?' she said. 'It won't hurt your relationship with the sow. I think I remember somebody cranking a whole bunch of electricity into your batteries. Wouldn't you like a little sport fuck on the side?'

I opened her car door and fitted my hand tightly around her upper arm. Her skin whitened around the edges of my fingers. Pieces of torn color floated behind my eyes, like the tongues of orange flame you see inside the smoke of an oil fire, and I heard whirring sounds in my ears, like wind blowing hard inside a conch shell. I saw the top of the attorney's body across the car's rooftop, saw his Humpty-Dumpty head and wide tie and high collar, saw his mouth opening and a fearful light breaking in his eyes.

'There's no problem, Counselor. I just want to make sure y'all don't accuse us of a lack of courtesy in Iberia Parish,' I said, and sat the woman down hard in the passenger seat. Her sunglasses fell off her nose into her lap. 'Happy motoring, Marie. It's a grand day. Stay the fuck away from my house. Next time down, it's under a black flag.'

chapter twenty-four

Late that afternoon Lieutenant Rankin of the Toronto Police Department called back and told me everything he had learned from others and the case record about the death of a robbery detective named James Mervain.

'This is what it comes down to,' he said. 'Mervain was one of those fellows whose life seemed to be going out of control – booze, a brutality charge, a wife in the sack with another cop, some suspicions that maybe he was gay – so when he got a little shrill, people dismissed what he had to say. You with me?'

'Yes.'

'He'd been working with a recruit named Kuhn or Koontz. Maybe he knew the guy off the job, too, through some kind of gay connection ...'

'I don't understand, you're not sure of the name?'

'That's what's strange. A couple of cops around here still remember this recruit, and they're sure the name was Kuhn or Koontz, but the name's not in the computer. Maybe it got wiped out, I don't know. Anyway, Mervain started telling people that Kuhn, or whatever his name was, had some problems; in particular, he liked to hurt people. But if that was true, he never did it on the job. Which made everybody think Mervain had a secret life, out there in the gay bars somewhere, and he had some kind of personal or sexual grievance with this fellow.

'Then some rather serious weapons were stolen from a

departmental arms locker – ten-gauge pumps, stun guns, three-fifty-sevens, nine-millimeter automatics, armor-piercing ammunition, stuff like that. Mervain maintained Kuhn was behind it. Actually, a custodian was arrested for it, but he died before he went to trial. This is about the time Kuhn disappeared, at least as far as anyone remembers.

'Then Mervain seemed to go crazy. He got arrested for drunk driving, he got beat up in a bar, he'd come to work so hungover nobody could talk to him till noon without getting their heads snapped off. He put his name on mailing lists of a half dozen hate groups, then he'd bring all this Nazi literature to the office and try to convince people Kuhn was part of an international conspiracy to bring back the Third Reich. The department sent him to a psychologist, but he just became more obsessed.

'Then one Monday he didn't come in to work. His ex-wife had no idea where he was, his apartment was empty, and some kids had stripped his car. Two weeks later the owner of a skid-row hotel called us. Maggots were crawling out from under the door crack in one of the rooms. Our people had to break open the door with a sledge. Mervain had nailed boards across the jamb. How much do you want in the way of detail?'

'Go ahead,' I said.

'The detective who did the investigation is still with the department. He says he never had a case like it before or since. Mervain hung himself, naked, upside down by the ankles with piano wire, then put a German Luger into his eye socket and let it off.'

'You're telling me y'all put this down as a suicide?'

'Forensics showed there's no question he fired the gun. The door was nailed shut. The window was locked from the inside. Both his personal and professional life were a disaster. How would you put it down?'

I tapped a paper clip on my desk blotter.

'Look, it bothered other people at the time, but there

was no indication that anyone else could have been in that room,' he said.

'What do you mean *bothered*?'

'The room was full of Nazi and hate literature. The walls and floors were papered with it. But all his clothes, except what he'd been wearing, were gone. So were his billfold and the notebook that he always carried.'

'Does anyone remember what this man Kuhn looked like?'

'Two cops used the same words – "a big blond guy."'

'I'm going to fax y'all a composite. Would you send me everything you have on the Mervain case?'

'Sure. Look, there's one other thing. A couple of days after the death was ruled a suicide, the desk clerk called and said Mervain's coat was on the back of a chair in the lobby. He wanted to know what he should do with it.'

'Yes?'

'There was a napkin from a gay bar in one of the pockets. Mervain had written a note on it. Somebody stuck it in the case folder. I'll read it to you. "Schwert ... Schwert ... Schwert ... His name is Schwert. I have become his fool and slave. I know he's out there now, flying in the howling storm. No one believes, I see no hope." Sounds kind of sad, doesn't it? You have any idea what it might mean?'

'What was Mervain's educational background?'

'Let's see ... Bachelor's in liberal arts, a master's degree in administration of justice. Why?'

'I'm not sure.'

'Maybe we blew this one.'

'It's a big club. Thanks for your time, sir.'

Early the next morning I drove to New Orleans and, after going to the bail bonds office that fronted points for the Caluccis, I found Max at his mother's in an old residential neighborhood off Canal, not far from Mandina's restaurant. The house was late Victorian, with a wide gallery, a fresh coat of gray and white paint, and rose-bushes blooming all over the lawn.

The family was celebrating the birthday of a little boy and eating lunch on redwood picnic tables in the backyard. Balloons were tied to the trees and lawn furniture, and the tables were covered with platters of pasta and cream pastry, bowls of red sausage, beaded pitchers of lemonade and iced tea. Max Calucci sat in the midst of it all, in undershirt and slacks, the pads of hair on his brown shoulders as fine as a monkey's.

I had to hand it to him. His expression never changed when he saw me at the garden gate. He cut pieces of cake and handed them to the children, continued to tell a story in Italian to a fat woman in black and an elderly man on a thin walking cane, then excused himself, rubbed a little boy on the head, and walked toward me with a glass of lemonade in his hand.

'You got business with me?' he asked.

'If you've got business with Clete Purcel, I do.'

'He can't talk for himself?'

'You better hope he doesn't, Max.'

'Is this more hard guy stuff? You got your shovel with you?'

'Nope.'

His eyes were as black and liquid as wet paint.

'You got some kind of deal you want to cut? That why you're here?' he said.

'Maybe.'

He drank from his lemonade, his eyes never leaving mine. Then he pushed opened the short iron gate with his foot.

'It's a nice day, a special occasion. I got no bad feelings on a nice day like this. Eat a piece of cake,' he said.

'We can talk out here.'

'What, you too good to sit down at my nephew's birthday party?' he said.

I ate a custard-filled éclair in a sunny spot by the garden wall. The air was dry and warm, and the breeze blew through the banana trees along the wall and ruffled the water in an aboveground swimming pool. The guests around the tables were his relatives and family friends – working-class people who owned small grocery stores and cafés, carried hod, belonged to the plumbers' union, made the stations of the cross each Friday in Lent, ate and drank at every meal as though it were a pagan celebration, married once, and wore widow black with the commitment of nuns.

Max combed his hair back over his bald pate at the table, cleaned the comb with his fingers, then stuck the stub of a filter-tipped cigar in his mouth and motioned me toward a gazebo on the far side of the yard. The latticework was covered with purple trumpet vine; inside, the glass-topped table and white-painted iron chairs were deep in shadow, cold to the touch.

Max lit his cigar and let the smoke trail out of his mouth. His shoulders were brown and oily-looking against the white straps of his undershirt.

'Say it,' he said.

'I hear you and Bobo put out an open contract on Clete.'

'You get that from Lonighan?'

'Who cares where it came from?'

'Lonighan's a welsher and a bum.'

I leaned forward and rubbed my hands together.

'I'm worried about my friend, Max.'

'You should. He's got a radioactive brain or something.'

'I'm not here to defend what he does. I just want you guys to take the hit off him.'

'He's the victim? Have you seen my fucking car? It ain't a car no more. It's a block of concrete.'

'Come on, Max. You guys started it when you leaned on his girlfriend.'

'That's all past history. She paid the loan, she paid the back vig. All sins forgiven.'

'Here's the deal. You and Bobo tried to take out Nate

Baxter. I think you probably did this without consent of the Commission. What if some reliable information ends up in their hands about a couple of guys in New Orleans trying to cowboy a police administrator?'

'That's what you got to work my crank with?' he said.

'Yeah, I guess so.'

'Then you got jack shit.'

'What's going to make you happy, Max?'

He smiled. I felt my pulse swelling in my throat; I rubbed the top of my knuckles with my palm. I kept my eyes flat and looked at the curtain of trumpet vine that puffed in the breeze.

'I want the two hundred large Tommy Lonighan owes me and Bobo,' he said. 'That fucking mick is gonna die and take the debt to the grave. You twist him right, we get our money, then I don't have no memory about troubles with Clete Purcel.'

'Big order, Max.'

'You know anything easy? Like they say, life's a bitch, then you get to be dead for a long time.'

The ash from his cigar blew on my slacks. I brushed it off, then put on my sunglasses and looked out into the sunlight.

'What, you sentimental about Lonighan or something?' he said.

'No.'

'That's good. Because he's been jobbing you. Him and Hippo Bimstine, both.'

'Oh?'

'That's a surprise? People like you rip me up, Robicheaux. You think Jews are martyrs, the Irish are fun guys singing "Rosie O'Grady" on the corner, and Italians are colostomy bags. Tell me I'm wrong.'

'You were going to say something about Tommy Blue Eyes?'

'Yeah, he got his fat mick mush full of booze and was laughing about how you trust Hippo Bimstine and think he's big shit because he's got all these liberal causes.'

'I see.'

'You see? I don't think you see shit. Lonighan says Hippo stole some stuff out of the public library about that Nazi sub so you wouldn't find out what's inside it.'

'No kidding?'

'*Yeah*, no fucking kidding.'

I leaned forward and picked at the calluses on my palm. The breeze was drowsy with the smell of chrysanthemums and dead birthday candles.

'You and I have something in common,' I said.

'I don't think so.'

'I went down on a murder beef once. Did you know that?'

'I'm supposed to be impressed?'

'Here's the trade, Max. Take the contract off Clete and I stay out of your life.'

'You ain't in my life.'

'Here's the rest of it.'

'I ain't interested,' he said. 'I tell you what. It's my nephew's birthday, you came out to my mother's house and showed respect, you didn't act like the drunk fuck everybody says you are. That means I'm letting all this stuff slide, and that includes what you done to me out at Lonighan's place. So you can tell dick-brain the score's even, he's getting a free pass he don't deserve, I got businesses to run and I don't have time for this shit. Are we clear on this now?'

'I hope you're a man of your word, Max.'

'Fuck you and get outta here.'

When I opened the gate and let myself out, I noticed a tangle of ornamental iron roses tack-welded in the center of the pikes. The cluster was uneven where one rose had been snapped loose from its base. I rubbed the ball of my thumb over the sharp edges of the broken stem and looked back at Max. His eyes had never left me. He rotated an unlit cigar in the center of his mouth.

The AA meeting is held on the second floor of a brick

church that was used as a field hospital for Confederate wounded in 1863, then later as a horse stable by General Banks's Union cavalry. Outside, the streets are wet and cool and empty, the storefronts shuttered under the wood colonnades, the trees still dripping with rain against a sky that looks like a red-tinged ink wash.

It's a fifth step meeting, one in which people talk about stepping across a line and admitting to God, themselves, and another person the exact nature of their wrongs. For many, it's not an easy moment.

Some of them are still zoned out, their eyes glazed with residual fear; those sent by the court try to hide the resentment and boredom in their faces; others seem to have the exuberance and confidence of airplane wing walkers.

Bootsie sits next to me, her hands folded tightly in her lap. She showered after supper and put on makeup and a new yellow dress, but in her cheeks are pale discolorations, like slivers of ice, and there's a thin sheen of perspiration at her temples.

'You don't have to say anything. Just listen,' I whisper to her.

They start to unload. Some of it seems silly – overdue library books, cavalier attitudes toward bills – then it turns serious and you feel embarrassed and voyeuristic; you find your eyes dropping to the floor, and you try not to be affected by the level of pain in the speaker's voice.

The details sometimes make the soul wince; then you remember some of the things you did, or tried to do, or could have done, while drunk and you realize that what you hear in this room differs only in degree from the moral and psychological insanity that characterized your own life.

Only one speaker makes use of euphemism. That's because he's told his story before and he knows that not everyone in the room will be able to handle it. He was eighteen years old, ripped on reefer and pills, when he pushed a blindfolded VC suspect out the door of a Huey at five hundred feet; he so impressed the ARVN and American officer onboard that they had him do it twice more the same afternoon.

Bootsie's eyes are filled with hidden thoughts. I slide my hand down her forearm and take her palm in mine. Her eyes move to the doorway and the darkened stairway at the front of the room. Her breath catches in her throat.

'What is it?' I ask.

Her eyes close, then open, like a doll's.

'A man at the door. Dave, I think—'

'What?'

'It was *him*.'

I get up from the folding chair and walk across the oak floor to the front of the room. I step through the open door, walk down the darkened stairway. The door to the street is open, and rain is blowing out of the trees onto the lawn. The violet air smells of wet stone and burning leaves.

I go back upstairs, and Bootsie looks at me anxiously. I shake my head.

Before the meeting ends, it's obvious she wants to speak. She raises her chin, her lips part. But the moment passes, and she lowers her eyes to her lap.

Later the room is empty. I turn out the lights and prepare to lock up. In the hallway downstairs she puts her arms around me and presses her face into my chest. I can feel her back shaking under my hands. A loose garbage can lid is bouncing down the street in the darkness.

'I feel so ashamed,' she says. Her face is wet against my shirt.

I went in to work early and looked at the notes I had taken during my conversation with the lieutenant at the Toronto Police Department.

It was time to try something different. On my yellow legal pad I made a list of aliases that Will Buchalter might have used. As a rule, the aliases used by a particular individual retain similarities in terms of initials or sound and phonetic value, or perhaps even cultural or ethnic identification, in all probability because most career criminals have a libidinal fascination with themselves.

I tried W. B. Kuhn, William Coon, Will Kuntz, Bill Koontz, then a dozen other combinations, making use of the same first and last names, in the same way that you would wheel pari-mutuel numbers in trying to hit a quiniela or a perfecta at the racetrack.

But more than a name it was a literary allusion written by the dead Canadian detective on the barroom napkin that gave me a brooding sense I almost did not want to confirm.

I began writing out the word *Schwert* with the combinations of first names and initials that I had already listed. The sheriff walked into my office with a cup of coffee in his hand and looked over my shoulder.

'That looks like alphabet soup,' he said. 'You going to run that through the NCIC?'

'Yeah, I want to go through the feds in New Orleans, too.'

'It can't hurt.' He gazed through the window at a black trusty in jailhouse issue sawing a yellowed palm frond from the tree trunk.

'You don't sound enthusiastic,' I said.

'I've got bad news. The tail we put on your girlfriend … She went through the front door of a supermarket in Lafayette, then out the back and *poof* … Gone.'

'Who was the tail?'

'Expidee Chatlin.'

I pressed my fingers into my temples.

'I didn't have anybody else available,' the sheriff said. 'I don't think it would have come out any different, anyway, Dave. Your gal's mighty slick.'

'I'd really appreciate your not calling her *my* gal or girlfriend.'

'Any way you cut it, she's one smart broad and she

took us over the hurdles. That's just the way it plays out sometimes.'

'Too often.'

'Sir?'

I tried to concentrate on my legal pad.

'You and Bootsie have had a bad time. I don't think you should blame others for it, though,' he said.

'That wasn't my intention, Sheriff.' I could hear his leather gunbelt creak. I wrote the words *William B. Schwert* on the pad. He started to walk out of the room, then stopped.

'What've you got there, exactly?' he said.

'A Toronto cop wrote something on a napkin before he was found hanging by his ankles with a nine-millimeter round through his eye.' I glanced back at my notes. '"I know he's out there now, flying in the howling storm."'

'So?'

'It's from a poem by William Blake. It's about evil. As I remember it, it goes "O Rose, thou art sick.

The invisible worm
That flies in the night
In the howling storm

Has found out thy bed
Of crimson joy,
And his dark secret love
Does thy life destroy."'

'No, you misunderstood me, Dave. I was looking at the name you just wrote down there ... Schwert. You never took any German at school?'

'No.'

'It means "sword," podna.'

He drank from his coffee cup and tapped me lightly on the shoulder with the flat of his fist.

But before I would get anything back from the FBI or the National Crime Information Center in Washington,

D.C., Clete Purcel would write a new chapter in the history of the New Orleans mob and outdo even Clete Purcel.

chapter twenty-five

Clete had been eating breakfast in Igor's on St. Charles, his porkpie hat tipped down over one eye, when two of Max Calucci's bodyguards came in and sat at the table next to him. They were in a good mood, expansive, joking with the waitress, relaxed in Clete's presence. One of them accidentally knocked his chair into Clete's.

'Sorry, Purcel. Don't be getting the wrong signal. It ain't that kind of day,' he said.

Clete chewed his food and looked back at the men silently.

'I'm saying we got the word, okay?' the man said. He grinned.

Clete wiped his mouth with his napkin.

'There's some kind of comedy act here I don't know about?' he said.

'Cool your ovaries down. You want to join us? Your breakfast is on me.'

'I'll eat at that table after it gets scrubbed down with peroxide.'

'Suit yourself. It's a beautiful day. Why fuck a beautiful day?'

'Yeah, it was.'

The two men laughed and looked at their menus. Clete set his knife and fork down on his plate and put a matchstick in the corner of his mouth.

'Are we working on new rules here?' he said.

'Give it a break, Clete. You want some tickets to the LSU–Ole Miss game? Look, we're glad to hear it's over, that's all,' the second man said.

Clete removed the matchstick from his mouth and studied it.

'Who gave you permission to call me by my first name, and what's this stuff about something being over?' he said.

'Sorry we bothered you, Purcel,' the first man said. 'Robicheaux don't want to tell you he did a sit-down, that's between you and him. Hey, somebody got my fat ass out of the skillet, I'd count my blessings.'

The following is my best re-creation of the events, as described by Ben Motley and Lucinda Bergeron, that happened later out by Lake Pontchartrain.

Clete parked his convertible two blocks from Max Calucci's home, then took a cab to a construction site one mile away, on Robert E. Lee Boulevard, where the Caluccis supplied all the heavy equipment to the builder. He leaned against the trunk of a palm tree across the street, sucking on a think stick of peppermint candy, enjoying the morning, inhaling the breeze off the lake.

Then he casually strolled across the boulevard, the peppermint stick pointed upward like an erection, and hot-wired an enormous earthmover. It was outfitted with a steel blade that could strip baked hardpan down to bedrock, a great, saw-toothed bucket that could break and scoop up asphalt highway like peanut brittle, and huge balloon tires with studded welts for scouring trenches through piles of crushed stone and angle iron.

Before anyone realized what was happening, Clete had wheeled around the corner into the midday traffic and was hammering full throttle down the boulevard toward Max's house, diesel smoke flattening in a dirty plume from the stack.

The gateman at Max's was the first to see, or hear, the earthmover thundering down the quiet, oak-shaded residential street. Then, inside the steel-mesh protective cage, he recognized the powder blue porkpie hat, the round, pink face with the gray scar through one eyebrow like a strip of inner tube patch, and the massive shoulders that seemed about to split the seams on the Hawaiian shirt.

By this time the gateman was grabbing at the telephone box inset in the brick pillar by the edge of the driveway. But it was too late; Clete lowered the saw-toothed bucket, swung the earthmover into the drive, and blew the gates off their hinges.

No one at the house – the Vietnamese gardeners, three of Max's hired gumballs, a couple of coked-out dancers suntanning topless by the pool – could believe what was happening. Clete, bent low, like an ape, over the controls, headed across the lawn, grinding through flower beds, the patio furniture by the pool, crashing through a corner of the gazebo, splintering a birdbath into ceramic shards, raking off sprinkler heads, shredding garden hoses into chopped rubber bands.

He made a wide circle of lawn destruction and came to a halt twenty yards from the columned portico at the front of the house, the cap on the stack bubbling quietly. He lowered the bucket to clear his field of vision, sighted on the front entrance, raised the bucket into position again, shifted down, and gave it the gas.

The bucket exploded a hole the size of a garage door through the front wall. Then Clete backed off, gunning the engine, crunching over the crushed cinder blocks and plaster, got a good running start, and plunged into the house's interior.

He made U-turns, shifted from reverse to first, backed through walls and wet bars and bathrooms, ripped water pipes and drain lines out of the floors, and ground washing machines, television sets, and microwaves into sparking piles of electrical junk. He seemed to pause for a moment, perhaps to get his bearings, then he crashed through Max's mirror-walled bedroom, dropped the grader blade into position, and raked the eighteenth-century tester and oak floors through the French doors onto a domed sunporch, where he swung the bucket in a wide arc and sent cascades of glass onto the lawn.

By this time the gumballs and the topless suntanners were racing for the street. Clete bounced out onto the backyard, strips of fabric flying from the stack and the driver's cage like medieval streamers. He lit a cigarette with his Zippo, fitted his porkpie hat down on his brow, then demolished the garages and the garden shed, dropped the bucket squarely on top of a new Chrysler, ripped a long slice out of the greenhouse, and plowed trenches bristling with severed pink roots where hedges had been.

The Romans at Carthage couldn't have done a more thorough job.

Then he got down from the machine and strolled across the flattened fence at the back of the property toward his automobile, his hands in his pockets, gazing at the white chop out on the lake. Geysers of water from broken pipes in the yard were fountaining in the sunlight, glistening on the grass, blowing in the cool air like an unloosed rainbow.

After I heard from both Ben Motley and Lucinda Bergeron, I got an unexpected call.

'What do you want, Nate?' I said.

'Guess.'

'You got me.'

'You'd better tell that crazy sonofabitch to come in.'

'Tell him yourself.'

'Great suggestion. Except when we showed up at his apartment with a warrant last night, he climbed out the window and went across the rooftops. You're mixed up in this, Robicheaux. Don't pretend you're not.'

'I'm not.'

'You know how I can always tell when a drunk is lying? His lips are moving.'

'What else can I do for you this morning?'

'Tell that fat fuck you call a friend that he comes in or

he gets no guarantees out on the street. You got my drift?'

'This must bother you, Nate.'

'What?' he said.

'Turning on your own people, taking it on your knees from the mob, doing grunt work for Max Calucci after he tried to have you whacked out.'

I could hear him breathing in the receiver, could almost smell the heat and nicotine coming through the perforations.

'Listen to me very carefully,' he said. 'The insurance adjuster estimates that Fuckhead did around a half million dollars' damage to that house. State Farm is not the Mafia, Robicheaux. They're corporate citizens, and they get seriously pissed and make lots of trouble when they have to pay out five hundred thousand large because a lunatic thinks he can wipe his shit on the furniture.'

'I'll pass on your remarks. Thanks for calling.'

'You never listen, do you? If I learn you have contact with Purcel and you don't report it, I'm charging you with aiding and abetting and being an accomplice after the fact.'

'Your problem isn't with me or Clete, Nate. When you took juice from the wise guys, you mortgaged your butt all the way to the grave,' I said, and hung up.

I went to the rest room and rinsed my face. I let the water run a long time. I even rinsed my ear where I had held the telephone receiver. Then I cupped a handful of water on the back of my neck and dried my skin with a handful of paper towels.

'You run the four-minute mile or something?' another detective said.

'That's right,' I said, and looked at him in the mirror.

'Who kicked on *your* burner?' he said.

Ten minutes later, my phone rang again.

'The wrong kind of people are looking for you,' I said. Through the receiver I could hear seagulls squeaking in the background.

'You heard about it?' Clete said.

'What do you think?'

'It'll cool down. It always does.'

'Baxter's got no bottom. He'll take you out, Clete.'

'You shouldn't try to cut deals with the greasebags on behalf of your old podjo.'

'Do you have a death wish? Is that the problem?'

'You want to go fishing? If the wind drops, I'm going after some specs in a couple of hours.'

'Fishing?'

'Yeah.'

I propped my forehead on my fingers and stared into space.

'You need any money?' I said.

'Not right now.'

'Why'd you do it, Clete? Baxter says the insurance company wants to hang you out to dry.'

'Who cares? They shouldn't do business with a bucket of shit like Max Calucci. You've had your shield too long, Streak. You're starting to think like an administrator.'

'What's that mean?'

'You think you or Motley or Lucinda Bergeron were ever going to get a search warrant on Max and Bobo? With Nate Baxter on their pad?'

'You were tossing the place with an earthmover?'

'So it was a little heavy-handed. But dig this. Just before I gutted Max's den, I emptied everything out of his desk into a garbage bag. I also took his Rolodex and all the videocassettes off the shelves. One of these videos is a documentary about this primitive Indian tribe down in South America. Before the missionaries got to them, these guys were known as the worst human beings on earth. They shrank heads and sawed people into parts; sometimes they'd boil them alive. They'd even kill their own children.'

'Go on.'

'They'd also cut the hearts out of their victims. What's

320

Max doing with a tape like that? The mob's into anthropology?'

'You've queered it as evidence.'

'Nobody else cares, Dave. Except for you and Motley and Lucinda, everybody in New Orleans is happy these black pukes could find new roles as organ donors. History lesson, big mon. When they talk law and order, they mean Wyatt Earp leaving hair on the walls.'

Across the street, a black kid was flying a blood red kite high against a shimmering blue sky.

chapter twenty-six

The information requests that I had made about a possible suspect named Schwert were answered, at first, in a trickle, in increments, unspecifically, as though we were pursuing a shadow that had cast itself over other cases and files without ever becoming a solid presence.

Then the computer printouts, the faxes, and the phone calls began to increase in volume, from the FBI, the NCIC, the Bureau of Alcohol, Tobacco and Firearms, the Immigration and Naturalization Service, and finally Interpol.

The sheriff looked down at the clutter of paper on my desk.

'Where'd you get your filing system? It looks like Fibber McGee's closet,' he said. He glanced up at my face. 'Sorry, that's one of those generational jokes, I guess.'

'The first time the name William Schwert shows up is in some phone taps the FBI and ATF had on some neo-Nazis in Idaho during the mideighties,' I said. 'Then ATF found it in the pocket of a guy who blew his face off while he was building a bomb in his basement in Portland.'

'Yeah, I think I remember that. He and some other guys were going to dynamite a synagogue?'

'That's right.'

'Schwert was involved?'

'No one's sure.'

The sheriff tilted his head quizzically.

'In a half dozen cases it's like he's standing just on the edge of the picture but he doesn't leave footprints,' I said.

The sheriff sniffed and blew his nose in a Kleenex.

'It doesn't sound like this is helping us a lot,' he said.

'It gets more interesting. The guy named Schwert seems to spend a lot of time overseas. Interpol has been tracking him for fifteen years. Berlin, London, Madrid, any place there're skinheads, Nazis, or Falangists.'

The light in the sheriff's eyes sharpened. He began poking in the papers on my desk.

'Where is it?' he said.

'What?'

'The Interpol jacket. The mug shots.'

'There aren't any. Nobody's nailed him.'

'This isn't taking us anywhere, Dave. It looks like what you've got here is more smoke. We don't even know if Schwert is Buchalter.'

'Interpol says a guy named Willie Schwert broke out of an asylum for the criminally insane in Melbourne, Australia, seventeen years ago. He tore the window bars out of a maximum security unit with his bare hands.'

'Then where's the sheet?'

'The records on the guy are gone. A fire in their computer system or something.'

'What is it, a computer virus wiping out all the information on this character?'

'You're not impressed?' I said.

'I wish I could say I was.'

'It's the same guy.'

'You're probably right. And it does diddle-squat for us. He's still out there, fucking up people in any way he can. I wish Purcel had dropped the hammer on this guy when he had him at close range ... Pardon my sentiment. I'm becoming convinced I'm not emotionally suited for this job.'

'The people who are shouldn't be cops, Sheriff,' I said.

* * *

323

That evening, as Bootsie and I washed the dishes at the sink, the breeze through the screen was dry and warm and the clouds above my neighbor's tree line looked like torn plums in the sun's afterglow. Her hands were chaffed, her knuckles white in the dishwater. For a second time, she began to wash a saucer I had already dried. I took it from her hand and placed it back on the drain rack.

'You want to go to a meeting?' I asked.

'Not tonight.'

'You tired?'

'A little.'

'Do you want to lie down?' I said. I rested my hand on the top of her rump.

'Not really. Maybe I'll just read.' Her eyes focused on a solitary mockingbird that stood in the middle of the picnic table.

I nodded.

'I don't seem to have any energy,' she said. 'I don't know what it is.'

'Long day,' I said, and dried my hands and turned away from her.

'Yes,' she said. 'I guess that's it.'

Later, after she and Alafair had gone to bed, I sat in the living room by myself and stared at the television screen. A gelatinous fat man, with the toothy smile of a chipmunk, was denigrating liberals and making fun of feminists and the homeless. His round face was bright with an electric jeer when he broached the subject of environmentalists and animal rights activists. His live audience squealed with delight.

Eighteen million people listened to him daily.

I turned off the set and went into the kitchen. The moon was down, and I could hear the tree limbs outside the window knocking together in the wind. When the phone rang on the counter, I knew who it would be. I almost looked forward to the encounter, like a man who has formed a comfortable intimacy with his bête noire.

His voice was indolent and ropy with saliva when he spoke. In the background I could hear the flat, tinny sound of Bix Beiderbecke's 'In a Mist.'

'I never saw tracks on your arm, Will. Do you shoot up in the thighs?'

'You never know.'

'How'd you get my number?' I said.

'People like to please. Not too much gets denied me, Dave.'

'It sounds like you might have done a good load of China pearl. Not a good sign for a guy who likes control.'

'Why did you do it?'

'What?'

'You spit in my face. When I tried to create a tender moment inside our pain.'

'I guess you're just that kind of guy. Besides that, you're probably insane.'

The phonograph stopped and started over again. Beiderbecke's trumpet rose off the record like sound ringing through crystal. Buchalter swallowed wetly, his mouth close to the receiver.

'It's not too late for us,' he said.

'It is for you, partner. Your threads are unraveling. We've got a make on you from Toronto and Interpol; we know about the asylum you broke out of in Australia. You're about to slide down the big ceramic bowl, Will.'

'You don't understand power. I can caress you in ways that'll make you beg for death. The auto garage was nothing.'

'Get off it, Buchalter. You're a hype. You're one day away any time your connection wants you.'

I heard his throat working again, words forming, then sticking unintelligibly in his mouth. Someone pulled the receiver from his hand.

'The wifey plowed again, Dave?' she said. Her voice was sweaty and hoarse, like a person high on her own glandular energies. 'You should have taken me up on my invitation. It'd give you something to fantasize about.'

'Your boyfriend's tracked shit over two continents, Marie,' I said. 'It looks like you're going to take the bounce with him.'

'Can she have orgasms while she's on the grog?'

'Save the comic book dialogue for after your trial. There's an amateur theatrical group at the women's prison in St. Gabriel. You'll fit right in.'

'I keep having this dream. There's a pump handle in it. It feels hard in my hand, and it has moisture dripping off it. I wake up all hot, thinking of a big dark policeman. I get hot even talking about it. What's my dream mean, Dave?'

'I'll say adios now, Marie. Then I'll unplug the phones. Enjoy the time you have left with Buchalter. I bet he really knows how to capture a lady's heart.'

There was a pause, then I heard a match strike against an abrasive surface, the match head hissing, and her breath exhaling.

'Run the coordinates in the personals of *The Times-Picayune*,' she said. 'If you don't, we reach out and touch someone. No, not the sow or the little girl. Maybe the boogie and her son; maybe your uncontrollable friend, Purcel. Will would love to spend a few hours alone with Mr. Purcel.'

'Be careful what you pray for.'

'You're so clever. And the wifey so sweet. I'm glad you're in the tropics where the sheep don't freeze up.'

I eased the receiver down in the cradle, then unplugged the phone jacks in both the kitchen and living room.

I undressed down to my skivvies and sat on the bed next to Bootsie in the dark. She was sleeping on her stomach, and I ran my hand down the smooth taper of her back and over her rump and bare thighs. Her skin felt hot, almost feverish, but she did not respond to my touch. Outside the window, the trees thrashed and swelled in the dry wind. I lay on top of the sheets and stared upward into the darkness, the backs of my fingers resting against Bootsie's leg, the words of the woman named Marie Guilbeaux like an obscene tongue in my ear.

The next morning I got up early and drove back to New Orleans. I stopped first at the library, or morgue, of *The Times-Picayune*, then drove down St. Charles and found Hippo Bimstine working behind the candy counter at one of his drugstores in the Garden District. He wore a starched gray apron over his white shirt and tie and rotund stomach, and his hair was oiled and combed as tight as wire, his thick neck talcumed, his face cheerful and bright.

Hippo had the confident and jolly appearance of a man who could charm a snake into a lawn mower.

'Another nice day,' he said.

'It sure is,' I said.

'So why the dark look? You dump some money at the track?' His smile was inquisitive and full of play.

'I guess I get down when I find out a friend has tried to blindside me.'

'What are you talking here?' He tried to look me steadily in the eyes.

'Max Calucci's been saying peculiar things about you, Hippo.'

'Consider the source.'

'I am. He's got no reason to lie. He says Tommy Lonighan told him you removed some stuff about the Nazi U-boat from the public library.'

'I'm under arrest for library theft?'

'Buchalter and his buttwipes used up my sense of humor, partner.'

'We're talking in hieroglyphics here. You're mystifying me, Dave.'

'I found a nineteen fifty-six *States-Item* story on Jon Matthew Buchalter's death in the files at *The Times-Picayune*. When *The States-Item* folded, all its records were kept by *The Picayune*. But I was careless and missed the story the first time around. I have a feeling it's the one you took from the public library.'

'So you tripped over some big revelation from a rag of thirty-five years ago?'

'Not really. Jon Buchalter was raving on his deathbed about a large gold swastika on board a downed U-boat. Is that the secret you've been keeping from me?'

He considered for a moment and scratched at his neck with one finger. 'Yeah, that's about it. You satisfied?'

'No.'

'It's supposed to weigh forty-two pounds. It's got a gold wreath around it, and the wreath is set with jewels. Big fucking deal, huh?'

'You were willing to let me get involved with Nazis so you could salvage the gold in a World War II wreck?'

'You got some kind of malfunction with your thought processes, Dave. You keep forgetting it was you tried to squeeze every spendolie you could from a finder's fee.'

'I don't let my friends hang their butts in the breeze for money, either, Hippo.' I picked up a roll of mints from the counter and set a half-dollar down on the glass. 'Thanks for your time. See you around.'

I turned to go. Outside, the streetcar rattled down the neutral ground in the sunshine.

'You righteous cocksucker,' he said behind me. A woman with a magazine cupped in her hand replaced it on the rack and walked away.

'Excuse me?' I said.

'When you guys got nothing to support your own argument against a Jew, you always take your shot about money. It takes a while, but you always get to it.'

'You set me up, Hippo.'

'Fuck you I did.' He came around the edge of the counter. He touched his finger against my breastbone. 'You want the rest of the story? The gold in that swastika was pried out of the mouths of Polish Jews. It was a gift from Heinrich Himmler himself. You know what else's supposed to be in that sub? Hitler's plan for the United States. I don't let any man talk down to me because I'm a Jew, Dave. I don't want you in my store.'

'I'll try my best to stay out of your life.'

He went back behind the counter and began knocking open rolls of change and shaking them into the cash drawer. Then he stopped and slammed the drawer shut with the flat of his pudgy hand. I walked outside, my face burning, the eyes of a half dozen people fastened upon me.

Lucinda Bergeron was sanding the wood steps on the back of her house. The air was sunny and warm, and her hair looked damp and full with the heat from her body and her work. She wore flip-flops and a denim shirt that hung over her pink shorts, and blades of grass stuck to the tops of her feet. She kept glancing up at me while she sanded. The tiny gold chain and cross around her neck were haloed with perspiration against her black skin.

'You go back on duty tomorrow?' I said.

'That's right. All sins forgiven.'

'How do you feel?'

'You know, one foot in front of the other, a day at a time, all that jazz.'

I brushed off a step where she had already sanded and sat down. She wiped her eyes on her sleeve and wrapped a fresh piece of sandpaper around a block of wood. She made a circle with her thumb and forefinger and smoothed the paper against the grain.

'I want you to be careful, Lucinda.'

'Worry about yourself, hotshot.'

'It's a mistake to be cavalier about Buchalter, or Schwert, or whatever his name is. There's nothing predictable about this guy or the woman working with him.'

She raised her eyes to mine while her arm and hand kept a steady motion against the step. 'I can't tell you how much I'd love the opportunity,' she said.

'When you're forced to ... to pop a cap in the line of duty, something happens to you, at least if you're not a sociopath yourself. The next time it goes down, you get sweaty, you hesitate, you doubt your motivations. It's a dangerous moment.'

'You think I'll freeze up?'

'You tell me.'

'I don't have doubts about the man who hurt my child, believe me.'

'When are you going to quit calling Zoot a child?'

'When I feel like it, Mr. Smart-ass.' She smiled, then worked the nozzle loose from the hose, turned on the faucet, and drank, with her body bent over, the backs of her thighs tight against her shorts, the water arching bright across her mouth. She wet a paper towel and wiped her face and neck and dropped it into a paper sack filled with garden cuttings.

'I have some tea made. Come inside,' she said.

The porcelain and yellow plastic surfaces of her kitchen gleamed in the sunlight through the windows, and the sills rang with red and blue dime-store vases. I sat at the breakfast table and watched her twist a handful of ice cubes in a towel and batter them on a chopping board with a rolling pin, then fill two tall glasses with the crushed ice and mint leaves and tea. The straps of her bra made a hard line across the wash-faded thinness of her denim shirt.

She turned toward me with the drink glasses in each hand. Her eyes looked at mine, and her expression sombered. She sat down across from me and folded her hands.

'I think you're a good person, Dave. That means some things aren't your style,' she said.

'I look like I have a clandestine agenda?'

'I've lived single for a long time. You recognize certain things in people. Even without being told.'

'I don't know if that's too complimentary.'

'Purcel was here yesterday.'

'There's a warrant on him.'

'I'm still suspended. I should worry about a warrant on Clete Purcel?'

'Why was he here?'

'He says one of the Caluccis' greasers will testify Nate Baxter's on a pad. He told me about your trouble at home.'

'Maybe some people should stay out of my private life.'

'Oh, that's perfect. Your closest friends shouldn't worry about you or try to help you?'

I felt my lips crimp together. I looked away from her unrelenting stare.

I stood up and took my seersucker coat off the back of the chair.

'Give me a call if Buchalter shows up,' I said, and walked toward the front door.

She followed me. The sun made slats of light on her face, causing her to squint as she looked up at me.

'Don't leave like this,' she said.

I took a breath. Her hair was scintillated with silver threads and curved thickly on her cheeks.

'What am I supposed to say, Lucinda?'

'Nothing. You're a good man. Good men don't need to say anything.'

The door was wide open so that nothing she did was hidden from view. She put her arms around my neck and bent my face to hers, raising herself on the balls of her feet, her knees pinching together, her thighs flexing and pressing against me unavoidably; then she kissed me on the cheeks, the bridge of the nose, the eyes, and finally once, a light adieu, on the mouth, as her hands came loose from my neck and my face felt as though it were covered with hot red dimes.

chapter twenty-seven

The chorus that condemns violence is multitudinous and unrelenting. Who can disagree with the sentiment? I think we're after the wrong enemy, though. It's cruelty, particularly when it's mindless and visited upon the defenseless, that has always bothered me most about human failure. But my viewpoint isn't exceptional. Anyone in law enforcement, social work, or psychiatric rehab of any kind carries with him or her a mental notebook whose pages never dim with the years.

Sometimes in the middle of the night I remember cases, or simply incidents, of twenty years ago that come aborning again like sins which elude remission, except either the guilt is collective in nature or the deed such a pitiful and naked admission of our tribal ignorance and inhumanity that the mere recognition of it leads to self-loathing.

Stephen Crane once suggested that few people are nouns; instead, most of us are adverbs, modifying a long and weary sequence of events in which the clearly defined culprit, with black heart and demonic intent, seldom makes himself available for the headsman.

I remember: a cop in the Lafayette police station laughing about how a friend rubbed his penis all over a black woman's body; a black street gang who videotaped their beating of a retarded Pakistani so they could show their friends their handiwork; an infant burned all over his body, even between his toes, with lighted cigarettes; a prosperous middle-class couple who forced the husband's parents to eat dog food; high school kids who held a drunk against a barroom picture window, then punched him through the glass; women and children sodomized, a coed shot through the face in Audubon Park (after she had surrendered her money), animals set on fire, a wounded cop flipped over on his back by his assailant, who then put a pillow under his head and slit his throat with a string knife.

I sincerely believe that we're attracted to films about the Mafia because the violence and evil portrayed in them seems to have an explanation and a beginning and an end. It's confined to one group of people, who in their fictional portrayal even have tragic proportions, and we're made to believe the problem is not endemic to the species.

But I think the reality is otherwise.

A random act of cruelty opened a door in the case I probably would not have gone through by myself.

It had started to sprinkle when I stopped at Igor's on St. Charles for a po'-boy sandwich and to call Bootsie and tell her I was headed home.

'Call Ben Motley, Dave. He's left two messages,' she said.

'What's he want?'

'Something about Tommy Lonighan.'

'How you doing?'

'Fine.'

'You want to go out to eat tonight?'

'Sure. What's the occasion?' she said.

'Nothing special.'

'Is anything wrong?'

'No, why do you think that?'

'Because you always suggest going out to dinner when you feel guilty about something.'

'Not me.' I looked out at the rain striking against the half-opened windows of the streetcar.

'I'm sorry about last night,' she said.

'See you later, kiddo.'

'Hang on to your butt in the Big Sleazy.'

That's more like it, Boots, I thought.

I called Motley at headquarters in the Garden District.

'I got a strange story for you, Robicheaux,' he said. 'We've had some fag bashers running around the city. A couple of them are UNO pukes; the others are just ugly and stupid or probably latent queerbait themselves. Anyway, they're always on the prowl for fresh meat down in the Quarter. This time they picked up a transvestite on Dauphine and took him to a camp out in St. Charles Parish. I think he blew a couple of them, then they got him stinking drunk, pulled his clothes off, and poured pig shit and chicken feathers all over him. Nice boys, huh?

'Anyway, the transvestite is no ordinary fruit. He looks like Frankenstein in a dress and panty hose. He starts sobering up and realizes this isn't a Crisco party. That's when he starts ripping puke ass, I mean busting slats out of the walls with these guys. The pukes made an instant conversion to law and order and called the sheriff's office.

'Right now Frankenstein's in a holding cell, scared shitless. Guess who he called to bail him out?'

'Lonighan?'

'Right. Then twenty minutes go by, and guess who calls back on the fruit's behalf?'

'I don't know, Ben.'

'A lawyer who works for the Calucci brothers. That's when the St. Charles sheriff called us. Why do the Caluccis want to help a cross-dresser with feathers and pig flop in his hair?'

'Is the guy's name Manuel?'

'Yeah, Manuel Ruiz. The sheriff thinks he's a lobotomy case. He's probably illegal, too.'

'How long has he been in custody?'

'Two hours.'

'I'll get back to you. Thanks, Ben.'

An hour later Manuel Ruiz was still in the holding cell, a narrow, concrete, barred room with a wood bench against one wall and a drain hole and grate in the floor. There were dried yellow stains on the grate and on the cement around the hole. He was barefoot and wore a black skirt with orange flowers on it and a torn peasant blouse with lace around the neck; his hair was matted and stuck together in spikes. His exposed chest looked as hard and flawless in complexion as sanded oak.

'You remember me, Manuel?' I asked.

The eyes were obsidian, elongated, unblinking, lidless, his wide, expressionless mouth lipsticked like a fresh surgical incision.

'I just talked with the prosecutor's office,' I said. 'The boys aren't pressing charges. You can go home with me if you want.'

The skin at the corner of one eye puckered, like tan putty wrinkling.

'Or you can wait for the Caluccis' lawyer to get here. But he left word he's running late.'

'Caluccis no good. No want.' His voice sounded as though it came out of a cave.

'Not a bad idea. The other problem we might have is the INS, Manuel.'

He continued to stare at me, as though I were an anomaly caged by bars and not he, floating just on the edge of memory and recognition.

'Immigration and Naturalization,' I said, and saw the words tick in his eyes. 'Time to get out of town. Hump it on down the road. *¿Vamos a casa?* Tommy's house?'

He hit at a fly with his hand, then looked at me again and nodded.

'I'll be back in a minute,' I said.

I walked back to the jailer's office. The jailer, a crew-cut man with scrolled green tattoos and black hair on his arms, sat behind his desk, reading a hunting magazine.

335

By his elbow, a cigar burned in an ashtray inset in a lacquered armadillo shell.

'He's agreed to leave with me,' I said. 'How about a towel and a bar of soap and some other clothes?'

'He hosed down when he come in.' He looked back at his magazine, then rattled the pages. 'All right. We want everybody tidy when they leave. Hey, Clois! The Mexican's going out! Walk him down to the shower!' He looked back down at his magazine.

'What about the clothes?'

'Will you mail them back?'

'You got it.'

'Clois! Find something for him to wear that don't go with tampons!' He smiled at me.

It was cool and raining harder now as we drove toward New Orleans on old Highway 90. Manuel sat hunched forward, his arm hooked outside the passenger's door, his jailhouse denim shirt wet all the way to the shoulder. We crossed a bridge over a bayou, and the wind swirled the rain inside the cab.

'How about rolling up the window?' I said.

'Don't want smell bad in truck,' he said.

'You're fine. There's no problem there. Roll up the window please.'

He cranked the glass shut and stared through the front window at the trees that sped by us on the road's edge and the approaching gray silhouette of the Huey Long Bridge.

'Do you do some work for the Calucci brothers, Manuel?' I said.

'*Trabajo por* Tommy.'

'Yeah, I know you work for Tommy. But why do Max and Bobo want to get you out of jail, partner?'

His jug head remained motionless, but I saw his eyes flick sideways at me.

'Max and Bobo don't help people unless they get something out of it,' I said.

He picked up the paper sack that held his soiled clothes and clutched it in his lap.

'Where you from, Manuel?'

His face was dour with fatigue and caution.

'I'm not trying to trap you,' I said. 'But you're living with bad people. I think you need help with some other problems, too. Those boys who took you out in the marsh are sadists. Do you understand what I'm saying to you?'

But if he did, he gave no indication.

I shifted the truck into second and began the ascent onto the massive steel bridge that spanned the Mississippi. Down below, the water's surface was dimpled with thousands of rain rings, and the willow and gum trees on the bank were deep green and flattening in the wind off the gulf.

'Look, Manuel, Tommy Lonighan's got some serious stuff on his conscience. I think it's got to do with dope dealers and the vigilante killings in the projects. Am I wrong?'

Manuel's hands closed on the sack in his lap as though he were squeezing the breath out of a live animal.

'You want to tell me about it?' I said.

'¿Quién es usted?'

'My name's Dave Robicheaux. The man you saw at Tommy's house.'

'No. Where work? Who are?'

'I live in New Iberia. I'd like to help you. That's on the square. Do you understand me?'

'I go to jail because of boys?'

'Forget those guys. They're pukes. Nobody cares about them.'

'No jail?'

'That's right. What do you know about the vigilante, Manuel?'

He twisted his face away from me and stared out the passenger window, his lips as tight as the stitched mouth on a shrunken head. His leathery, work-worn hands looked like starfish clutched around the sack in his lap.

It was still raining a half hour later when I drove down Tommy Lonighan's drive, past the main house to the cottage where Manuel lived. Steam drifted off the coral-lined goldfish ponds; the door to the greenhouse banged like rifle shots in the wind. I cut the engine. Manuel sat motionless, with his hand resting on the door handle.

'Good luck to you,' I said.

'Why do?'

'Why do what?'

'Why help?'

'I think you're being used.' I took my business card out of my wallet and handed it to him. 'Call that telephone number if you want to talk.'

But it was obvious that he had little comprehension of what the words on the card meant. I slipped my badge holder out of my back pocket and opened it in front of him.

'I'm a police officer,' I said.

His hairline actually receded on his skull, like a rubber mask being stretched against bone; his nostrils whitened and constricted, as though he were inhaling air off a block of ice.

'All cops aren't bad, Manuel. Even those guys at the jail wanted to help you. They could have called Immigration if they had wanted.'

Bad word to use. The top of his left thigh was flexed like iron and trembling against his pants leg. I reached across him and popped the door open.

'Adios,' I said. 'Stay away from the pukes. Stay off Dauphine Street. Okay? Good-bye. *Hasta* whatever.'

I left him standing in the rain, his black hair splayed on his head like running paint, and drove back down the driveway. The gateman, a rain hat pulled down on his eyes, opened up for me. I rolled my window down as I drew abreast of him.

'Where's Tommy?' I said.

'He went out to the St. Charles Parish jail to pick up the Indian. He's gonna be a little pissed when he gets back.'

'It's not Manuel's fault.'

'Tell me about it. I'm working his shift. The guy's a fucking savage, Robicheaux. He eats mushrooms off the lawn, he's got a fucking blowgun in his room.'

Way to go, Robicheaux, I thought. You frighten and confuse a retarded man, then leave him to the care of a headcase like Tommy Lonighan.

'Leave the gate open,' I said.

I made a U-turn in the street and headed back up the drive. I got out of the truck, a newspaper over my head, and walked toward Manuel's cottage. Then I stopped. At the rear of the greenhouse, kneeling in the rain, Manuel was chopping a hole through the roots of a hibiscus bush with a gardener's trowel. When the hole was as deep as his elbow, he dropped the trowel inside and began shoving the mound of wet dirt and torn roots in on top of it. The hibiscus flowers were red and stippled with raindrops, puffing and swelling in the wind like hearts on a green vine.

Ten minutes later I called Ben Motley from a pay phone outside a drugstore. A block away I could see the water whitecapping out on Lake Pontchartrain and, in the distance, the lights glowing like tiny diamonds on the causeway.

'Get a warrant on Tommy Lonighan's place,' I said.

'What for?'

I told him what I had seen and where they should dig.

'The vigilante is some kind of headhunter or cannibal?' he said.

'I don't know, Ben. But if you bust him, don't let the Caluccis or their lawyer bond him out.'

'The poor ignorant fuck.'

Welcome to Shit's Creek, Manuel.

chapter twenty-eight

The word *death* is never abstract. I think of my father high up on the night tower, out on the salt, when the wellhead blew and all the casing came out of the hole, the water and oil and sand geysering upward through the lights just before a spark flew from a metal surface and ignited a flame that melted the steel spars into licorice; I think of his silent form, still in hobnailed boots and hard hat, undulating in the groundswell deep under the gulf, his hand and sightless face beckoning.

Death is the smell that rises green and putrescent from a body bag popped open in a tropical mortuary; the luminescent pustules that cover the skin of VC disinterred from a nighttime bog of mud and excrement when the 105's come in short; the purple mushrooms that grow as thick and knotted as tumors among gum trees, where the boys in butternut brown ran futilely with aching breasts under a rain of airbursts that painted their clothes with torn rose petals.

But there are other kinds of endings that serve equally well for relocating your life into a dead zone where there seems to be neither wind nor sound, certainly not joy, or even, after a while, the capacity to feel.

You learn that the opposite of love is not hate but an attempt at surrogate love, which becomes a feast of poisonous flowers. You learn to make love out of need, in the dark, with the eyes closed, and to justify it to yourself, with a kiss only at the end. You learn that that old human enemy, ennui, can become as tangible and ubiquitous a presence in your life as a series of gray dawns from which the sun never breaks free.

I wasn't going to let it happen.

Bootsie and I met at a dance on Spanish Lake in the summer of '57. It was the summer that Hurricane Audrey killed over five hundred people in Louisiana, but I'll always remember the season for the twilight softness of its evenings, the fish fries on Bayou Teche and crab boils out on Cypremort Point, the purple and pink magic of each sunrise, the four-o'clocks that Bootsie would string in her hair like drops of blood, and the rainy afternoon we lost our virginity together on the cushions in my father's boathouse while the sun's refraction off the water spangled our bodies with brown light.

It was the summer that Jimmy Clanton's 'Just a Dream' played on every jukebox in southern Louisiana. I believed that death happened only to other people, and that the season would never end. But it did, and by my own hand. Even at age nineteen I had learned how to turn whiskey into a weapon that could undo everything good in my life.

'What're you thinking about, bubba?' Bootsie said behind me.

'Oh, just one thing and another.' I stopped cleaning the spinning reel that I had taken apart on top of the picnic table. The air was wet and close, the willows dripping with water along the coulee.

'I called you twice through the window and you didn't hear me.'

'Sorry. What's up?'

'Nothing much. What's up with you?'

I turned around and looked at her. She wore a pair of white shorts and a T-shirt that was too small for her, which exposed her navel and her tapered, brown stomach.

'Isn't anything up with you?' she asked, and rested one

knee on the bench, her arms on my shoulders, and leaned her weight into my back.

'What are you doing?' I said.

'Ummm,' she answered, and her hand moved down my chest.

I reached behind me and held the backs of her thighs and arched my neck and head between her breasts. She widened her legs and drew me tightly against her.

'Let's go inside,' she said, her voice husky and close to my ear.

'Alafair'll be home in a half hour.'

'A half hour will do just fine,' she said.

She drew the curtains in the bedroom, undressed completely, and pulled back the bedspread. Her skin was flushed and hot when I touched her.

'Are you okay, Boots?'

She pressed me down on the pillows and got on top of me, then cupped my sex with both hands and put it inside her. Her mouth opened silently, then her eyes became veiled and unfocused and she propped herself on her arms above me and adjusted her weight so that I was deep inside her, lost now in a place where breath and the heart's blood and the thin sheen of sweat on our bodies all became one. The only sound I could hear was a moist *click* in her throat when she swallowed, and the wind arching a thick, rain-slick oak limb against the window.

She came before I did, her breasts and nipples hard between her stiffened arms, her mouth wide, her hair curled damply on her cheeks. Then I felt it build and crest inside me, my loins dissolving like a hot ember burning through parchment. A sound unlike my own voice rose from my throat, and I pulled her close against me, my face buried in her hair, my mouth pressed like a hungry child's against her ear, while outside mockingbirds lifted clattering into the lavender sky.

I had believed that my will alone could solve the problem in our lives. As I lay beside her on top of the sheets, I realized that, as usual, I was wrong. But at a moment like that, who cares where gifts come from?

At five the next morning Clete Purcel knocked on my back screen. He wore canvas boat shoes without socks, a pair of baggy safari shorts covered with snap-button pockets, his porkpie hat, and a sleeveless purple and gold Mike the Tiger jersey wash-faded to the thinness of cheesecloth. His face was unshaved and bright with fresh sunburn.

'You're not going to dime me, are you, Streak?'

'What do I know about warrants in Orleans Parish?' I stepped outside into the blue coolness of the morning and eased the screen shut behind me. 'Bootsie and Alf are still asleep. Let's walk down to the dock.'

We went down the slope through the deep shadow of the trees, stepping over the trip wire I had strung for Buchalter. Clete kept cracking his knuckles, as though they were big walnut shells. His eyes were red and irritated along the rims, as though he were hungover, but I could smell no alcohol on him.

'You look like you're getting a lot of sun,' I said.

'Why not? Life in the Quarter was turning me into a fat slug, anyway.'

Inside the shop I poured coffee and hot milk for both of us, and we took it out on one of the spool tables by the water. He unsnapped a pocket on his shorts and unfolded a nautical chart on the table.

'Can you show me where that sub is?' His eyes looked at the chart and not at me.

'What are you up to?'

'What do you care?'

'You look wired, Clete. What's wrong?'

'I've got a warrant on me, my business is in the toilet, Nate Baxter's trained shitheads'll probably try to smoke me on sight, and you ask what's wrong?'

I smoothed the chart flat with my palm. The marsh was emerald green after last night's rain, and the cypress knees along the bayous were grained and dark and shining with water from a passing boat's wake.

'Don't get in any deeper,' I said.

'In for a penny, in for a pound. You going to show me where it is or not?' He lit an unfiltered cigarette and flicked the match hard into the air.

I took a mechanical pencil from my shirt pocket and made three marks on the chart.

'These are the places where either I saw it or Hippo's friend pinged it. You can see the pattern. There's probably a trench that bleeds back off the continental shelf. A guy with a depth finder could set up a zigzag pattern and probably locate it. Unless it drops off the shelf and only gets blown back in by a storm.'

He stared down at the chart, his hat cocked over one eye.

'What are you going to do?' I asked.

'Maybe I should remodel it with some C-4.'

'Is the preacher mixed up in this?'

'Not yet. But he was sure beautiful on the radio last night, you know, that call-in show where the geek in the street gets to express his opinion. Brother Oswald is telling people the Beast is about to rise from the sea.' He looked at me and tried to smile. 'Maybe he's talking about my ex.'

'What are you hiding from me, partner?'

He arched his cigarette out on the bayou and watched it hiss in the water and float downstream.

'I've got to quit this. My lungs feel like they've got battery acid in them,' he said.

'What's the gig, Clete?'

'I got to boogie, noble mon,' he said.

'Eat some breakfast.'

'Got to make it happen, Streak. Like you used to say, miles before I sleep and all that stuff. Hang loose.'

'How's Martina?'

He walked toward his convertible without answering, then turned, winked, and gave me the thumbs-up sign.

* * *

Just before noon, Ben Motley called me at the office.

'We got the trowel,' he said.

'Go on ...'

'The blade was clean, but there was dried blood in a crack between the handle and the shaft. The lab says it's human.'

'What else?'

'Two types. One match. With a guy who had his heart taken out against the wall of the St. Louis Cemetery.'

'Why not two matches?'

'You're assuming we've found all the victims.'

'Where's Manuel?'

'In custody ... This one doesn't make me feel too good, Robicheaux. The guy's got strained carrots for brains. The interpreter says he speaks some Indian dialect from down in the fucking Amazon.'

'You think it's too easy?'

'I think maybe we're talking patsy here. Hey, Lonighan's a prick but he was genuinely upset, like in a personal way, when he found out we were charging the kid with murder. Does that sound like Tommy Bobalouba to you?'

Not bad, Mots, I thought.

'Have you had any contact with Clete Purcel?' I said.

'Who?'

'He found a videotape on South American Indians, a documentary of some kind, in Max Calucci's house.'

'There's static on the line. I couldn't hear what you said. You got me? I didn't fucking hear that, Robicheaux.'

'Lonighan borrowed two hundred thou for his casino from the Calucci brothers. I have a feeling he was paying the debt by helping them set up the brown scag trade in the projects.'

'You tell Purcel he tries to put turds in the punch bowl on this one, he won't have to worry about Nate Baxter. I'll send his butt to Angola myself.'

'Rough words, Mots.'

'What you don't understand is Purcel doesn't take a guy down because the guy broke the law. He takes him down because he doesn't like the guy. That's why he'll never carry a shield again.'

'How do you think the case against the Indian is going to stand up?'

'Circumstantial evidence, a retard on the stand, a defense attorney who lets the jury know the retard is a grunt for a rich gangster who actually drowned somebody with a fire hose and got away with it. Take a guess how the jury might vote.'

'Thanks for all the good news.'

'It's not all bad. The word on the street is Lonighan's dying.'

'For some reason that doesn't fill me with joy, partner.'

'Lonighan's mixed up with the Caluccis and the dope trade in the projects. Those black kids we bust all the time, they weren't addicts when they came out of their mamas' womb. Believe it or not, even those dead dealers had families, Robicheaux.'

Why argue with charity? I eased the receiver down in the cradle and stared out the window at the palm trees rattling in the wind. The bottom of the sky looked green over the gulf.

What was Clete Purcel doing?

I went home for lunch. When I came back the sheriff stopped me at the watercooler.

'The FBI just relayed some stuff to us from Interpol. They've got a fix on the woman,' he said.

'What?'

'Read it. It's on your desk. I thought stuff like that only went on in the Barker family.' He walked away and left me staring after him.

The statement from Interpol consisted of four paragraphs. There was nothing statistical or demonstrable about the information in them. As with all the other documents in the case, it was as though the writer were trying to describe an elusive presence that had been mirrored only briefly in the eyes of others.

But the images he used weren't those of the ordinary technical writer; they remained in the memory like splinters under the skin.

Two undercover antiterrorist agents in Berlin believed that the man known as William Buchalter and Willie Schwert and other variations operated inside a half dozen neo-Nazi groups with a half sister named Marie. A skinhead in a beer garden told a story of an initiation into a select inner group known in England and the United States as the Sword. A kidnapped Turkish laborer had knelt trembling on the dirt floor of a potato cellar, his wrists wired behind him, a burlap sack pulled over his face, while the initiates pledged their lives to the new movement. Then the woman named Marie had set the kidnapped man on fire.

I opened and closed my mouth, as though my ears were popping from cabin pressure in an airplane, and continued to read. The details in the last paragraph gave another dimension to the sweaty, hoarse voices that I had heard over the telephone.

The sheriff stood in my doorway with a coffee cup in his hand.

'You think that's our phony nun?' he said.

'Yeah, I do.'

'You believe that stuff at the end of the page?'

'They're perverse people. Why should anything they do be a surprise?'

'Did you know Ma Barker and one of her sons were incestuous? They committed suicide by machine-gunning each other. They were even buried together in the same casket, to keep the tradition intact. That's a fact.'

'Interesting stuff,' I said.

'You've got to have some fun with it or you go crazy. I got to tell you that?'

'No, you're right.'

He walked over and squeezed me on the shoulder. I

could smell his leather gunbelt and pipe tobacco in his clothes.

'You sleeping all right at night?' he said.

'You bet.'

He grunted under his breath.

'That's funny, I don't. Well, maybe we'll drop that pair in their own box. Who knows?' he said.

He walked his fingernails across my desk and went back out the door.

The best lead on Buchalter, the only one, really, was still music.

Brother Oswald Flat, I thought.

I got his telephone number from long-distance information.

'Didn't you say you played with Jimmy Martin and the Sunny Mountain Boys?' I asked.

'What about hit?'

'Did you ever have any connection with jazz or blues musicians?'

'Son, I like you. I really do. But a conversation with you is like trying to teach someone the recipe for ice water.'

'I'm afraid I'm not following you.'

'That's the point. You never do.'

'I'll try to listen carefully, sir, if you can be patient with me.'

'Music's one club. Hit's like belonging to the church. Hit don't matter which room you're in, long as you're in the building. You with me?'

'You know some jazz musicians?'

'I'll have a go at hit from a different angle,' he said. 'I used to record gospel at Sam Phillip's studio in Memphis. You know who else recorded in that same studio? Elvis Presley, Carl Perkins, Johnny Cash, Jerry Lee Lewis, Jimmy Lee Swaggert. You want me to go on?'

'I think Will Buchalter has some kind of involvement with historical jazz or blues. But I don't know what it is.'

The phone was silent.

'Reverend?'

'Why didn't you spit hit out?'

This time I didn't answer. His voice had changed when he spoke again.

'I won't interrupt you or insult you again,' he said.

I recounted the most recent late-night phone call, with Beiderbecke's 'In a Mist' playing in the background; Buchalter's knowledge of early Benny Goodman and the proper way to handle old seventy-eights; the Bunk Johnson record that someone had left playing on my phonograph.

'You impress me, son. You *know*,' Oswald Flat said.

Again, I was silent.

'An evil man cain't love music,' he said. 'He's interested in hit for some other reason.'

'I think you're right.'

'There's a band plays on Royal Street. I mean, out in the street, when the cops put the barricades up and close off the traffic. They got a piano on a truck, a Chinese kid playing harmonica, some horns, a colored, I mean a black, man on slide guitar. The black man comes to my church sometimes. But he don't live in New Orleans. He's in Morgan City.'

'Yes?'

'If I call and see if he's home, can you meet me there in a couple of hours?'

'I think you'd better clarify yourself.'

'That's all you get. Holler till your face looks like an eggplant.'

'This is part of a police investigation, Reverend. You don't write the rules.'

'He's been in the penitentiary. He won't talk to you unless I'm there. You want my he'p or not?'

The black man's name was Jesse Viator, and he lived in a dented green trailer set up on concrete blocks thirty feet from the bayou's edge. He had only three teeth in his mouth, and they protruded from his gums like the hooked teeth in the mouth of a barracuda. We sat on old movie theater seats that he had propped up on railroad ties in his small, tidy backyard. A shrimp boat passed with its lights on, and near the far bank swallows were swooping above an oil barge that had rusted into a flooded shell.

Jesse Viator was not comfortable in the presence of a police officer.

'You remember that man you told me about, the one wanted you to record, the fellow you said bothered you the way he looked at you?' Brother Oswald said.

'Yeah, dude was up to no good,' he said.

'Why did you think that?' I asked. I smiled.

'Some people got their sign hanging out,' he answered. He pulled at the soft flesh under his chin and looked out at the bayou.

'Why was he up to no good, Jesse?' I said.

'Dude didn't say nothing mean. He was polite. But it was like there was heat in his face,' Viator said. 'Like a dry pan been setting on the gas burner.'

I showed him the composite drawing of Buchalter. He held it in the light from his trailer and studied it. His grizzled pate shone like tan wax.

'You do them composites with a machine, right? So a lot of them look alike,' he said.

'Who's the worst guy you ever met inside?' I said.

'They only get so bad. Then they all about the same. They end up in Camp J.'

'The guy I'm looking for is worse than anybody in Camp J. Do you believe me when I say that?'

He took the drawing back from my hand and tilted it to catch the light from the trailer. He tapped on the edges of the face. 'What's that?' he said.

'You tell me,' I said.

'Dude had dirt in his skin, what d' you call 'em, blackheads or something, made him look like he was wearing a mask around his eyes. Look, it was t'ree, four mont's back. I stopped thinking about it.'

'Tell him the rest of hit, Jesse,' Oswald Flat said.

'There ain't no *rest*,' he said. 'Dude say he give me a hundred dollars to record. I tole him I ain't interested. That's it. I don't want to talk about it no more.'

'Are you scared of this man?' I said, and kept my eyes on his.

He took a breath that was between anger and exasperation.

'You know the feeling that dude give me? It was like when a guy get made a slave up at Angola. When somebody turn out a kid, rape him, then tell him, Haul your lil ass down the Walk. In a half hour come back with ten dollars. In another half hour, I want ten dollars more, then I want ten dollars more after that, or the next thing go in your mouth got a sharp point on it and it don't come out. That's what that dude's eyes made me think of.'

He became morose and sullen and would say little more. The moon was up, and road dust and a sheen of diesel oil floated on the dead current close under the willows. The air was cool and humid and smelled of bait shrimp someone had left in a bucket. I asked the reverend to wait for me out front.

'What'd you fall for, Jesse?' I said.

'Guy tried to joog me at a dance. I didn't want to, but I put him down. Lawyer tole me to plea to manslaughter.'

'You have a family?'

'My wife's at the Charity. She got heart trouble. Our two daughters is growed up and married, in California.'

'The man I want molested my wife. I'll show you what he does when he gets his hands on people.' I stood up from my chair.

'What you doing, man? Hey, you taking off your—'

'Buchalter used an electrical generator on me, Jesse. That's where he attached the terminals. It's quite an experience.'

He propped his hands on his thighs, twisted in his

chair, and focused his eyes on a cane pole that was stuck deep in the roots of a cypress tree.

'Man, I'm serious, I don't want no more to do with this,' he said.

'You had this guy made from the jump. You've got to help me, Jesse.'

He wiped at his face as though insects were in his eyes.

'Dude comes up to me on Royal, right after the gig, offers me a hundred bucks to play a half hour of my slide at his studio. I say, A hundred bucks don't cut making a tape. He says it's a demo, he's gonna offer it around, he's doing me a favor, usually a guy's got to pay for his own demo.

'I'm looking into that cat's face, I'm thinking he ain't ever gonna use the word *nigger*, he ain't gonna call me boon or tree climber or spear chucker, that ain't his way. He got that lil smile playing around the corner of his mouth, just like them guys in the AB look at you up at the farm. They'll hoe next to you in the soybean row, won't say nothing to you, chopping all the time like their mind is full of cool thoughts. That night you go in the shower and that same dude waiting for you with a shank in his hand.'

'You've got to give me something, Jesse.'

'He say his studio was one hour away. One hour there, one hour back. He winked at me when he said it.'

'I think you're holding back on me.' I kept my eyes locked on his.

'I ain't. He called once, man, right here at the trailer. I tole him I still ain't interested. It sound like he was outdoors, pay phone maybe. I could hear waves flopping, like on a beach.'

'He never mentioned a place? How about Grand Isle?'

'Not unless they moved Grand Isle over to Miss'sippi.'

'I'm not with you.'

'That day on Royal. I didn't pay the car no mind, but the plates was from Miss'sippi. That good enough? 'Cause that's all there is.'

I gave him my business card and picked up my coat from the chair. He looked out into space while his hand closed and opened on the card. Then he pressed it back into my palm.

'My wife deserve a trip after all the sickness she been having. I think we going out to visit our children in California. Be gone quite a while. You understand what I'm saying?'

The next afternoon, which was Friday afternoon, Ben Motley called me from New Orleans.

'Max Calucci dropped the charges against Purcel for destroying his house,' he said.

'Quite a change of heart.'

'What's your take on it?'

'He probably started sweating marbles when he heard Lonighan's Indian was in custody. That is, if he's mixed up in the vigilante killings. The last thing he needs now is legal involvement with the prosecutor's office. What's the insurance carrier, State Farm, going to do?'

'They're out of luck if they want to put it on Purcel. The witnesses now say they don't remember what the guy on the grader looked like. But they're sure it wasn't Purcel. I left a message on his recorder, but he didn't call back.'

'He's holed up in a fish camp someplace.'

'I went by his office. A secretary, a temp, was in there. She said he retrieved the message off the machine. Why doesn't he answer his calls?'

'I don't know, he's a little irresponsible sometimes. What's the status on Manuel Ruiz?'

'No bond. We're holding him for the INS. By the way, tell Purcel it's all right he doesn't call me back. Since he's already got such good friends in the department. Like Nate Baxter.'

I left a message for Clete at both his office and his apartment.

That evening I put on my gym shorts and running

shoes and did three sets of dead lifts, bench presses, and curls in the backyard. My neighbor was burning a pile of dried honeysuckle, and the air was hazy and sweet with the smoke.

Tie it down, *think*, I told myself. What were the ongoing connections in the Buchalter case?

Music, and now geography.

Two of Buchalter's hired meltdowns, Jack Pelley and Charles Sitwell, had been in the rock 'n' roll band in the Block at Angola. Buchalter evidently prowled stores that handled old records, like Jimmie Ryan's, and had tried to make a studio recording of the slide guitarist Jesse Viator.

He had been driving a car with Mississippi plates, had access to a studio an hour from New Orleans, and had made a telephone call within earshot of a beach.

The German skinhead who had been run down by his friends out on the salt had been diving from a cabin cruiser he and his friends had stolen from a berth in Biloxi.

Hippo Bimstine's friends had broken up a meeting of a hate group with baseball bats and expropriated their Nazi film footage in a cinder-block house north of Pascagoula.

I lowered the bar to my thighs, then curled it into my chest, released it slowly again, pausing in midair as the muscles in my arms burned and filled with blood. The air felt as cool as a knife blade in my lungs.

Maybe the circle was starting to tighten on Will Buchalter.

Before we went to bed, Bootsie and I ate a piece of pie at the kitchen table.

'Is something bothering you?' she said.

'I thought Clete might call.'

'Clete has his own way of doing things.'

'You're right about that.'

That night the wind blew hard out of the south, and I could hear our rental boats knocking against the pilings in the dock. Then it began to rain, and in my sleep I heard another sound, a distant one, metal striking methodically against metal, one pinging blow after another, muffled by the envelope of water it had to travel through.

In my dream I saw a group of Nazi sailors huddled in a half-flooded compartment, salt water pinwheeling through the leaks above their heads, their faces white with terror in the dimming light while they breathed their own stink and the coldness crept above their loins and one man kept whanging a wrench against the bulkhead.

I woke from the dream, my chest laboring for air. Through the clicking of the rain in the trees, I could still hear the rhythmic *twang* of metal hitting against metal. I slipped on my loafers and khakis, pulled a raincoat over my head, and, with a flashlight in my hand, ran from the back door to the collapsed barn by my duck pond. A sheet of corrugated tin roofing, purple with rust, was swinging from a broken beam against the remains of my father's old hay baler.

I pulled the broken beam and sheet of tin loose from the pile and threw them out into the field.

But I couldn't shake the dream. Why? What did I care about the fate of Nazis drowned fifty years ago?

The dream was not about submariners. Someone close to me was in trouble, maybe because of information I had given him, and I was trying to deny that simple fact.

Where was Clete Purcel?

chapter twenty-nine

Tommy Lonighan had turned up the heat inside his glassed-in sunporch, even though it was seventy-five degrees outside and he was wearing sweatpants and a long-sleeved flannel shirt. My face was moist with heat, but his skin looked dry and gray, almost flaccid, as though his glands had stopped secreting; he sat forward on his reclining chair, his eyes still trying to follow the action in a movie playing on his VCR, a furious conclusion working in his face.

'This is a piece of crap,' he said, pulled the cassette from the VCR, and flung it clattering into a pile of other cassettes. 'You saw that movie *Reservoir Dogs*? It's sickening. A bunch of made guys are beating up and torturing a cop. No mobbed-up guys would do something like that. The guy who wrote this don't know dick about crime. You know what I think, it's the guy wrote this is sick, not the fucking criminals.'

'Can you help me find Clete or not?'

'Where do you find an elephant? You go to the circus. How should I know where he is? Ask his punch, the one getting in my face about Jews.'

'I went by Martina's apartment this morning. No one's seen her in two or three days.'

''Cause she's with Purcel. 'Cause he's got a warrant on him, he don't wake up with a boner?'

'You're unbelievable, Tommy.'

'If Max or Bobo did something to him, I'd a heard about it, and I ain't.' He freed something from a nostril and sniffed dryly. 'Can I tell you something? I don't give a shit, either. I wish the Caluccis would try to hit somebody now. Maybe they'd get taken down like they deserve.'

'You're talking about my friend.'

'I should worry about Purcel? I got maybe three, four months, then the doctor says he'll start me on morphine. Maybe it ain't gonna do the job, either. You know why I got all this grief in my life? It's punishment 'cause I got mixed up with those fucking greasebags. They're immoral, they got no honor, they—'

'Then why not dime 'em and be done with it, Tommy?'

'I thought you knew.' His eyes were close-set, like BB's. Blotches of color broke in his face. 'You guys don't use telephones, you don't talk to each other?'

'What is it?' I said.

'Late yesterday, I spilled my guts, everything,' he said. 'I haven't been charged yet, but they'll do that Monday.'

I waited. The room was ablaze with sunlight and color – the deep blue tile floor, the cane deck furniture and canary yellow cushions – but in its midst Tommy looked stricken, like a man who had mistakenly thought the source of his abiding shame had at least become known and accepted if not forgiven.

'Max and Bobo wanted to scare the coloreds out of the trade in the projects,' he said. 'They used Manny to do three guys. They told him these coloreds were evil spirits and had to be killed 'cause they were selling dope and corrupting little kids. He comes from a bunch of headhunters or cannibals that's got a flower and death cult or something. Or maybe Max made him think he did after he got ahold of this documentary on these prehistoric people that's running around in South America. I don't know about that stuff.'

He scowled into space. White clouds were tumbling in the sky, leaves blowing across the freshly clipped lawn.

'You think I'm toe jam, don't you?' he said.

I kept my face empty and brushed at the crystal on my watch with my thumb.

'A couple of button guys did the other hits, I heard Jamaicans out of Miami,' he said. 'It's been putting boards in my head. I feel miserable. It's like nothing's any good anymore. There's some kind of smell won't wash out of my clothes. Here, you smell it?'

He extended his shirt cuff under my nose.

'Where you going?' he said.

'I've got to find Clete.'

'Stay. I'll fix some chicken sandwiches.'

'Sorry.'

He blew his nose in a Kleenex and dropped the Kleenex in a paper bag full of crumpled tissue, many of them flecked with blood.

'You seen Hippo?' he said.

'We're not on good terms, I'm afraid.'

'He ain't such a bad guy.' He stared disjointedly at the leaves blowing against the windows. 'You see him again, tell him I said that.'

'Sure.'

'You want to take some movie cassettes? I get them for two bucks from a guy sells dubs in Algiers.'

'Dubs?'

'What world you hang out in, Dave? Anything that's electronically recorded today gets dubbed and resold. Those music tapes you see in truck stops, you think Kenny Rogers sells his tapes for three-ninety-five? What, I'm saying the wrong thing again?'

'No, I just haven't been thinking clearly about something, Tommy. See you around.'

I went by Clete's office on St. Ann in the Quarter. It was locked, the blinds drawn, the mailbox inside the brick archway stuffed with letters. I used a pay phone in Jackson Square to call Ben Motley at his home.

'Why didn't you tell me Lonighan made a statement yesterday?' I said.

'It happened late. I don't know how it's going to go down, anyway ... Look, the bottom line is Lonighan implicated himself and the Indian. Lonighan's already a dead man, and the Indian's a retard. The interpreter says he'll testify he works for Spiderman if you want him to. The prosecutor's office isn't calling news conferences.'

'What's the status on the Caluccis?'

'That's what I'm trying to tell you, Robicheaux. There isn't any. We'll see what happens Monday. But we got an old problem, too. The Caluccis go down, Nate Baxter goes down. He's going to screw up the investigation any way he can.'

I felt my hand squeeze tightly around the receiver. The sunlight through the restaurant window was like a splinter of glass in the eye.

'Cheer up,' he said. 'We're getting there.'

'Purcel's completely off the screen.'

'Cover your own ass for a change. You know how Purcel'll buy it? He'll catch some kind of incurable clap when he's a hundred and fifty. Call me Monday.'

I drove up St. Charles to Hippo's drugstore. He was sitting in the shade on a collapsible metal chair by the entrance, eating a spearmint snowball. Two streetcars were stopped at a sunny spot on the neutral ground, loading and unloading passengers. At first he ignored me and continued to eat the ice out of the paper cone; then he smiled and aimed his index finger and thumb at me like a cocked pistol.

'A weird place to sit, Hippo,' I said.

'Not for me. I love New Orleans. Look up and down this street – the trees, the old homes, the moss in the wind. There's not another street like it in the world.' He reached next to him and popped open a second metal chair. 'Sit down. What can I do for you?'

'You're okay, Hippo.'

'Why not?' His eyes squinted into slits with his smile.

'You know about almost every enterprise on the Gulf Coast, don't you?'

'Business is like spaghetti ... pull on one piece, you move the whole plate.'

'Let me try a riddle on you. Mobbed-up guys don't torture cops, do they?'

'Not unless they're planning careers as crab bait.'

'Buchalter's not mobbed-up.'

'That's a breakthrough for you?'

'But what if Buchalter was selling duplicated recordings of historical jazz, or making blues tapes and screwing the musician on the copyright?'

'Dubs are in. Some lowlifes tried to get me to retail them in my drugstores. I don't think there's any big market for historical jazz, though.'

'Stay with me, Hippo. A guy selling dubs would have to piece off the action or be connected, right?'

'If he wants to stay in business.'

'So Buchalter's not part of the local action. Where's the biggest market for old blues and jazz?'

His eyes became thoughtful. 'He's selling it in Europe?'

'I think I've got a shot at him.'

He took another bite out of his cone and sucked his cheeks in.

'You want some backup? From guys with no last names?' he asked.

'Buchalter probably has a recording studio of some kind over on the Mississippi coast. I can go over there and spend several days looking through phone books and knocking on doors.'

He nodded without replying.

'Or I can get some help from a friend who has a lot of connections on the coast.'

'I provide information, then me and my friends get lost, that's what you're saying?'

'So far we don't have open season on people we don't like, Hippo.'

He crumpled up the paper cone in his hand, walked to a trash receptacle, and dropped it in.

'We'll use the phone at my place,' he said.

It didn't take long. He made four phone calls, then a half hour later a fax came through his machine with a list of addresses on it. He handed it to me, his sleek, football-shaped head framed by the corkboard filled with death camp photos behind him.

'There're seven of them, strung out between Bay St. Louis and Pascagoula,' he said. 'It looks like you get to knock on lots of doors, anyway.'

I folded the fax and put it in my coat pocket.

'Did you hear about Tommy Bobalouba?' I said.

'He knew he had cancer two years ago. He shouldn't have fooled around with it.'

'That's kind of rough, Hippo.'

'I'm supposed to weep over mortality? Do you know what's going on in that mick's head? I win, he loses. But he wants me to know I win only because he got reamed by the Big C.'

'I saw him just a little while ago. He said you're not a bad guy. He wanted you to know he said that.'

He snipped off the tip of a cigar with a small, sharp tool, and didn't raise his eyes. He kept sucking his lips as though he had just eaten a slice of raw lemon rind.

It was three o'clock when I stopped at Bay St. Louis. The bay was flat and calm, the long pier off old ninety dotted with fishermen casting two-handed rods and weighted throw nets into the glaze of sunlight on the surface; but in the south the sky was stained a chemical green along the horizon, the clouds low and humped, like torn black cotton.

The first address was a half block from the beach. The owners were elderly people who had moved recently from Omaha and had opened a specialty store that featured Christian books and records. They had bought the building two years ago from a man who had operated a recording studio at that address, but he had gone into bankruptcy and had since died.

I had a telephone number for the next address, which was in Pass Christian. I called before getting back on the highway; a recorded voice told me the number was no longer in service.

Thanks, Hippo.

I called his house to ask about the source of his information. His wife said he had left and she didn't know when he would be back. Did she know where he was?

'Why do you want to know?' she asked.

'It's a police matter, Mrs. Bimstine.'

'Do you get paid for solving your own problems? Or do you hire consultants?'

'Did I do something to offend you?'

She paused before she spoke again. 'Somebody called from the hospital. Tommy Lonighan's in the emergency room. He wanted to see Hippo.'

'The emergency room? I saw Lonighan just a few hours ago.'

'Before or after he was shot?'

She hung up.

It was starting to rain when I drove into Gulfport to check the next address. The sky was gray now, and the beach was almost empty. The tide was out, and the water was green and calm and dented with the rain, but in the distance you could see a rim of cobalt along the horizon and, in the swells, the triangular, leathery backs of stingrays that had been kicked in by a storm.

I was running out of time. It was almost five o'clock, and many of the stores were closing for the weekend. At an outdoor pay phone on the beach, I called the 800 number for Federal Express and asked for the location of the largest Fed Ex station in the area.

There was only one, and it was in Gulfport. The clerk at the station was young and nervous and kept telling me that I should talk to his supervisor, who would be back soon.

'It's an easy question. Which of your customers sends the greatest volume of express packages overseas?' I said.

'I don't feel comfortable with this, Officer. I'm sorry,' he said, a pained light in his eyes.

'I respect your integrity. But would you feel comfortable if somebody dies because we have to wait on your supervisor?'

He went into the back and returned with a flat, cardboard envelope in his hand. He set it on the counter.

'The guy owns a music business in Biloxi,' he said. 'He sends a lot of stuff to Germany and France.'

'You know this guy?'

'No, sir.' His jawbone flexed against his skin.

'But you know something about him?'

He cleared his throat slightly. 'One of the black drivers said he'd quit before he'd go back to the guy's store.'

The sender's name on the envelope was William K. Guilbeaux.

Before driving into Biloxi, I called Hippo's house again. This time *he* answered. There was static on the line, and the rain was blowing in sheets against the windows of the phone booth.

'I can't understand you,' I said.

'I'm saying he had a priest with him. You're a Catholic, I thought you'd appreciate that.'

'Tommy's—'

'He had a priest there, maybe he'll get in a side door up in heaven. The spaghetti head didn't have that kind of luck, though.'

'What?'

chapter thirty

On Saturdays Max and Bobo Calucci usually had supper, with their girlfriends and gumballs, at a blue-collar Italian restaurant off Canal near the New Orleans Country Club. It was a place with checker-cloth-covered tables, wood-bladed ceiling fans, Chianti served in wicker-basket bottles, a brass-railed mahogany bar, a TV sports screen high overhead, and a good-natured bartender who had once played for the Saints.

An off-duty uniformed police officer stood guard at the front door. The patrons were family people, and white; they celebrated birthdays and anniversaries at the restaurant; the mood was always loud and happy, almost raucous. It was like going through a door into a festive and carefree New Orleans of forty years ago.

Tommy Lonighan was by himself when he arrived in a rental stretch limo. Tommy Bobalouba, the stomp-ass kid from Magazine who could knock his opponent's mouthpiece into the fourth row, stepped out on the curb with the perfumed and powdered grace of castle Irish. He looked like an elegant resurrection of the 1940s, in a tailored white suit with purple pinstripes, a wide scarlet polka-dot tie, oxblood loafers, his face ruddy with a whiskey flush, his blue eyes as merry as an elf's. His lavender shirt seemed molded to his powerful physique.

Outside his shirt and under his tie, he wore a gold

chain with what looked like two mismatched metal objects attached to it.

The cop at the door, who was nearing retirement, grinned and feigned a prizefighter's stance with him. When he walked through the tables, people shook his hand, pointed him out to each other as a celebrity; the bartender shouted out, 'Hey, Tommy, Riddick Bowe was just in here looking for you! He needs some pointers!'

Tommy sipped a whiskey sour at the bar, with one polished loafer on the rail, his smile always in place, his face turned toward the crowd, as though the collective din that rose from it was an extension of the adulation that had rolled over him in a validating crescendo many years ago, when thousands in a sweaty auditorium chanted, 'Hook 'im, Bobalouba! Hook 'im, Bobalouba! Hook 'im, Bobalouba!'

He gazed at the Caluccis' table with goodwill, bought a round for the bar, dotted a shrimp cocktail with Tabasco sauce, and ate it with a spoon like ice cream.

Then one of Max's people, a pale, lithe Neapolitan hood named Sal Palacio, walked up to him, his palms open, a question mark in the center of his face.

'We got a problem, Tommy?' he said.

'Not with me you don't,' Tommy answered, his dentures showing stiffly with his smile.

'Because Max and Bobo are wondering what you're doing here, since it ain't your regular place, you hear what I'm saying?'

Tommy looked at a spot on the wall, his eyelids fluttering. 'I need a passport in New Orleans these days?' he said.

'They said to tell you they got no hard feelings. They're sorry things ain't worked out, they're sorry you're sick, they don't want people holding no grudges.'

Tommy cocked his fists playfully; Sal's face popped like a rubber band.

'Man, don't do that,' he said.

'Take it easy, kid,' Tommy said, brushing Sal's stomach with his knuckles. 'You want a drink?'

'I got to ask you to walk into the washroom with me.'

'Hey, get this kid,' Tommy said to the people standing around him. 'Sal, you don't got a girlfriend?'

'It ain't funny, Tommy.'

Tommy pulled back his coat lapels, lifted his coattails, slapped his pockets, turned in a circle.

'Sal, you want to put your hand in my crotch?' he asked.

'You're a fucking lunatic,' he answered, and walked away.

But the Caluccis were becoming more and more nervous, self-conscious, convinced that each time Lonighan spoke into a cluster of people at the bar and they laughed uproariously, the Caluccis were the butt of the joke.

Max stood up from his chair, a bread stick in one hand, a pitcher of sangria in the other, working his neck against the starch in his collar.

'Hey, Tommy,' he said, over the heads of people at the other tables. 'You don't want to have a drink with your friends, you crazy guy?'

Tommy walked toward the Calucci table, still smiling, a dream-like luster in his eyes, his cheeks glowing from a fresh shave. He patted Max on the shoulders, pressed him into his chair, bent down and whispered in his ear, as though he were confiding in an old friend.

Few people noticed Tommy's left hand biting into the back of Max's neck or the charged and fearful light in Max's eyes, or Tommy raising his right knee and slipping a .38 one inch from the cloth holster strapped to his calf.

Then the conversation at the other tables died; people stopped eating and became immobile in their chairs, as though they were part of a film winding down on a reel; waiters set down their trays and remained motionless in the aisles. Tommy pushed Max's face into his plate as though he were bending the tension out of a spring.

The cop at the door had stepped inside out of the rain. He stared dumbfounded at Lonighan.

'Walk back outside, Pat. Or I pop him right now. I swear to God I will,' Tommy said.

'You're having some kind of breakdown, Tommy. This ain't your way,' Sal Palacio said.

'Put your piece in the pitcher, Sal. You other two fucks do the same,' Tommy said.

Sal and the other two bodyguards dropped their pistols into the sangria. Tommy twisted the barrel of the .38 into the soft place behind Max's ear and clicked back the hammer.

'This guy here, the one with the linguine in his face, him and his brother been killing the colored dealers in the projects,' he said. 'You think the city's shit now, wait till you see what it's like when the Caluccis got the whole dope trade to themselves.'

'Tommy, you're taking us all over the edge here,' the cop at the door said, his mouth parting dryly after his words had stopped.

'Hey, Pat, tell Nate Baxter I just fucked his meal ticket,' Tommy said, and pulled the trigger.

Max's mouth opened sideways on his plate, like that of a fish that had been thrown hard upon the bank. Tommy pulled the trigger again, with people screaming now, this time the barrel a half inch from the crown of Max's skull. A tuft of Max's hair jumped as though it had been touched by a puff of wind.

Then, with Bobo under the table and the cop drawing his weapon, Tommy went through the curtained hallway behind him, stepped inside the men's room, and bolted the door.

For some reason he did it in a toilet stall, seated on top of the stool, with his trousers still on, the revolver pointed awkwardly toward his throat. The impact of the round wedged his head into the corner of the stall; the recoil sent the .38 skittering in a red trail across the tiles; the hemorrhage from the wound covered his chest like a scarlet bib. Later the coroner lifted the gold chain from his neck with a fountain pen. Attached to it were a lead-colored army dog tag and a small gold boxing glove from the Golden Gloves of 1951.

I wondered if Tommy heard the roar of the crowd just as his thumb tightened inside the trigger housing, or the echo of Chinese bugles and small arms through a frozen arroyo, or perhaps the squeal of an ice truck's brakes on a street full of children in the Channel; or if he stared into the shadows, seeking the epiphany that had always eluded him, and saw only more shadows and motes of spinning dust and the graffiti scratched into the paint on the door, until he realized, just as the hammer snapped down on the brass cartridge, that the eruption of pain and fear and blood in his chest was simply the terminus of an ongoing war that he had waged for a lifetime against his own heart.

Later I mentioned my thoughts to Hippo.

'Don't complicate that dumb mick, Dave. He even screwed up his own suicide,' he answered. Then, with his face turned so I couldn't see his eyes, 'He apologized before he checked out. Just him and me in the room. Just like when we were boys.'

And he walked away.

chapter thirty-one

The music store was located between an auto garage and a boarded-up café on a nondescript street north of Biloxi. It was still raining; only two cars were parked on the street, and the sidewalks were empty. A block farther north, there was a string of gray clapboard and Montgomery Ward brick houses, their lawns choked with weeds. A neon beer sign burned in the gloom above a pool hall that had virtually no patrons. The street reminded me of a painting I had once seen by Adolf Hitler; it contained buildings but no people. It was the kind of neighborhood where one's inadequacies would never find harsh comparisons.

Was this music store, with cracked and taped windows, moldy cardboard cartons piled by the front door, the headquarters of Will Buchalter, a man who moved like a political disease through a dozen countries?

I remembered a story about the Israeli agents who captured Adolf Eichmann as he was returning from his job in an automobile plant somewhere in South America. One of the agents was young and could not quite accept the fact that he was now face-to-face with the man who had murdered his parents.

'What job do you perform at the auto plant?' he asked.

'I'm one of the chrome polishers. We polish all the chrome surfaces on the new automobiles,' Eichmann answered.

According to the story, the agent began to weep.

The door to the store was locked, but I could see a man moving around behind a counter. The wind was blowing a wet, acrid stench through the space between the buildings. I tapped on the glass.

The man inside waved his hand negatively. I tapped again. He walked toward me, saying the word *Closed* so I could read his lips. He wore a sleeveless flannel shirt and black jeans that sculpted his sex. His blond hair was coated and waved with gel, his white arms wrapped with tattoos of green and red dragons.

I shook the doorknob when he tried to walk away.

'I'm a friend of Will's,' I said.

'He's gone,' the man said through the glass.

'Open up. I've got to leave him a message.'

'Sorry, we're closed. I don't know how else to say it.'

'Where's Marie?'

'Come back Monday,' he said, and dropped the venetian blinds down the glass.

I got back in my truck and drove three blocks up the street. Then I circled back, parked at the end of the alley, and walked toward the rear of the store under the eaves of the buildings. A rusted-out trash barrel was smoldering in the rain, and again I smelled a moist, acrid odor that was like the smell of a dead bat in an incinerator.

Just as I reached inside my raincoat for my .45, he stepped out the back door with a sack of trash in his hands. I slipped my hand back out of my coat and fixed a button with it.

'What's with you?' he said.

'I got to be back at the halfway house by dark, you hear what I'm saying?'

'No.'

'Maybe you think you're doing your job, but you're starting to piss me off,' I said.

'*Excuse* me.'

'Look, I was supposed to connect with him when I got out. I just had six fucking years of putting up with smart-ass watermelon pickers. I'm begging you, buddy, don't fuck up my day any worse than it already has been.'

'All right, I'm sorry, but it don't change anything. I got to lock up. Will ain't here. Okay? See the man Monday.'

He dropped the paper bag into the trash barrel and turned to go back inside. I shoved him hard between the shoulder blades, followed him inside, and laid the muzzle of the .45 against the back of his neck.

'Get down on your knees,' I said.

'I don't know who you are but—'

'You've got a serious hearing problem,' I said, kicked him behind the knee, and pushed him into the counter. His eyes widened with pain when his knees hit the floor.

'Where is he?' I said.

'He don't tell me that kind of stuff. I work for *him*, he don't work for me. Who are you, man?'

'What do you care, as long as you get to live?'

'I just finished a bit myself. Why you twisting me? Take your shit to Will.'

'But you're the only guy around,' I said. 'Which means you're all out of luck.'

I pulled my cuffs off my belt and hooked up his wrists. He was facedown now, his eyelids fluttering against the dust and oil on the floor. The rain and the smoke from the trash barrel blew through the back door.

'What's that smell?' I said.

He bit down on his bottom lip.

I glanced around the store. The interior was cluttered with boxes of old seventy-eight records. In one corner was a glassed-in sound booth with an instrument panel and an elevated microphone inside. A mop inside a pail of dirty water was propped against a closed side door. I pulled back the slide on the .45 and eased a round into the chamber.

'I bought this in Bring Cash Alley in Saigon for twenty-five dollars,' I said. 'No registration, completely cold, you get my drift?'

His eyes squeezed shut, then opened again. 'Don't do this to me, man. Please,' he said.

My hand was tight and sweating on the knurled grips of the .45. I looked through the front window at the rain falling in the street. In the distance a stuck car horn was blaring, a stabbing, unrelieved sound in the inner ear like fingernails on a blackboard.

I eased the hammer back into place, clicked on the safety, and slipped the .45 back into my belt holster.

'I'm a police officer,' I said. 'Do you believe me when I say that?'

'Bust me. I ain't arguing.'

'But I'm beyond my parameters here. Do you know what that means?'

His eyes were filled with confusion.

'Will Buchalter and his sister have hurt my family,' I said. 'So we're not working on conventional rules anymore. Do you believe me when I say that?'

'Yes, sir. You got no trouble from me.'

'So what's that smell?'

'I was just trying to clean up ... The guy gets crazy sometimes ... He started hitting her with his fists for no reason, then he went in there with some scissors. I didn't have anything to do with it, man.'

'Hit who?'

'The broad ... I thought that's why you were here. The broad he's been holding.' He stared at the look on my face. 'Oh shit, man, this ain't my doing. You got to believe that.'

I scraped the pail and mop out of the way with my foot and opened the side door.

She was tied to a chair with clothesline, her mouth and eyes wrapped with silver tape, her reddish hair shorn and hacked to the scalp. One nostril was caked with dried blood, her neck and shoulders marbled with bruises the color of pomegranates. She turned her head toward my sound, like a blind person, her nostrils dilating with fear.

'Martina?' I said, my heart dropping.

She tried to talk through the tape.

I removed it first from her eyes, then her mouth. Her right eye was swollen shut, the inside of her lips gashed, her teeth pink, as though they had been painted with Mercurochrome. I opened my Puma knife and sliced the rope from the arms and back of the chair. She held me around the waist while I stroked her shorn head.

'It's all right,' I said. 'We'll get you to a hospital. I'll have somebody stay with you. You hear me? Buchalter's gone. Everything's going to be okay.'

She turned her face up to me. Her left eyeball jittered, as though a nerve in it were impaired. 'Where's Clete?' she said.

'I don't know. But we'll find him.'

'The man who beat me, he told me about the things he was going to do to Clete. He has pictures of what he's done to people.'

She leaned forward with her face in her hands, sobbing. There were white places the size of nickels with raw cuts inside them all over her scalp.

'I'll be right back,' I said.

The man in cuffs on the floor was trembling.

'I took her to the bathroom, I give her food when I wasn't supposed to,' he said.

'Where's your phone?'

'On the desk,' he said, exhaling the words like a man who knows the fury and intensity of the world is about to move past him.

I called 911 and asked for an ambulance and a sheriff's car.

'Here's how it shakes out, partner,' I said to the man on the floor. 'You're probably going down as an accessory to assault and battery, kidnapping, and anything else the locals can dream up. But no matter how you cut it, it's a serious bounce. You want to tell me where he is, I'll see what I can do for you later.'

'He knows how to get to people. Anywhere. Lockdown, isolation, Witness Protection Program. There's

373

white guys even paid the Black Guerrillas to protect them. It didn't work.'

'Last chance.'

'Him and Marie, this morning, they got excited about something in a newspaper. Then they took off.'

'Where's the newspaper?'

'I burned it in the trash barrel. With her hair I swept up. I was trying to keep the place clean, and I go down on a kidnapping beef. You tell me that's fair, man.'

I heard sirens in the distance, outside the window, a black man was looking up the street.

'I don't want to be rough on you, but I'd reconsider my attitude about cooperating,' I said to the man in handcuffs. 'When we nail Buchalter, he's going to find out we talked to you first. Who do you think he's going to blame his problems on?'

His face turned ashen.

I rode in the ambulance with Martina to the hospital, then used the phone at the Harrison County Sheriff's Department to call home and Clete's office. I recorded a long message on his machine, assured him Martina was going to be all right, and left him the number of the hospital.

But I would soon discover that I wasn't thinking clearly. I called Ben Motley.

'It's Saturday afternoon. Believe it or not, Robicheaux, I'd like forty-eight hours without thinking about pus bags.'

'Buchalter doesn't take weekends off,' I said.

'You got the woman back. You traced Buchalter to his nest. Count your blessings. Ease up.'

'Now's the time to staple him to the wall, Ben. Call Fart, Barf, and Itch in New Orleans for me.'

'What else?'

'Nothing.' Then I happened to glance at a deputy across the room who was eating a sandwich with his feet on the desk and reading the sports page in the newspaper.

'Wait a minute. Do you have this morning's *Times-Picayune*?'

'What do you want?'

'Look in the personals for me.'

'That's what they do when they're bored over in Vice.'

'Come on, Ben.'

He put down the phone, then I heard newspaper pages rattling.

'Do you see anything in there that looks peculiar?' I said.

'That's like asking if there's any washroom graffiti that shouldn't be on a Hallmark card,' he said. 'Hold on … Here's one that's all numbers. No message, just numbers.'

'Read them.' I could hear my own breath in the phone. I wrote the numbers down as he read them off. 'Those are the coordinates for that Nazi sub, Ben. You check with *The Times-Picayune*, you'll find Clete ran that ad.'

'I don't get it.'

'Buchalter kidnapped Martina and forced Clete to find out where I'd seen the sub. I gave him the coordinates. But it took a couple of days for the ad to come out. Look, we need to get a boat or a chopper out there.'

'Call your own department.'

'We don't have anything available.'

'You think I can snap my fingers on Saturday afternoon and come up with a boat or a helicopter? We don't have jurisdiction out on the salt, anyway.'

'You don't understand. I left a message on Clete's machine. I told him Martina's all right. As soon as he retrieves the message, you know where he's headed.'

'So let him light up the fun house. It's what Purcel does best.'

'He might lose, too. I need a boat.'

'You won't get it from me this weekend.'

'Motley—'

'It's *Motley* now? Why don't you call Nate Baxter? See what kind of help you get.'

I started back home. It was getting dark now, and the palm trees along the highway were beating in the wind, the rain spinning in my headlights. It would take me at least four and a half hours to reach New Iberia, then another seven, maybe more, with the bad weather, to get my boat down Bayou Teche and into the gulf south of Grand Isle.

I pulled into a filling station by the Pearl River and called Lucinda Bergeron's house. The gum trees around the phone booth were green and brightly lit by the filling station's signs, and the leaves were ripping like paper in the wind.

'Zoot?'

'Hey, Mr. Dave, what's happenin'?'

'Where's your mom?'

'She ain't here. Something wrong?'

'I've got to get ahold of her. I need a boat.'

'She went to the grocery. What kind of boat you looking for?'

'A fast one,' I said.

'You ax the right man.'

'Oh?'

'I tole you at your house. But you wasn't listening real good, remember? I worked on all kinds of boats.'

'Who owns this boat, Zoot?'

'A man who don't mind lending it, I promise. When you coming?'

An hour and a half later I parked the truck at a boatyard way out in Jefferson Parish. It had quit raining; and the sky was dark, and water was dripping off the tin shed where Zoot waited in a cabin cruiser with the interior lights on. I took my Japanese field glasses from the glove compartment, then unlocked the iron box welded to the bed of my pickup and removed my old army field jacket and the AR-15 and my Remington twelve-gauge with the barrel sawed off right in front of the pump that I had wrapped in a canvas duffel bag. I dropped a box of

.223 rounds and a box of double-ought buckshot into the bag and pulled the drawstring. When I walked out onto the dock under the shed I saw that Zoot wasn't alone.

'Hello, Lucinda,' I said, stepping down into the boat.

She was dressed in jeans, a purple sweater, and a nylon NOPD windbreaker. Zoot fixed his attention on the clearing sky, tapping his palms on the wheel, whistling quietly.

'What would you like to hear from me first?' she said.

'I beg your pardon?'

'You call my house and ask a seventeen-year-old to provide a boat for you?' she said.

'Believe what you want, Lucinda. I'm not up to an argument tonight.'

'You were willing to bring a minor and civilian into a potentially dangerous situation? With no consultation with anyone else?'

'I couldn't get a boat from Motley. I don't have time to go back to New Iberia. You think it's right Purcel may be out there by himself?'

'I can't quite tell you how angry I am,' she said.

'Then why'd you let him come?'

She didn't answer. I lowered my voice. 'Maybe nobody's out there. Maybe I should have waited for you to come home. Maybe I should have gone back to New Iberia,' I said. 'I did what I thought was best.'

I waited. Her arms were folded across her chest, her hands cupped on her elbows. I looked at Zoot, and he turned over the engines and backed us out of the slip. The wind was cool and damp and smelled of salt and dead gars that had been hit by boat propellers. Lights flickered across the clouds in the south.

We headed down Bayou St. Denis. It was a beautiful boat, custom-built with teakwood and mahogany panels in the cabin, brightwork that had the soft glow of butter, wide beds down below, sonar, a pump toilet, a small galley, and twin two-hundred-horsepower Evinrude outboard engines that could hit fifty knots. When we entered Barataria Bay, Zoot tried to open her up.

'The chop's too heavy. You're going to beat us to death, partner,' I said.

The glass was beaded with the spray off the bow. The moon had broken from behind the clouds, and our wake glistened behind us like a long brown and silver trough. Zoot wore a black knitted cap rolled up on top of his head and chewed on a matchstick. When he eased back on the throttle, I saw the two ignition wires wrapped together and swinging loose at the bottom of the instrument panel.

'What kind of engineering do we have here, Zoot?' I said, raising my finger toward the wires.

'The man out of town right now. He forgot to leave the key where it's always at,' he said.

'I see.'

'That's a fact. He lets me take it all the time. I'll introduce y'all sometime.'

'That's very kind of you.'

I looked down below at Lucinda, who was sitting on a cushioned storage locker with her legs crossed, staring straight ahead. Her nickel-plated .357 revolver glinted in her belt holster. I realized that I had read her wrong.

I walked down the steps and sat on a bunk across from her. I could feel the steady vibration of the bow coursing through the chop.

'You're over the black dude in the motel?' I said.

Her mouth parted slightly.

'It's like anything else. It passes,' I said.

The skin wrinked at the corner of her left eye.

'The first time a guy dealt the play on me, I thought I'd wake up with his face in front of me every day of my life,' I said. 'Then one day it was gone. Poof. Three years later I put another guy down.'

'Why are you doing this?' she said.

'Because this boat's a little warm.'

'It's a little ...'

'Right. Warm. Not hot exactly. Terms like *borrowed* and *lend-lease* come to mind,' I said, and leaned forward on my hands. 'You've got your own agenda tonight, Lucinda.'

'He tortured my son.'

'You know when a good cop does it by the numbers? The day he thinks he *shouldn't* do it by the numbers.'

'I get this from the friend and advocate of Clete Purcel? Wonderful.'

'Don't let Buchalter remake you in his image.'

She looked into my face for a long time.

'Your advice is always good, Dave,' she said. 'But it's meant for others. It has no application for yourself, does it?'

We stared silently at each other as the hull of the boat veered toward the cut at Grand Terre.

It was a strange, cold dawn. With first light the sky looked streaked with india ink, then the wind dropped suddenly and the sun came up red and molten on the gulf's watery rim. The tide was coming in, rose-dimmed, heavy with the fecund smell of schooled-up trout, flecked with foam toward the shore, the air loud with the cry of gulls that glided and dipped over our wake. I watched the gray-green landmass of Louisiana fall away behind us.

Zoot stood erect in front of the wheel, his hooded workout jersey zipped up to his chin, his long hands resting lightly on the spokes. He had cranked open the glass, and the skin of his face looked taut and bright with cold.

'How you doing, Skipper?' I said.

'Not bad. She asleep?'

'Yes.'

'You know what she said about you the other day?'

'I wouldn't want to guess.'

'She say, "He's probably crazy but I wouldn't mind if I'd met him before he was married." '

'You'd better not be giving out your mama's secrets,' I said.

'Why you think she tell it to me?' he said.

Through my field glasses I could see the black, angular silhouettes of two abandoned drilling platforms against the sun and a freighter with rusty scuppers and a Panamanian flag to the far west. Zoot cut back on the throttle, and we rocked forward on our own wake.

'Look at the sonar, Mr. Dave,' he said. 'We're in about forty feet now. But see where the line drops? That's a trench. I been over it before. It runs maybe two miles, unless it drifts over with sand sometimes.'

'You're pretty good at this.'

'I ain't even gonna say nothing. You and her just alike. Got one idea about everything, so every day you always surprised about something.'

'I think you're probably right.'

'*Probably*?' He shook his head.

But I wasn't listening now. Just off the port bow, beyond one of the drilling platforms, I saw the low, flat outline of a salvage vessel, one that was outfitted with side booms, dredges, and a silt vacuum that curved over the gunwale like the body of an enormous snake. I sharpened the image through the field glasses and saw that the ship was anchored bow and stern and was tilted slightly to starboard, as though it were straining against a great weight.

Then I saw something move on the drilling platform closest to us. I stepped outside the cabin and refocused the field glasses. The tide was washing through the pilings at the base of the platform, and upside-down in the swell, knocking against the steel girders, was the red and white hull of a capsized boat. I moved the glasses up a ladder to the rig itself and held them on a powerful, sunburned, bare-chested man whose Marine Corps utilities hung just below his navel.

'What is it?' Lucinda said behind me. The side of her face was printed with lines from her sleep.

I handed the glasses to her.

'Take a look at that first rig,' I said.

She balanced herself against the sway of the deck and peered through the glasses.

'It's Clete Purcel,' she said. 'He looks half frozen.'

'With a sunk boat,' I said. 'Clete's no sailor, either. Which means he probably went out with somebody who didn't make it to that ladder.'

'Who?'

'I don't like to think about it.'

'Who?'

'The elderly preacher comes to mind.' I went back inside the cabin. 'Zoot, take us on into the rig. But try to keep it between us and that salvage ship so whoever's onboard doesn't get a good look at us.'

'It's Buchalter and them Nazis?' he said. I saw his long, ebony hands tighten involuntarily on the wheel.

'Maybe it's just an ordinary salvage group trying to raise some drilling equipment.'

'There's some oil field junk down out here, but not yonder, Mr. Dave.'

'Okay, podna.'

'I know what you got in that canvas bag. If the time come, is one of them for me?'

'You have any experience with firearms?'

'A lot.'

'With what kind?'

'The kind you shoot things wit' … Me and my cousin, we gone under the Huey Long Bridge and shot bottles all over the place.'

'Look, Zoot, we want the people on that salvage boat to think we're a fishing party. Can you set the outriggers and put some trolling rods in the sockets while I take the wheel?'

'Sure,' he said, but his eyes were still on the canvas bag.

'Just keep your hood tied on your head, too, in case they put binoculars on us.'

'You ain't gonna let me have one of them guns?'

'If that's Buchalter out there, we'll call the Coast Guard.'

'Then why you bring all them guns?'

I'd never guess you were Lucinda's son, I thought to myself.

I kept the bow pointed in a straight line at the rig and the salvage ship. The sun had broken through a bank of lavender and black clouds, and you could see flying fish and the stringlike tentacles and swollen pink air sacs of Portuguese man-o'-wars in the swell. The day should have warmed, but the wind had risen again and the tidal current looked green and cold flowing under the oil platform, rolling the capsized boat against the pilings and the steel ladder.

To the south there was a frothy white line along the horizon where the waves were starting to cap.

Zoot worked his way forward onto the bow, and I cut the gas and let the cabin cruiser drift into the ladder that extended out of the water, upward to the platform where Clete Purcel was leaning over the rail, staring down at us, the sandy curls of hair on his shoulders and chest blowing dryly in the wind.

He came down the ladder fast, his face pointed downward, his love handles flexing, his huge buttocks working as he clanged onto each rung. When he dropped onto the bow, he kept his face pointed in the opposite direction from the salvage ship and made his way aft along the side of the cabin.

His teeth were chattering when he came through the hatchway.

'Streak, I love you,' he said. 'I knew my old podjo wouldn't let me down. I ain't kidding you, I was turning to an ice cube up there. I tried to wrap myself up in a piece of canvas, but it blew away.'

'What happened?'

'It's Buchalter. We found him about three this morning,' he said, pulling a blanket around his shoulders.

'We came up on him from the south. I thought we had him. There's a metal stairs on his port side. We were going to drift up to it, then take them from behind while all that machinery was roaring. Except we hit a log and punched a hole in the hull.'

He sat on top of a locker filled with life vests and scuba gear and worked the stopper from a bottle of Cutty Sark he had taken from the liquor cabinet. The scar through his eyebrow and across the bridge of his nose looked like a stitched strip of pink rubber.

'Who's *we*, Clete?'

'Brother Oswald.' His voice changed when he said the words. His eyes looked away from me, then at Lucinda and Zoot. Then he looked at the deck. He lifted the bottle to his mouth.

'Why didn't you wait?' I said.

'For what? The guy to blow the country?'

'You could have waited,' I said.

'Get real, Streak. You nail this guy under a black flag or he'll live to piss on your grave.'

'What's a black flag?' Zoot said.

Clete started to raise the Scotch again, then the color drained out of his face and he went through the hatchway and threw up over the stern. He came back inside, wiping his mouth with a towel.

'Excuse me, I swallowed some oil out there,' he said. 'When the boat turned over, I hung on to it. Brother Oswald had on a life preserver. He was drifting right past that stairs I was talking about. He didn't come out north of the ship, either.'

'You mean he's onboard with Buchalter?' Lucinda said.

'The tide was coming in real strong. He couldn't be anywhere else,' Clete said. 'I would have seen him. I know I would have.'

'I'll give our position to the Coast Guard,' I said.

'The old guy kept talking about Gog and Magog. What's Gog and Magog?' Clete said.

'It's a biblical prophesy about the war between good and evil,' I said.

'I don't know about no black flags and Magogs, but there's something I ain't mention yet,' Zoot said.

We all stared at him. In the silence a wave broke across the bow and streaked the glass.

'The radio don't work,' he said.

chapter thirty-two

I was crouched behind Clete on the steps of the small passageway that gave onto the bow. He had put on my raincoat and a red wool shirt he found in a closet. His big hands were clenched on the stock and pump of the twelve-gauge shotgun. I could hear him breathing with expectation.

He glanced backwards at me and started to smile. Then stopped.

'Why the scowl, mon?'

'This is your fault.'

'I don't read it that way.'

'Why didn't you go take care of Martina? Why'd you have to go out on the salt with a fanatical old man?'

'I don't like what you're saying to me, Streak.'

'Too bad.'

'Remember the dude in New Iberia General? He got a hypodermic load of roach paste. Buchalter *ends* here.'

I punched him on the shoulder with my finger.

'We need to understand something, Clete. You're not going to re-create the O.K. Corral out here.'

He twisted around on his haunches.

'What do you want to do?' he said. 'Go all the way back to land to notify the Coast Guard, then hope they're not a hundred miles away? The old man's on his own up there. We go in there and blow up their shit.'

I punched him with one finger, hard, on the shoulder

again. He turned and slapped my hand away, his green eyes suddenly disturbed and dark, as though he were looking at someone he didn't know.

'This whole gig started with you tearing up the Calucci brothers,' I said. 'It's not going to end that way. We're putting Buchalter in a cage.'

'Tell it to the Rotary Club,' he said, and looked upward toward the closed hatch.

We could hear Zoot cutting back the gas now, the exhaust pipes throbbing at the waterline, echoing off the steel hull of the salvage ship. Then we heard Lucinda making her way forward, picking up the bowline off the deck, as though it were natural to tie onto the metal steps that zigzagged down the side of the ship.

Clete eased the hatch upward a half inch.

'We found an injured man on an oil platform! We need your radio!' Lucinda shouted.

There was no answer. We could hear the sounds of an air compressor, a winch grinding, chains rattling through pulleys, a diesel engine working hard.

'It's a boat hand who doesn't know what to do,' Clete said. 'He probably went for somebody else.' He looked back at me again. 'Lighten up. I figure no more than five of them, including the diver in the water. Easy odds, mon.'

But the creases in the back of his neck were bright with sweat, his knuckles white and ridged on the shotgun's stock.

'We're calling it in for you!' someone yelled down at Lucinda.

'I'm a nurse! I need to describe his condition! I think he's had a coronary!'

'We're radioing your message! You can't come onboard!'

The hull bumped against the rubber tires that were roped to the bottom of the steps.

'Repeat ... You can't come onboard! No one but

company personnel are allowed! Your message is being transmitted!'

'This man may die!'

Clete's eyes were level with the crack between the deck and the hatch.

'She's tying on. That broad's got ice water in her veins,' he whispered. 'That's it, Lucinda, get on the steps, do it, do it, do it, do it....'

'Mr. Dave, leave me something 'case I got to come after y'all.'

I turned around. It was Zoot, bent down below the level of the passageway in the cabin.

'If it goes sour, partner, you get help,' I said.

It was very fast after that.

'Party time,' Clete said, and charged out onto the bow with the shotgun at port arms.

Lucinda had already reached the top of the stairs and was on the deck of the salvage ship, her .357 pointed straight out in front of her with both hands, her hair whipping in the wind, while she shouted at two paralyzed deckhands, 'Police officer, motherfucker! Down on your face, hands laced behind your neck! Are you deaf? Down on your face! Now! Or I blow your fucking head off!'

I hit the stairs running, right behind Clete, my .45 flopping in the pocket of my field jacket. I had already chambered a round in the AR-15, and my hand was squeezed tight on the grip and inside the trigger guard, my thumb poised on the safety. I could hear waves bursting against the stern and hissing along the hull.

The salvage ship was old, covered with tack welds, the scuppers orange with corrosion, the paint blistered and soft and flaking under the hand, the glass in the pilothouse oxidized and dirty with oil. The hatch to the engine room was open, and from belowdecks I could smell electrical odors, diesel fuel, stagnant water in a sump, a salty, rotten stench like a rat that's been caught in machinery.

Lucinda was standing above the two deckhands, her

weapon moving back and forth between them while she worked her cuffs off her belt. I took them from her hand, hooked up one man, pulled his arm through a rail on the gate to the steps, then snipped the loose cuff on the second man's wrist.

'Where's the old-timer?' I said.

One man was bald and wore a chin beard; the other had an empty eye socket that was puckered and sealed shut as though it had been touched with a hot instrument. The bald man twisted his head and looked indifferently toward the south, where lightning was pulsating amid muted thunder on the horizon.

'Look at me when I talk to you,' I said. 'Where's the old man?'

He slowly turned his head and let his eyes drift over both me and Lucinda.

'Fuck you, nigger lover,' he said.

Then I heard Clete's weight shift above me and looked up just as he threw the shotgun against his shoulder and aimed at a man in a canvas coat and rain hood who stood in silhouette by the stern with a blue-black automatic in his hand.

Clete fired twice. Part of the double-ought buckshot razored lines of paint off the bulkhead like dry confetti, then the man in the canvas coat was knocked backwards as though he had been jerked by an invisible cable wrapped around his chest.

Clete ejected the spent easing onto the deck, pumped a fresh round into the chamber, then pressed two more shells into the magazine with his thumb.

'Three down,' he said. 'Streak, you and Lucinda go around the bow. I'll come up the other side. Watch the bridge. Don't let 'em get behind you.'

He didn't wait for an answer. He moved toward the stern, bearlike, his shotgun back at port arms, his scalp showing white in the wind, his utilities stiff with salt.

Lucinda glanced down at the cabin cruiser, which was rolling in the swells while Zoot kept gunning the engines to keep the stern from swinging into the salvage ship's hull.

'He's all right,' I said. 'My dad used to always say, "Don't ever treat brave people as less than what they are." '

'Cover your own ass,' she said.

We moved toward the bow. I could feel the deck vibrating under me from the machinery roaring on the other side of the ship. I paused at the steps that led onto the pilothouse, worked my way up them until I could see inside, then moved quickly through the open hatch.

I looked at the shape in the corner and lowered my rifle. I heard Lucinda behind me.

'Oh God,' she said.

'Check the starboard side,' I said, and knelt next to Brother Oswald. He lay on top of an oil-grimed tarp, his poached, round face filled with the empty, stunned, disbelieving expression that I had seen once in the faces of villagers who had been killed by airbursts in a rice field.

A switchblade knife, a made-in-Korea gut-ripper that you can buy for five dollars in Laredo, had been driven to the hilt just above his right lung. He had pressed a rag around the wound, and the rag had become sodden and congealed as though it had been dipped in red paint. I put my ear to his mouth and felt his breath touch my skin.

'We're going to medevac you out of here, partner,' I said. 'You hear me? We're going to secure the ship, then have you on a chopper in no time.'

His tongue stuck to his mouth when he tried to speak. I leaned down close to his face again. His breath smelled like dried flowers.

'... after the wrong one,' he whispered.

'I don't understand,' I said.

'Hit's the woman ... She can speak in tongues ... I heard her talk on the radio ...'

'Who did this to you, Reverend?'

His lips moved, but no sound came out. His pale eyes looked like they were drowning.

'I can't see anybody on the starboard side,' Lucinda said.

I raised Brother Oswald's head with my palm, bunched up the tarp like a pillow, then turned his head sideways so his mouth could drain. I picked up the AR-15. The plastic stock felt cold and light and smooth in my hands.

'You know how to get the Coast Guard on the radio?' I said to Lucinda.

'Yes.'

'Tell them we're thirty miles south of Grand Isle. Describe the two oil platforms, and they'll know where to go.'

She nodded toward Brother Oswald, the question in her face.

I *don't know*, I said with my lips.

A moment later I crossed the deck in front of the pilothouse. I stepped out into the open, the iron sights of the AR-15 aimed at whoever might be standing between me and the stern.

But there was no one, except Clete Purcel, who was on one knee, his back toward me, amid a tangle of hoses, ropes, scuba and acetylene tanks, and salvage nets in pools of water. Two giant side booms towered above him, their cables almost bursting with the great weight anchored to them. Then beneath the sliding waves, the foam curling off the stern, the clouds of seaweed in the swells, glowing dimly under a bank of underwater lamps, I saw the long, tapered outline of the U-boat. It looked like the top of an enormous sand shark that had been torn out of the silt. I could see the forward deck gun shaggy with moss and crustaceans, air bubbles stringing from the torpedo tubes in the bow, the crushed steel flanges at the top of the conning tower, and the indistinct and dull glimmer of a swastika painted on the plates.

Clete's right arm was working furiously at a task that his body concealed from view. Then I saw the gasoline-powered generator and the air compressor just beyond where he was crouched on the deck, and I realized what he was doing.

I ran toward him, the rifle hanging loosely from my hand. With his single-bladed Case knife he had already sawed halfway through the air hose and the safety rope attached to it. The escaping pressure had blown a bare spot on the deck like a clean burn.

'Don't do it, Clete!'

'Too late, mon. Buchalter is about to do the big gargle.' He stood erect, ripped his knife through the remainder of the hose, and flung it like a severed snake into the water.

I stared over the side. Framed in silhouette against the bank of underwater lights, just aft of the conning tower, was a steel-mesh diver's platform, held aloft by a cable. In the middle of the platform, a diver in canvas suit, weighted boots, and hard hat was looking upward frantically, while a forgotten acetylene torch bounced like a sparkler across the sub's deck and the severed air hose spun limply downward into the darkness.

I dropped the rifle to the deck and tried to work the levers on the winch and spool that controlled the cable to the platform. I pushed the levers the wrong way, then corrected them and felt the engine buck into gear and start to retrieve the diver from below.

'Sorry, Dave, but this is one time you're wrong,' Clete said, pulling a fire ax from the wall above me. He tore all the connecting wires out of the winch's engine. Suddenly the spool locked in place, and the cable squeaked and oscillated slightly from side to side at the tip of the boom and trembled rigidly at the waterline. Then he swung the ax overhand into the spool and sheared the cable as neatly as you would coat hanger wire. It whipped free from the pulley on the boom and disappeared beneath the waves.

'It's homicide, Clete.'

'The hell it is. There's still at least one guy loose. All I did was keep a player off the board.'

But the story under the waves wasn't over. The platform had tipped sideways before it plummeted to the bottom, and the diver had managed to land on the deck, just behind the conning tower. I could see the brass helmet, the face glass, and the white hands waving in the tidal current, like a cartoon figure struggling at the bottom of a well.

I stripped off my field jacket, picked up a scuba tank and diving mask off the deck, checked the air gauge, and slipped my arms through the straps. I tied one end of a rope to the winch and the other around my waist.

'When I jerk, you pull us up,' I said.

'Big mistake,' Clete answered.

'I'll live with it. Don't let me down, Cletus.' He shrugged his shoulders and shook his head. I fitted the air hose into my mouth and went over the side.

The coldness was like a fist in the stomach, then I felt currents tear at me from several directions and I heard metal ringing, cable clanging on steel, plates grinding, perhaps a long-silenced propeller gouging a trench in packed sand, and I realized that the storm in the south was already destabilizing the sub's environment and was twisting the keel against the cables that Buchalter's crew had secured to the bow and stern.

I had no weight belt or flippers and had to struggle to gain depth. I blew the mask clear and swam deeper into the vortex of gold and brown light and spinning silt until I was only five feet away from the drowning figure in the diving suit. My head was aching with the cold, my teeth locked on the rubber mouthpiece to keep them from chattering, my ears pinging from the water pressure.

Then I saw what we had interrupted. The plates in the hull, just aft of the tower, probably already weak with strain and corrosion, had been cut with acetylene torches and prized out of the spars with jacks, exposing a compartment whose escape hatch into the tower was locked shut.

A battery-powered underwater light burned amid the drifting silt and softly molded skeletons of a dozen Nazi submariners.

Their uniforms were green rags now, their faces a yellow patina of pickled skin, their atrophied mouths puckered with rats' teeth.

I swam behind the diver, untied the rope from my waist, and slipped it under the canvas arms of the diver's suit, then knotted it hard in the spine. I felt the sub shift on its keel in a sudden surge of coldness from the gulf's bottom. As the deck listed to port, the diver turned in a slow pirouette and looked through the glass into my face.

The water had risen inside the suit to her neck, and her red hair floated like strands of dried blood against the glass. Her chin was twisted upward into the air, her cheeks pale, her mouth working like a guppy's.

It was too late to spin the wing nuts off the helmet and place my air hose in her mouth. I jerked hard on the rope and felt it come taut as Clete started to retrieve it topside. Then I tried to push both me and the woman who called herself Marie Guilbeaux to the surface.

Then, inches from my face, I saw the salt water climb to the top of the glass and immerse her head as though it were a severed and preserved specimen in a laboratory, her hair floating about her in a dark web. She fought and twisted, tried to hold her breath, her eyes bulging in their sockets; then a broken green balloon slipped suddenly from her mouth into the top of the helmet. Her arms locked about my neck in an almost erotic embrace, her body gathering against mine, her lips meshed against the glass like torn fruit, the teeth bare now, the loins shuddering, a wine-dark kiss from the grave.

A moment later I felt Clete stop pulling on the rope, then it was slipping free over the side of the salvage ship, curling down out of the waves toward me. I released the body of the woman called Marie Guilbeaux and watched it spin downward, the puffed arms extended sideways like a scarecrow's, the weighted boots pulling it past the bank of lights into the darkness, until the rope snapped taut again, and Marie's drowned figure swung back and forth against the bottom of the sub's hull.

I blew my glass clear again and swam upward to the surface. I popped through a wave into the wind, the groan of cables straining from the side booms, my mask streaked with water, my eyes searching the deck for Clete and Lucinda.

They were nowhere in sight. I climbed back aboard, breathless with cold, and slipped the straps to the air tank off my back. My AR-15 was gone.

I put on my field jacket, buttoned it against the wind, and took the .45 from the side pocket. A hollow-point round was already in the chamber. I cocked back the hammer and moved toward the stern, past the air compressor, the gasoline-powered generator, the winches, the piles of salvage nets and coils of acetylene hose, my shoulder brushing lightly against the base of the pilothouse, past an entrance to a room throbbing with the diesel motors that powered the side booms, past the galley, past a machine shop, finally to an open hatch that gave onto a small confined area that served as crew quarters.

No one.

I went inside the crew's quarters. It smelled of unwashed bedding and expectorated snuff. A color photograph of a nude black woman torn from a magazine was glued against one bulkhead. I went through another open hatch into a passageway that traversed the interior of the ship and led back toward the pilothouse and the bridge. The bulkheads were gray and cold with moisture, the deck patterned with the wet imprints of tennis shoes.

I opened or went through each hatch along the passageway.

Nothing.

The end of the passageway was unlighted, shrouded in gloom, as indistinct as fog. I didn't notice the broken lightbulb glass until the sole of my shoe came down on a piece of filament and cracked it against the deck. By then it was too late.

Buchalter stepped out from behind an open storage locker door, the stock of the AR-15 tight against his shoulder and cheek, one green eye as hard and bulbous as an egg behind the iron sights.

'You lose again, Dave. Throw it away,' he said, and kicked the door shut behind him, allowing me to see Lucinda and Clete on their knees by the ladder that led into the pilothouse, their fingers hooked behind their necks. There was a raw, skinned area above Clete's left eye.

'You want to take a chance and plant one in them?' Buchalter said.

'Don't give up your piece, Streak!' Clete shouted.

I held the .45 out to my side, bent slightly with my knees, and placed it carefully on the deck. Buchalter wore combat boots and khakis, a heavy gray wool shirt, and long underwear buttoned to the throat. His cheeks and chin were gold with the beginnings of a beard, the spray of blackheads fanning from his eyes like powder burns.

I smelled a bright, clean odor in the air, one that travels to the brain as quickly as a slap. Like the smell of white gas.

'Your friend killed my sister, Dave. What do you think of that?' he said. He looked at me with his lopsided grin.

'We tried to save her,' I said.

'Come join us,' he said.

'Maybe I shouldn't.'

'Oh, yes. It won't be complete without you. You and I have a date. All three of you do.' His thick tongue worked itself wetly along his lips.

'He soaked us with gasoline, Dave. Run!' Lucinda said.

'You know you're not going anywhere, Dave. Come

closer. That's it, come on. The little boy is always inside the man. Don't be ashamed. You'd be surprised what people are willing to do under the right circumstances.' He held the rifle against his side by the pistol grip and worked a Zippo lighter out of his left pocket with his thumb.

'One's a Negro, the other a gentile who has intercourse with a Jew,' he said. 'They're going to die, anyway. Would you like to watch their performance with me, or be part of it? Nobody'll know, either, Dave.'

He pursed his lips and sucked in his cheeks, as though a mint lay on his tongue.

'The Coast Guard's on the way, Will.'

'I guess we should finish quickly then. Even when they catch my kind, you know what they do with us. Government hospitals. Clean drugs, maybe a horny nurse who needs a few extra dollars. Come on, kneel down with your friends, now.'

The heel of one boot clanked against a gasoline can. But then I heard another sound, too – behind me, at the far end of the passageway, a clumsy thud like an awkward person tripping across the bottom of a hatchway.

Buchalter heard it too, and his eyes shot past me, trying to focus on an image that they couldn't quite accept.

'Duck, Mr. Dave!'

I dropped to the deck, curling in an embryonic ball, waiting for the quick, sharp report of the AR-15. Instead, I heard a sound like a strand of broken piano wire whizzing through the air.

I stared down the passageway at the frozen silhouette of Zoot Bergeron, the discharged speargun held in front of him.

I grabbed the .45 from the deck just as Will Buchalter stumbled along the bulkhead, through the gloom, toward the ladder, partly obscured by the open door on a locker. Then I saw both his hands clenched on the aluminum shaft that protruded from his mouth. He careened up the ladder, the tendons in his shoulders and neck knotted like the roots in a tree stump, his hands gathered in front of his mouth, his combat boots ringing like hammers on the iron steps.

I fired twice through the hatchway into the pilothouse and heard the hollow points shatter panes of glass out on the deck.

'Sorry, Streak. He came up behind me while I was pulling on that rope,' Clete said.

'Get the rifle,' I said, and went up the ladder after Buchalter.

But the chase was not to be a long one.

I found him out on the deck, his back slumped against the rail, like a lazy man taking a nap, the spearpoint protruding from the back of his neck in a bloody clot, the shaft trembling slightly with the vibrations from the engine room. His eyes were open and empty, staring at nothing, the gold down on his chin slick with the drainage from his wound.

It started to rain, and the spray off the stern was blowing hard in the wind. A cable snapped loose from a side boom and was gone below the water's surface in the wink of an eye.

I heard Clete behind me.

'Did you hit him?' he said.

'Nope.'

'A bad way for the black kid to get started,' he said, and looked at me.

I glanced up at the broken windows in the pilothouse. Lucinda and Zoot were still below.

'Let's do it,' I said.

We pulled Buchalter away from the rail and laid him flat on the deck, then rolled him over the side. His shirt was puffed with air, and a wave scudded the upper portion of his body along the hull of the ship; his mouth was locked open around the spear shaft as though he were yawning or perhaps considering one final thought before the waves pressed him under in a cascade of dirty foam.

'That storm looks mean. Time to cut loose from the Katzenjammer Kids,' Clete said. He paused. 'Is there some paperwork later that's going to cause a problem for me?'

'What do I know?' I said. I shielded my eyes against the rain and watched as he sliced the line that held the suspended body of the woman who called herself Marie Guilbeaux, shut down motors, released winches, chopped cables and ropes in half, his sandy hair blowing in the wind, his Marine Corps utilities flapping and flattening against his legs.

I felt the deck pitch under me when all the cables had snapped free from the submarine's weight. For just a moment I watched the mud and blackened seaweed and oil trapped in sand churn in clouds out of the gulf's bottom, and I knew that down below the U-boat's crew and Buchalter and his sister were setting sail again. But it wasn't a time to muse upon old historical warnings about protean creatures who rise from biblical seas or slouch toward Bethlehem to be born again.

Instead I mounted the steps into the pilothouse, where Lucinda and her son had fixed a blanket under Oswald Flat's head and pulled a second one up to his chin. They stood at one of the shattered windows, Zoot with his arm on his mother's shoulders, looking at a Coast Guard helicopter that was flying toward us from the east, just ahead of the impending storm.

Zoot's eyes searched my face.

'You saved our butts, partner, but you missed Buchalter completely,' I said.

'Then why ain't I seen the spear?'

'Who cares, podna? It's yesterday's box score now,' I said.

Down below, Clete stretched his big arms and shoulders, clenched the deck rail, and spit over the side.

'Good guys *über alles*,' he called up to us.

'What's that mean?' Zoot said.

'I think that's German for *Semper fi*, Mac,' I said, and hit him on the arm, trying not to intrude upon the affectionate smile in his mother's eyes.

epilogue

The winter was mild that year; the days were balmy, the grass in the fields a soft green, the nights touched with a faint chill, a hint of smoke from a stump fire in my neighbor's pasture. Even during duck season, when the marsh should have been gray and thick with mist, the skies remained a porcelain blue and the cypress and gum and willow trees seemed to stay in leaf through Christmas, almost right up to the spring rains that begin in late February.

There was only one day when I truly felt winter's presence, and that presence was in the heart rather than the external world. For our anniversary Bootsie and Alafair and I treated ourselves to a weekend at the Pontchartrain Hotel on St. Charles Avenue. We were having supper at an outdoor café down the street, and the day had been warm and bright, the camellia bushes thick with newly opened pink and blue flowers, the wonderful old green-painted iron streetcars clattering down the neutral ground under the overhang of the oak trees. Then the sun dropped behind the rooftops, the air became cold and heavy, and suddenly there was no traffic or sound in the streets, only dust and scraps of newspaper whirling in the wind through the tunnel of trees.

This is what it could become, I thought. All we had to do was stop believing in ourselves and let the charlatans and the manipulators convince us they have the answers that we don't. They aren't fashioned from anvil and chain in a devil's forge, either. Judas Iscariot was us; there was no metaphysical mystery to Will Buchalter and his sister and the Calucci brothers. Their souls had the wingspan of moths; they functioned because we allowed them to and gave them sanction; they stopped functioning when that sanction was denied.

'What's wrong, Dave?' Alafair said from across the table.

'Nothing, little guy. Everything seemed too quiet for a minute.'

'Then let's go hear the band at Preservation Hall,' she said.

'I think that's a fine idea,' I said, and rubbed the silky smooth top of her head.

One beautiful evening that spring we went to the New Orleans Jazz and Heritage Festival at the Fairgrounds. The Fat Man was up on the stage with his band, his sequined sports coat painted with a lavender glow, sweat streaking his walrus face like lines of clear plastic, his pudgy hands and ringed sausage fingers pounding on the piano keys. People began dancing in the infield, jitterbugging like kids out of the 1940s, doing the bop, the dirty boogie, the twist, the shag, arms and legs akimbo, full of fun and erotic innocence.

Everyone was there for it – Clete and Martina, Batist, Lucinda and Zoot (who wore his Marine Corps Reserve uniform), Pearly Blue and her ex-con pals from the Work the Steps or Die, Motherfucker group, Ben Motley, Hippo Bimstine and his family, black and white people, visitors from Europe, Japanese businessmen, zydeco and Dixieland musicians, granola hippies, Bourbon Street strippers, cross-dressers, French Quarter hookers, coon-ass bikers, Jimmie Ryan and Count Carbonna, the meltdowns, religious crazoids with placards warning of apocalyptic destruction, even Brother Oswald Flat and his wife, who strolled about the grounds, sharing a bag of pork rinds. The music rose into the sky until it seemed to fuse with the gentle and pervasive light spreading far beyond the racetrack, over oak-lined streets, paintless wood houses with galleries and green window shutters, elevated highways, the Superdome, the streetcars and palm-dotted neutral ground of Canal, the scrolled iron balconies, colonnades, and brick chimneys in the Quarter, Jackson Square and the spires of St. Louis Cathedral, the Café du Monde, the wide mud-churned sweep of the Mississippi, the shining vastness of the wetlands to the south, and eventually the Gulf of Mexico, where later the moon would rise like an enormous pearl that had been dipped in a glass of burgundy.

It's funny what can happen when you lay bare the heart and join the Earth's old dance through the heavens.

chapter one

I had seen a dawn like this one only twice in my life: once in Vietnam, after a Bouncing Betty had risen from the earth on a night trail and twisted its tentacles of light around my thighs, and years earlier outside of Franklin, Louisiana, when my father and I discovered the body of a labor organizer who had been crucified with sixteen-penny nails, ankle and wrist, against a barn wall.

Just before the sun broke above the Gulf's rim, the wind, which had blown the waves with ropes of foam all night, suddenly died and the sky became as white and brightly grained as polished bone, as though all color had been bled out of the air, and the gulls that had swooped and glided over my wake lifted into the haze and the swells flattened into an undulating sheet of liquid tin dimpled by the leathery backs of stingrays.

The eastern horizon was strung with rain clouds and the sun should have risen out of the water like a mist-shrouded egg yolk, but it didn't. Its red light mush-roomed along the horizon, then rose into the sky in a cross, burning in the center, as though fire were trying to take the shape of a man, and the water turned the heavy dark color of blood.

Maybe the strange light at dawn was only coincidence and had nothing to do with the return to New Iberia of Megan Flynn, who, like a sin we had concealed in the

3

confessional, vexed our conscience, or worse, rekindled our envy.

But I knew in my heart it was not coincidence, no more so than the fact that the man crucified against the barn wall was Megan's father and that Megan herself was waiting for me at my dock and bait shop, fifteen miles south of New Iberia, when Clete Purcel, my old Homicide partner from the First District in New Orleans, and I cut the engines on my cabin cruiser and floated through the hyacinths on our wake, the mud billowing in clouds that were as bright as yellow paint under the stern.

It was sprinkling now, and she wore an orange silk shirt and khaki slacks and sandals, her funny straw hat spotted with rain, her hair dark red against the gloom of the day, her face glowing with a smile that was like a thorn in the heart.

Clete stood by the gunnel and looked at her and puckered his mouth. 'Wow,' he said under his breath.

She was one of those rare women gifted with eyes that could linger briefly on yours and make you feel, rightly or wrongly, you were genuinely invited into the mystery of her life.

'I've seen her somewhere,' Clete said as he prepared to climb out on the bow.

'Last week's *Newsweek* magazine,' I said.

'That's it. She won a Pulitzer Prize or something. There was a picture of her hanging out of a slick,' he said. His gum snapped in his jaw.

She had been on the cover, wearing camouflage pants and a T-shirt, with dog tags around her neck, the downdraft of the British helicopter whipping her hair and flattening her clothes against her body, the strap of her camera laced around one wrist, while, below, Serbian armor burned in columns of red and black smoke.

But I remembered another Megan, too: the in-your-face orphan of years ago, who, with her brother, would run away from foster homes in Louisiana and Colorado,

4

until they were old enough to finally disappear into that wandering army of fruit pickers and wheat harvesters whom their father, an unrepentant IWW radical, had spent a lifetime trying to organize.

I stepped off the bow onto the dock and walked toward my truck to back the trailer down the ramp. I didn't mean to be impolite. I admired the Flynns, but you paid a price for their friendship and proximity to the vessel of social anger their lives had become.

'Not glad to see me, Streak?' she said.

'Always glad. How you doin', Megan?'

She looked over my shoulder at Clete Purcel, who had pulled the port side of the boat flush into the rubber tires on my dock and was unloading the cooler and rods out of the stern. Clete's thick arms and fire-hydrant neck were peeling and red with fresh sunburn. When he stooped over with the cooler, his tropical shirt split across his back. He grinned at us and shrugged his shoulders.

'That one had to come out of the Irish Channel,' she said.

'You're not a fisher, Meg. You out here on business?'

'You know who Cool Breeze Broussard is?' she asked.

'A house creep and general thief.'

'He says your parish lockup is a toilet. He says your jailer is a sadist.'

'We lost the old jailer. I've been on leave. I don't know much about the new guy.'

'Cool Breeze says inmates are gagged and handcuffed to a detention chair. They have to sit in their own excrement. The U.S. Department of Justice believes him.'

'Jails are bad places. Talk to the sheriff, Megan. I'm off the clock.'

'Typical New Iberia. Bullshit over humanity.'

'See you around,' I said, and walked to my truck. Rain was pinging in large, cold drops on the tin roof of the bait shop.

'Cool Breeze said you were stand-up. He's in lockdown

now because he dimed the jailer. I'll tell him you were off the clock,' she said.

'This town didn't kill your father.'

'No, they just put me and my brother in an orphanage where we polished floors with our knees. Tell your Irish friend he's beautiful. Come out to the house and visit us, Streak,' she said, and walked across the dirt road to where she had parked her car under the trees in my drive.

Up on the dock, Clete poured the crushed ice and canned drinks and speckled trout out of the cooler. The trout looked stiff and cold on the board planks.

'You ever hear anything about prisoners being gagged and cuffed to chairs in the Iberia Parish Prison?' I asked.

'That's what that was about? Maybe she ought to check out what those guys did to get in there.'

'She said you were beautiful.'

'She did?' He looked down the road where her car was disappearing under the canopy of oaks that grew along the bayou. Then he cracked a Budweiser and flipped me a can of diet Dr Pepper. The scar over his left eyebrow flattened against his skull when he grinned.

The turnkey had been a brig chaser in the Marine Corps and still wore his hair buzzed into the scalp and shaved in a razor-neat line on the back of his neck. His body was lean and braided with muscle, his walk as measured and erect as if he were on a parade ground. He unlocked the cell at the far end of the corridor, hooked up Willie Cool Breeze Broussard in waist and leg manacles, and escorted him with one hand to the door of the interview room, where I waited.

'Think he's going to run on you, Top?' I said.

'He runs at the mouth, that's what he does.'

The turnkey closed the door behind us. Cool Breeze looked like two hundred pounds of soft black chocolate poured inside jailhouse denims. His head was bald, lacquered with wax, shiny as horn, his eyes drooping at the corners like a prizefighter's. It was hard to believe he was a second-story man and four-time loser.

'If they're jamming you up, Cool Breeze, it's not on your sheet,' I said.

'What you call Isolation?'

'The screw says you asked for lockdown.'

His wrists were immobilized by the cuffs attached to the chain around his waist. He shifted in his chair and looked sideways at the door.

'I was on Camp J up at Angola. It's worse in here. A hack made a kid blow him at gunpoint,' he said.

'I don't want to offend you, Breeze, but this isn't your style.'

'What ain't?'

'You're not one to rat out anybody, not even a bad screw.'

His eyes shifted back and forth inside his face. He rubbed his nose on his shoulder.

'I'm down on this VCR beef. A truckload of them. What makes it double bad is I boosted the load from a Giacano warehouse in Lake Charles. I need to get some distance between me and my problems, maybe like in the Islands, know what I saying?'

'Sounds reasonable.'

'No, you don't get it. The Giacanos are tied into some guys in New York City making dubs of movies, maybe a hundred t'ousand of them a week. So they buy lots of VCRs, cut-rate prices, Cool Breeze Midnight Supply Service, you wit' me?'

'You've been selling the Giacanos their own equipment? You're establishing new standards, Breeze.'

He smiled slightly, but the peculiar downward slope of his eyes gave his expression a melancholy cast, like a bloodhound's. He shook his head.

'You still don't see it, Robicheaux. None of these guys are that smart. They started making dubs of them kung fu movies from Hong Kong. The money behind them kung fus comes from some very bad guys. You heard of the Triads?'

'We're talking about China White?'

'That's how it gets washed, my man.'

I took out my business card and wrote my home number and the number of the bait shop on the back. I leaned across the table and slipped it in his shirt pocket.

'Watch your butt in here, Breeze, particularly that ex-jarhead.'

'Meet the jailer. It's easy to catch him after five. He like to work late, when they ain't no visitors around.'

Megan's brother Cisco owned a home up Bayou Teche, just south of Loreauville. It was built in the style of the West Indies, one story and rambling, shaded by oaks, with a wide, elevated gallery, green, ventilated window shutters, and fern baskets hanging from the eaves. Cisco and his friends, movie people like himself, came and went with the seasons, shooting ducks in the wetlands, fishing for tarpon and speckled trout in the Gulf. Their attitudes were those of people who used geographical areas and social cultures as playgrounds and nothing more. Their glittering lawn parties, which we saw only from the road through the myrtle bushes and azalea and banana trees that fringed his property, were the stuff of legend in our small sugarcane town along the Teche.

I had never understood Cisco. He was tough, like his sister, and he had the same good looks they had both inherited from their father, but when his reddish-brown eyes settled on yours, he seemed to search inside your skin for something he wanted, perhaps coveted, yet couldn't define. Then the moment would pass and his attention would wander away like a balloon on the breeze.

He had dug irrigation ditches and worked the fruit orchards in the San Joaquin and had ended up in Hollywood as a road-wise, city-library-educated street kid who was dumbfounded when he discovered his handsome face and seminal prowess could earn him access to a movie lot, first as an extra, then as a stuntman.

It wasn't long before he realized he was not only braver than the actors whose deeds he performed but that he was more intelligent than most of them as well. He co-wrote scripts for five years, formed an independent production group with two Vietnam combat veterans, and put together a low-budget film on the lives of migrant farmworkers that won prizes in France and Italy.

His next film opened in theaters all over the United States.

Now Cisco had an office on Sunset Boulevard, a home in Pacific Palisades, and membership in that magic world where bougainvillea and ocean sun were just the token symbols of the health and riches that southern California could bestow on its own.

It was late Sunday evening when I turned off the state road and drove up the gravel lane toward his veranda. His lawn was blue-green with St. Augustine grass and smelled of chemical fertilizer and the water sprinklers twirling between the oak and pine trees. I could see him working out on a pair of parallel bars in the side yard, his bare arms and shoulders cording with muscle and vein, his skin painted with the sun's late red light through the cypresses on the bayou.

As always, Cisco was courteous and hospitable, but in a way that made you feel his behavior was learned rather than natural, a barrier rather than an invitation.

'Megan? No, she had to fly to New Orleans. Can I help you with something?' he said. Before I could answer, he said, 'Come on inside. I need something cold. How do you guys live here in the summer?'

All the furniture in the living room was white, the floor covered with straw mats, blond, wood-bladed ceiling fans turning overhead. He stood shirtless and barefooted at a wet bar and filled a tall glass with crushed ice and collins mix and cherries. The hair on his stomach looked like flattened strands of red wire above the beltline of his yellow slacks.

'It was about an inmate in the parish prison, a guy named Cool Breeze Broussard,' I said.

He drank from his glass, his eyes empty. 'You want me to tell her something?' he asked.

'Maybe this guy was mistreated at the jail, but I think his real problem is with some mobbed-up dudes in New Orleans. Anyway, she can give me a call.'

'Cool Breeze Broussard. That's quite a name.'

'It might end up in one of your movies, huh?'

'You can't ever tell,' he replied, and smiled.

On one wall were framed still shots from Cisco's films, and on a side wall photographs that were all milestones in Megan's career: a ragged ditch strewn with the bodies of civilians in Guatemala, African children whose emaciated faces were crawling with blowflies, French Legionnaires pinned down behind sandbags while mortar rounds geysered dirt above their heads.

But, oddly, the color photograph that had launched her career and had made *Life* magazine was located at the bottom corner of the collection. It had been shot in the opening of a storm drain that bled into the Mississippi just as an enormous black man, in New Orleans City Prison denims strung with sewage, had burst out of the darkness into the fresh air, his hands raised toward the sun, as though he were trying to pay tribute to its energy and power. But a round from a sharpshooter's rifle had torn through his throat, exiting in a bloody mist, twisting his mouth open like that of a man experiencing orgasm.

A second framed photograph showed five uniformed cops looking down at the body, which seemed shrunken and without personality in death. A smiling crew-cropped man in civilian clothes was staring directly at the camera in the foreground, a red apple with a white hunk bitten out of it cupped in his palm.

'What are you thinking about?' Cisco asked.

'Seems like an inconspicuous place to put these,' I said.

'The guy paid some hard dues. For Megan and me, both,' he said.

'Both?'

'I was her assistant on that shot, inside the pipe when those cops decided he'd make good dog food. Look, you think Hollywood's the only meat market out there? The cops got citations. The black guy got to rape a sixteen-year-old white girl before he went out. I get to hang his picture on the wall of a seven-hundred-thousand-dollar house. The only person who didn't get a trade-off was the high school girl.'

'I see. Well, I guess I'd better be going.'

Through the French doors I saw a man of about fifty walk down the veranda in khaki shorts and slippers with his shirt unbuttoned on his concave chest. He sat down in a reclining chair with a magazine and lit a cigar.

'That's Billy Holtzner. You want to meet him?' Cisco said.

'Who?'

'When the Pope visited the studio about seven years ago, Billy asked him if he had a script. Wait here a minute.'

I tried to stop him but it was too late. The rudeness of his having to ask permission for me to be introduced seemed to elude him. I saw him bend down toward the man named Holtzner and speak in a low voice, while Holtzner puffed on his cigar and looked at nothing. Then Cisco raised up and came back inside, turning up his palms awkwardly at his sides, his eyes askance with embarrassment.

'Billy's head is all tied up with a project right now. He's kind of intense when he's in preproduction.' He tried to laugh.

'You're looking solid, Cisco.'

'Orange juice and wheat germ and three-mile runs along the surf. It's the only life.'

'Tell Megan I'm sorry I missed her.'

11

'I apologize about Billy. He's a good guy. He's just eccentric.'

'You know anything about movie dubs?'

'Yeah, they cost the industry a lot of money. That's got something to do with this guy Broussard?'

'You got me.'

When I walked out the front door the man in the reclining chair had turned off the bug light and was smoking his cigar reflectively, one knee crossed over the other. I could feel his eyes on me, taking my measure. I nodded at him, but he didn't respond. The ash of his cigar glowed like a hot coal in the shadows.

also available from
THE ORION PUBLISHING GROUP

All Orion/Phoenix titles are available at your local bookshop or from the following address:

Littlehampton Book Services
Cash Sales Department L
14 Eldon Way, Lineside Industrial Estate
Littlehampton
West Sussex BN17 7HE
telephone 01903 721596, *facsimile* 01903 730914

Payment can either be made by credit card (Visa and Mastercard accepted) or by sending a cheque or postal order made payable to *Littlehampton Book Services*.
DO NOT SEND CASH OR CURRENCY.

Please add the following to cover postage and packing

UK and BFPO:
£1.50 for the first book, and 50P for each additional book to a maximum of £3.50

Overseas and Eire:
£2.50 for the first book plus £1.00 for the second book and 50p for each additional book ordered

---

BLOCK CAPITALS PLEASE

name of cardholder ....   *delivery address*
                      ....   *(if different from cardholder)*

address of cardholder ....

....

....

....

postcode ....   *postcode* ....

☐ I enclose my remittance for £.................................

☐ please debit my Mastercard/Visa (delete as appropriate)

card number ⬚⬚⬚⬚⬚⬚⬚⬚⬚⬚⬚⬚⬚⬚⬚⬚

expiry date ⬚⬚⬚⬚

signature ....

prices and availability are subject to change without notice